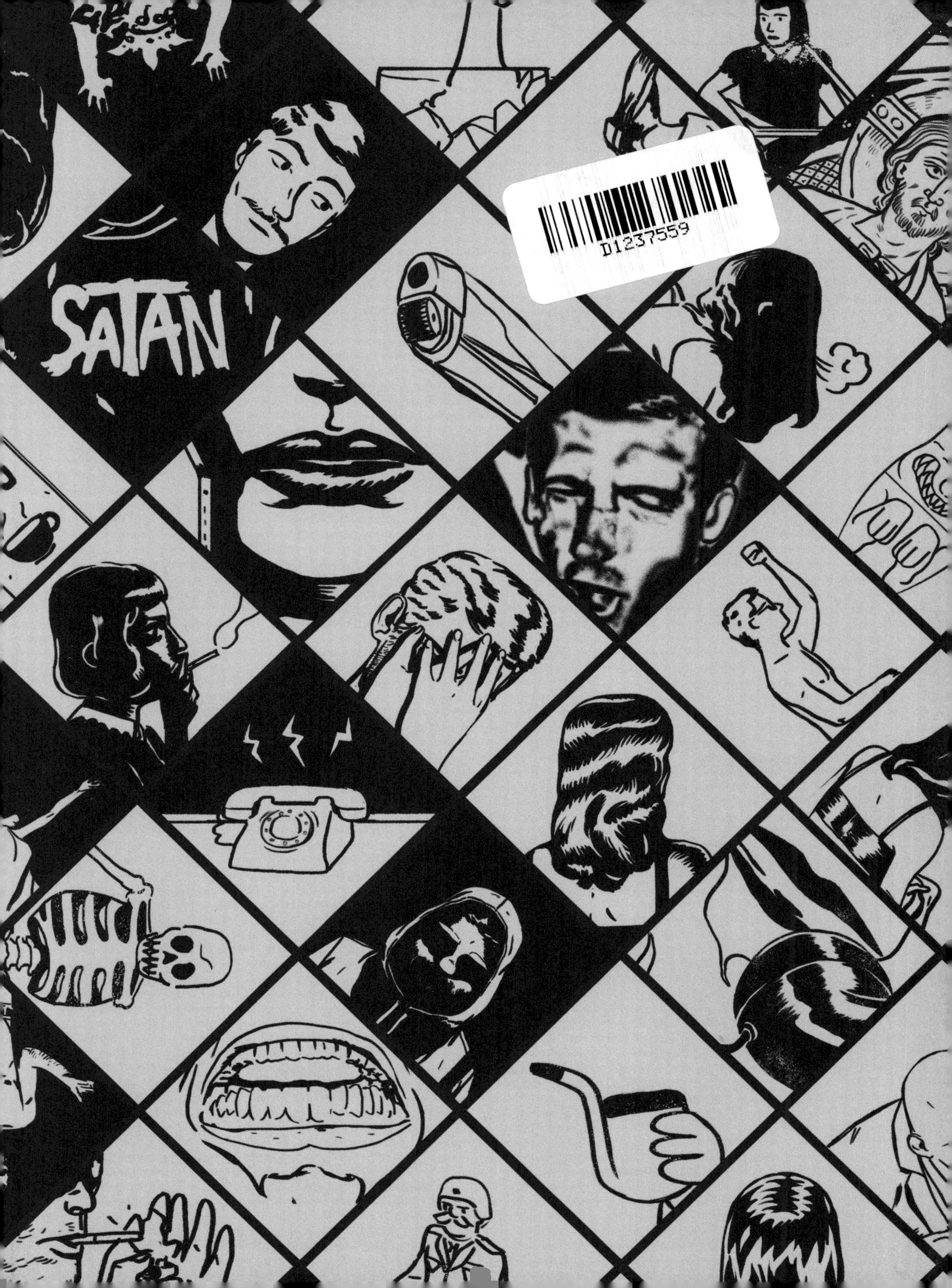
SATAN

TUMULT

This book is dedicated to Christian Ward.
Without you, it wouldn't have happened.

First published by
SelfMadeHero
139-141 Pancras Road
London NW1 1UN
www.selfmadehero.com

Written by John Harris Dunning
Illustrations by Michael Kennedy

Publishing Director: Emma Hayley
Sales & Marketing Manager: Sam Humphrey
Editorial & Production Manager: Guillaume Rater
UK Publicist: Paul Smith
US Publicist: Maya Bradford
Designer: Txabi Jones
With thanks to: Dan Lockwood

A CIP record for this book is available from the British Library

ISBN: 978-1-910593-48-6

10 9 8 7 6 5 4 3 2 1

Printed and bound in Slovenia

TUMULT

JOHN HARRIS DUNNING
MICHAEL KENNEDY

SELF
MADE
HERO

Midway upon the journey of our life
I found myself within a forest dark,
For the straightforward pathway had been lost.
Inferno, Canto One

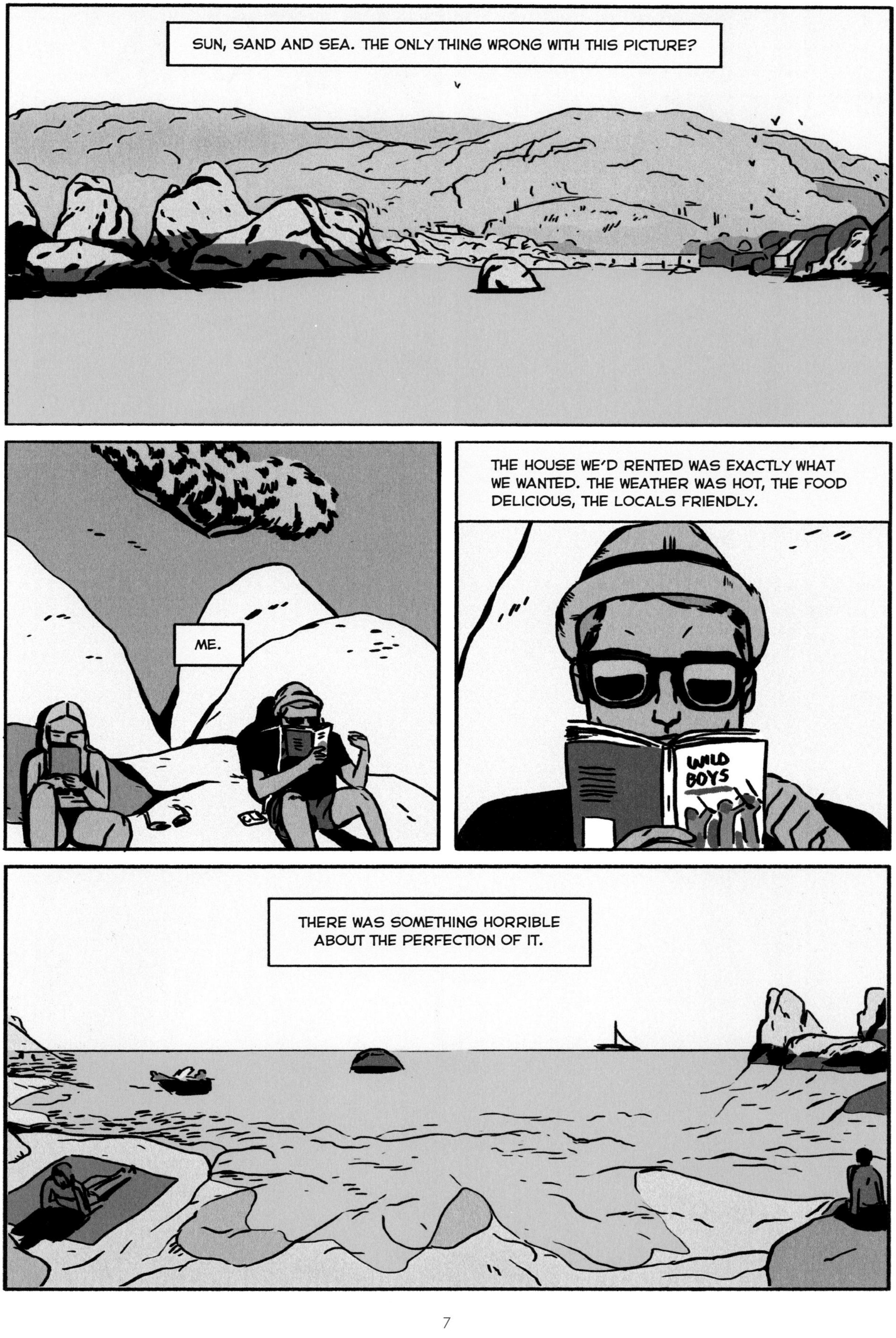
SUN, SAND AND SEA. THE ONLY THING WRONG WITH THIS PICTURE?
ME.
THE HOUSE WE'D RENTED WAS EXACTLY WHAT WE WANTED. THE WEATHER WAS HOT, THE FOOD DELICIOUS, THE LOCALS FRIENDLY.
WILD BOYS
THERE WAS SOMETHING HORRIBLE ABOUT THE PERFECTION OF IT.

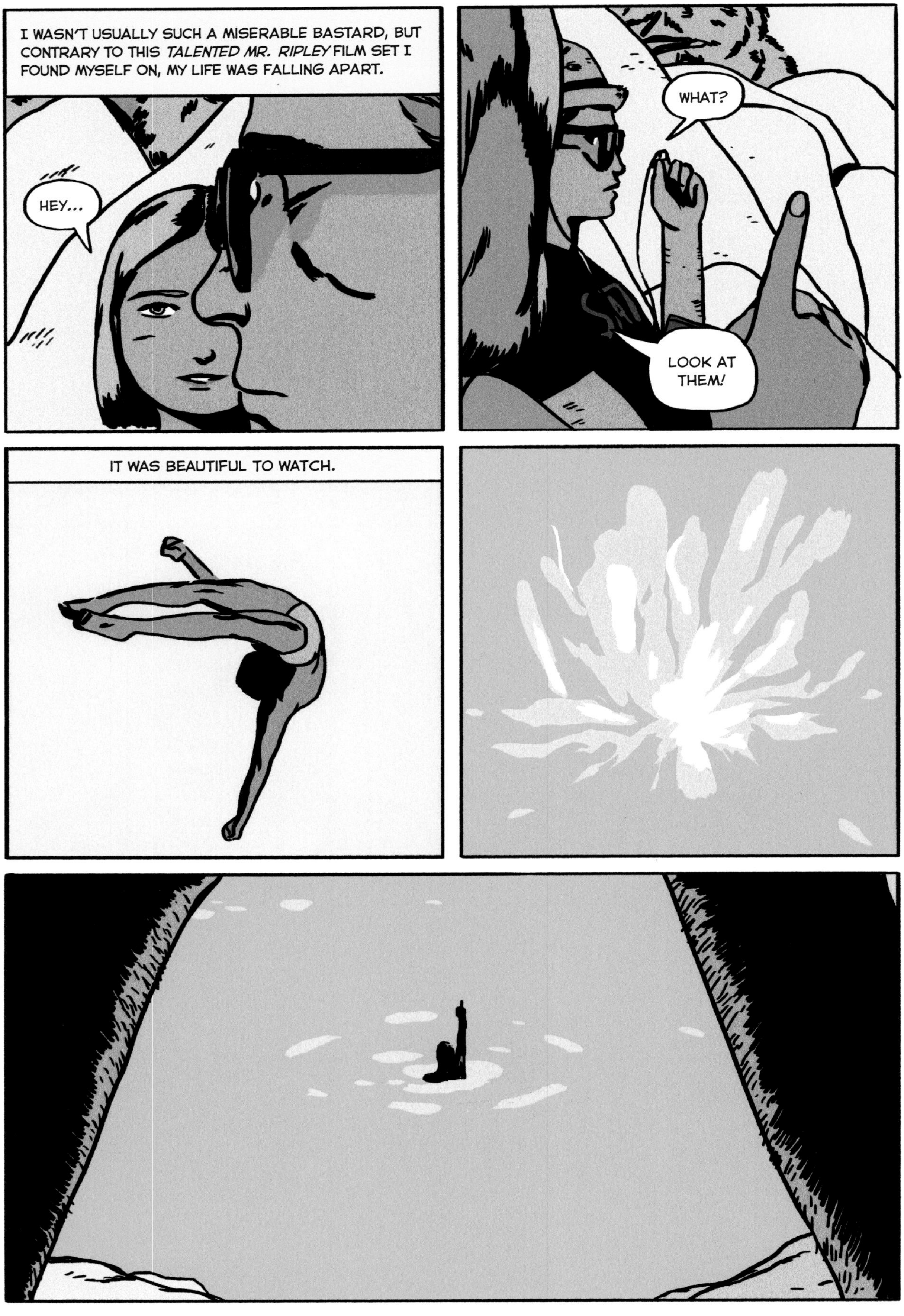
I WASN'T USUALLY SUCH A MISERABLE BASTARD, BUT CONTRARY TO THIS *TALENTED MR. RIPLEY* FILM SET I FOUND MYSELF ON, MY LIFE WAS FALLING APART.
HEY...
WHAT?
LOOK AT THEM!
IT WAS BEAUTIFUL TO WATCH.

COME ON, LET'S HAVE A GO.

HOW HARD COULD IT BE IF THOSE LITTLE JERKS WERE DOING IT? SURE, THEY WERE YOUNGER THAN ME, BUT SO WHAT? I WAS A MAN, SOMETHING THEY WERE ONLY PLAYING AT.

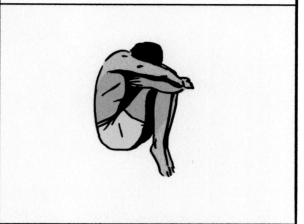

HANGOVERS TOOK LONGER TO RECOVER FROM, AND I HAD TO PUT IN A BIT OF WORK TO STAY IN SHAPE, BUT I WAS EVERY BIT THEIR EQUAL.

I STILL HAD IT IN ME TO FEEL THAT CAREFREE.

TO TAKE THE LEAP.

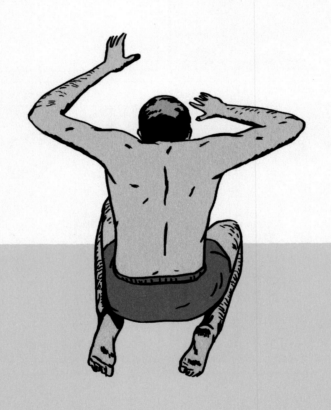

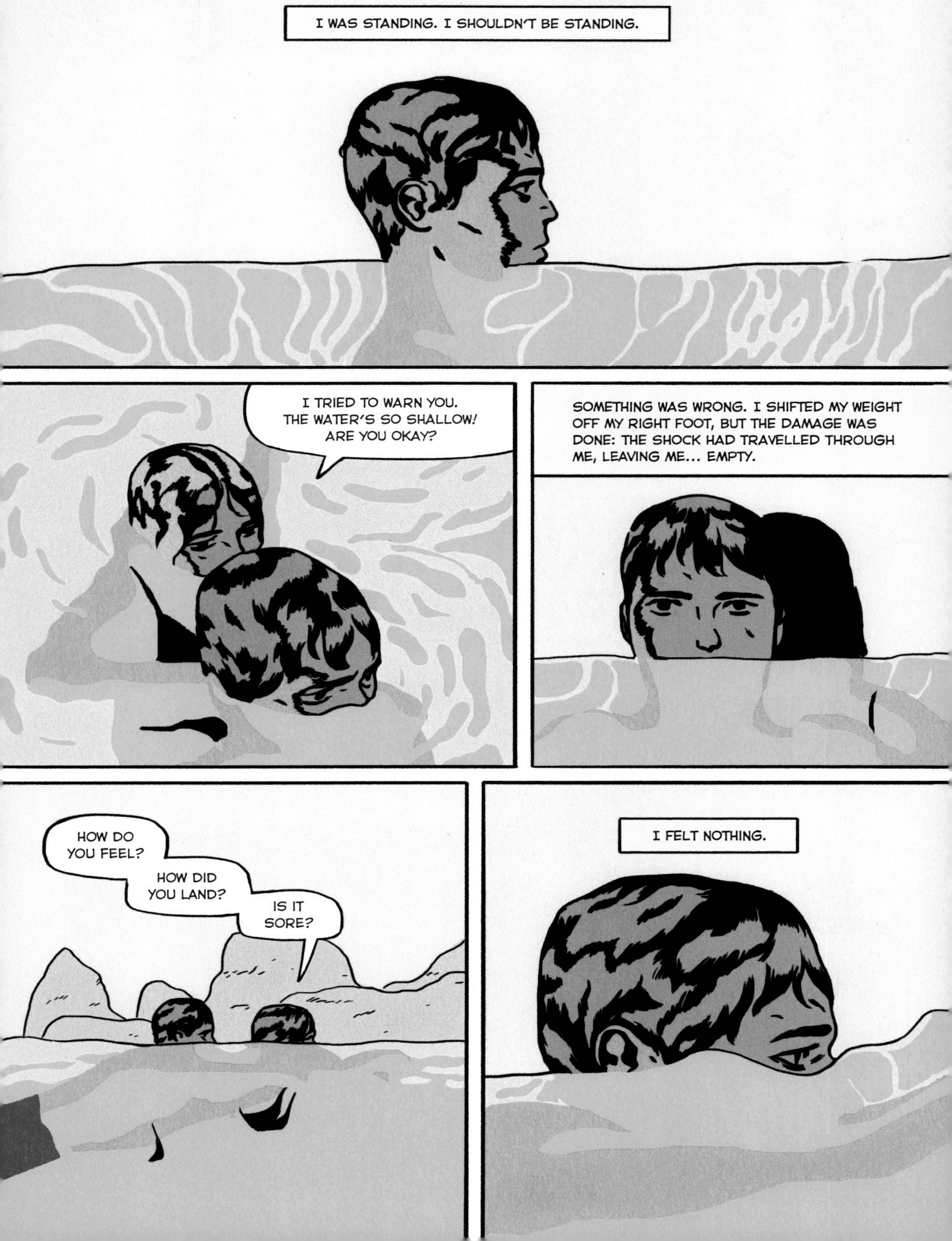
I WAS STANDING. I SHOULDN'T BE STANDING.
I TRIED TO WARN YOU. THE WATER'S SO SHALLOW! ARE YOU OKAY?
SOMETHING WAS WRONG. I SHIFTED MY WEIGHT OFF MY RIGHT FOOT, BUT THE DAMAGE WAS DONE: THE SHOCK HAD TRAVELLED THROUGH ME, LEAVING ME... EMPTY.
HOW DO YOU FEEL?
HOW DID YOU LAND?
IS IT SORE?
I FELT NOTHING.

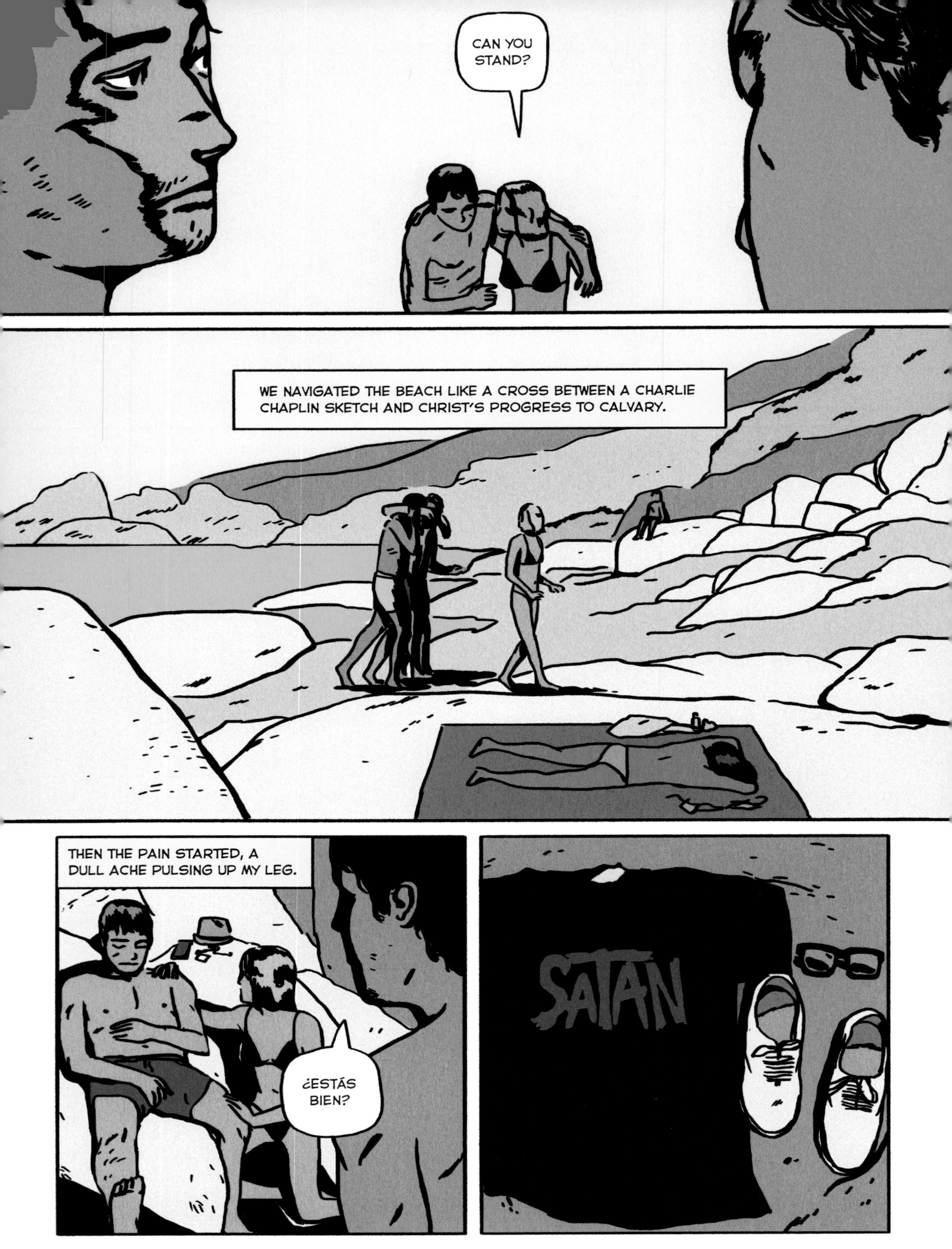
CAN YOU STAND?
WE NAVIGATED THE BEACH LIKE A CROSS BETWEEN A CHARLIE CHAPLIN SKETCH AND CHRIST'S PROGRESS TO CALVARY.
THEN THE PAIN STARTED, A DULL ACHE PULSING UP MY LEG.
¿ESTÁS BIEN?
SATAN

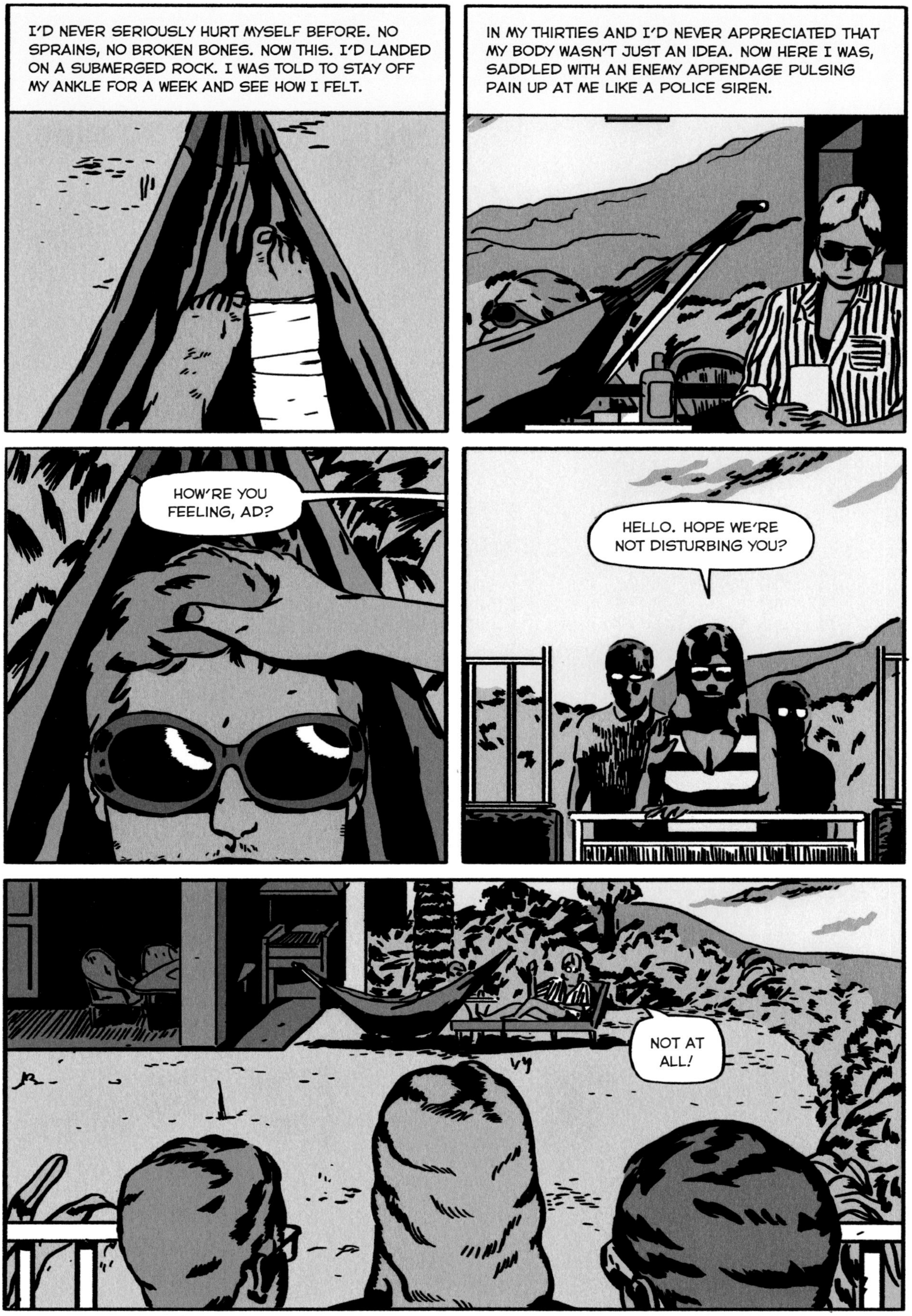
I'D NEVER SERIOUSLY HURT MYSELF BEFORE. NO SPRAINS, NO BROKEN BONES. NOW THIS. I'D LANDED ON A SUBMERGED ROCK. I WAS TOLD TO STAY OFF MY ANKLE FOR A WEEK AND SEE HOW I FELT.
IN MY THIRTIES AND I'D NEVER APPRECIATED THAT MY BODY WASN'T JUST AN IDEA. NOW HERE I WAS, SADDLED WITH AN ENEMY APPENDAGE PULSING PAIN UP AT ME LIKE A POLICE SIREN.
HOW'RE YOU FEELING, AD?
HELLO. HOPE WE'RE NOT DISTURBING YOU?
NOT AT ALL!

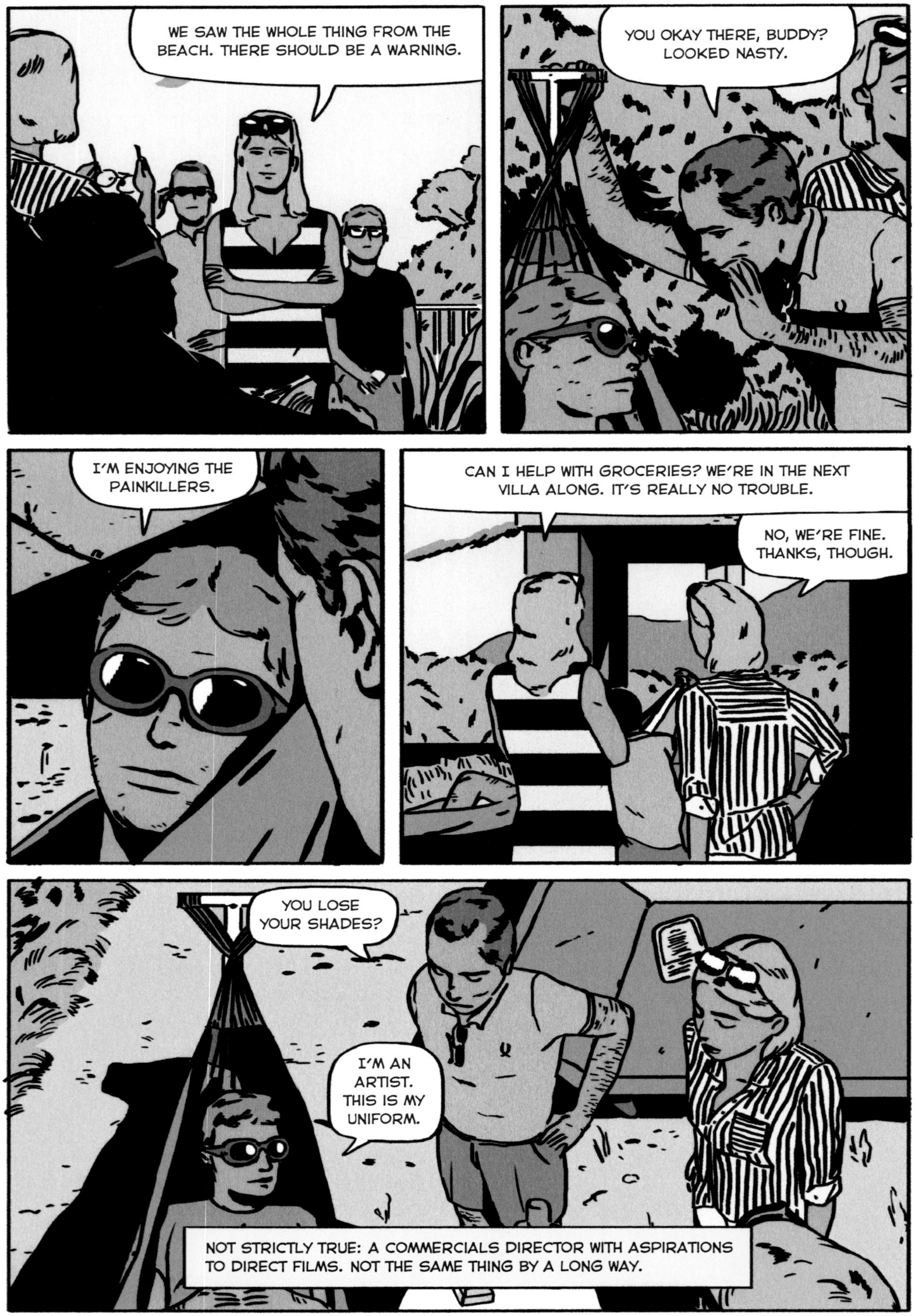
WE SAW THE WHOLE THING FROM THE BEACH. THERE SHOULD BE A WARNING.
YOU OKAY THERE, BUDDY? LOOKED NASTY.
I'M ENJOYING THE PAINKILLERS.
CAN I HELP WITH GROCERIES? WE'RE IN THE NEXT VILLA ALONG. IT'S REALLY NO TROUBLE.
NO, WE'RE FINE. THANKS, THOUGH.
YOU LOSE YOUR SHADES?
I'M AN ARTIST. THIS IS MY UNIFORM.
NOT STRICTLY TRUE: A COMMERCIALS DIRECTOR WITH ASPIRATIONS TO DIRECT FILMS. NOT THE SAME THING BY A LONG WAY.

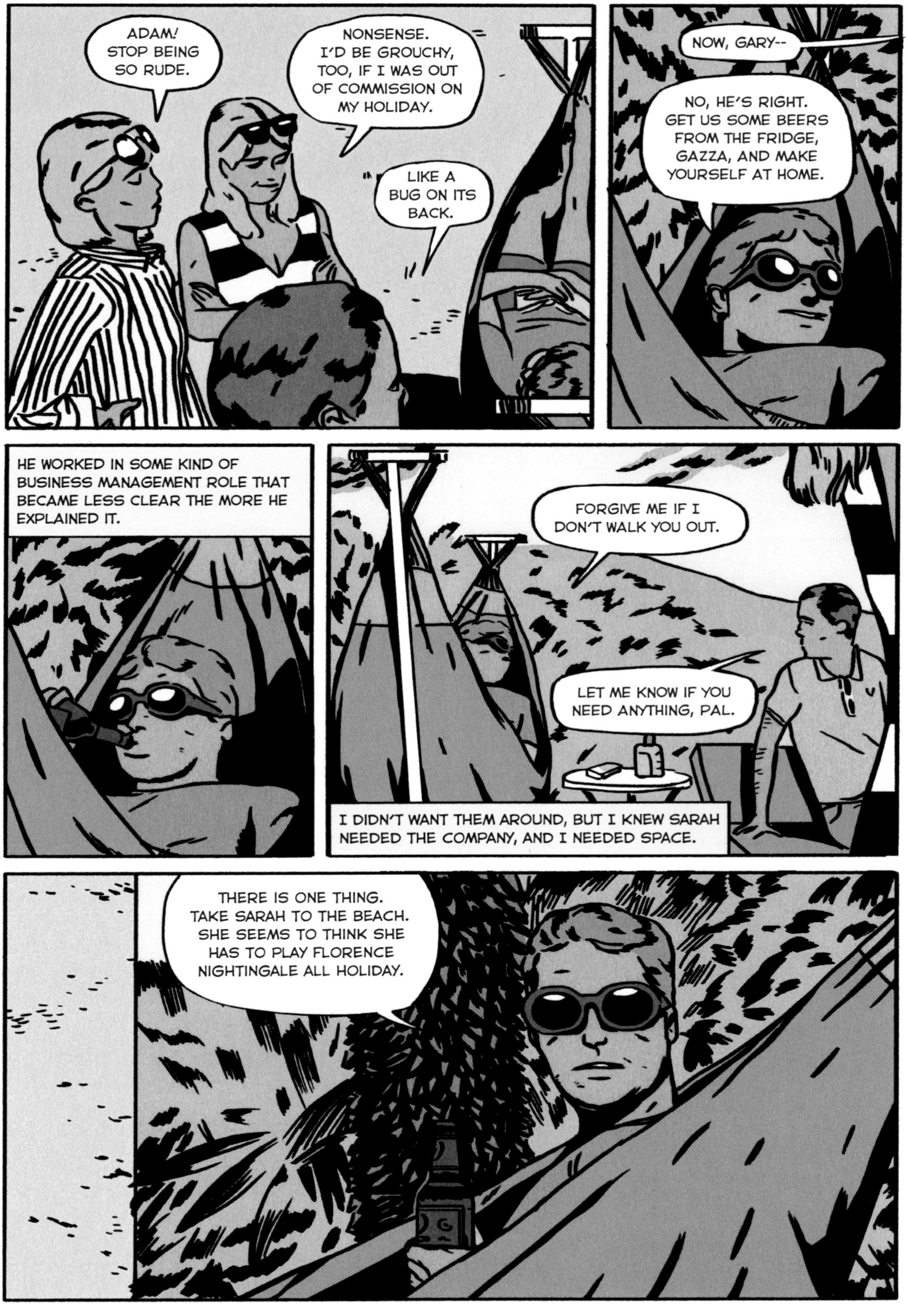
ADAM! STOP BEING SO RUDE.
NONSENSE. I'D BE GROUCHY, TOO, IF I WAS OUT OF COMMISSION ON MY HOLIDAY.
LIKE A BUG ON ITS BACK.
NOW, GARY--
NO, HE'S RIGHT. GET US SOME BEERS FROM THE FRIDGE, GAZZA, AND MAKE YOURSELF AT HOME.
HE WORKED IN SOME KIND OF BUSINESS MANAGEMENT ROLE THAT BECAME LESS CLEAR THE MORE HE EXPLAINED IT.
FORGIVE ME IF I DON'T WALK YOU OUT.
LET ME KNOW IF YOU NEED ANYTHING, PAL.
I DIDN'T WANT THEM AROUND, BUT I KNEW SARAH NEEDED THE COMPANY, AND I NEEDED SPACE.
THERE IS ONE THING. TAKE SARAH TO THE BEACH. SHE SEEMS TO THINK SHE HAS TO PLAY FLORENCE NIGHTINGALE ALL HOLIDAY.

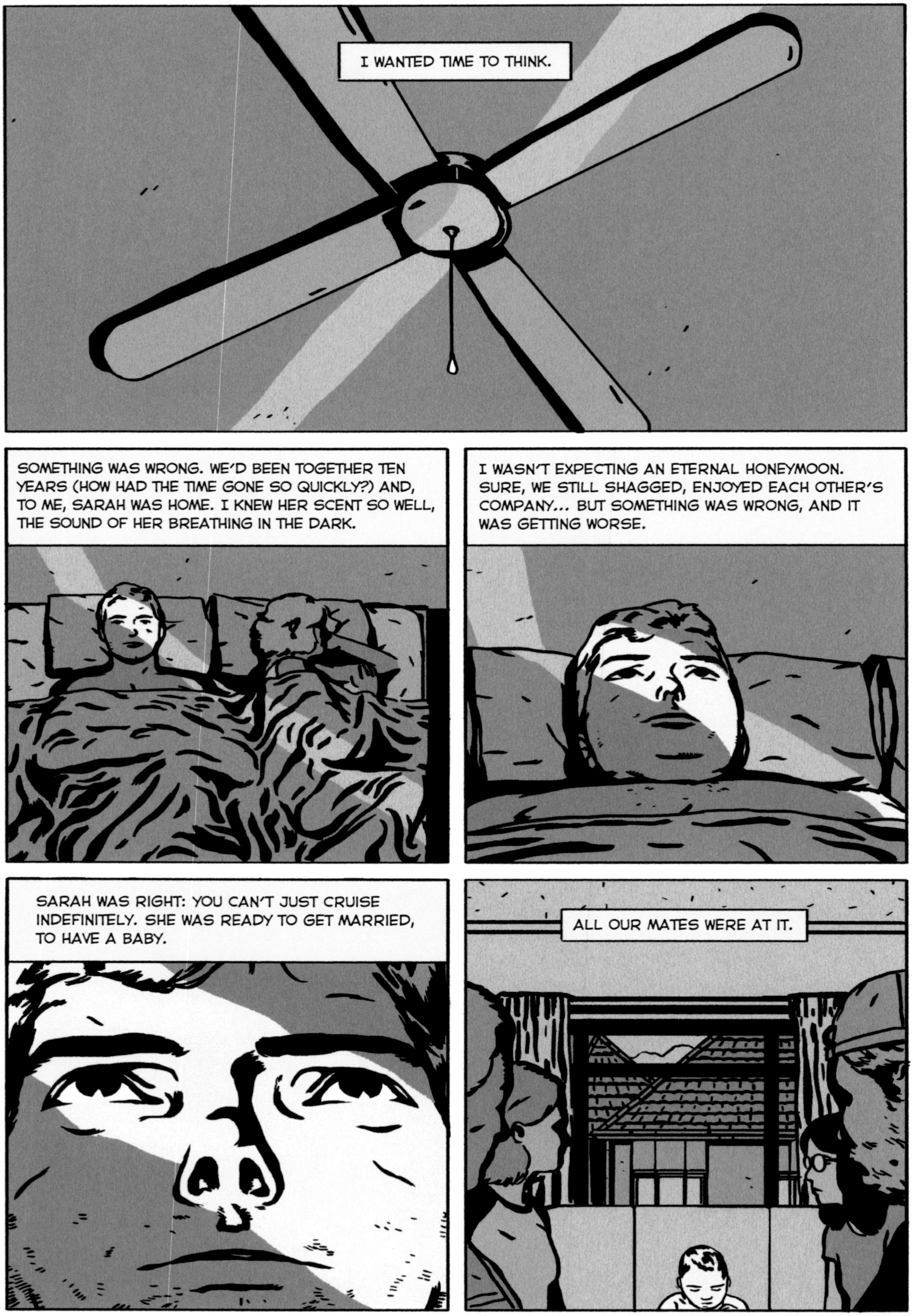
I WANTED TIME TO THINK.
SOMETHING WAS WRONG. WE'D BEEN TOGETHER TEN YEARS (HOW HAD THE TIME GONE SO QUICKLY?) AND, TO ME, SARAH WAS HOME. I KNEW HER SCENT SO WELL, THE SOUND OF HER BREATHING IN THE DARK.
I WASN'T EXPECTING AN ETERNAL HONEYMOON. SURE, WE STILL SHAGGED, ENJOYED EACH OTHER'S COMPANY... BUT SOMETHING WAS WRONG, AND IT WAS GETTING WORSE.
SARAH WAS RIGHT: YOU CAN'T JUST CRUISE INDEFINITELY. SHE WAS READY TO GET MARRIED, TO HAVE A BABY.
ALL OUR MATES WERE AT IT.

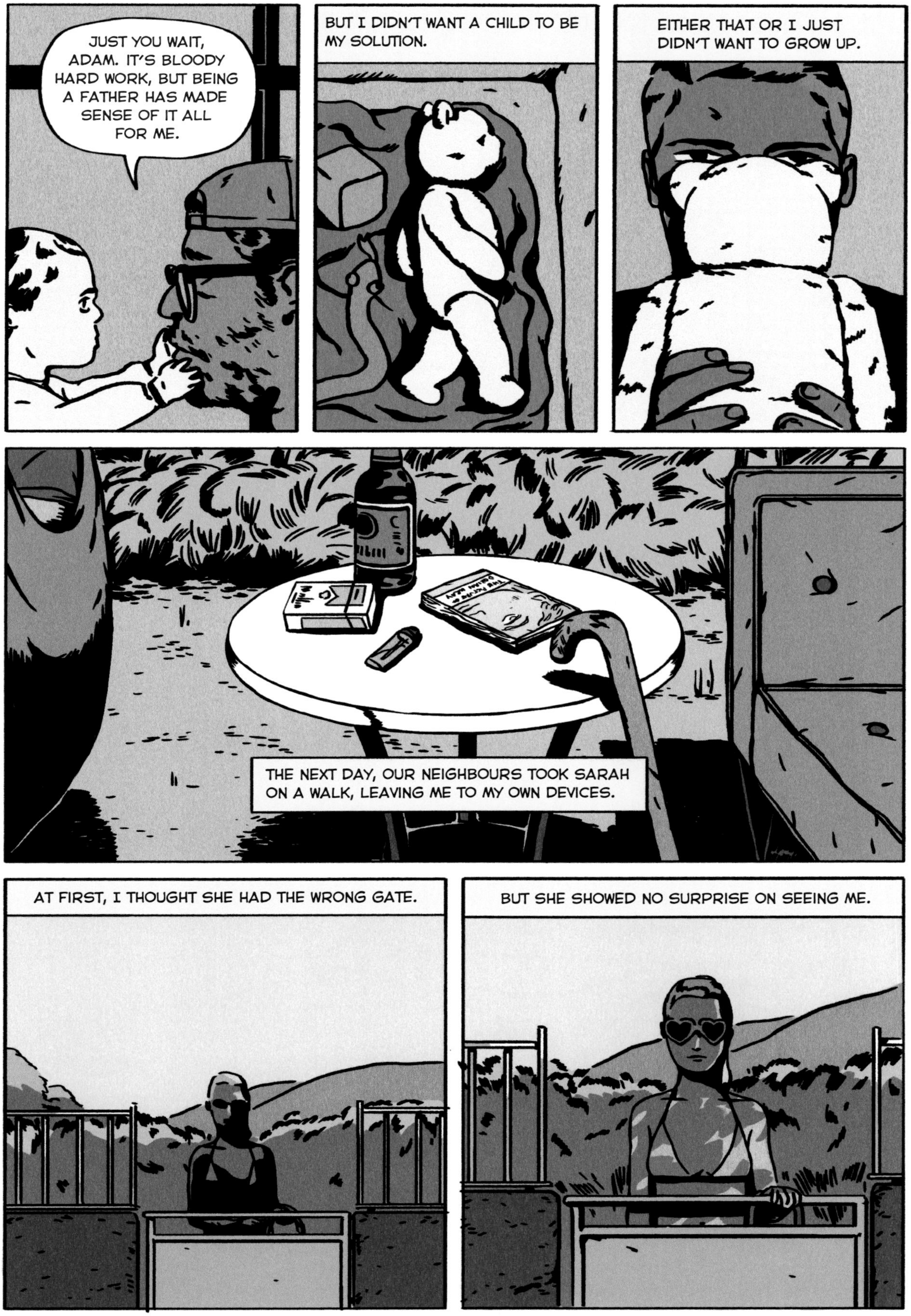
JUST YOU WAIT, ADAM. IT'S BLOODY HARD WORK, BUT BEING A FATHER HAS MADE SENSE OF IT ALL FOR ME.
BUT I DIDN'T WANT A CHILD TO BE MY SOLUTION.
EITHER THAT OR I JUST DIDN'T WANT TO GROW UP.
THE NEXT DAY, OUR NEIGHBOURS TOOK SARAH ON A WALK, LEAVING ME TO MY OWN DEVICES.
AT FIRST, I THOUGHT SHE HAD THE WRONG GATE.
BUT SHE SHOWED NO SURPRISE ON SEEING ME.

Panel 1: I'M TAMMY. THIS SEAT TAKEN? / BE MY GUEST. I'M ADAM.

Panel 2: I KNOW.

Panel 3: I WAS STILL NONE THE WISER AS TO WHO SHE WAS, BUT I WASN'T GOING TO BE THE FIRST TO CRACK IN THIS NOIR STAND-OFF.

Panel 4: CAN I HAVE ONE? / HELP YOURSELF.

Panel 5: SO, YOU FEELING BETTER? / NOT REALLY. BUT I'M GETTING USED TO IT, I GUESS.

Panel 6: MY FOLKS SAW YOU FALL. THEY SAID IT COULD HAVE BEEN MUCH WORSE.

Panel 7: OF COURSE! THAT'S WHO THIS MYSTERIOUS CREATURE WAS.

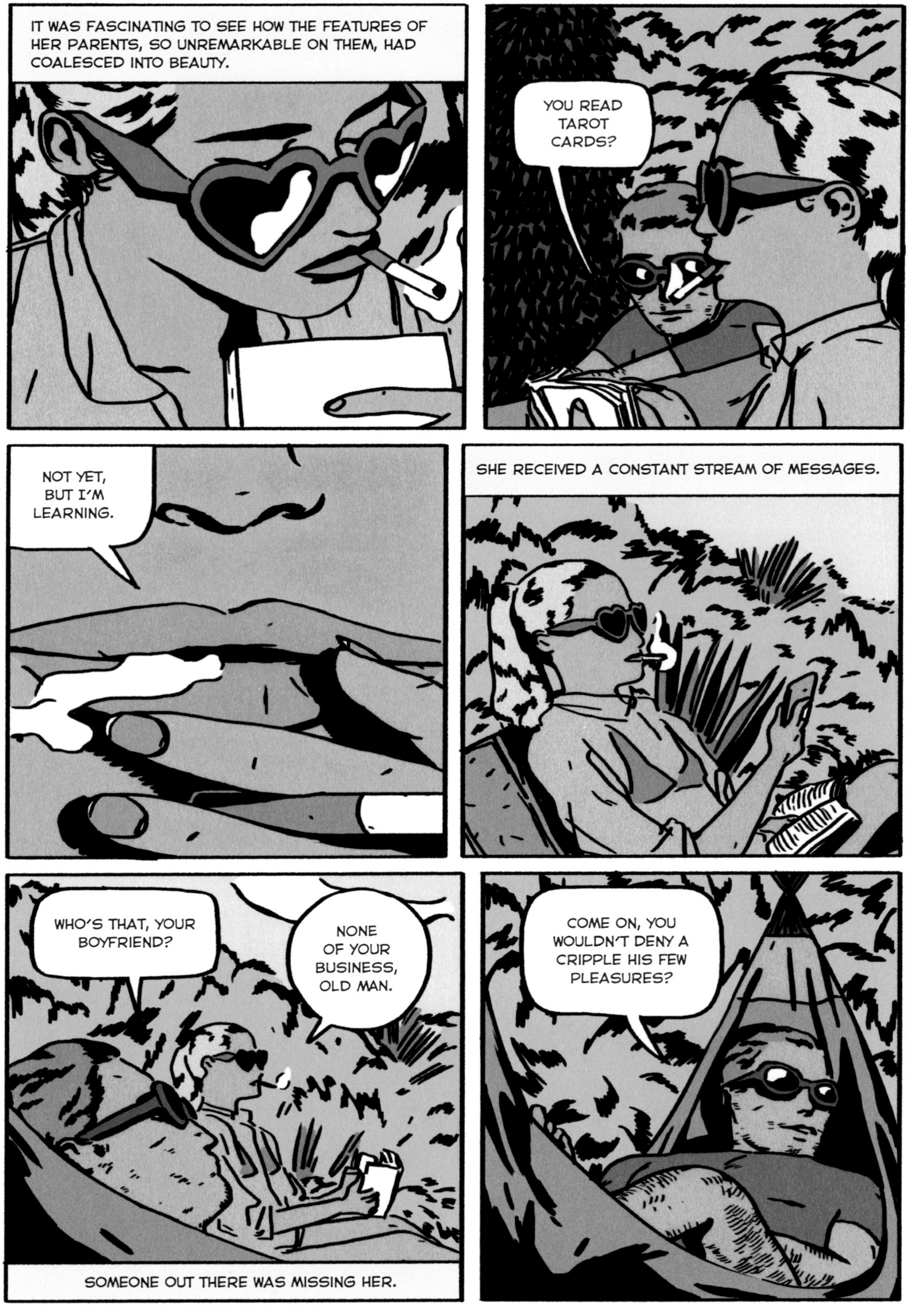
IT WAS FASCINATING TO SEE HOW THE FEATURES OF HER PARENTS, SO UNREMARKABLE ON THEM, HAD COALESCED INTO BEAUTY.
YOU READ TAROT CARDS?
NOT YET, BUT I'M LEARNING.
SHE RECEIVED A CONSTANT STREAM OF MESSAGES.
WHO'S THAT, YOUR BOYFRIEND?
NONE OF YOUR BUSINESS, OLD MAN.
SOMEONE OUT THERE WAS MISSING HER.
COME ON, YOU WOULDN'T DENY A CRIPPLE HIS FEW PLEASURES?

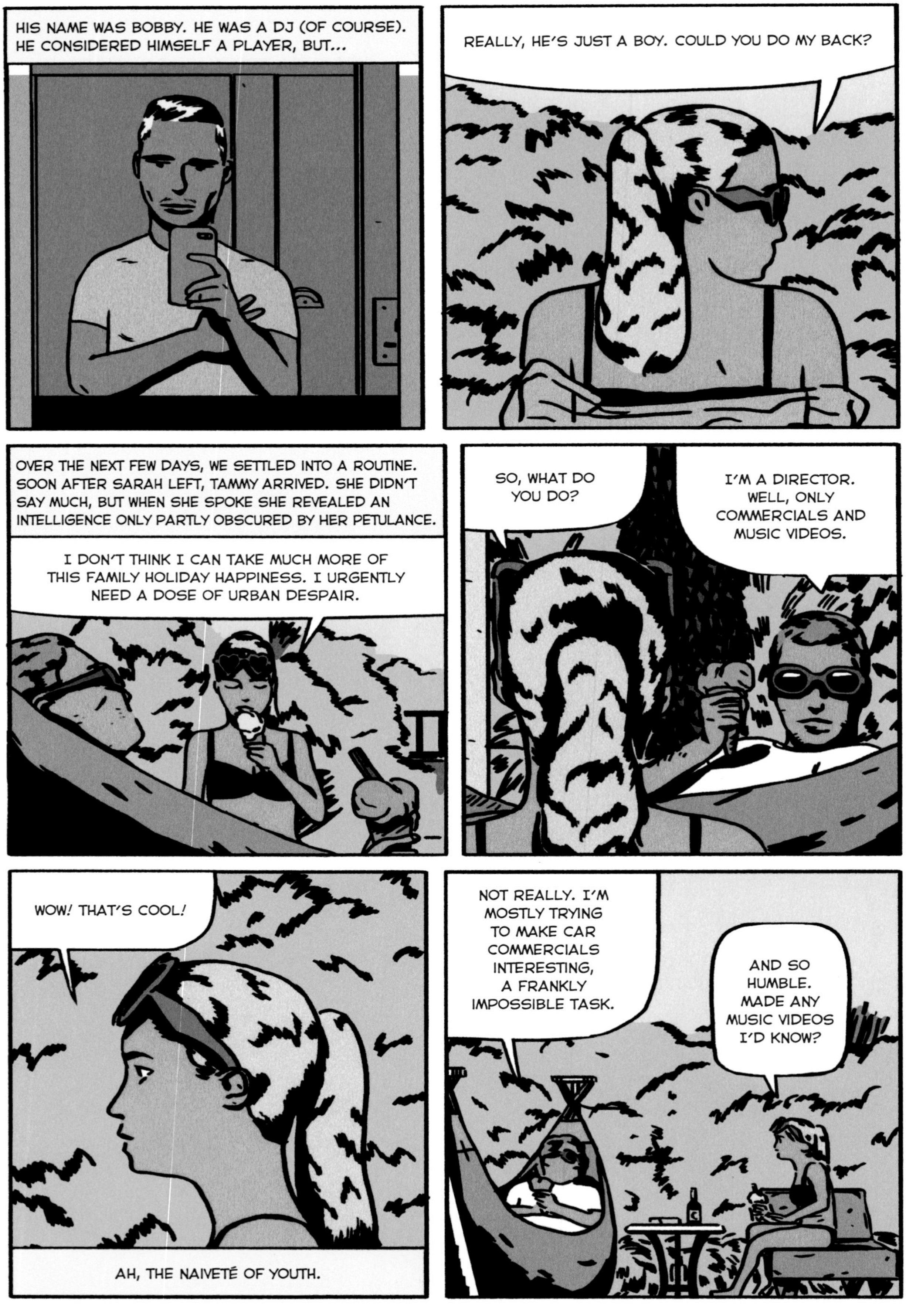
HIS NAME WAS BOBBY. HE WAS A DJ (OF COURSE). HE CONSIDERED HIMSELF A PLAYER, BUT...
REALLY, HE'S JUST A BOY. COULD YOU DO MY BACK?
OVER THE NEXT FEW DAYS, WE SETTLED INTO A ROUTINE. SOON AFTER SARAH LEFT, TAMMY ARRIVED. SHE DIDN'T SAY MUCH, BUT WHEN SHE SPOKE SHE REVEALED AN INTELLIGENCE ONLY PARTLY OBSCURED BY HER PETULANCE.
I DON'T THINK I CAN TAKE MUCH MORE OF THIS FAMILY HOLIDAY HAPPINESS. I URGENTLY NEED A DOSE OF URBAN DESPAIR.
SO, WHAT DO YOU DO?
I'M A DIRECTOR. WELL, ONLY COMMERCIALS AND MUSIC VIDEOS.
WOW! THAT'S COOL!
AH, THE NAIVETÉ OF YOUTH.
NOT REALLY. I'M MOSTLY TRYING TO MAKE CAR COMMERCIALS INTERESTING, A FRANKLY IMPOSSIBLE TASK.
AND SO HUMBLE. MADE ANY MUSIC VIDEOS I'D KNOW?

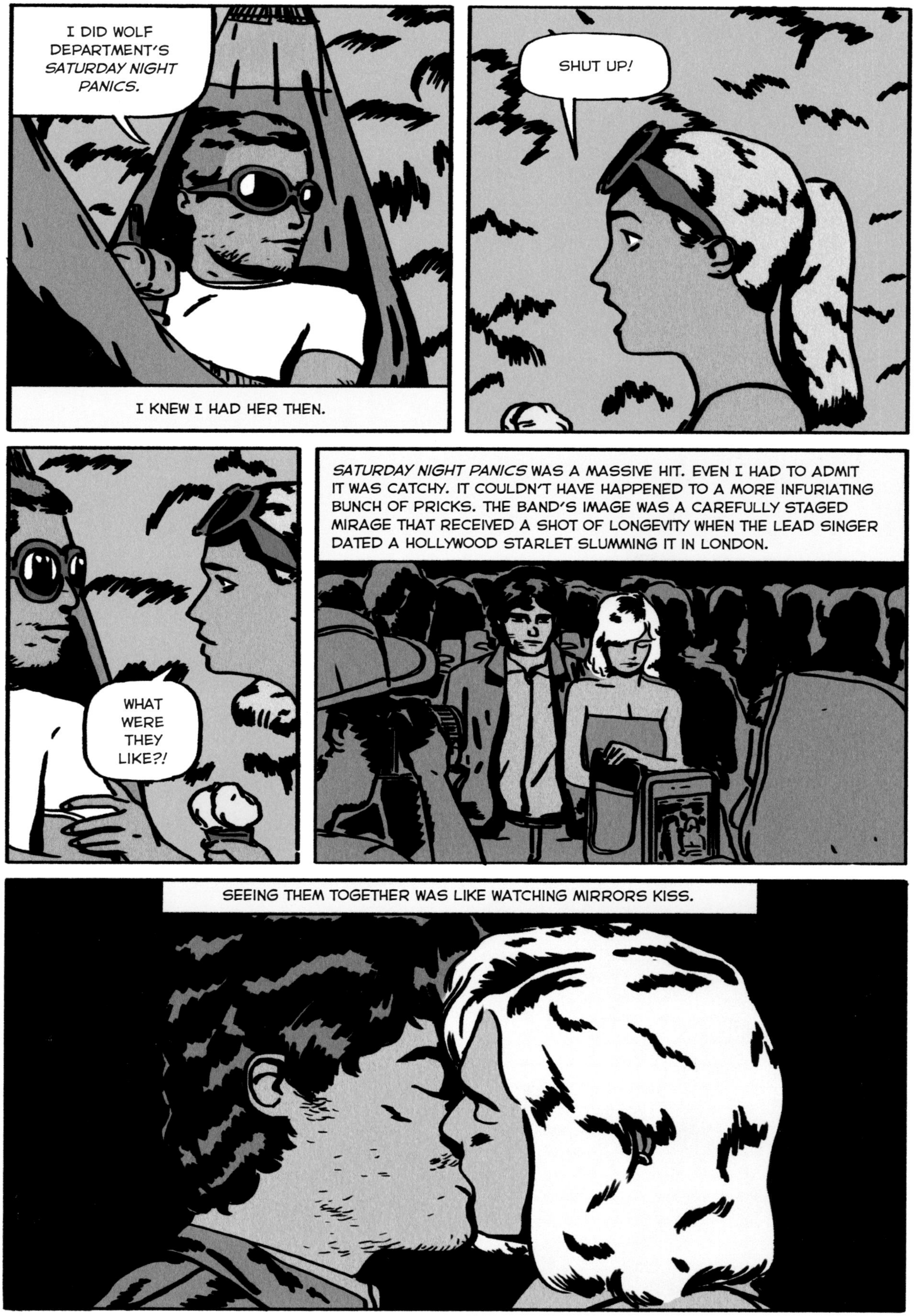
I DID WOLF DEPARTMENT'S *SATURDAY NIGHT PANICS.*
I KNEW I HAD HER THEN.
SHUT UP!
WHAT WERE THEY LIKE?!
SATURDAY NIGHT PANICS WAS A MASSIVE HIT. EVEN I HAD TO ADMIT IT WAS CATCHY. IT COULDN'T HAVE HAPPENED TO A MORE INFURIATING BUNCH OF PRICKS. THE BAND'S IMAGE WAS A CAREFULLY STAGED MIRAGE THAT RECEIVED A SHOT OF LONGEVITY WHEN THE LEAD SINGER DATED A HOLLYWOOD STARLET SLUMMING IT IN LONDON.
SEEING THEM TOGETHER WAS LIKE WATCHING MIRRORS KISS.

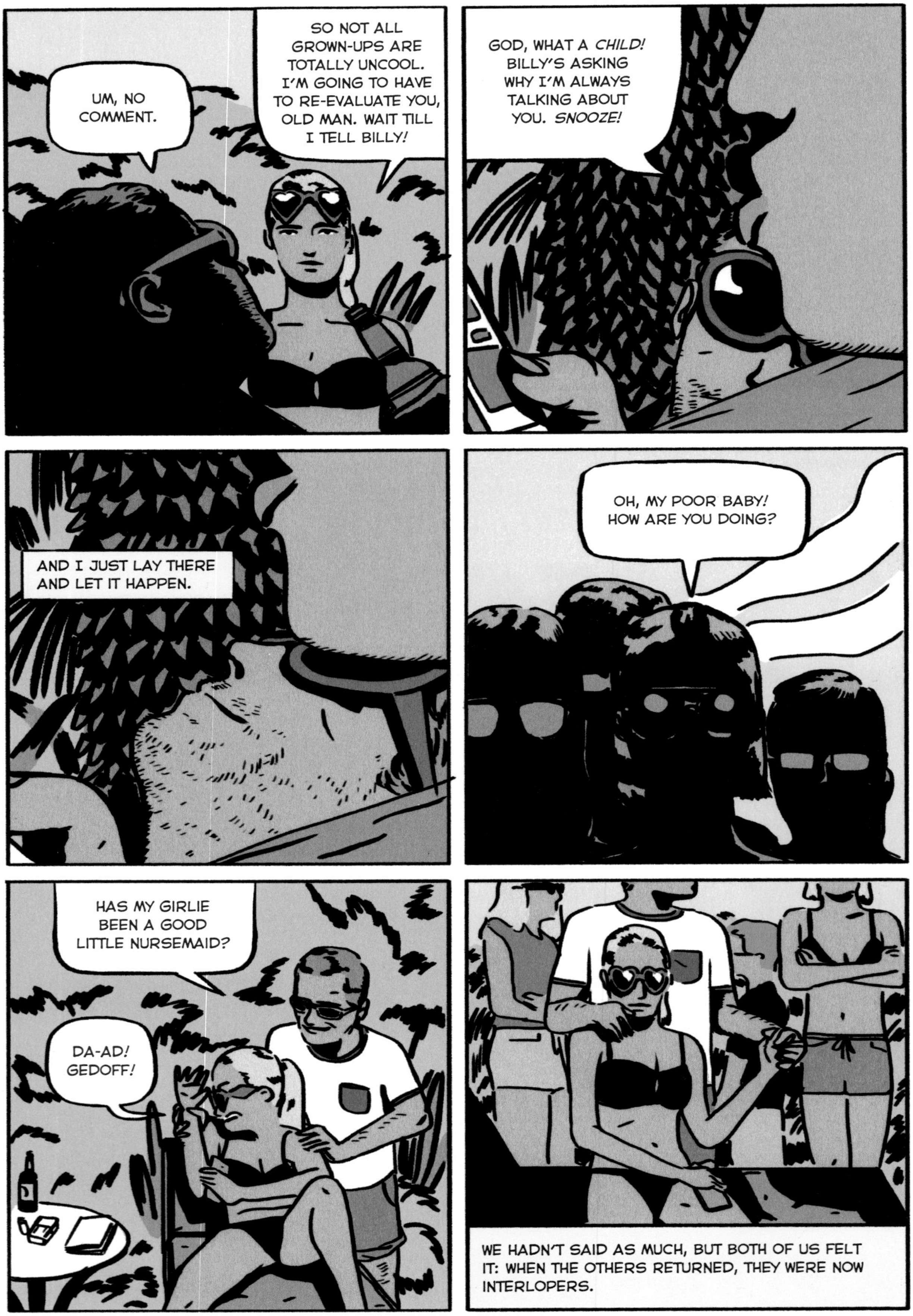
UM, NO COMMENT.
SO NOT ALL GROWN-UPS ARE TOTALLY UNCOOL. I'M GOING TO HAVE TO RE-EVALUATE YOU, OLD MAN. WAIT TILL I TELL BILLY!
GOD, WHAT A *CHILD!* BILLY'S ASKING WHY I'M ALWAYS TALKING ABOUT YOU. *SNOOZE!*
AND I JUST LAY THERE AND LET IT HAPPEN.
OH, MY POOR BABY! HOW ARE YOU DOING?
HAS MY GIRLIE BEEN A GOOD LITTLE NURSEMAID?
DA-AD! GEDOFF!
WE HADN'T SAID AS MUCH, BUT BOTH OF US FELT IT: WHEN THE OTHERS RETURNED, THEY WERE NOW INTERLOPERS.

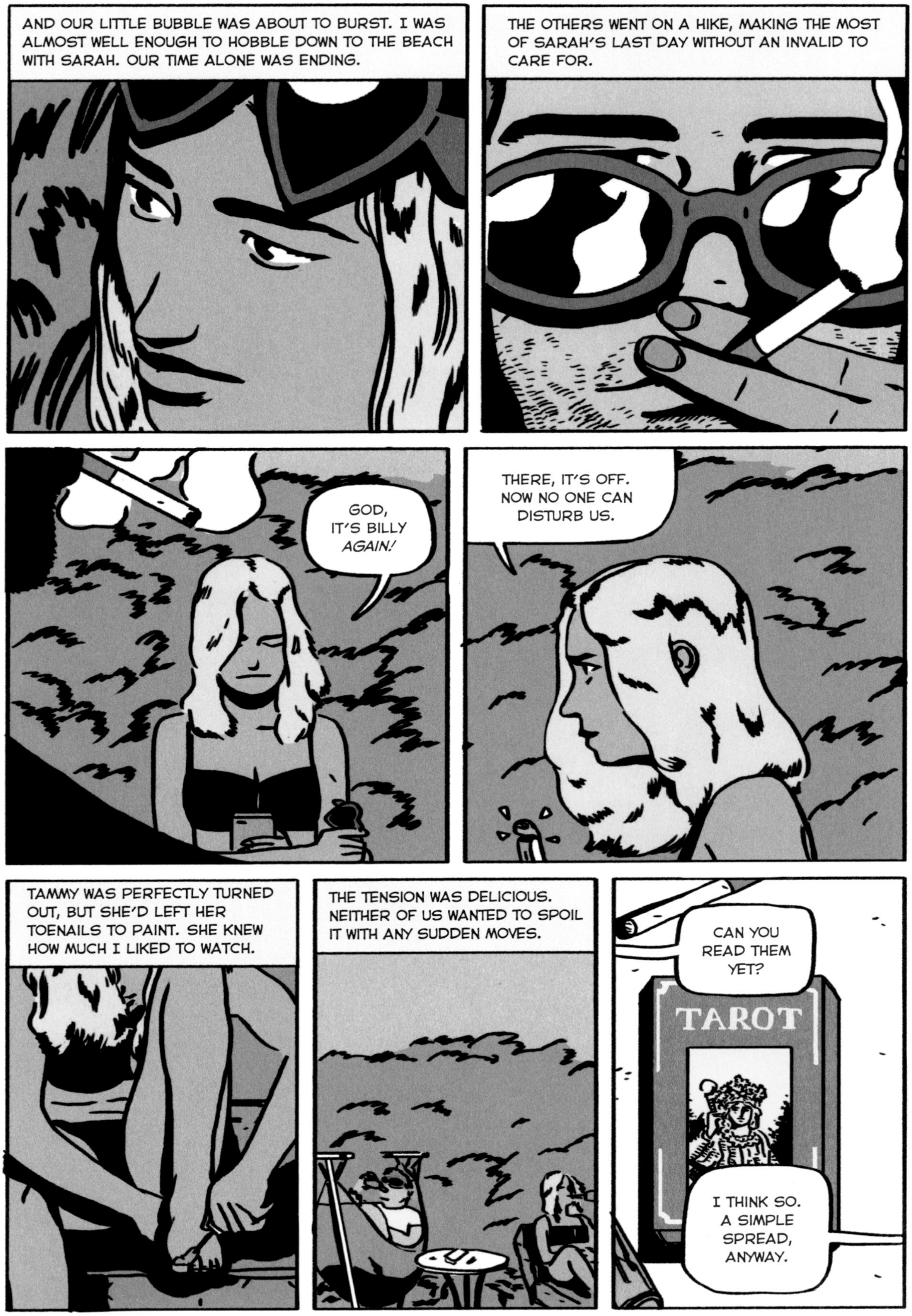
AND OUR LITTLE BUBBLE WAS ABOUT TO BURST. I WAS ALMOST WELL ENOUGH TO HOBBLE DOWN TO THE BEACH WITH SARAH. OUR TIME ALONE WAS ENDING.
THE OTHERS WENT ON A HIKE, MAKING THE MOST OF SARAH'S LAST DAY WITHOUT AN INVALID TO CARE FOR.
GOD, IT'S BILLY *AGAIN!*
THERE, IT'S OFF. NOW NO ONE CAN DISTURB US.
TAMMY WAS PERFECTLY TURNED OUT, BUT SHE'D LEFT HER TOENAILS TO PAINT. SHE KNEW HOW MUCH I LIKED TO WATCH.
THE TENSION WAS DELICIOUS. NEITHER OF US WANTED TO SPOIL IT WITH ANY SUDDEN MOVES.
CAN YOU READ THEM YET?
TAROT
I THINK SO. A SIMPLE SPREAD, ANYWAY.

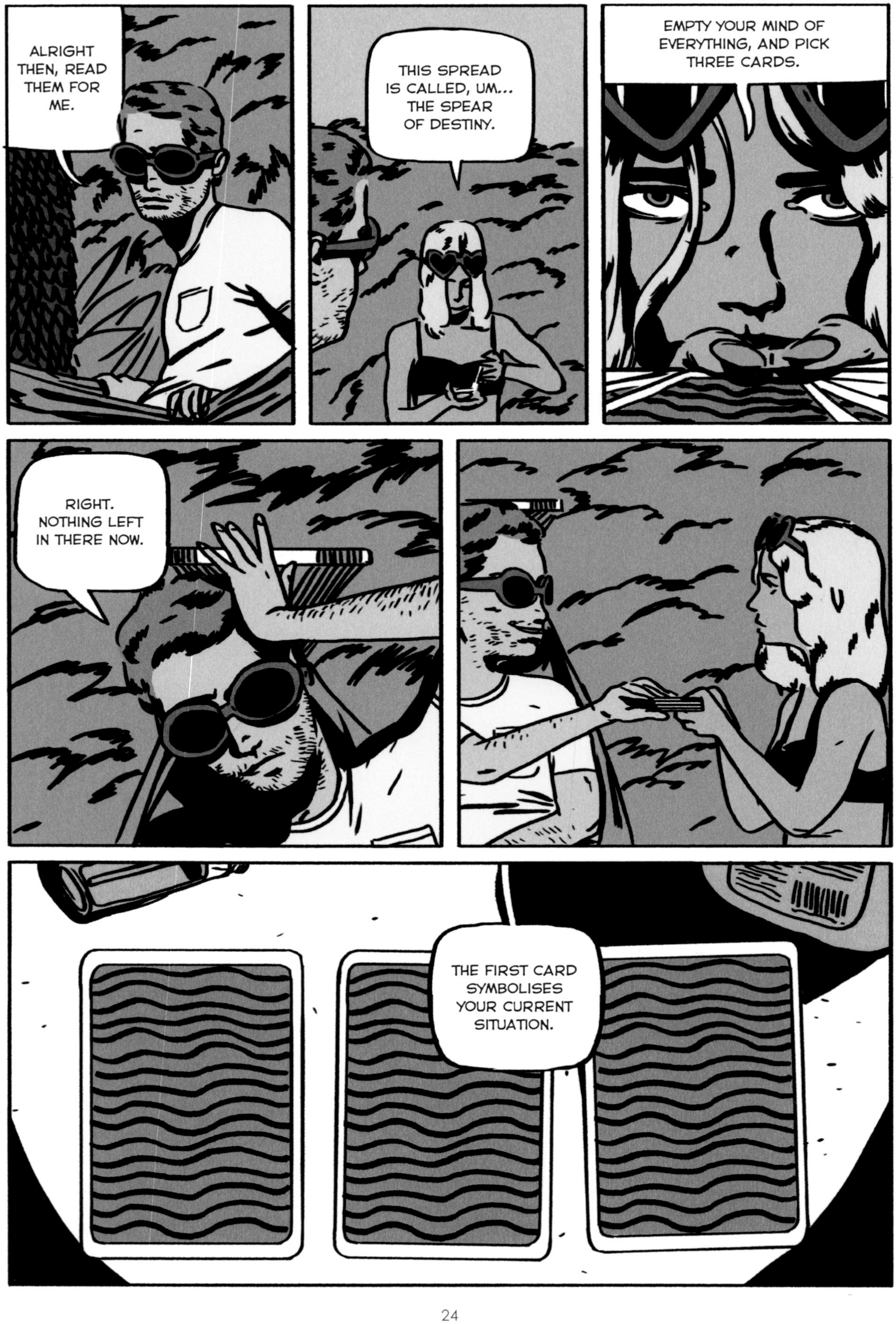
ALRIGHT THEN, READ THEM FOR ME.
THIS SPREAD IS CALLED, UM... THE SPEAR OF DESTINY.
EMPTY YOUR MIND OF EVERYTHING, AND PICK THREE CARDS.
RIGHT. NOTHING LEFT IN THERE NOW.
THE FIRST CARD SYMBOLISES YOUR CURRENT SITUATION.

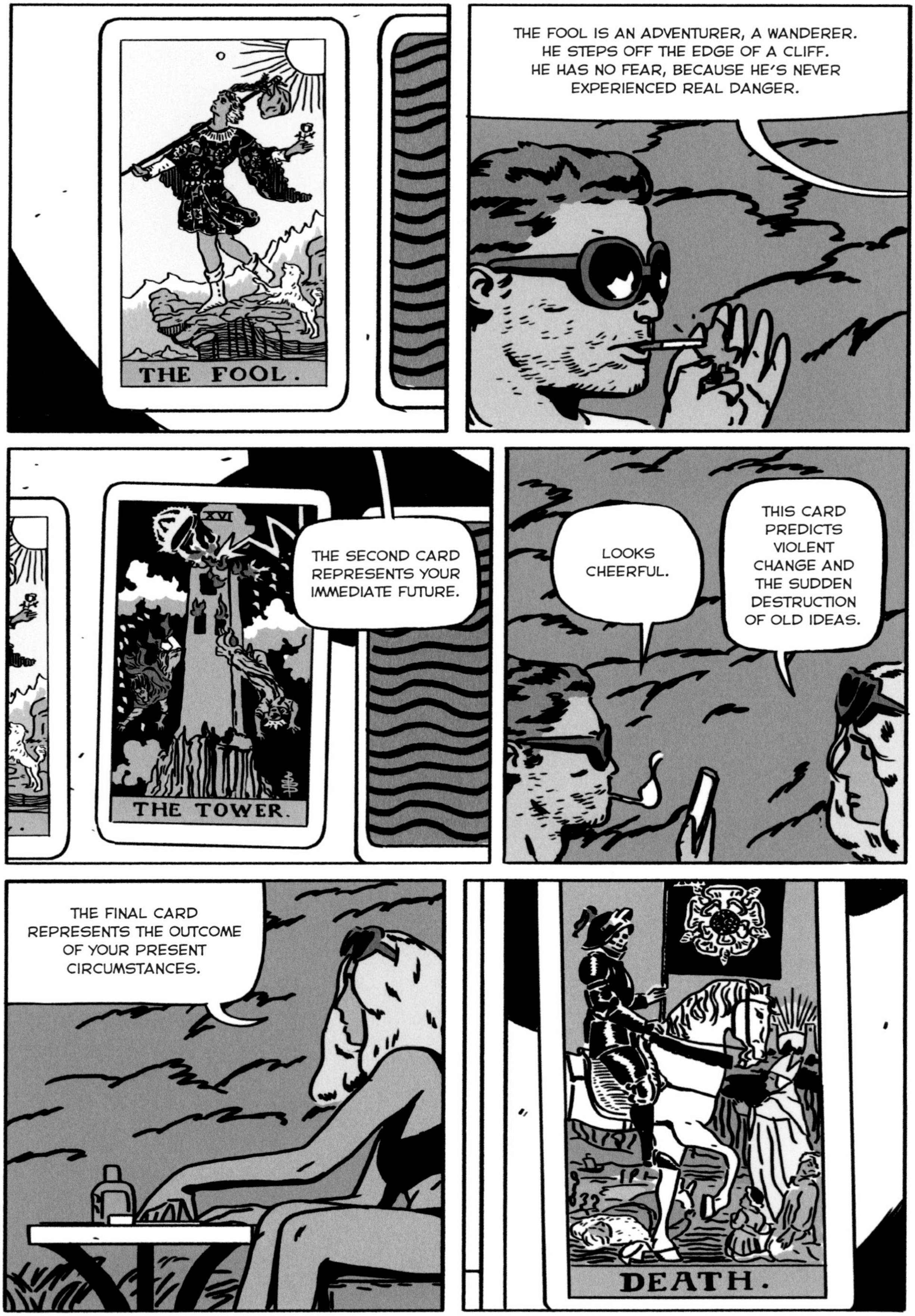
THE FOOL.
THE FOOL IS AN ADVENTURER, A WANDERER. HE STEPS OFF THE EDGE OF A CLIFF. HE HAS NO FEAR, BECAUSE HE'S NEVER EXPERIENCED REAL DANGER.
XVI
THE TOWER.
THE SECOND CARD REPRESENTS YOUR IMMEDIATE FUTURE.
LOOKS CHEERFUL.
THIS CARD PREDICTS VIOLENT CHANGE AND THE SUDDEN DESTRUCTION OF OLD IDEAS.
THE FINAL CARD REPRESENTS THE OUTCOME OF YOUR PRESENT CIRCUMSTANCES.
DEATH.

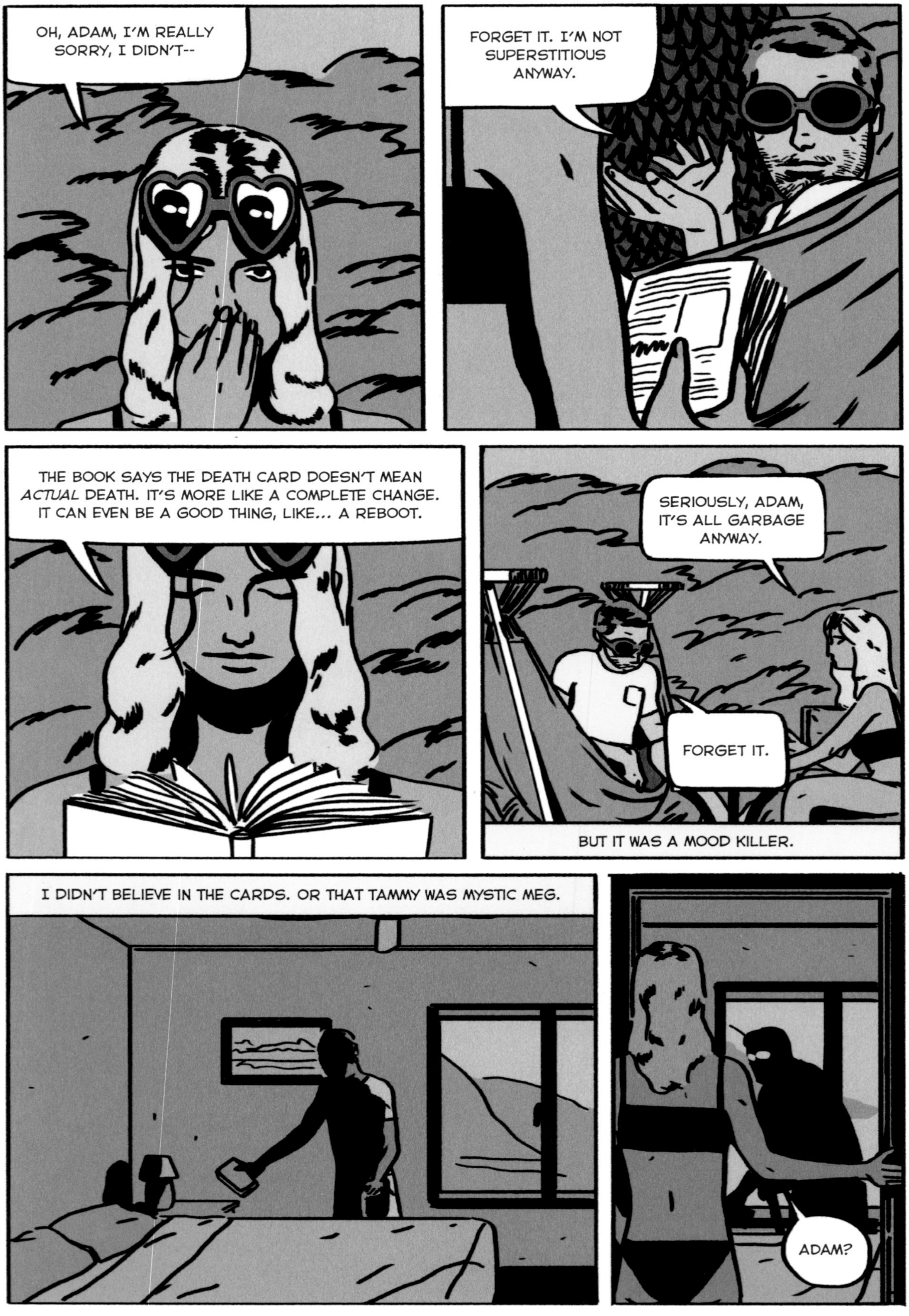
OH, ADAM, I'M REALLY SORRY, I DIDN'T--
FORGET IT. I'M NOT SUPERSTITIOUS ANYWAY.
THE BOOK SAYS THE DEATH CARD DOESN'T MEAN *ACTUAL* DEATH. IT'S MORE LIKE A COMPLETE CHANGE. IT CAN EVEN BE A GOOD THING, LIKE... A REBOOT.
SERIOUSLY, ADAM, IT'S ALL GARBAGE ANYWAY.
FORGET IT.
BUT IT WAS A MOOD KILLER.
I DIDN'T BELIEVE IN THE CARDS. OR THAT TAMMY WAS MYSTIC MEG.
ADAM?

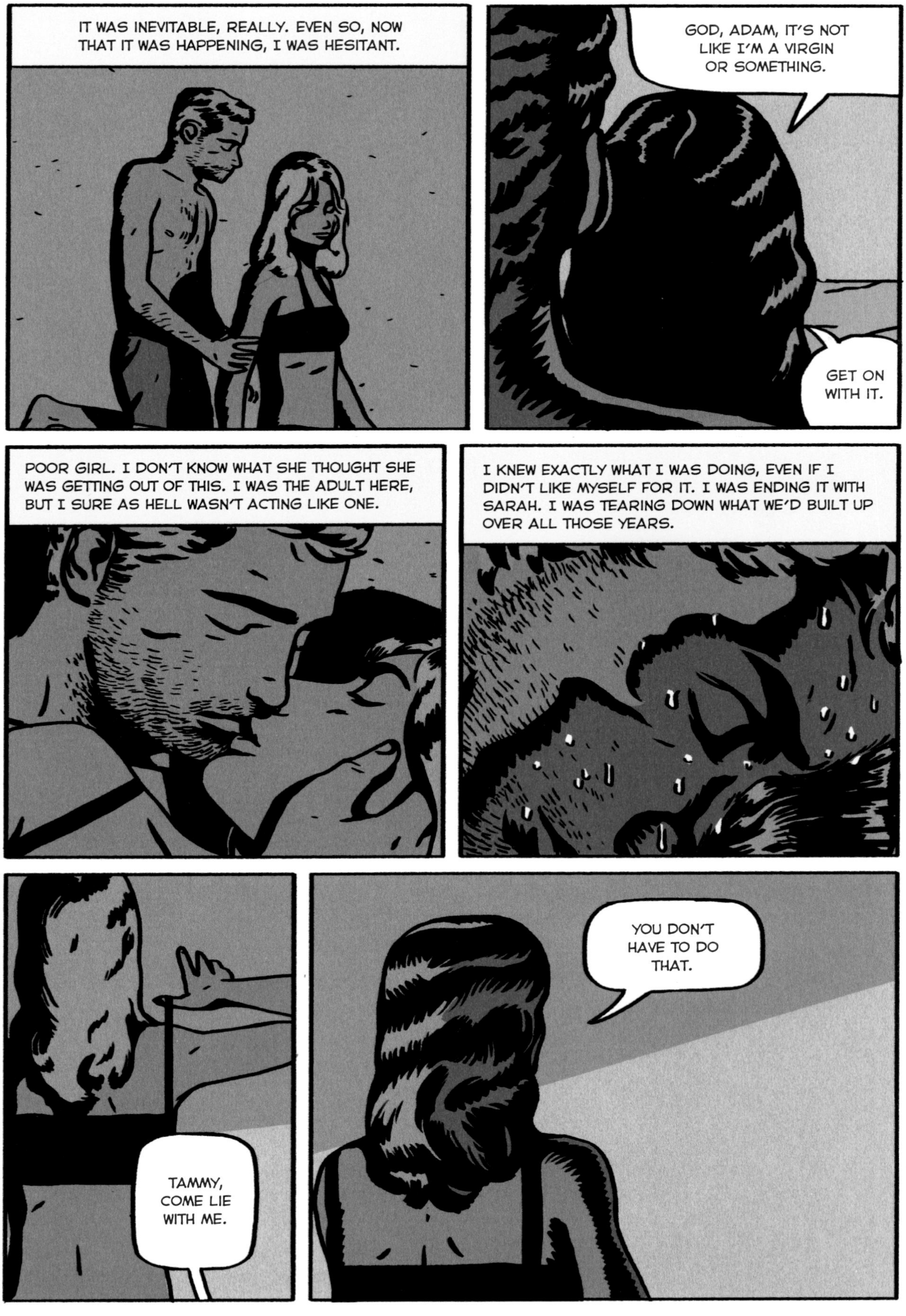
IT WAS INEVITABLE, REALLY. EVEN SO, NOW THAT IT WAS HAPPENING, I WAS HESITANT.
GOD, ADAM, IT'S NOT LIKE I'M A VIRGIN OR SOMETHING.
GET ON WITH IT.
POOR GIRL. I DON'T KNOW WHAT SHE THOUGHT SHE WAS GETTING OUT OF THIS. I WAS THE ADULT HERE, BUT I SURE AS HELL WASN'T ACTING LIKE ONE.
I KNEW EXACTLY WHAT I WAS DOING, EVEN IF I DIDN'T LIKE MYSELF FOR IT. I WAS ENDING IT WITH SARAH. I WAS TEARING DOWN WHAT WE'D BUILT UP OVER ALL THOSE YEARS.
TAMMY, COME LIE WITH ME.
YOU DON'T HAVE TO DO THAT.

I NEVER THOUGHT I'D BE THE BAD GUY IN THE STORY OF MY LIFE.

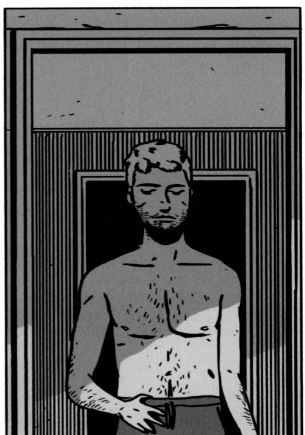

THE FOOL.

COULDN'T HAVE PUT IT BETTER MYSELF.

WHAT WAS TAMMY THINKING? WAS SHE PISSED OFF? ASHAMED?

I WAS SURE HER PARENTS – OR SARAH – WOULD NOTICE THE CHILL BETWEEN US.

BUT NONE OF THEM SEEMED TO. OR DIDN'T WANT TO.

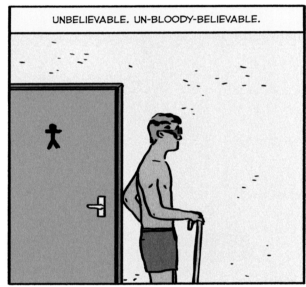

UNBELIEVABLE. UN-BLOODY-BELIEVABLE.

OI! HAND THEM OVER!

29

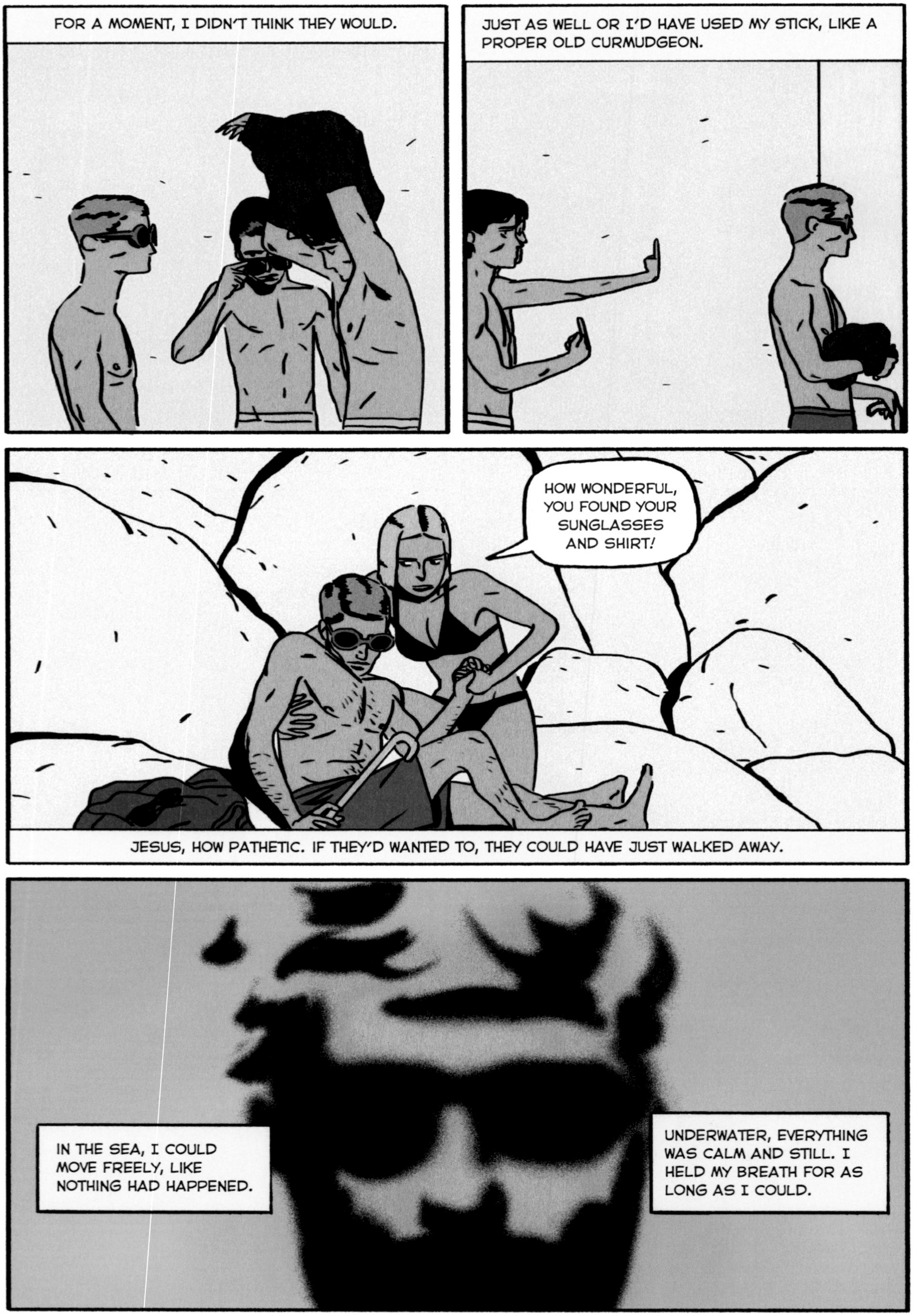
FOR A MOMENT, I DIDN'T THINK THEY WOULD.
JUST AS WELL OR I'D HAVE USED MY STICK, LIKE A PROPER OLD CURMUDGEON.
HOW WONDERFUL, YOU FOUND YOUR SUNGLASSES AND SHIRT!
JESUS, HOW PATHETIC. IF THEY'D WANTED TO, THEY COULD HAVE JUST WALKED AWAY.
IN THE SEA, I COULD MOVE FREELY, LIKE NOTHING HAD HAPPENED.
UNDERWATER, EVERYTHING WAS CALM AND STILL. I HELD MY BREATH FOR AS LONG AS I COULD.

ON THE FLIGHT HOME, I STARTED CRACKING UP IN EARNEST.

AS THE CABIN CREW SEALED THE DOOR, IT WAS LIKE SOMEBODY CUT OFF MY OXYGEN SUPPLY.

FEAR CRASHED IN AROUND ME LIKE A PHYSICAL FORCE.

I TRIED TO READ, TO GRAB AT ANYTHING THAT WOULD TAKE ME AWAY FROM THE HERE AND NOW, BUT LIKE A SWARM OF ANTS THE WORDS REFUSED TO HOLD STILL.

I TRIED TO THINK OF BLUE, ENDLESS BLUE, TO RECALL WHAT IT HAD BEEN LIKE FLOATING THERE UNDERWATER.

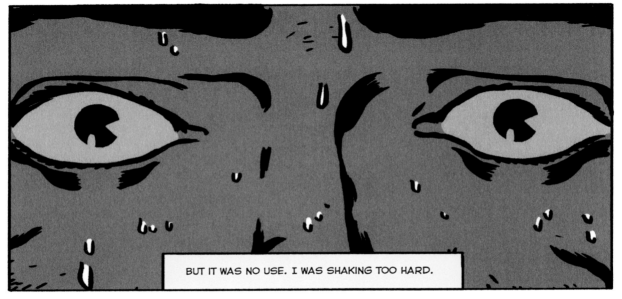

BUT IT WAS NO USE. I WAS SHAKING TOO HARD.

OH GOD, OH GOD...

ADAM, WHAT'S WRONG?!

IT WASN'T A PLEASANT FLIGHT HOME.

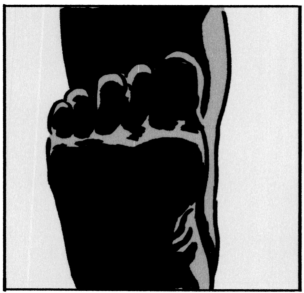

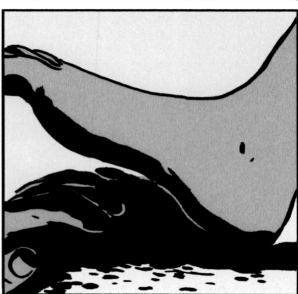

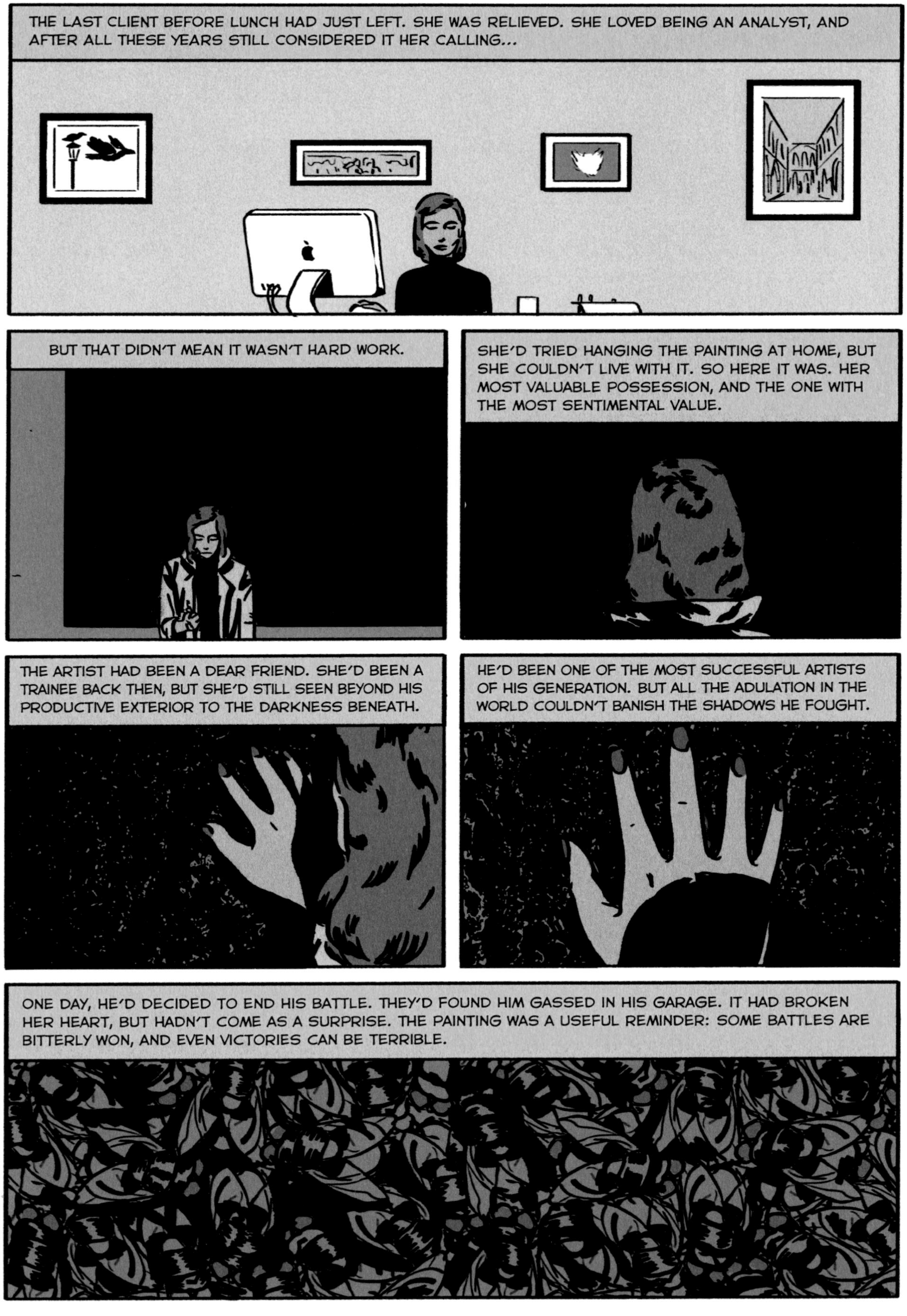

THE LAST CLIENT BEFORE LUNCH HAD JUST LEFT. SHE WAS RELIEVED. SHE LOVED BEING AN ANALYST, AND AFTER ALL THESE YEARS STILL CONSIDERED IT HER CALLING...
BUT THAT DIDN'T MEAN IT WASN'T HARD WORK.
SHE'D TRIED HANGING THE PAINTING AT HOME, BUT SHE COULDN'T LIVE WITH IT. SO HERE IT WAS. HER MOST VALUABLE POSSESSION, AND THE ONE WITH THE MOST SENTIMENTAL VALUE.
THE ARTIST HAD BEEN A DEAR FRIEND. SHE'D BEEN A TRAINEE BACK THEN, BUT SHE'D STILL SEEN BEYOND HIS PRODUCTIVE EXTERIOR TO THE DARKNESS BENEATH.
HE'D BEEN ONE OF THE MOST SUCCESSFUL ARTISTS OF HIS GENERATION. BUT ALL THE ADULATION IN THE WORLD COULDN'T BANISH THE SHADOWS HE FOUGHT.
ONE DAY, HE'D DECIDED TO END HIS BATTLE. THEY'D FOUND HIM GASSED IN HIS GARAGE. IT HAD BROKEN HER HEART, BUT HADN'T COME AS A SURPRISE. THE PAINTING WAS A USEFUL REMINDER: SOME BATTLES ARE BITTERLY WON, AND EVEN VICTORIES CAN BE TERRIBLE.

ALRIGHT, ISADORA?

ISADORA. SHE'D LOVED AND HATED HER NAME IN EQUAL MEASURE. IN HER TEENS, SHE'D FOUND ITS SINGULARITY A CURSE. AT UNIVERSITY, SHE'D CHERISHED IT FOR THE SAME REASON.

IT WAS SURELY NO COINCIDENCE THAT HER MOTHER HAD NAMED THE DAUGHTER WHO'D PREMATURELY ENDED HER OWN DANCE CAREER AFTER A DANCER SHE'D ADMIRED...

...A DANCER WHO'D DIED IN A FREAK ACCIDENT.

ISADORA DUNCAN'S SCARF HAD ANCHORED IN THE WHEEL OF HER SPEEDING CAR, SNAPPING HER NECK.

EVERY LUNCHTIME, BARRING AN EMERGENCY, SHE CAME HERE.

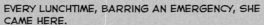

IT ALWAYS AMAZED HER THAT IN A CITY OF ALMOST NINE MILLION PEOPLE SO FEW USED THE HEATH ON WEEKDAYS.

WHY WERE HER THOUGHTS DRAWN BACK TO THE PAINTING?

MAYBE IT WAS BECAUSE SHE HAD HER OWN SHADOWS TO CONTEND WITH. THAT WAS THE THING WITH SHADOWS: YOU MIGHT NOT PAY ATTENTION TO THEM, BUT TURN AROUND AND THERE THEY WERE, JUST WHERE YOU LEFT THEM.

SHE'D NEVER FELT ENTIRELY COMFORTABLE ABOUT TAKING THE JOB, BUT WHAT HARM HAD COME OF IT? SHE'D HONESTLY DONE EVERYTHING SHE COULD TO HELP THE GIRL.

SHE'D NEVER BEEN ENTIRELY HONEST WITH HER, BUT WOULD THAT REALLY HAVE BEEN FOR THE BEST?

THERE WAS A SOFT SOUND, LIKE A CHILD IMITATING GUNFIRE.

THEN A STING, AND SOMETHING BLOSSOMED INSIDE HER.

IT WAS MORE SURPRISING THAN PAINFUL.

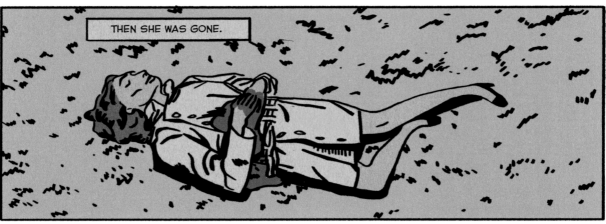

THEN SHE WAS GONE.

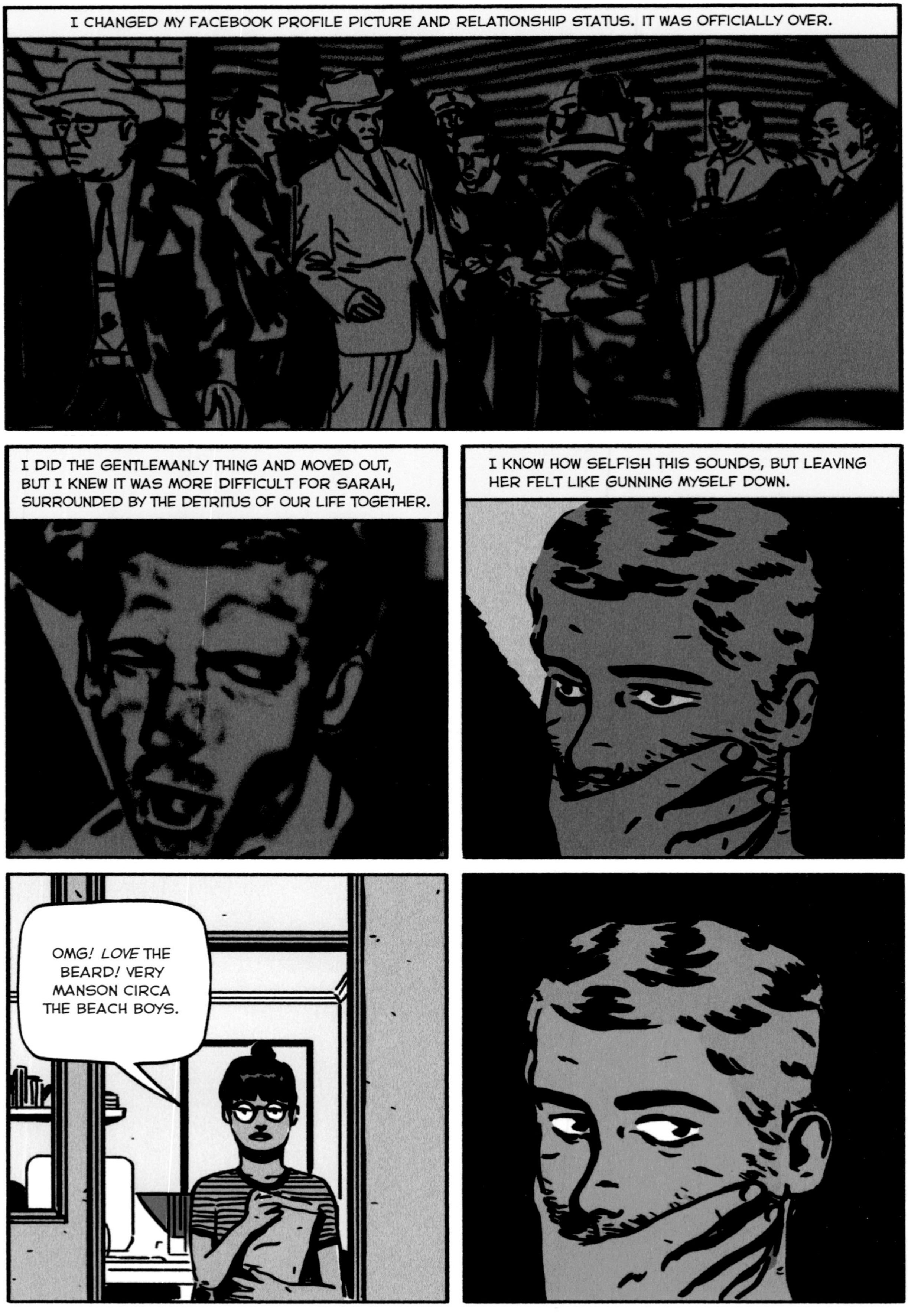
I CHANGED MY FACEBOOK PROFILE PICTURE AND RELATIONSHIP STATUS. IT WAS OFFICIALLY OVER.
I DID THE GENTLEMANLY THING AND MOVED OUT, BUT I KNEW IT WAS MORE DIFFICULT FOR SARAH, SURROUNDED BY THE DETRITUS OF OUR LIFE TOGETHER.
I KNOW HOW SELFISH THIS SOUNDS, BUT LEAVING HER FELT LIKE GUNNING MYSELF DOWN.
OMG! *LOVE* THE BEARD! VERY MANSON CIRCA THE BEACH BOYS.

AND HAVE I GOT *GREAT* NEWS FOR YOU!

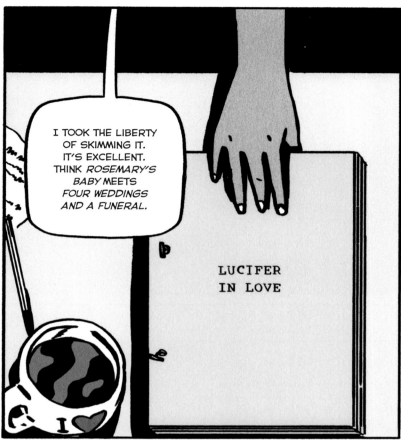

I TOOK THE LIBERTY OF SKIMMING IT. IT'S EXCELLENT. THINK *ROSEMARY'S BABY* MEETS *FOUR WEDDINGS AND A FUNERAL.*

LUCIFER IN LOVE

THIS WAS WHAT I'D BEEN WAITING FOR — A FEATURE FILM SCRIPT FROM ONE OF LONDON'S TOP AGENTS. I SHOULD HAVE FELT ON TOP OF THE WORLD.

CIFER IN LOVE

I FELT NOTHING.

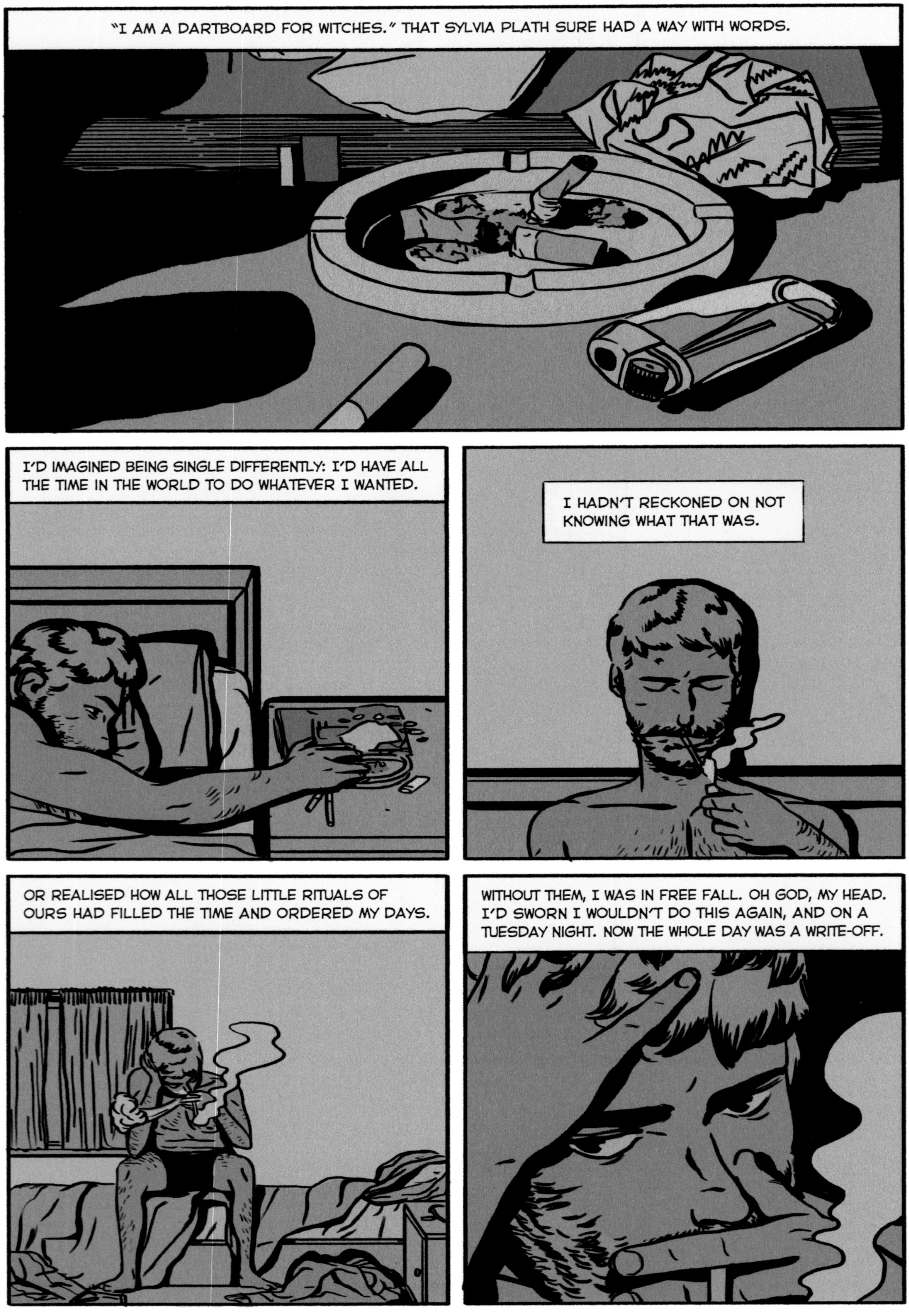
"I AM A DARTBOARD FOR WITCHES." THAT SYLVIA PLATH SURE HAD A WAY WITH WORDS.
I'D IMAGINED BEING SINGLE DIFFERENTLY: I'D HAVE ALL THE TIME IN THE WORLD TO DO WHATEVER I WANTED.
I HADN'T RECKONED ON NOT KNOWING WHAT THAT WAS.
OR REALISED HOW ALL THOSE LITTLE RITUALS OF OURS HAD FILLED THE TIME AND ORDERED MY DAYS.
WITHOUT THEM, I WAS IN FREE FALL. OH GOD, MY HEAD. I'D SWORN I WOULDN'T DO THIS AGAIN, AND ON A TUESDAY NIGHT. NOW THE WHOLE DAY WAS A WRITE-OFF.

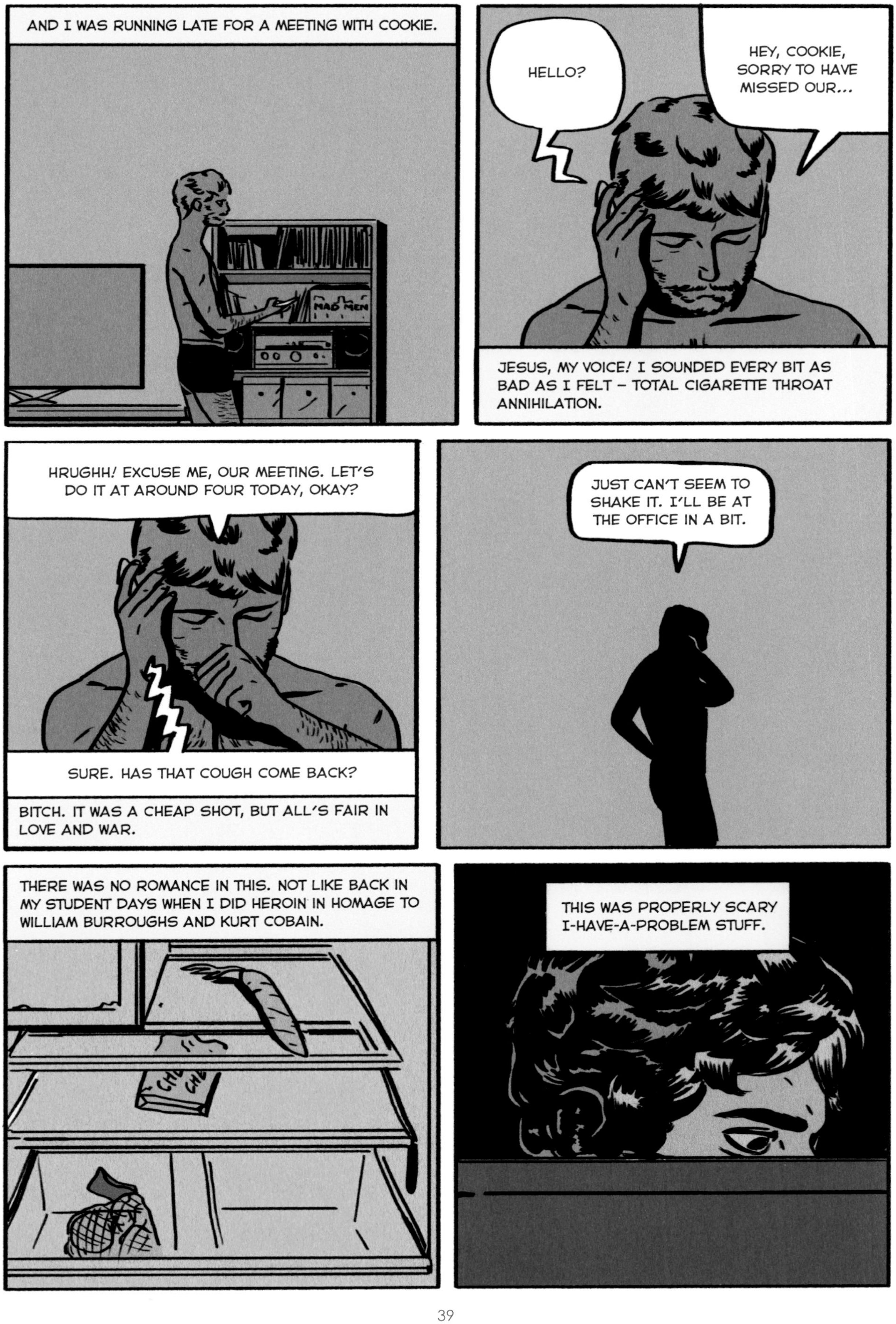
AND I WAS RUNNING LATE FOR A MEETING WITH COOKIE.
MAD MEN
HELLO?
HEY, COOKIE, SORRY TO HAVE MISSED OUR...
JESUS, MY VOICE! I SOUNDED EVERY BIT AS BAD AS I FELT – TOTAL CIGARETTE THROAT ANNIHILATION.
HRUGHH! EXCUSE ME, OUR MEETING. LET'S DO IT AT AROUND FOUR TODAY, OKAY?
SURE. HAS THAT COUGH COME BACK?
BITCH. IT WAS A CHEAP SHOT, BUT ALL'S FAIR IN LOVE AND WAR.
JUST CAN'T SEEM TO SHAKE IT. I'LL BE AT THE OFFICE IN A BIT.
THERE WAS NO ROMANCE IN THIS. NOT LIKE BACK IN MY STUDENT DAYS WHEN I DID HEROIN IN HOMAGE TO WILLIAM BURROUGHS AND KURT COBAIN.
THIS WAS PROPERLY SCARY I-HAVE-A-PROBLEM STUFF.

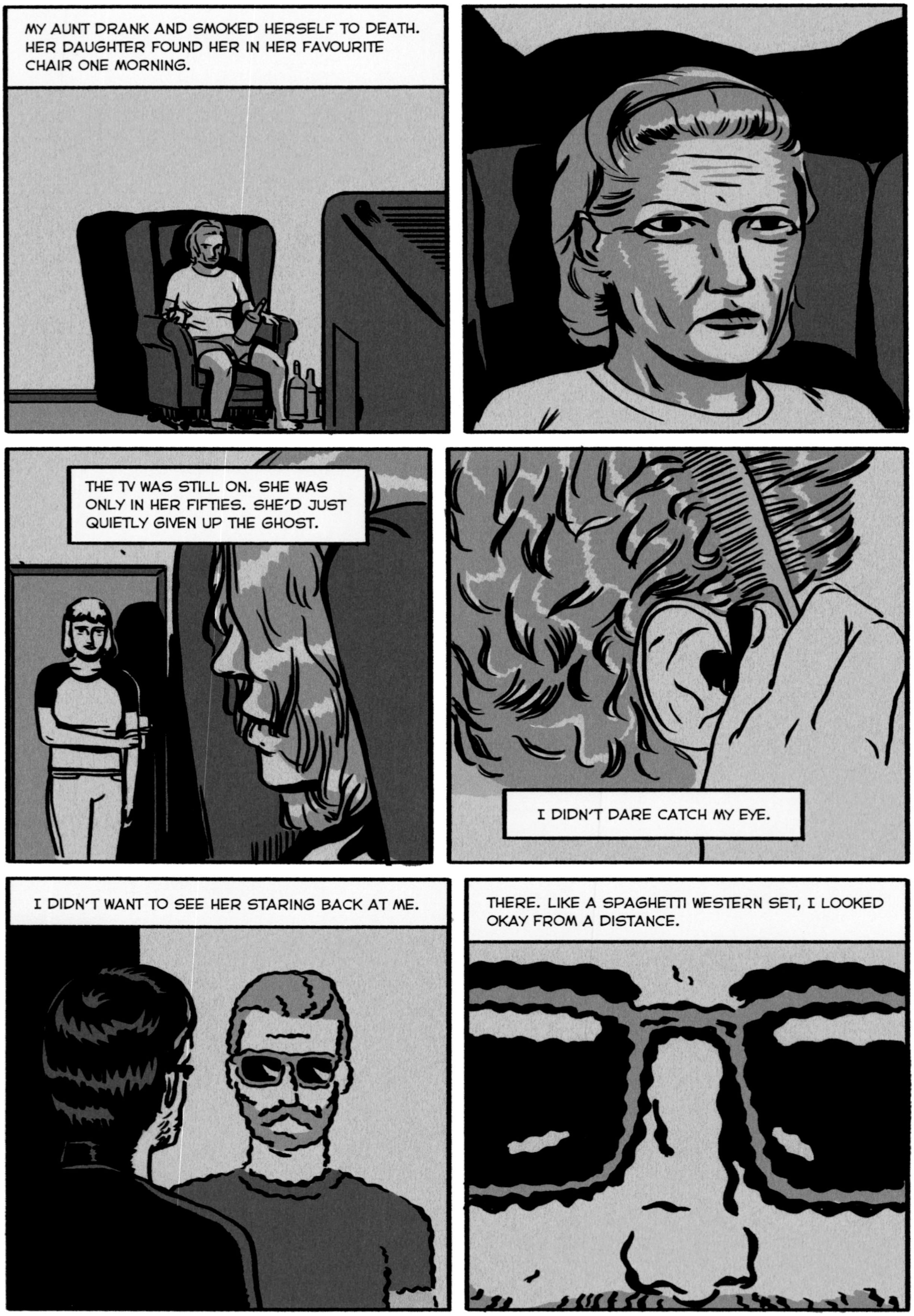
MY AUNT DRANK AND SMOKED HERSELF TO DEATH. HER DAUGHTER FOUND HER IN HER FAVOURITE CHAIR ONE MORNING.
THE TV WAS STILL ON. SHE WAS ONLY IN HER FIFTIES. SHE'D JUST QUIETLY GIVEN UP THE GHOST.
I DIDN'T DARE CATCH MY EYE.
I DIDN'T WANT TO SEE HER STARING BACK AT ME.
THERE. LIKE A SPAGHETTI WESTERN SET, I LOOKED OKAY FROM A DISTANCE.

THE PRIMARY THEME OF *PREDATOR* IS THE ESSENTIAL STRENGTH OF MAN TRIUMPHING OVER TECHNOLOGY.

"SURE, ARNIE'S HOODWINKED BY HIS MILITARY SUPERIORS TO GO ON WHAT SEEMS LIKE A SUICIDE MISSION, PITTING HIM AGAINST IMPOSSIBLE ODDS..."

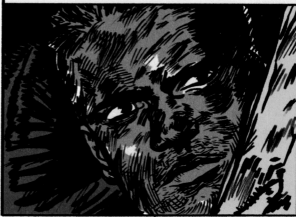

"...BUT WHEN IT COMES DOWN TO IT, HE BEATS THE HI-TECH ALIEN HUNTER BY SIMPLY COVERING HIMSELF IN MUD AND LETTING HIS MUSCLES DO THE REST."

"HERE ENDS THE LESSON."

ENOUGH OF THIS! WE NEED TO GET ON WITH PREPARATIONS.

MAREK AND I GREW UP TOGETHER IN DERBY, THEN WENT TO FILM SCHOOL IN LEEDS (HE DROPPED OUT). HE WAS ONE OF A RARE BREED: A LEADING MAN WHO CONSIDERS HIMSELF A CHARACTER ACTOR.

RIGHT, LIBERATE THOSE BEERS AND I'LL GET BOWLS FOR THE SNACKS.

NO ONE COULD DENY MAREK'S BRILLIANCE, BUT HIS RAVENOUS INTELLECTUAL CURIOSITY MEANT HE DIDN'T STICK AT ANYTHING FOR LONG.

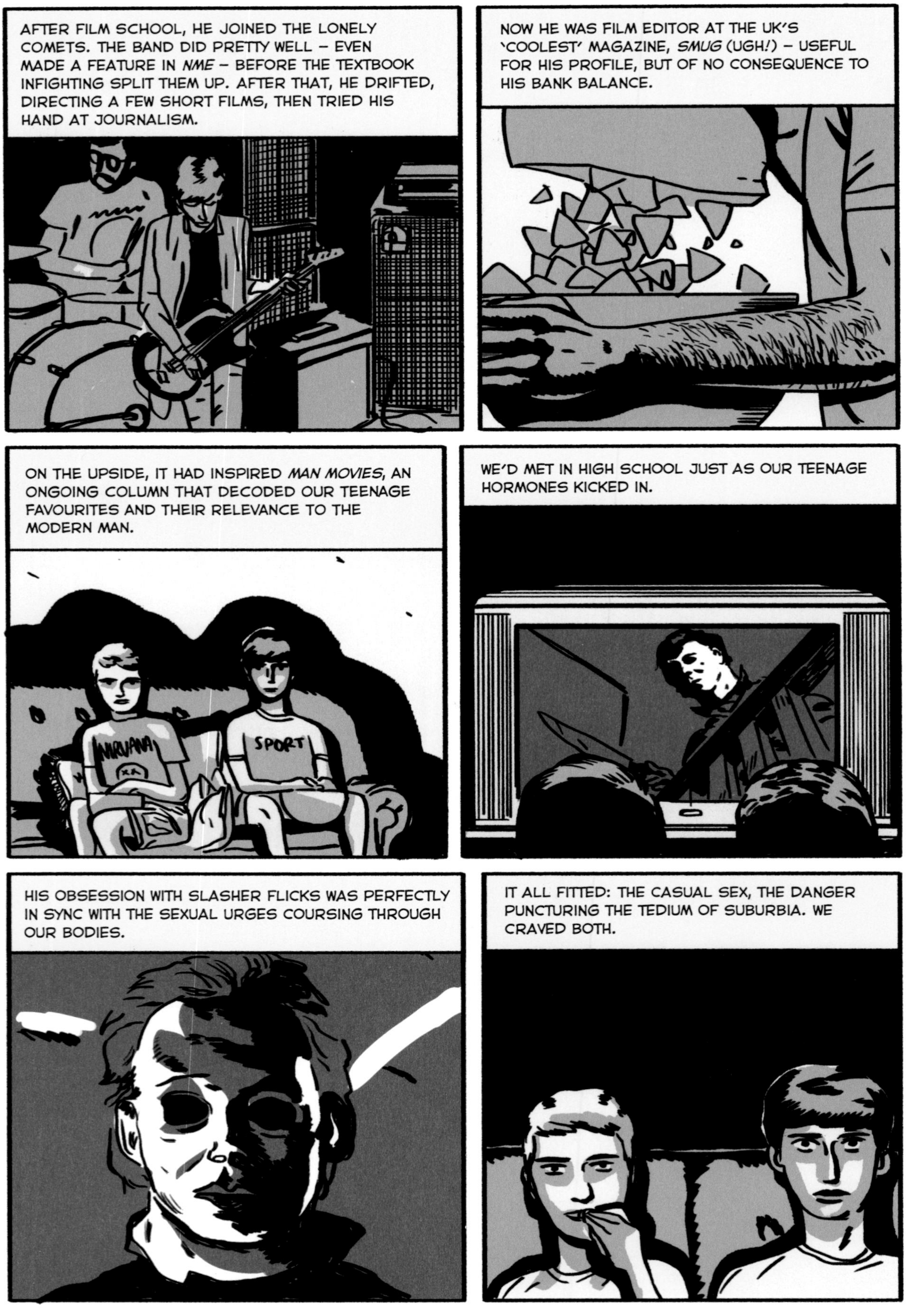
AFTER FILM SCHOOL, HE JOINED THE LONELY COMETS. THE BAND DID PRETTY WELL – EVEN MADE A FEATURE IN *NME* – BEFORE THE TEXTBOOK INFIGHTING SPLIT THEM UP. AFTER THAT, HE DRIFTED, DIRECTING A FEW SHORT FILMS, THEN TRIED HIS HAND AT JOURNALISM.
NOW HE WAS FILM EDITOR AT THE UK'S 'COOLEST' MAGAZINE, *SMUG* (UGH!) – USEFUL FOR HIS PROFILE, BUT OF NO CONSEQUENCE TO HIS BANK BALANCE.
ON THE UPSIDE, IT HAD INSPIRED *MAN MOVIES*, AN ONGOING COLUMN THAT DECODED OUR TEENAGE FAVOURITES AND THEIR RELEVANCE TO THE MODERN MAN.
NIRVANA
SPORT
WE'D MET IN HIGH SCHOOL JUST AS OUR TEENAGE HORMONES KICKED IN.
HIS OBSESSION WITH SLASHER FLICKS WAS PERFECTLY IN SYNC WITH THE SEXUAL URGES COURSING THROUGH OUR BODIES.
IT ALL FITTED: THE CASUAL SEX, THE DANGER PUNCTURING THE TEDIUM OF SUBURBIA. WE CRAVED BOTH.

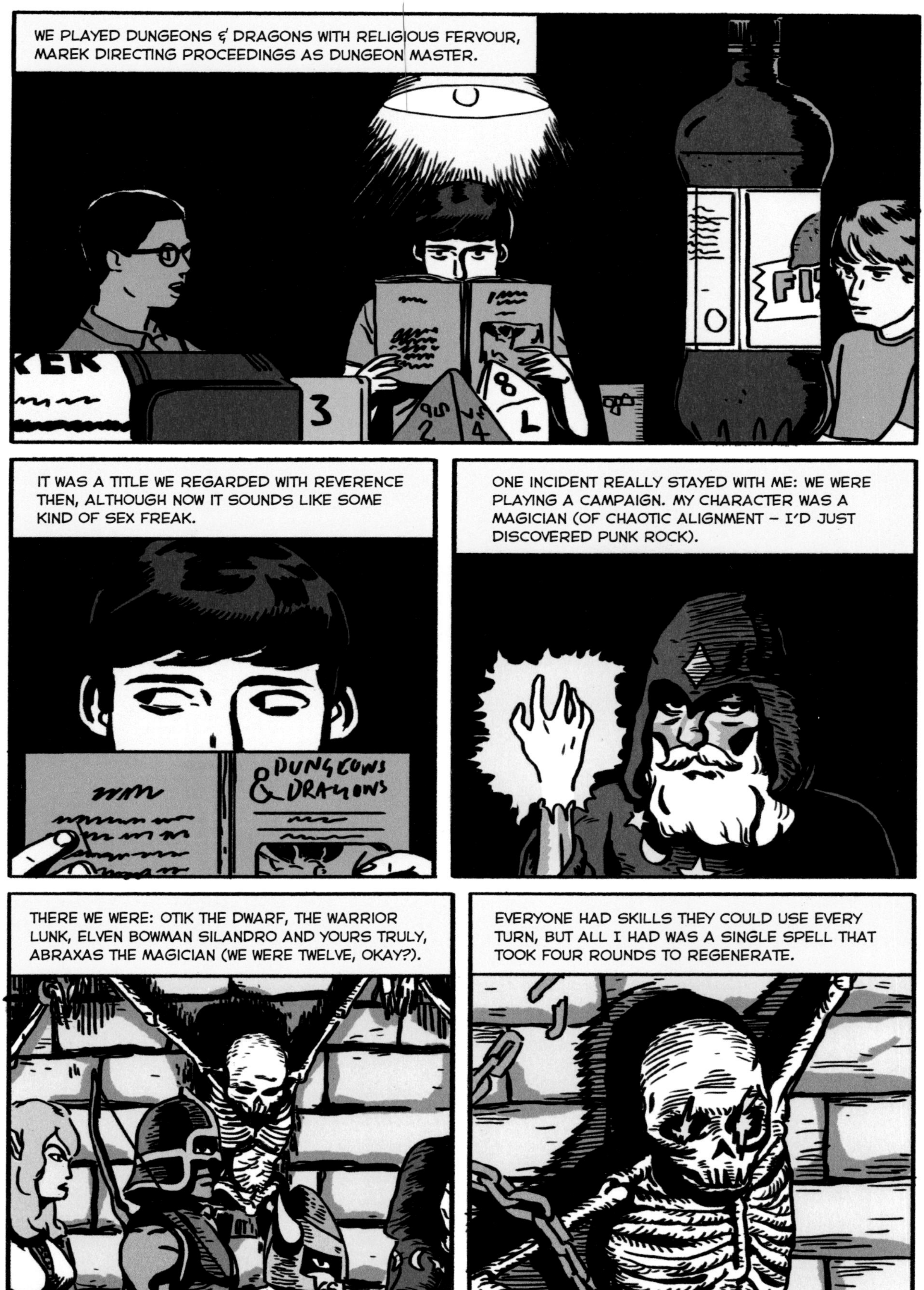

WE PLAYED DUNGEONS & DRAGONS WITH RELIGIOUS FERVOUR, MAREK DIRECTING PROCEEDINGS AS DUNGEON MASTER.
IT WAS A TITLE WE REGARDED WITH REVERENCE THEN, ALTHOUGH NOW IT SOUNDS LIKE SOME KIND OF SEX FREAK.
DUNGEONS & DRAGONS
ONE INCIDENT REALLY STAYED WITH ME: WE WERE PLAYING A CAMPAIGN. MY CHARACTER WAS A MAGICIAN (OF CHAOTIC ALIGNMENT – I'D JUST DISCOVERED PUNK ROCK).
THERE WE WERE: OTIK THE DWARF, THE WARRIOR LUNK, ELVEN BOWMAN SILANDRO AND YOURS TRULY, ABRAXAS THE MAGICIAN (WE WERE TWELVE, OKAY?).
EVERYONE HAD SKILLS THEY COULD USE EVERY TURN, BUT ALL I HAD WAS A SINGLE SPELL THAT TOOK FOUR ROUNDS TO REGENERATE.

THE GROUP LAID INTO OUR ENEMIES TIME AND TIME AGAIN, PROTECTING ME.

I REFUSED TO USE MY SPELL. AT THE CENTRE OF THIS DUNGEON LURKED OUR REAL ADVERSARY, THE BLACK WIZARD.

HE COULD STRIKE AT ANY TIME AND, WHEN HE DID, I WAS GOING TO BE READY.

AS THE QUEST WORE ON, ALL I COULD OFFER THE GROUP WAS MY HEALING ABILITIES.

YOUR SPELL ONLY TAKES A FEW ROUNDS TO REGENERATE...

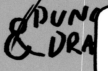

YEAH, GO ON. LET'S FRY THE NEXT MONSTER THAT GETS IN OUR WAY.

BUT I WAS CONVINCED THAT MAREK WAS TRYING TO BLUFF ME – AND I WASN'T ABOUT TO BE CAUGHT UNPREPARED.

ANYWAY, TO CUT A LONG QUEST SHORT, WE FINALLY FOUND THE BLACK WIZARD. THIS WAS IT – MY BIG MOMENT.

ONLY IT WASN'T. SILANDRO HAD PICKED UP A MAGIC ARROW ALONG THE WAY.

NOW HE TOOK A ONE-IN-A-HUNDRED CHANCE AND AIMED NOT AT THE SLUG CREATURE BUT AT THE BLACK WIZARD HIMSELF.

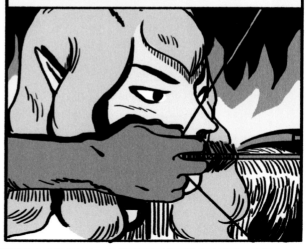

HE HOPED TO WOUND THE WIZARD, LEAVING HIM VULNERABLE TO MY ATTACK...

...BUT WITH CRAZY LUCK, HE FINISHED HIM OFF.

MY HOLDING BACK HAD BEEN FOR NOTHING.

I SHOULD HAVE LEARNED THAT LESSON, BUT TOO OFTEN SINCE THEN I'D DONE THE SAME THING. I'D WASTED SO MANY OPPORTUNITIES.

NOW WAS THE TIME TO CHANGE. NOW WAS THE TIME FOR *JEOPARDY*.

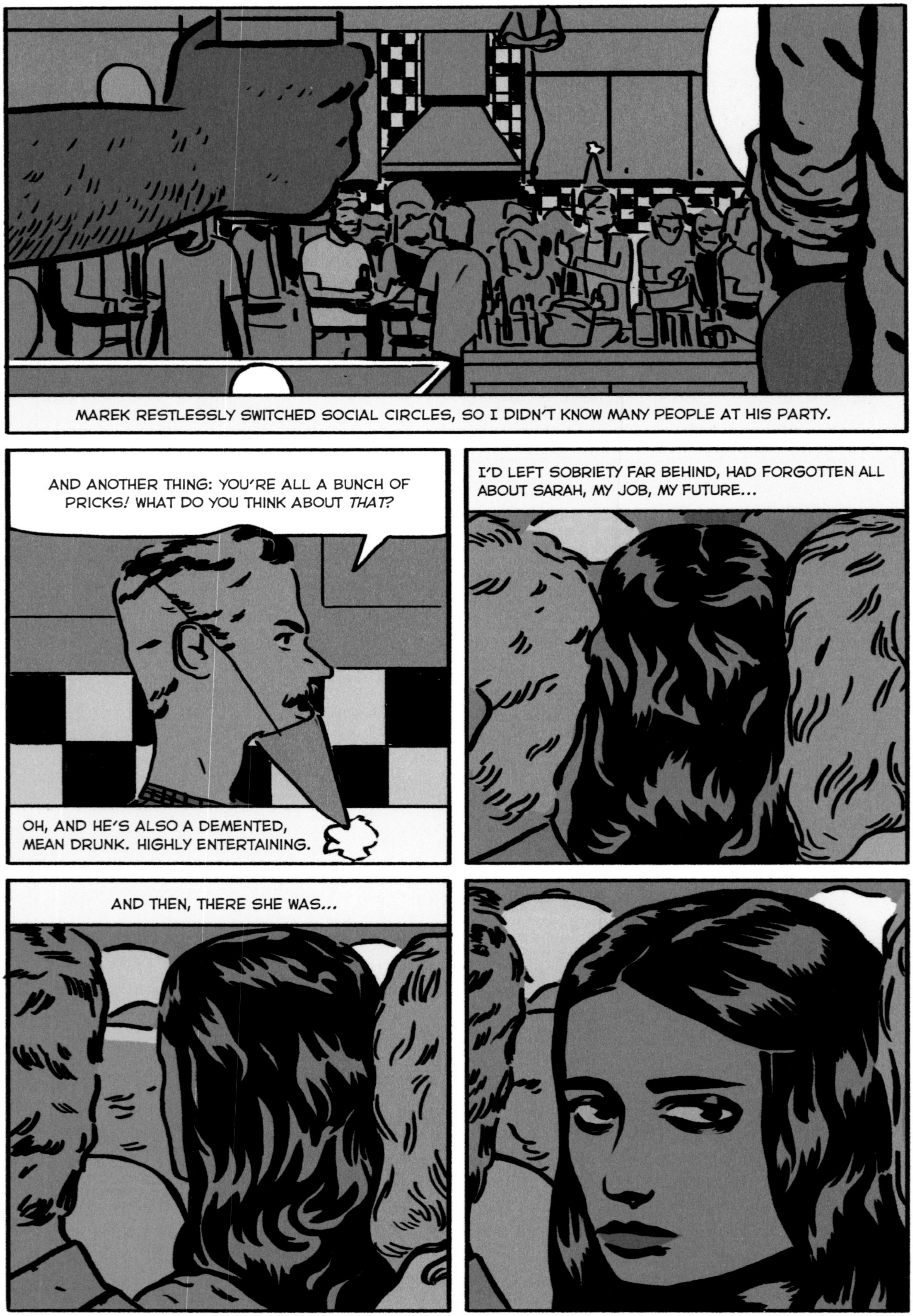
MAREK RESTLESSLY SWITCHED SOCIAL CIRCLES, SO I DIDN'T KNOW MANY PEOPLE AT HIS PARTY.
AND ANOTHER THING: YOU'RE ALL A BUNCH OF PRICKS! WHAT DO YOU THINK ABOUT *THAT*?
OH, AND HE'S ALSO A DEMENTED, MEAN DRUNK. HIGHLY ENTERTAINING.
I'D LEFT SOBRIETY FAR BEHIND, HAD FORGOTTEN ALL ABOUT SARAH, MY JOB, MY FUTURE...
AND THEN, THERE SHE WAS...

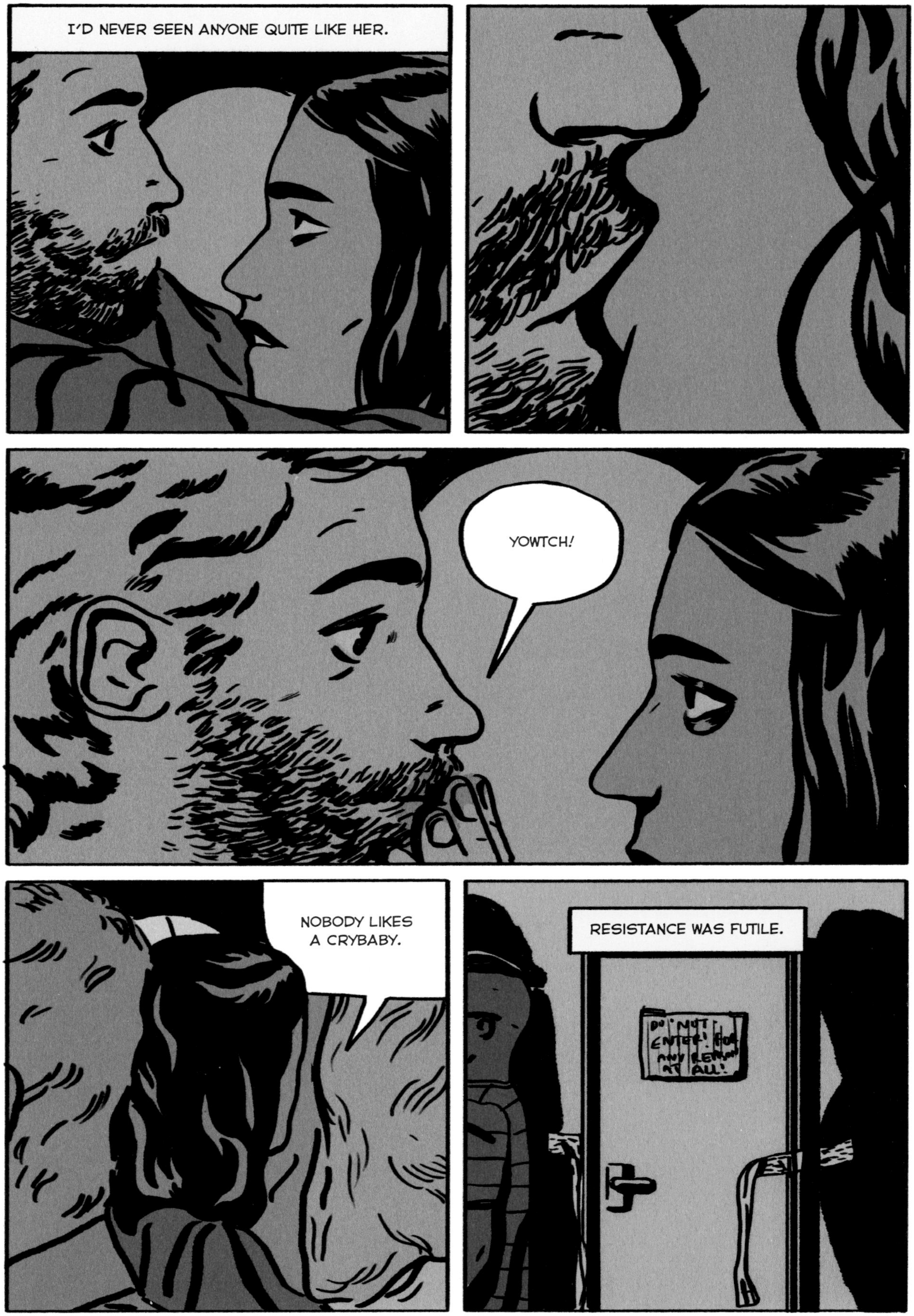
I'D NEVER SEEN ANYONE QUITE LIKE HER.
YOWTCH!
NOBODY LIKES A CRYBABY.
RESISTANCE WAS FUTILE.

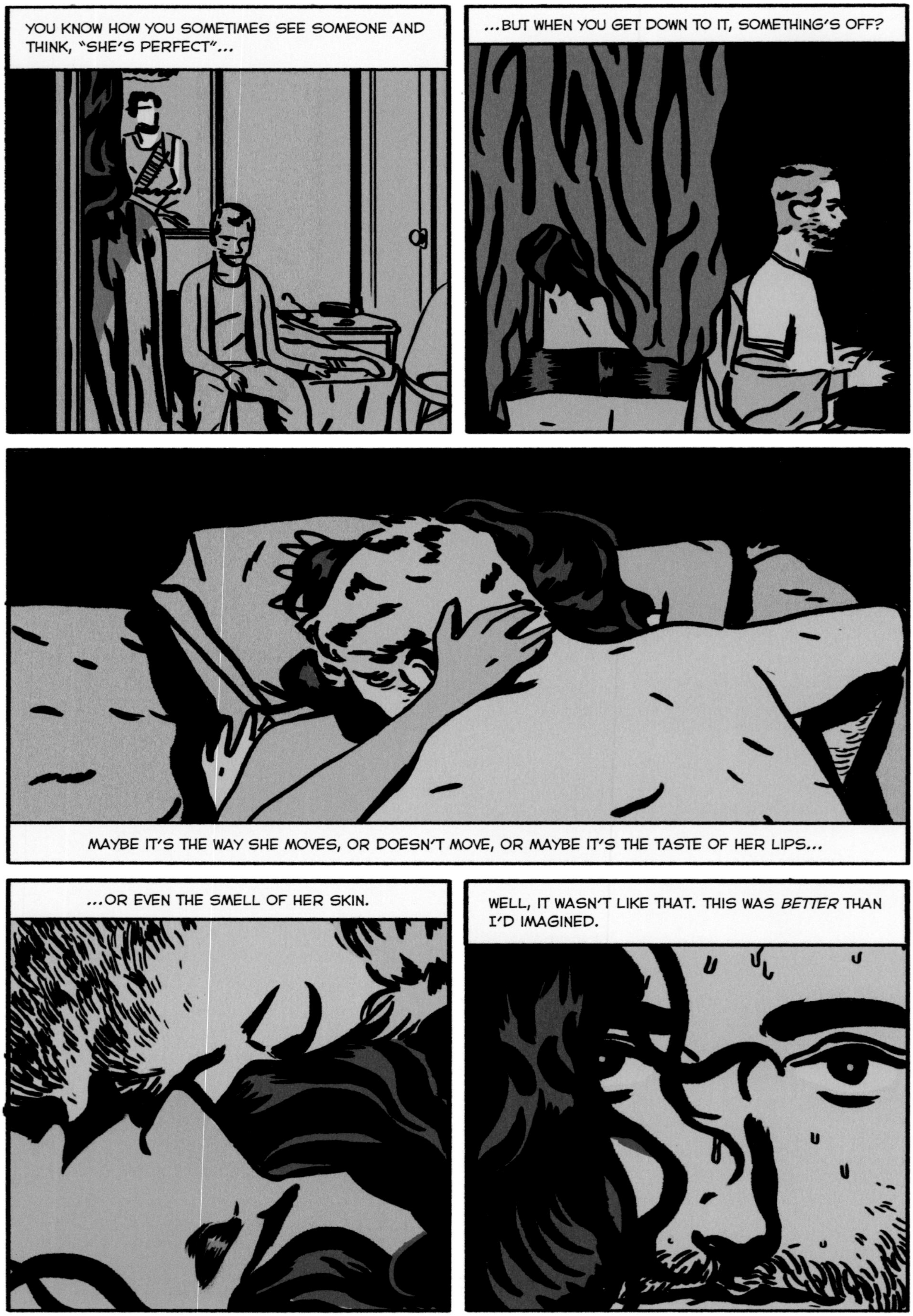
YOU KNOW HOW YOU SOMETIMES SEE SOMEONE AND THINK, "SHE'S PERFECT"...
...BUT WHEN YOU GET DOWN TO IT, SOMETHING'S OFF?
MAYBE IT'S THE WAY SHE MOVES, OR DOESN'T MOVE, OR MAYBE IT'S THE TASTE OF HER LIPS...
...OR EVEN THE SMELL OF HER SKIN.
WELL, IT WASN'T LIKE THAT. THIS WAS *BETTER* THAN I'D IMAGINED.

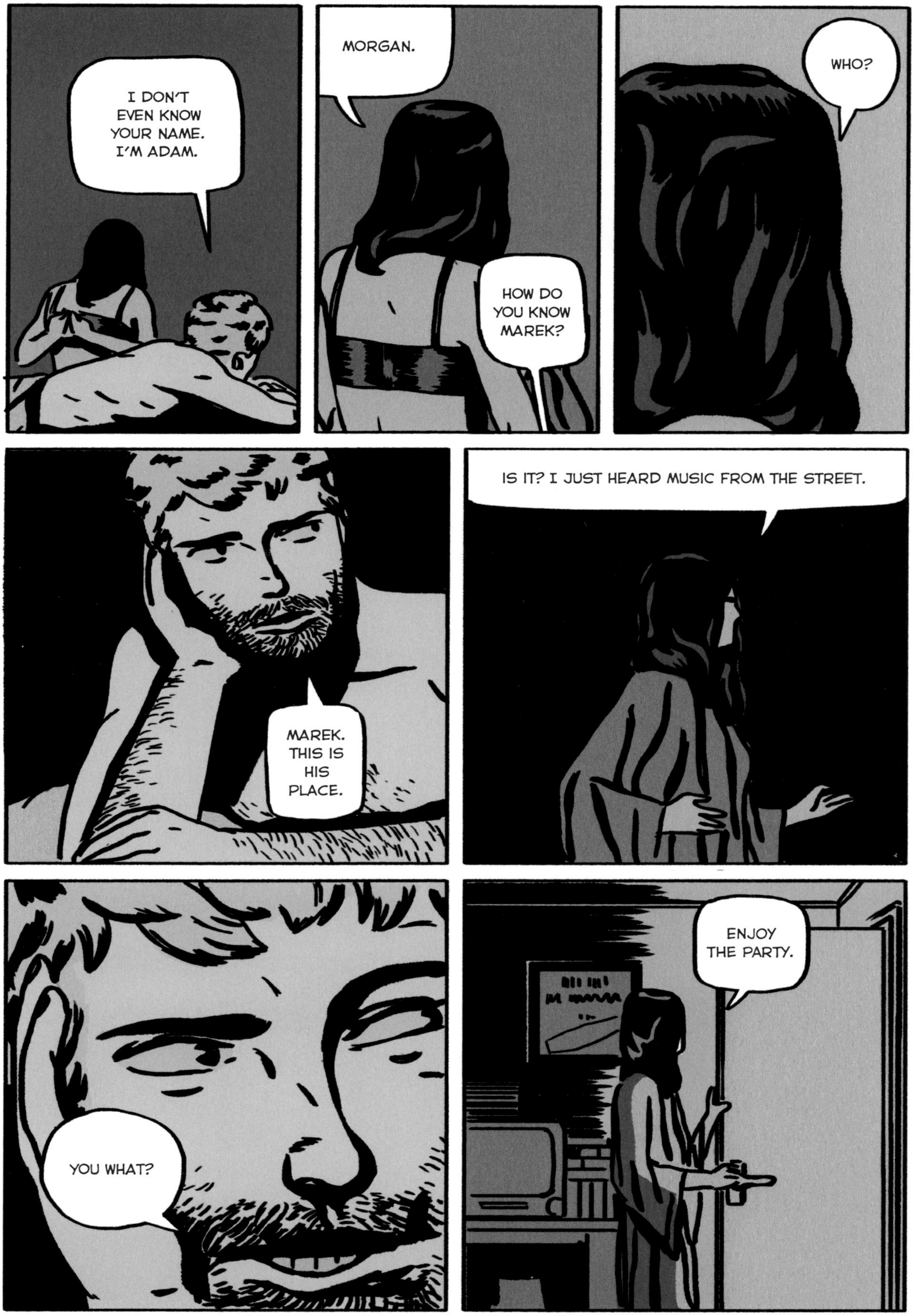
I DON'T EVEN KNOW YOUR NAME. I'M ADAM.
MORGAN.
HOW DO YOU KNOW MAREK?
WHO?
MAREK. THIS IS HIS PLACE.
IS IT? I JUST HEARD MUSIC FROM THE STREET.
YOU WHAT?
ENJOY THE PARTY.

THE EVENING ENDED IN CHAOS. I GOT EVEN DRUNKER. MAREK GOT INTO A FIGHT AND DRAGGED ME IN AFTER HIM.

I LET HER GO. I DIDN'T WANT TO DIMINISH THE ENCOUNTER BY TRYING TO REPEAT IT.

BY THE NEXT DAY, FIGHTING MY WAY THROUGH THE FOG OF A HANGOVER, I KNEW I'D MADE A MISTAKE.

DID YOU GET MUGGED?

YEAH. BY MYSELF.

GET A CHANCE TO READ THE SCRIPT?

YEAH. THAT'S WHY I LOOKED LIKE THIS. A HARD NIGHT'S READING.

OH, SHE PLAYED SWEET, BUT COOKIE HAD SHARK-LIKE AMBITION, AND RIGHT NOW I WAS HER MEAL TICKET. I WAS AMAZED SHE HADN'T JUST STUFFED MY CORPSE INTO THE STATIONARY CLOSET AND GOTTEN ON WITH THE FILM HERSELF.

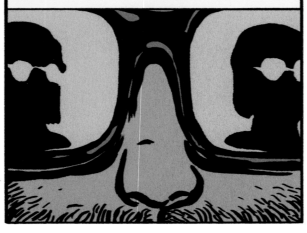

WELL, I'LL GO GET YOU A COFFEE AND YOU CAN MAKE A START, THEN.

THAT WAS IT! SHE WAS PLANNING TO SCALP MY BEARD AND STEAL MY CAREER!

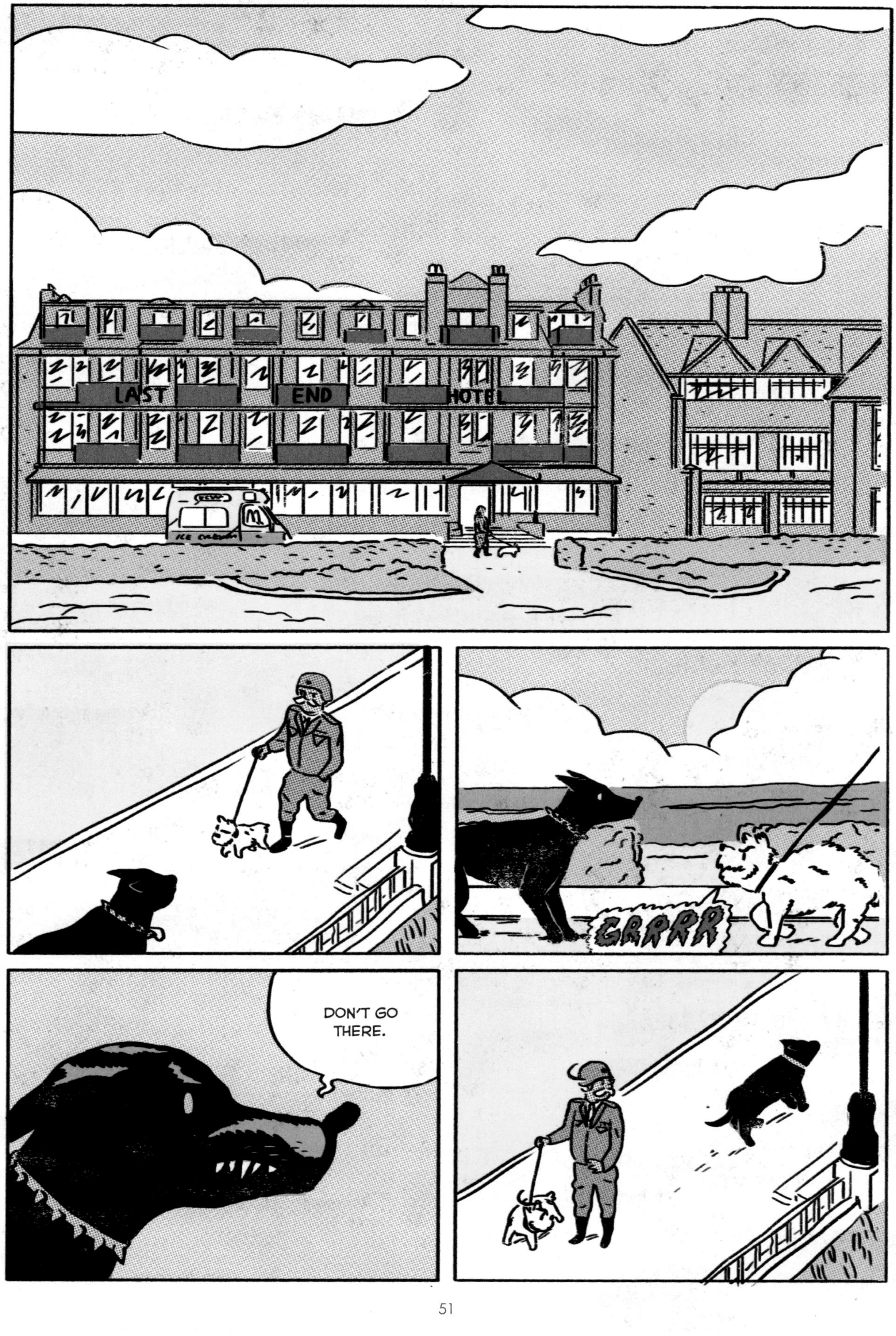
LAST END HOTEL
GRRRR
DON'T GO THERE.

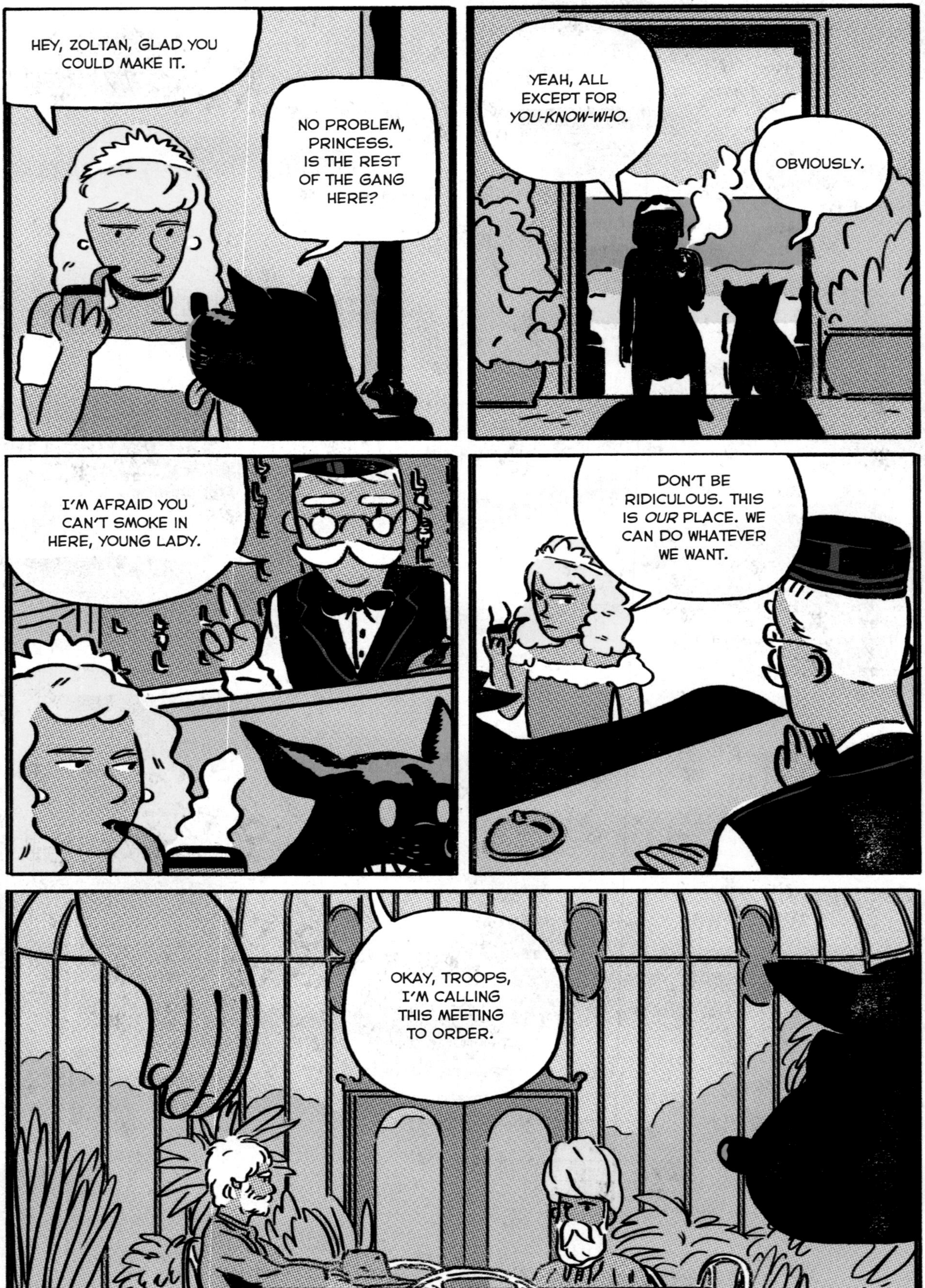
HEY, ZOLTAN, GLAD YOU COULD MAKE IT.
NO PROBLEM, PRINCESS. IS THE REST OF THE GANG HERE?
YEAH, ALL EXCEPT FOR *YOU-KNOW-WHO.*
OBVIOUSLY.
I'M AFRAID YOU CAN'T SMOKE IN HERE, YOUNG LADY.
DON'T BE RIDICULOUS. THIS IS *OUR* PLACE. WE CAN DO WHATEVER WE WANT.
OKAY, TROOPS, I'M CALLING THIS MEETING TO ORDER.

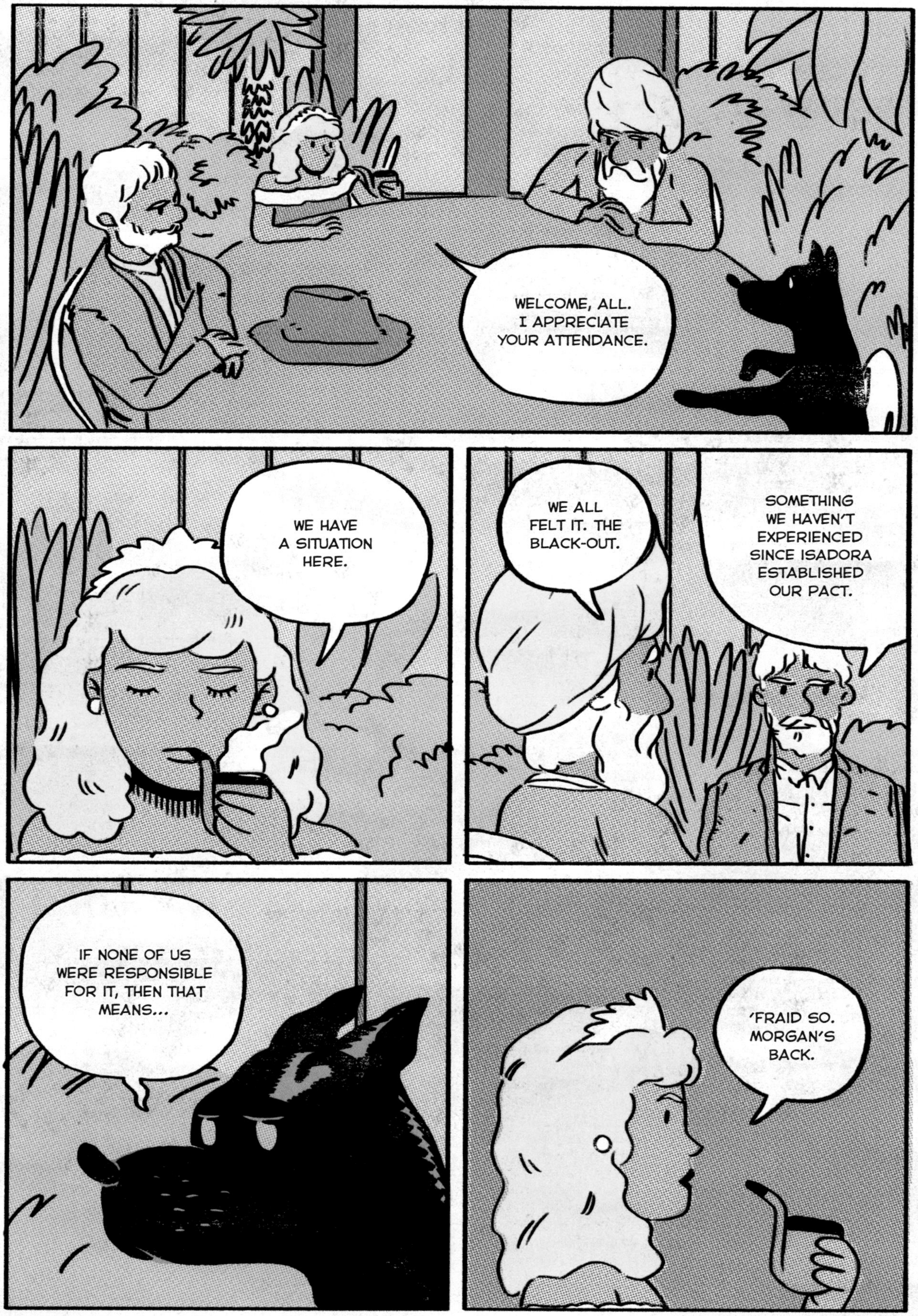
WELCOME, ALL. I APPRECIATE YOUR ATTENDANCE.
WE HAVE A SITUATION HERE.
WE ALL FELT IT. THE BLACK-OUT.
SOMETHING WE HAVEN'T EXPERIENCED SINCE ISADORA ESTABLISHED OUR PACT.
IF NONE OF US WERE RESPONSIBLE FOR IT, THEN THAT MEANS...
'FRAID SO. MORGAN'S BACK.

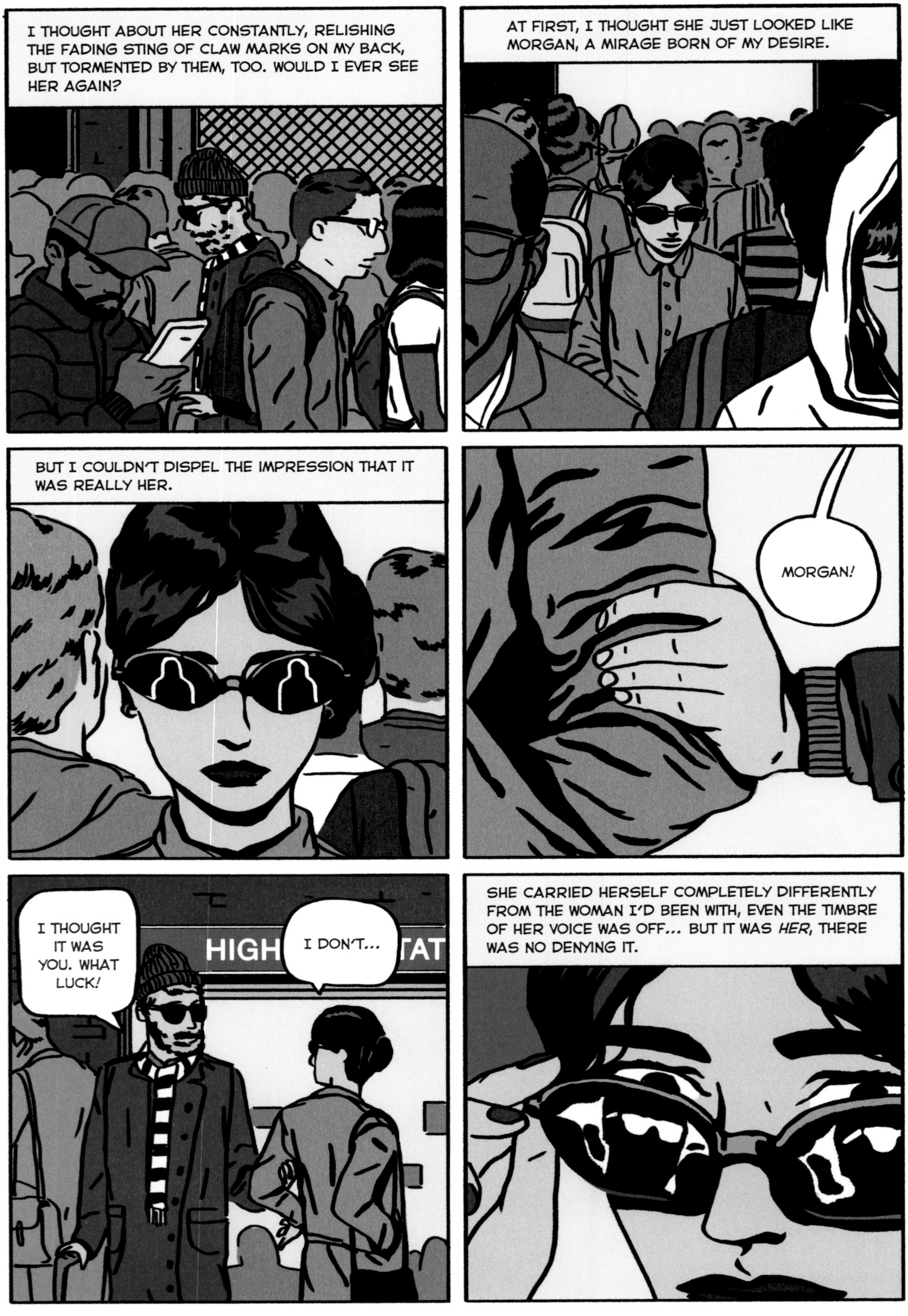

I THOUGHT ABOUT HER CONSTANTLY, RELISHING THE FADING STING OF CLAW MARKS ON MY BACK, BUT TORMENTED BY THEM, TOO. WOULD I EVER SEE HER AGAIN?
AT FIRST, I THOUGHT SHE JUST LOOKED LIKE MORGAN, A MIRAGE BORN OF MY DESIRE.
BUT I COULDN'T DISPEL THE IMPRESSION THAT IT WAS REALLY HER.
MORGAN!
I THOUGHT IT WAS YOU. WHAT LUCK!
HIGH
I DON'T...
TAT
SHE CARRIED HERSELF COMPLETELY DIFFERENTLY FROM THE WOMAN I'D BEEN WITH, EVEN THE TIMBRE OF HER VOICE WAS OFF... BUT IT WAS *HER*, THERE WAS NO DENYING IT.

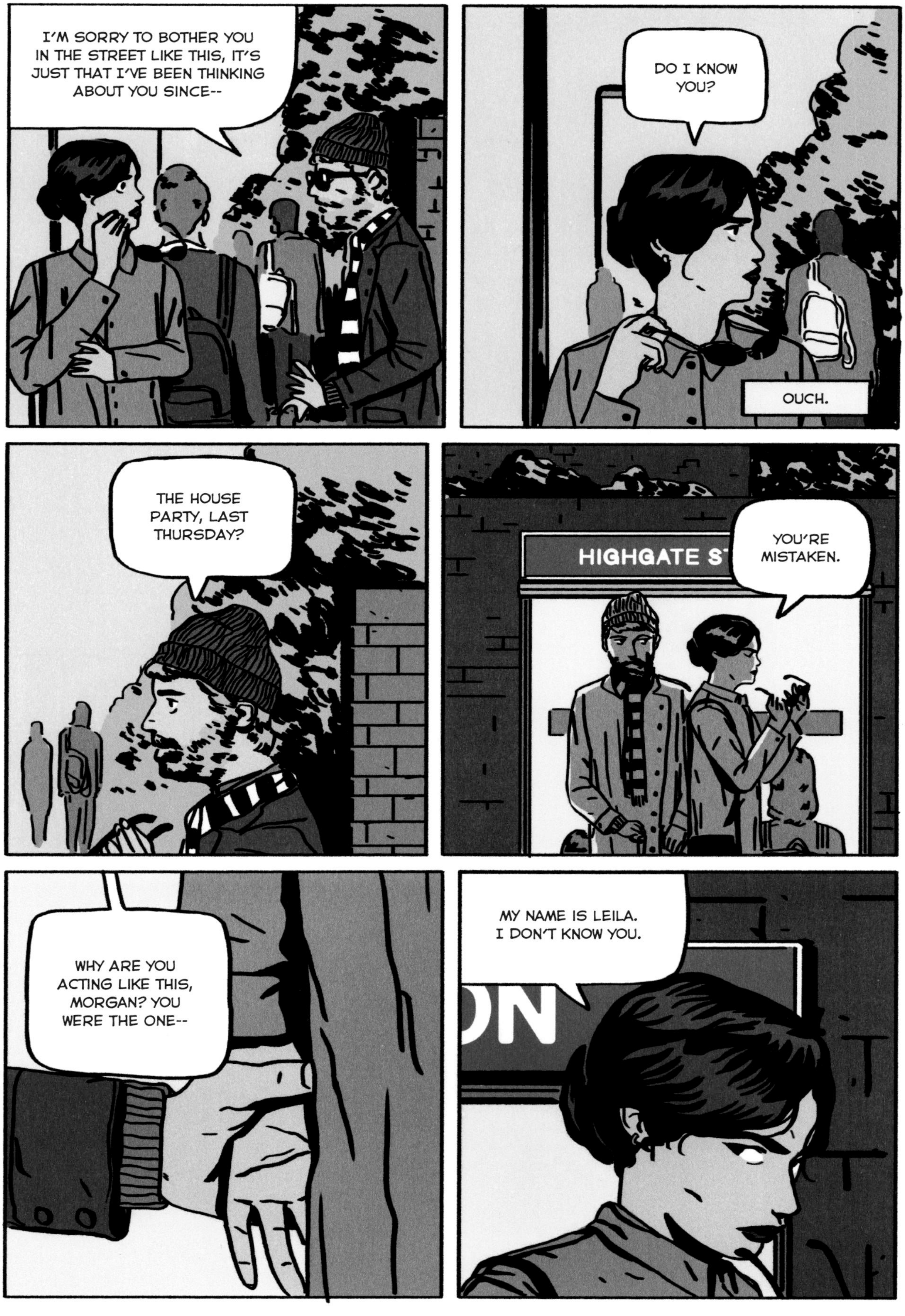
I'M SORRY TO BOTHER YOU IN THE STREET LIKE THIS, IT'S JUST THAT I'VE BEEN THINKING ABOUT YOU SINCE--
DO I KNOW YOU?
OUCH.
THE HOUSE PARTY, LAST THURSDAY?
HIGHGATE ST
YOU'RE MISTAKEN.
WHY ARE YOU ACTING LIKE THIS, MORGAN? YOU WERE THE ONE--
MY NAME IS LEILA. I DON'T KNOW YOU.
ON

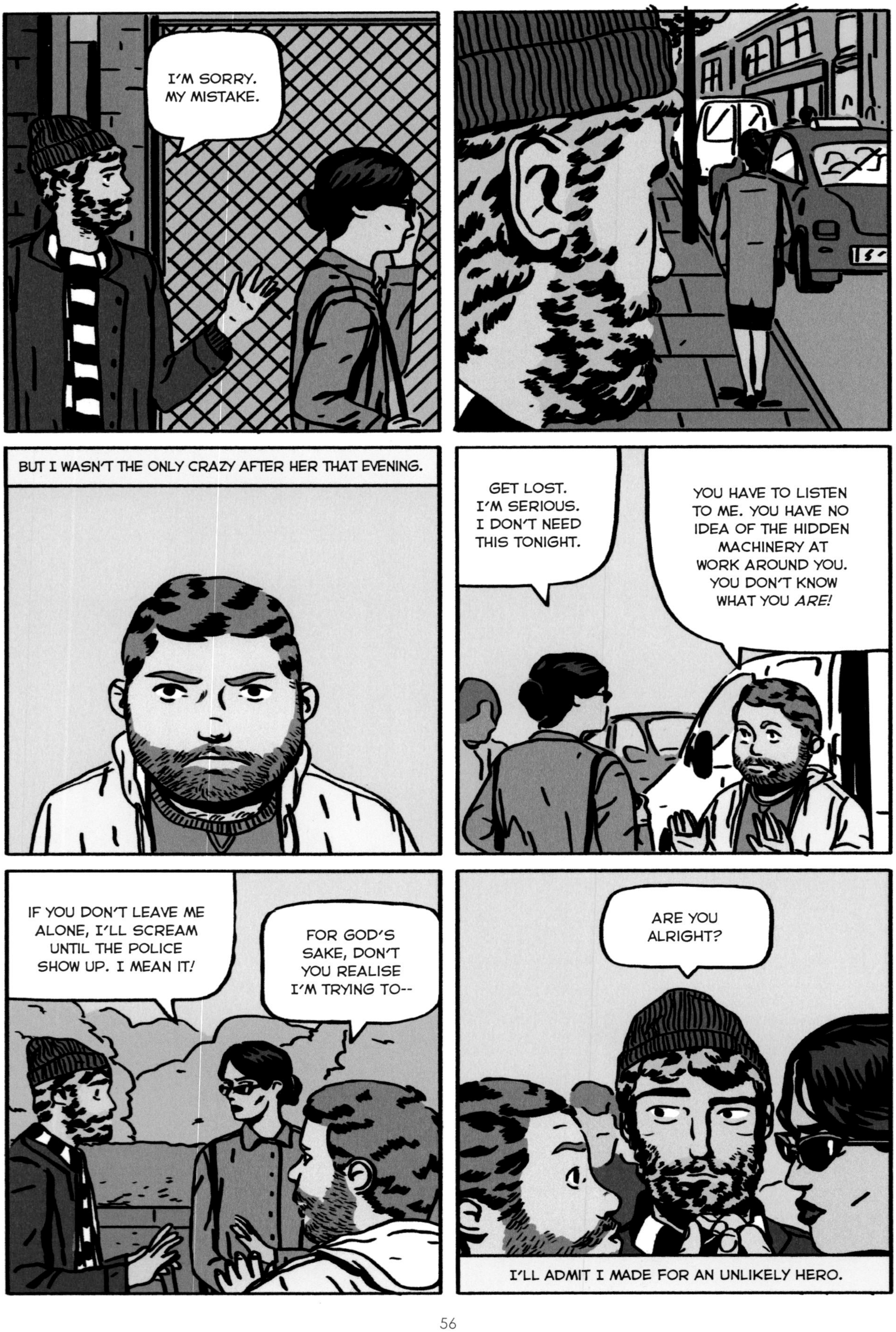
I'M SORRY.
MY MISTAKE.
BUT I WASN'T THE ONLY CRAZY AFTER HER THAT EVENING.
GET LOST. I'M SERIOUS. I DON'T NEED THIS TONIGHT.
YOU HAVE TO LISTEN TO ME. YOU HAVE NO IDEA OF THE HIDDEN MACHINERY AT WORK AROUND YOU. YOU DON'T KNOW WHAT YOU *ARE!*
IF YOU DON'T LEAVE ME ALONE, I'LL SCREAM UNTIL THE POLICE SHOW UP. I MEAN IT!
FOR GOD'S SAKE, DON'T YOU REALISE I'M TRYING TO--
ARE YOU ALRIGHT?
I'LL ADMIT I MADE FOR AN UNLIKELY HERO.

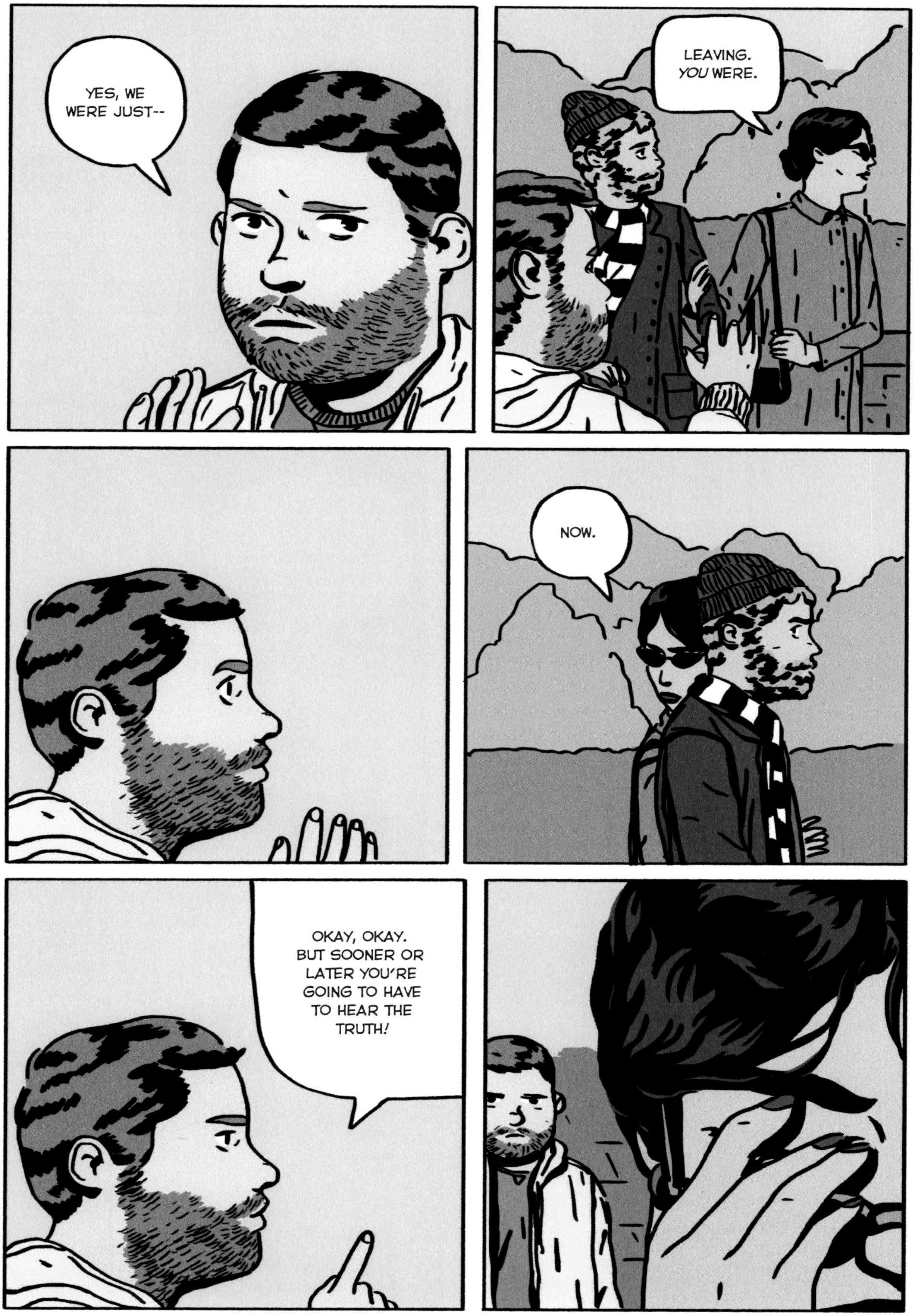
YES, WE WERE JUST--
LEAVING. *YOU* WERE.
NOW.
OKAY, OKAY. BUT SOONER OR LATER YOU'RE GOING TO HAVE TO HEAR THE TRUTH!

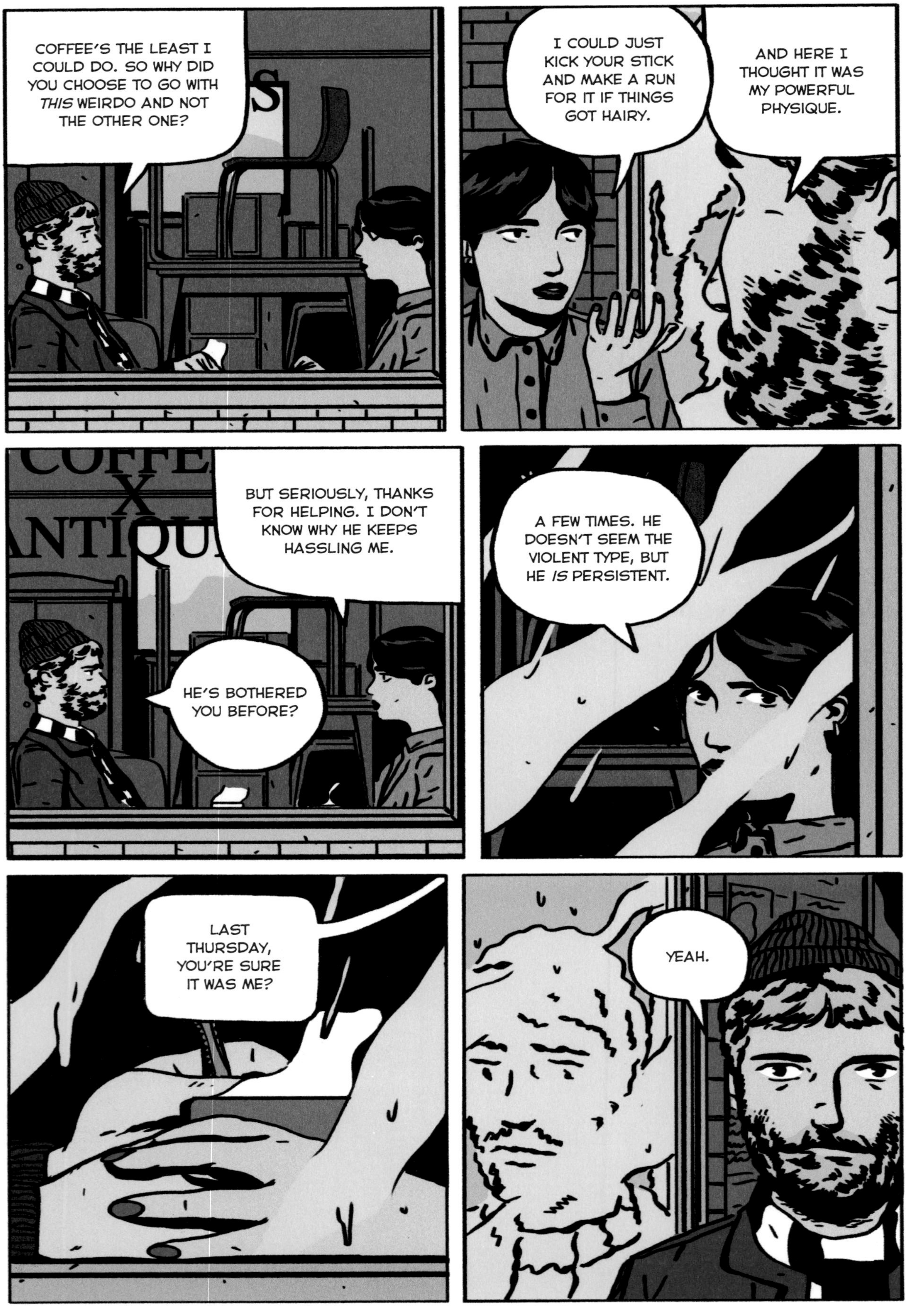
COFFEE'S THE LEAST I COULD DO. SO WHY DID YOU CHOOSE TO GO WITH *THIS* WEIRDO AND NOT THE OTHER ONE?
I COULD JUST KICK YOUR STICK AND MAKE A RUN FOR IT IF THINGS GOT HAIRY.
AND HERE I THOUGHT IT WAS MY POWERFUL PHYSIQUE.
COFFE
X
ANTIQU
BUT SERIOUSLY, THANKS FOR HELPING. I DON'T KNOW WHY HE KEEPS HASSLING ME.
HE'S BOTHERED YOU BEFORE?
A FEW TIMES. HE DOESN'T SEEM THE VIOLENT TYPE, BUT HE *IS* PERSISTENT.
LAST THURSDAY, YOU'RE SURE IT WAS ME?
YEAH.

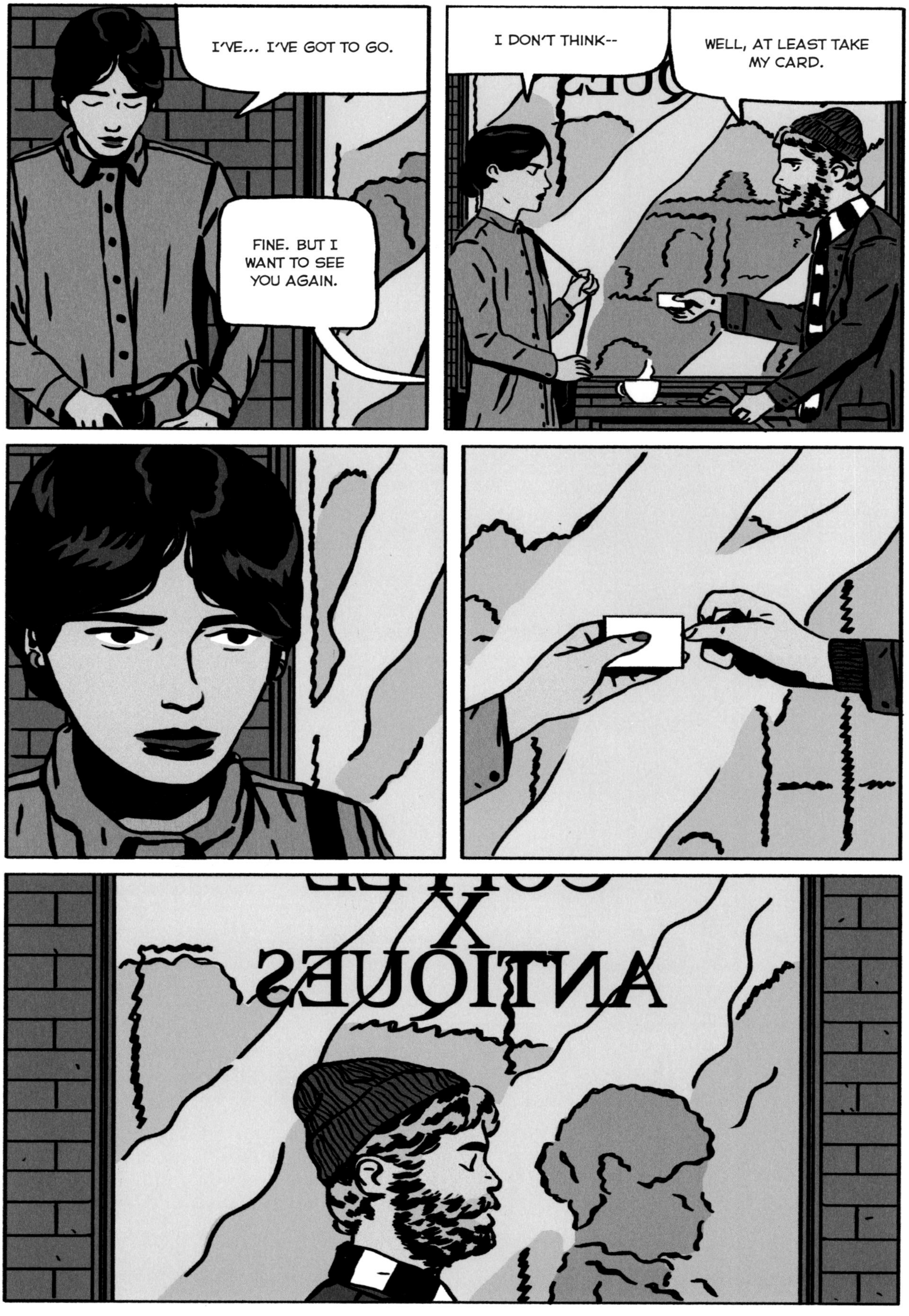
I'VE... I'VE GOT TO GO.
FINE. BUT I WANT TO SEE YOU AGAIN.
I DON'T THINK--
WELL, AT LEAST TAKE MY CARD.

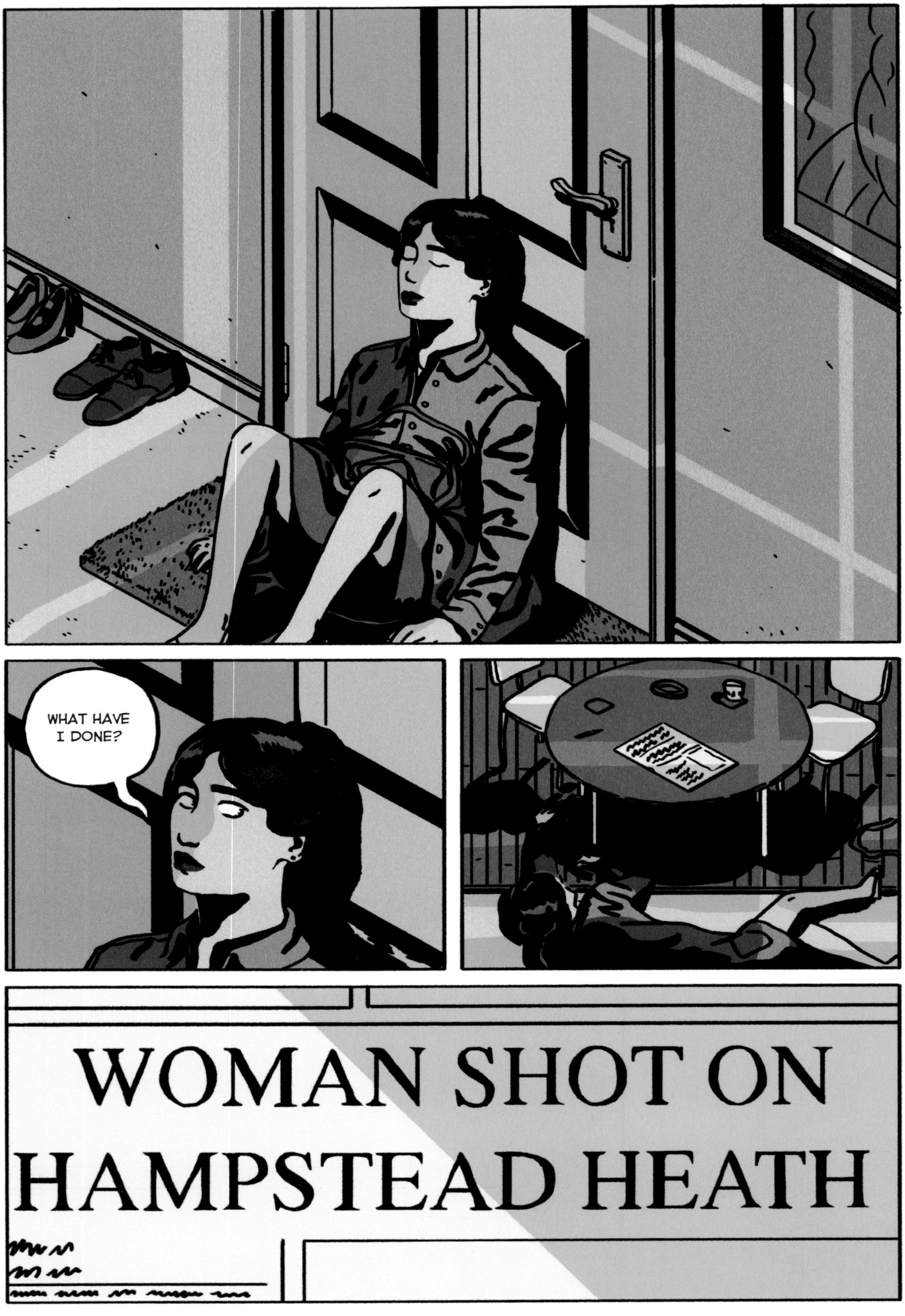
WHAT HAVE I DONE?
WOMAN SHOT ON HAMPSTEAD HEATH

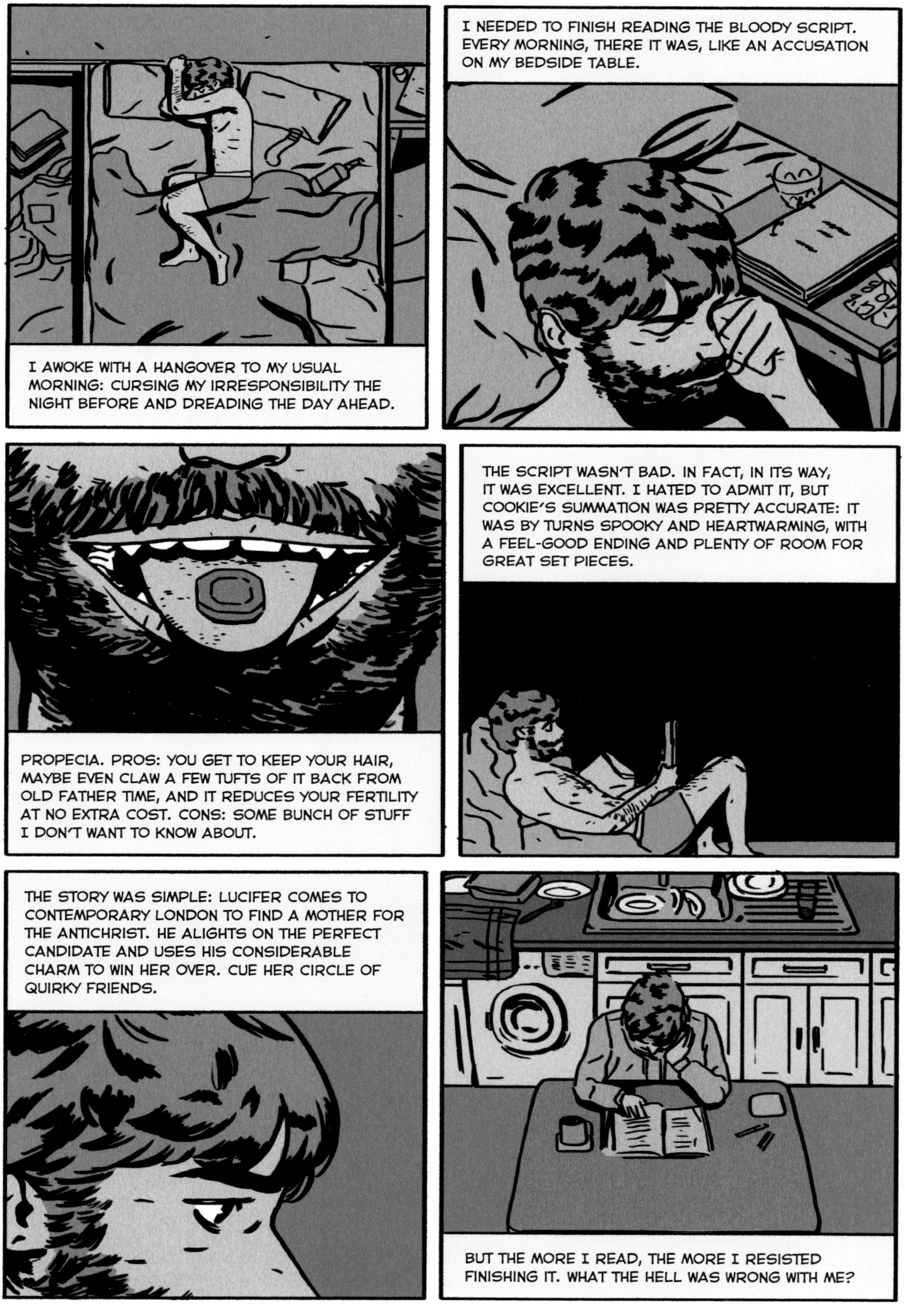
I AWOKE WITH A HANGOVER TO MY USUAL MORNING: CURSING MY IRRESPONSIBILITY THE NIGHT BEFORE AND DREADING THE DAY AHEAD.
I NEEDED TO FINISH READING THE BLOODY SCRIPT. EVERY MORNING, THERE IT WAS, LIKE AN ACCUSATION ON MY BEDSIDE TABLE.
PROPECIA. PROS: YOU GET TO KEEP YOUR HAIR, MAYBE EVEN CLAW A FEW TUFTS OF IT BACK FROM OLD FATHER TIME, AND IT REDUCES YOUR FERTILITY AT NO EXTRA COST. CONS: SOME BUNCH OF STUFF I DON'T WANT TO KNOW ABOUT.
THE SCRIPT WASN'T BAD. IN FACT, IN ITS WAY, IT WAS EXCELLENT. I HATED TO ADMIT IT, BUT COOKIE'S SUMMATION WAS PRETTY ACCURATE: IT WAS BY TURNS SPOOKY AND HEARTWARMING, WITH A FEEL-GOOD ENDING AND PLENTY OF ROOM FOR GREAT SET PIECES.
THE STORY WAS SIMPLE: LUCIFER COMES TO CONTEMPORARY LONDON TO FIND A MOTHER FOR THE ANTICHRIST. HE ALIGHTS ON THE PERFECT CANDIDATE AND USES HIS CONSIDERABLE CHARM TO WIN HER OVER. CUE HER CIRCLE OF QUIRKY FRIENDS.
BUT THE MORE I READ, THE MORE I RESISTED FINISHING IT. WHAT THE HELL WAS WRONG WITH ME?

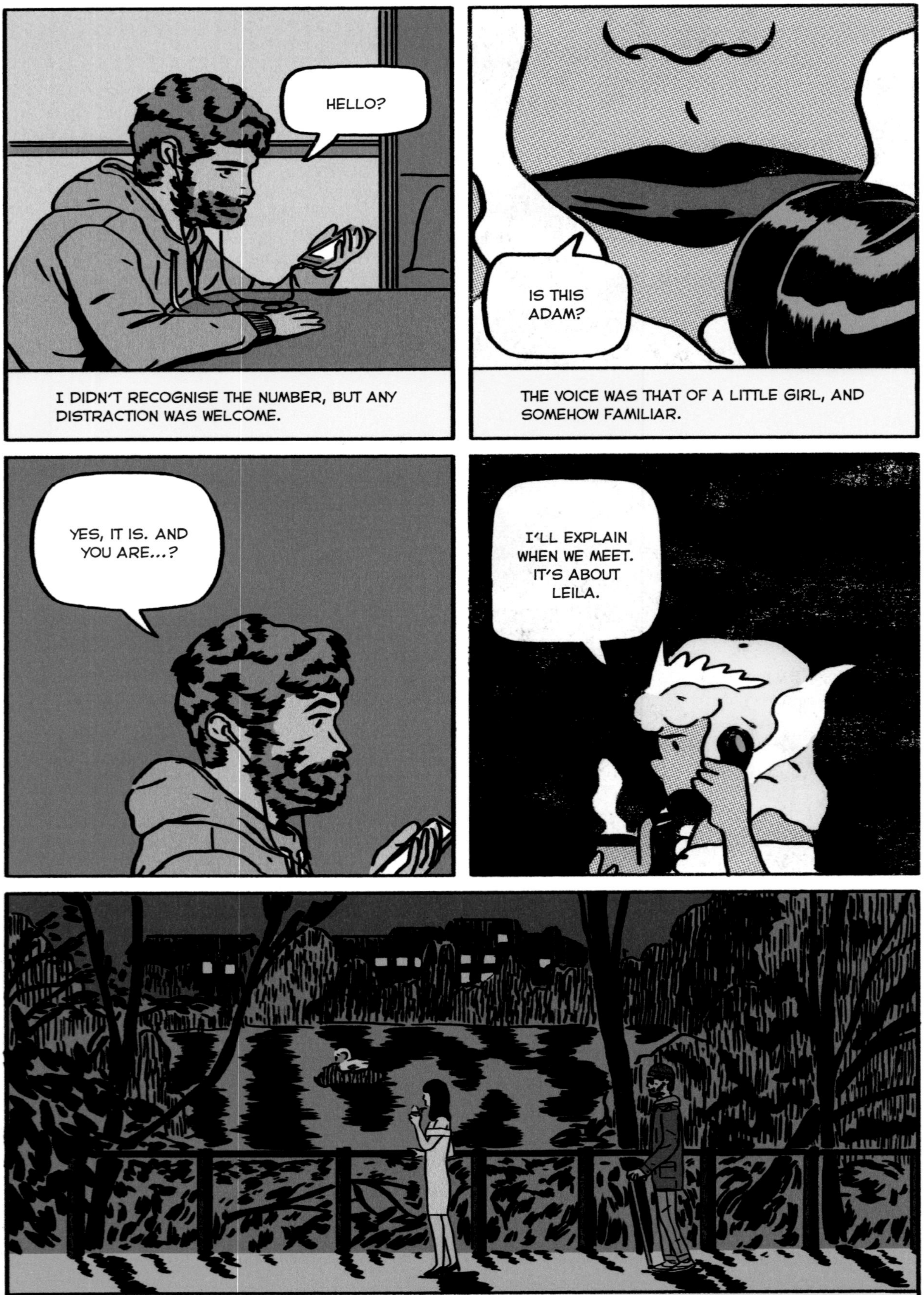
HELLO?
I DIDN'T RECOGNISE THE NUMBER, BUT ANY DISTRACTION WAS WELCOME.
IS THIS ADAM?
THE VOICE WAS THAT OF A LITTLE GIRL, AND SOMEHOW FAMILIAR.
YES, IT IS. AND YOU ARE...?
I'LL EXPLAIN WHEN WE MEET. IT'S ABOUT LEILA.
"HAMPSTEAD HEATH IN AN HOUR. THE CAUSEWAY RUNNING ALONG THE MIXED BATHING POND."

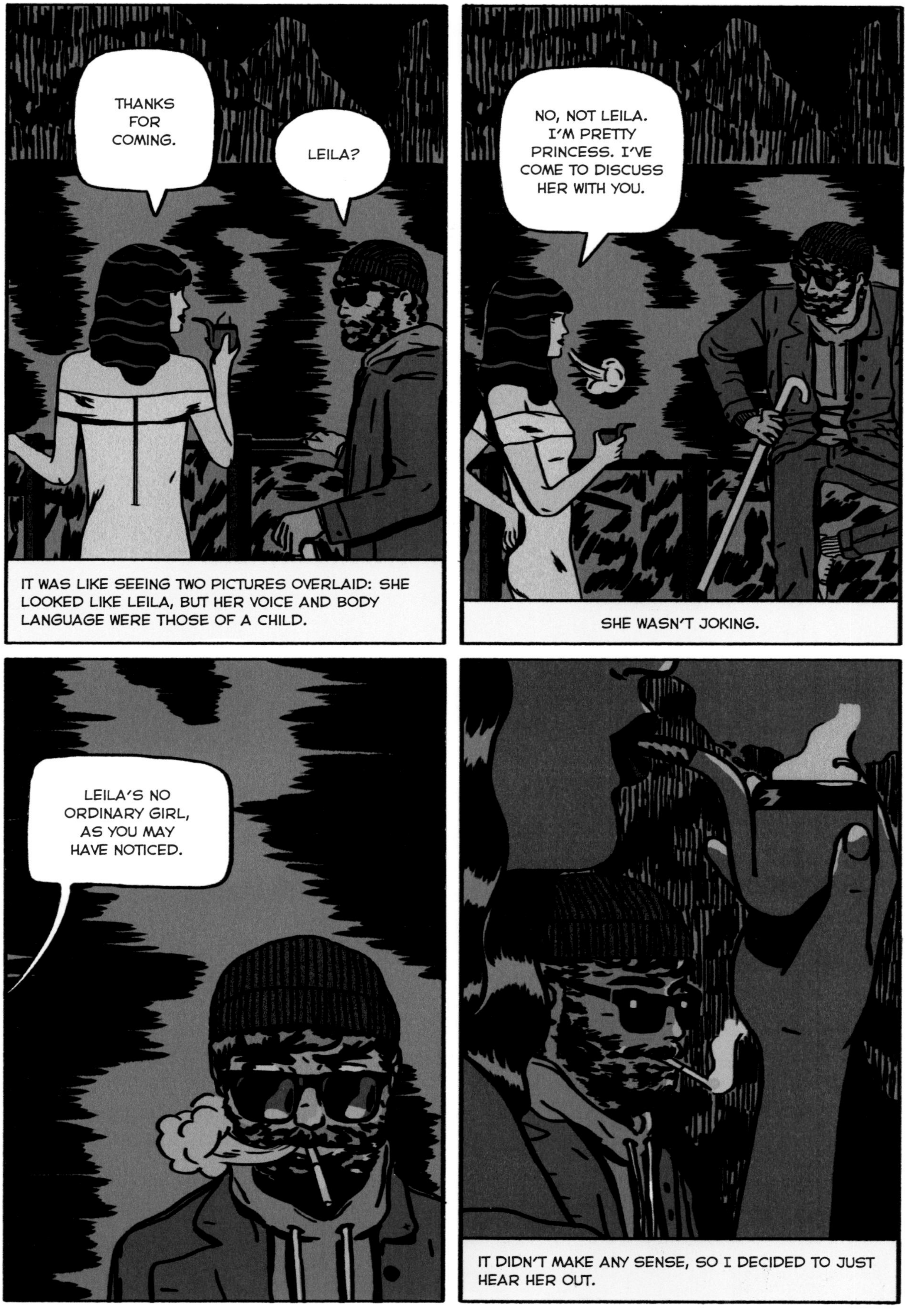
THANKS FOR COMING.
LEILA?
IT WAS LIKE SEEING TWO PICTURES OVERLAID: SHE LOOKED LIKE LEILA, BUT HER VOICE AND BODY LANGUAGE WERE THOSE OF A CHILD.
NO, NOT LEILA. I'M PRETTY PRINCESS. I'VE COME TO DISCUSS HER WITH YOU.
SHE WASN'T JOKING.
LEILA'S NO ORDINARY GIRL, AS YOU MAY HAVE NOTICED.
IT DIDN'T MAKE ANY SENSE, SO I DECIDED TO JUST HEAR HER OUT.

IT'S NOT UP TO ME TO TELL YOU THE
PARTICULARS, BUT I CAN TELL YOU THIS:
LEILA'S IN TROUBLE. SHE NEEDS A FRIEND.

I WANT YOU TO
KEEP AN EYE ON
HER FOR ME.

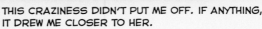

THIS CRAZINESS DIDN'T PUT ME OFF. IF ANYTHING,
IT DREW ME CLOSER TO HER.

I ALREADY
AM.

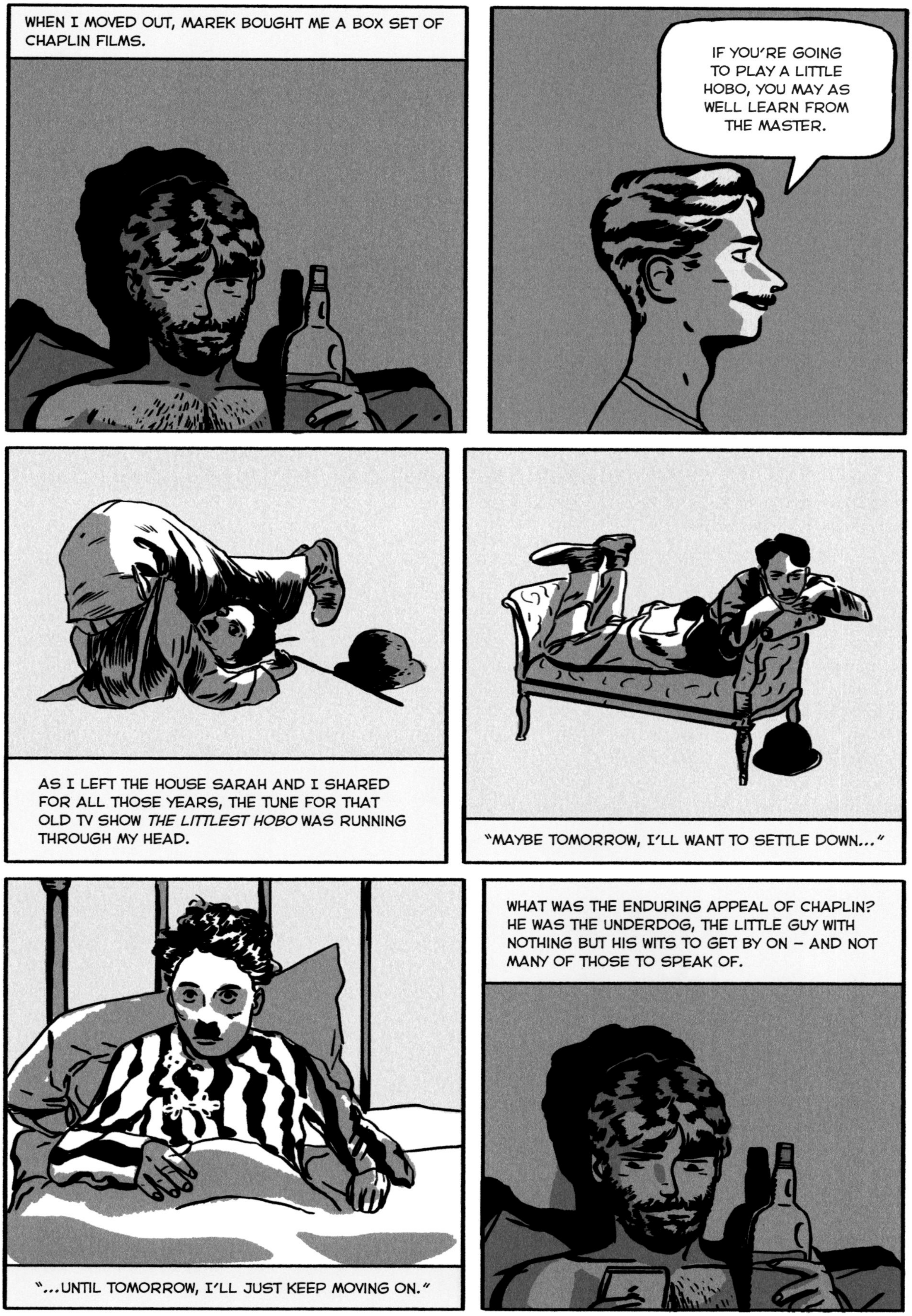
WHEN I MOVED OUT, MAREK BOUGHT ME A BOX SET OF CHAPLIN FILMS.
IF YOU'RE GOING TO PLAY A LITTLE HOBO, YOU MAY AS WELL LEARN FROM THE MASTER.
AS I LEFT THE HOUSE SARAH AND I SHARED FOR ALL THOSE YEARS, THE TUNE FOR THAT OLD TV SHOW *THE LITTLEST HOBO* WAS RUNNING THROUGH MY HEAD.
"MAYBE TOMORROW, I'LL WANT TO SETTLE DOWN..."
"...UNTIL TOMORROW, I'LL JUST KEEP MOVING ON."
WHAT WAS THE ENDURING APPEAL OF CHAPLIN? HE WAS THE UNDERDOG, THE LITTLE GUY WITH NOTHING BUT HIS WITS TO GET BY ON – AND NOT MANY OF THOSE TO SPEAK OF.

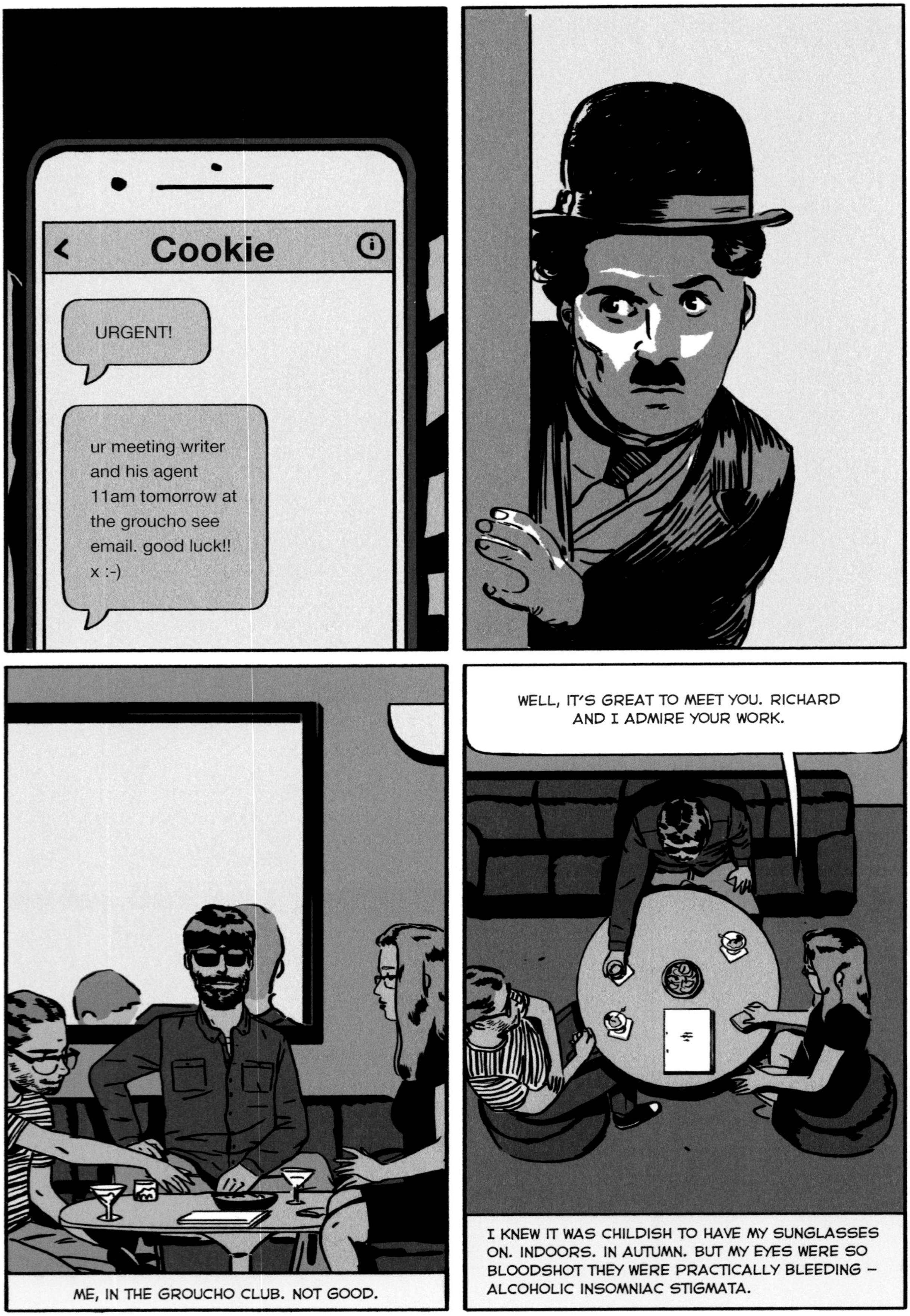
Cookie
URGENT!
ur meeting writer and his agent 11am tomorrow at the groucho see email. good luck!! x :-)
ME, IN THE GROUCHO CLUB. NOT GOOD.
WELL, IT'S GREAT TO MEET YOU. RICHARD AND I ADMIRE YOUR WORK.
I KNEW IT WAS CHILDISH TO HAVE MY SUNGLASSES ON. INDOORS. IN AUTUMN. BUT MY EYES WERE SO BLOODSHOT THEY WERE PRACTICALLY BLEEDING – ALCOHOLIC INSOMNIAC STIGMATA.

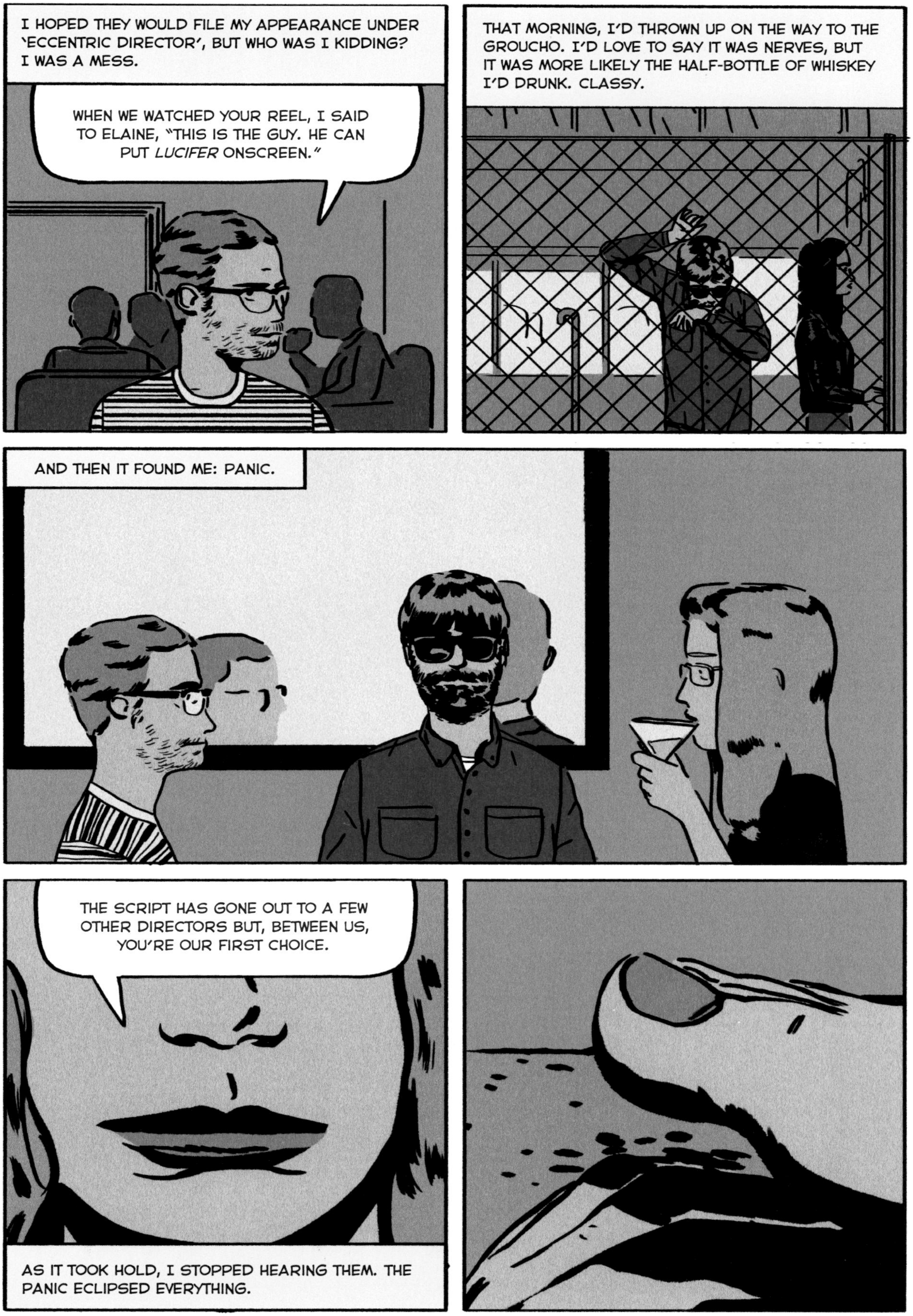
I HOPED THEY WOULD FILE MY APPEARANCE UNDER 'ECCENTRIC DIRECTOR', BUT WHO WAS I KIDDING? I WAS A MESS.
WHEN WE WATCHED YOUR REEL, I SAID TO ELAINE, "THIS IS THE GUY. HE CAN PUT *LUCIFER* ONSCREEN."
THAT MORNING, I'D THROWN UP ON THE WAY TO THE GROUCHO. I'D LOVE TO SAY IT WAS NERVES, BUT IT WAS MORE LIKELY THE HALF-BOTTLE OF WHISKEY I'D DRUNK. CLASSY.
AND THEN IT FOUND ME: PANIC.
THE SCRIPT HAS GONE OUT TO A FEW OTHER DIRECTORS BUT, BETWEEN US, YOU'RE OUR FIRST CHOICE.
AS IT TOOK HOLD, I STOPPED HEARING THEM. THE PANIC ECLIPSED EVERYTHING.

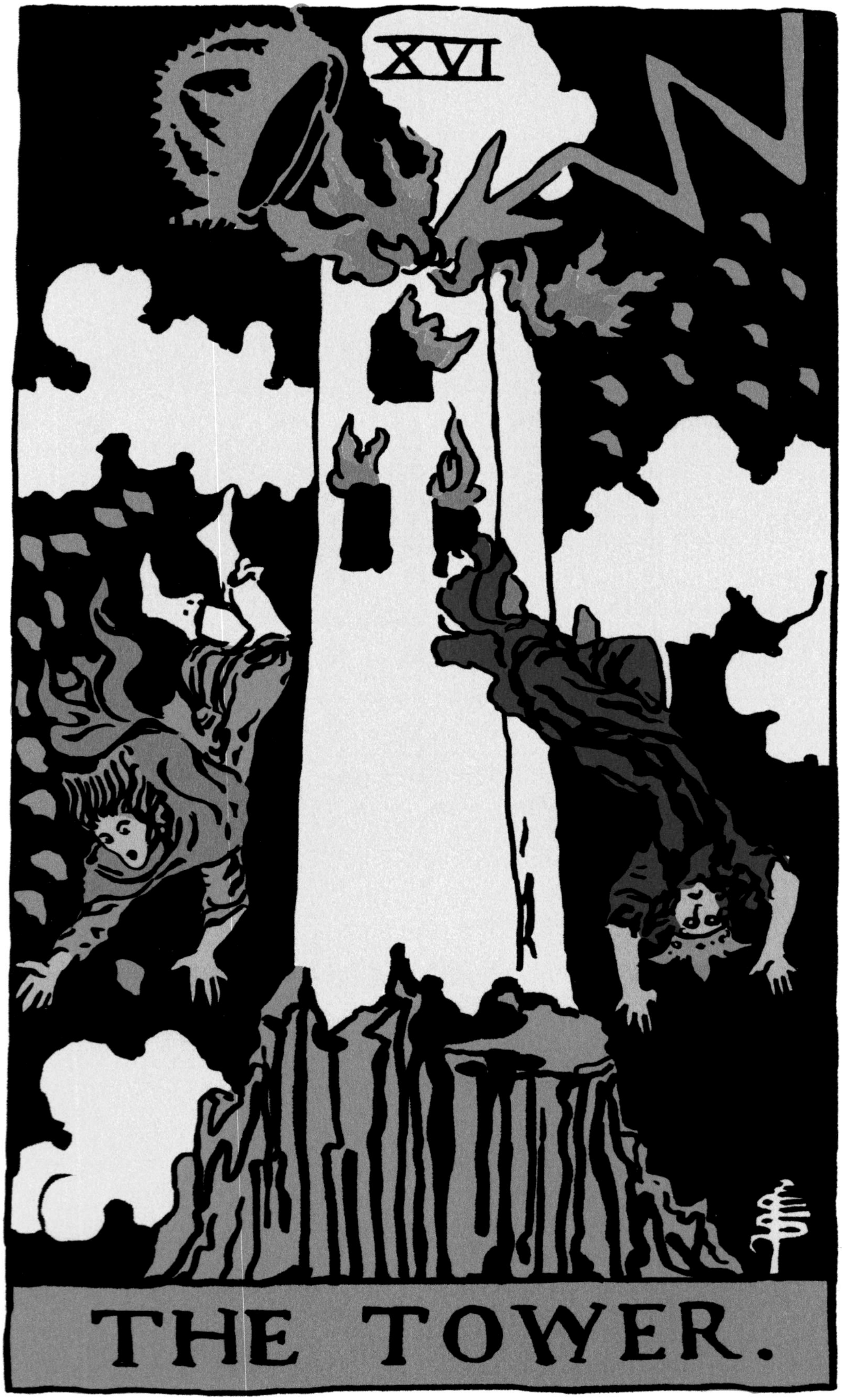
XVI
THE TOWER.

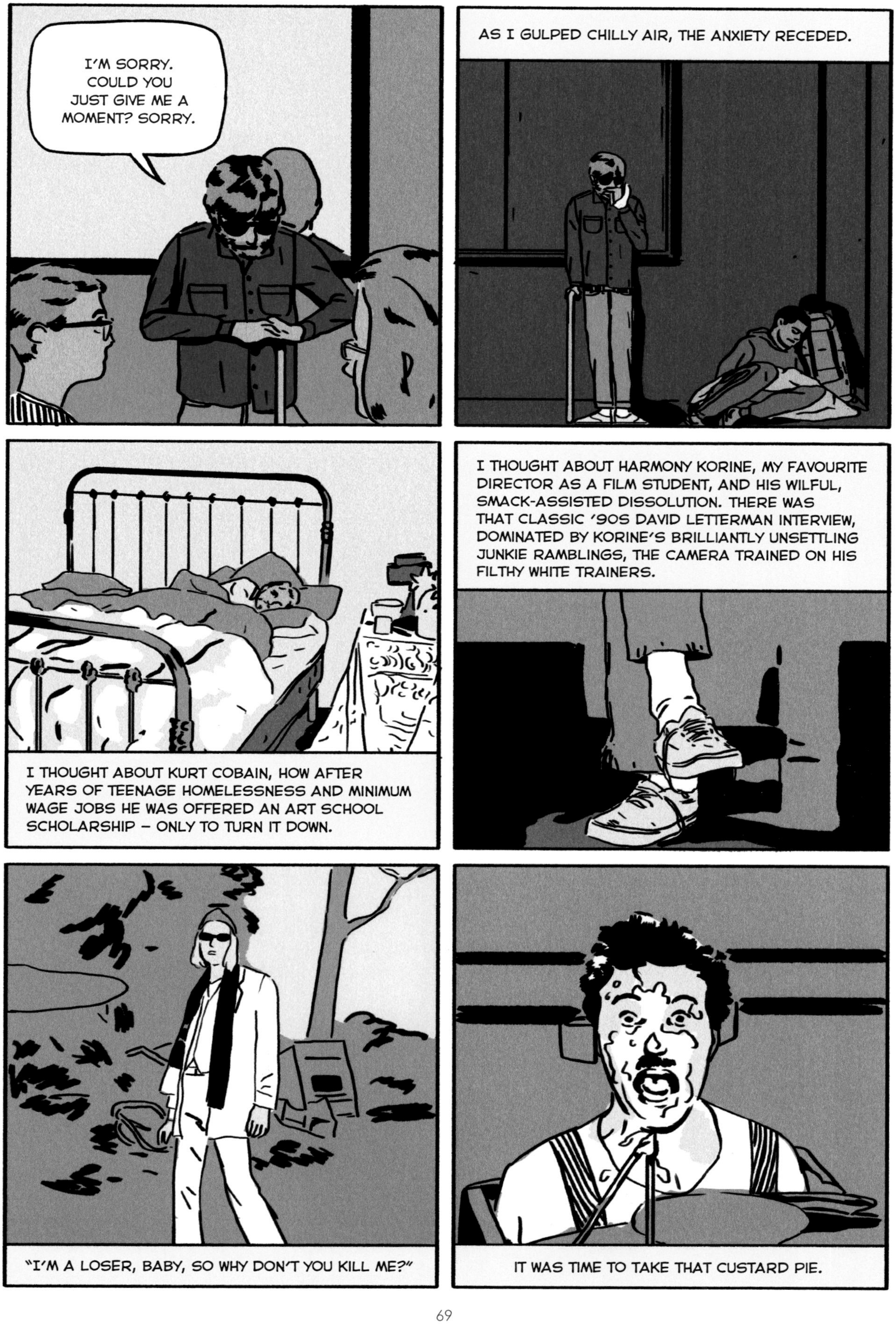
I'M SORRY. COULD YOU JUST GIVE ME A MOMENT? SORRY.
AS I GULPED CHILLY AIR, THE ANXIETY RECEDED.
I THOUGHT ABOUT KURT COBAIN, HOW AFTER YEARS OF TEENAGE HOMELESSNESS AND MINIMUM WAGE JOBS HE WAS OFFERED AN ART SCHOOL SCHOLARSHIP – ONLY TO TURN IT DOWN.
I THOUGHT ABOUT HARMONY KORINE, MY FAVOURITE DIRECTOR AS A FILM STUDENT, AND HIS WILFUL, SMACK-ASSISTED DISSOLUTION. THERE WAS THAT CLASSIC '90S DAVID LETTERMAN INTERVIEW, DOMINATED BY KORINE'S BRILLIANTLY UNSETTLING JUNKIE RAMBLINGS, THE CAMERA TRAINED ON HIS FILTHY WHITE TRAINERS.
"I'M A LOSER, BABY, SO WHY DON'T YOU KILL ME?"
IT WAS TIME TO TAKE THAT CUSTARD PIE.

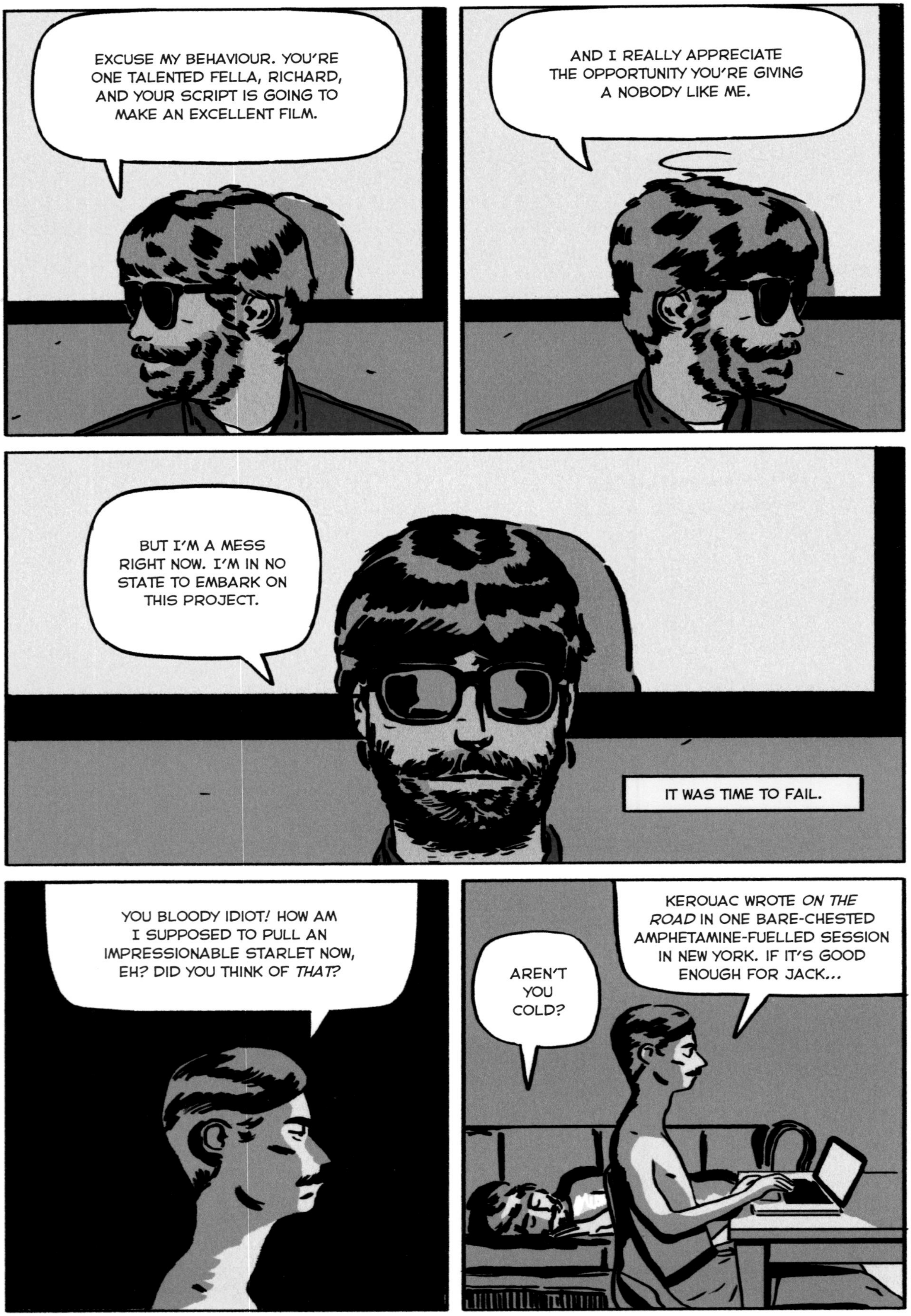
EXCUSE MY BEHAVIOUR. YOU'RE ONE TALENTED FELLA, RICHARD, AND YOUR SCRIPT IS GOING TO MAKE AN EXCELLENT FILM.
AND I REALLY APPRECIATE THE OPPORTUNITY YOU'RE GIVING A NOBODY LIKE ME.
BUT I'M A MESS RIGHT NOW. I'M IN NO STATE TO EMBARK ON THIS PROJECT.
IT WAS TIME TO FAIL.
YOU BLOODY IDIOT! HOW AM I SUPPOSED TO PULL AN IMPRESSIONABLE STARLET NOW, EH? DID YOU THINK OF *THAT*?
KEROUAC WROTE *ON THE ROAD* IN ONE BARE-CHESTED AMPHETAMINE-FUELLED SESSION IN NEW YORK. IF IT'S GOOD ENOUGH FOR JACK...
AREN'T YOU COLD?

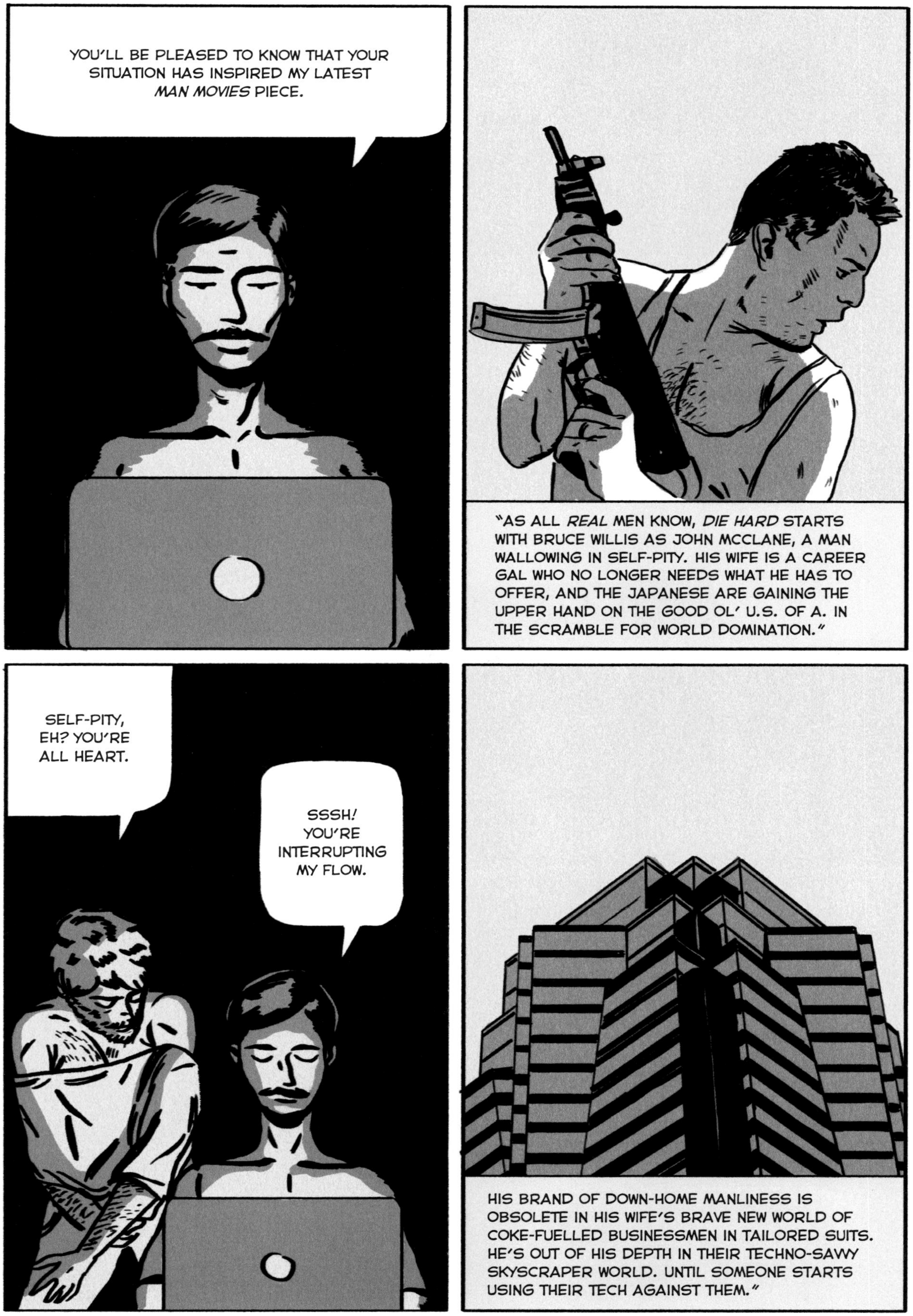
YOU'LL BE PLEASED TO KNOW THAT YOUR SITUATION HAS INSPIRED MY LATEST *MAN MOVIES* PIECE.
"AS ALL *REAL* MEN KNOW, *DIE HARD* STARTS WITH BRUCE WILLIS AS JOHN MCCLANE, A MAN WALLOWING IN SELF-PITY. HIS WIFE IS A CAREER GAL WHO NO LONGER NEEDS WHAT HE HAS TO OFFER, AND THE JAPANESE ARE GAINING THE UPPER HAND ON THE GOOD OL' U.S. OF A. IN THE SCRAMBLE FOR WORLD DOMINATION."
SELF-PITY, EH? YOU'RE ALL HEART.
SSSH! YOU'RE INTERRUPTING MY FLOW.
HIS BRAND OF DOWN-HOME MANLINESS IS OBSOLETE IN HIS WIFE'S BRAVE NEW WORLD OF COKE-FUELLED BUSINESSMEN IN TAILORED SUITS. HE'S OUT OF HIS DEPTH IN THEIR TECHNO-SAVVY SKYSCRAPER WORLD. UNTIL SOMEONE STARTS USING THEIR TECH AGAINST THEM."

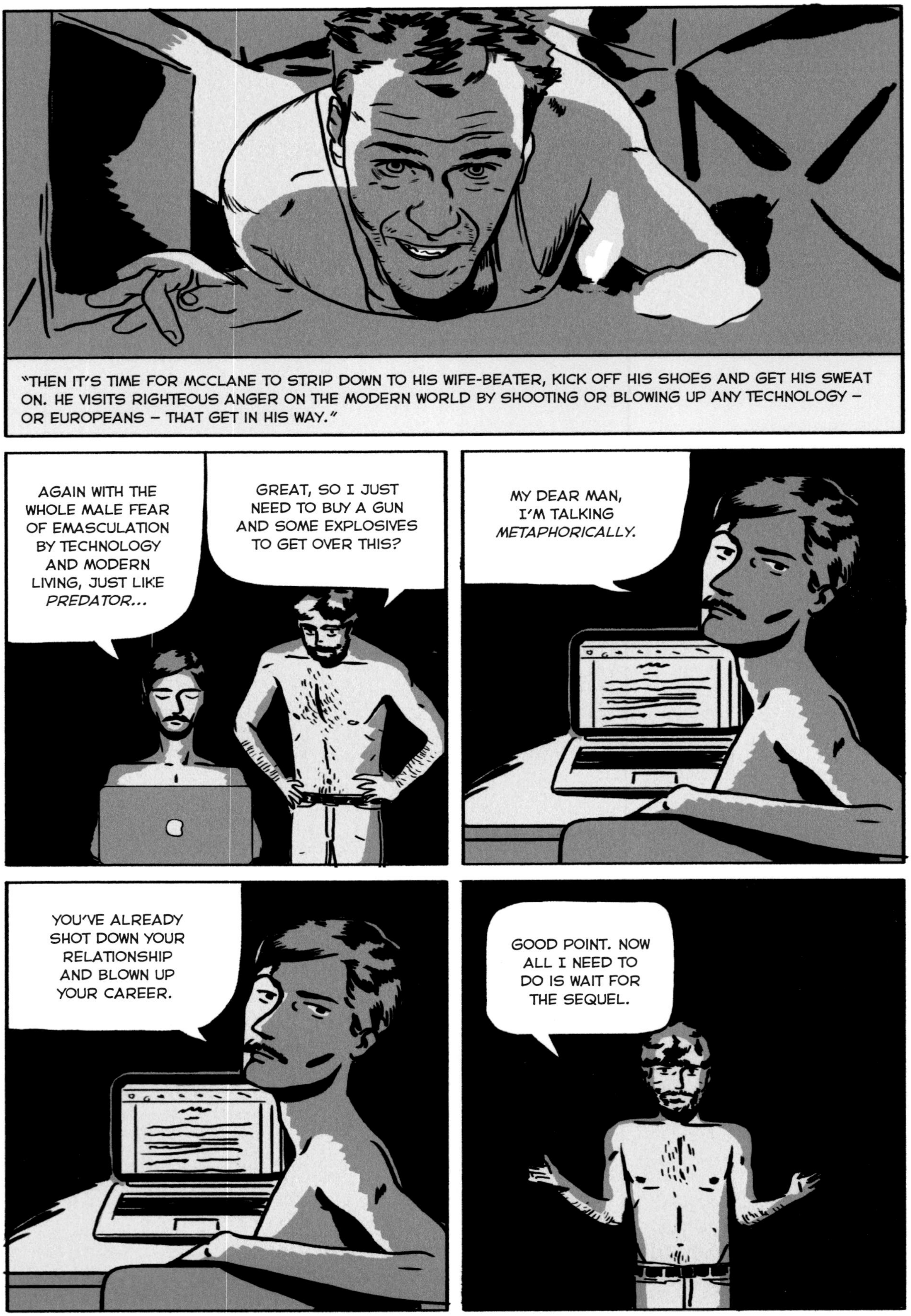
"THEN IT'S TIME FOR MCCLANE TO STRIP DOWN TO HIS WIFE-BEATER, KICK OFF HIS SHOES AND GET HIS SWEAT ON. HE VISITS RIGHTEOUS ANGER ON THE MODERN WORLD BY SHOOTING OR BLOWING UP ANY TECHNOLOGY – OR EUROPEANS – THAT GET IN HIS WAY."
AGAIN WITH THE WHOLE MALE FEAR OF EMASCULATION BY TECHNOLOGY AND MODERN LIVING, JUST LIKE *PREDATOR*...
GREAT, SO I JUST NEED TO BUY A GUN AND SOME EXPLOSIVES TO GET OVER THIS?
MY DEAR MAN, I'M TALKING *METAPHORICALLY*.
YOU'VE ALREADY SHOT DOWN YOUR RELATIONSHIP AND BLOWN UP YOUR CAREER.
GOOD POINT. NOW ALL I NEED TO DO IS WAIT FOR THE SEQUEL.

MULTIPLE PERSONALITY DISORDER, DISSOCIATIVE IDENTITY DISORDER, CALL IT WHAT YOU WILL – I'D HEARD OF IT, BUT I NEVER BELIEVED IT EXISTED, NOT REALLY.

THERE WERE THE FILMS *SYBIL* AND *THE THREE FACES OF EVE*, AND EVEN A CHARACTER WITH IT IN *DOOM PATROL*, A COMIC I READ AS A KID.

BUT THOSE WERE JUST PORTRAYALS OF IT REFRACTED THROUGH THE LENS OF POPULAR CULTURE. HERE, I WAS FACED WITH THE REAL THING.

THE IDEA WAS DECEPTIVELY SIMPLE: EXTREME TRAUMA EXPERIENCED BY A CHILD LED TO THE FRAGMENTATION OF IDENTITY.

THIS RESULTED IN A NUMBER OF PERSONALITIES WHO ASSISTED IN EXPERIENCING AND MANAGING THE UNBEARABLE PSYCHIC BURDEN.

THERE WERE A LOT OF CONFLICTING VIEWS ABOUT HOW IT SHOULD BE TREATED.

SOME QUESTIONED WHETHER IT EXISTED AT ALL.

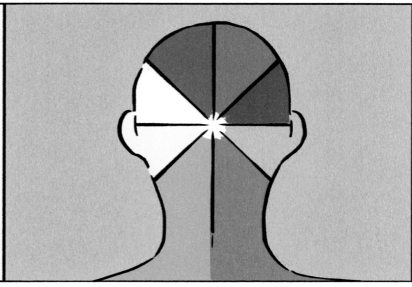

BUT I KNEW IT DID. I'D *SEEN* IT.

JESUS, LEILA, WHAT THE HELL HAPPENED TO YOU?

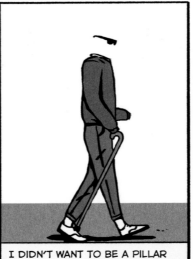

WITH THE FILM OFF MY PLATE, I FELT A FIERCE RELIEF. WHAT RACE WAS I RUNNING? WHO FOR?

I DIDN'T WANT TO BE A PILLAR OF THE COMMUNITY. I JUST WANTED TO DISAPPEAR.

I KNEW THAT NUMBER...

THANKS FOR COMING.

THANKS FOR ASKING ME. I COULD USE A DRINK.

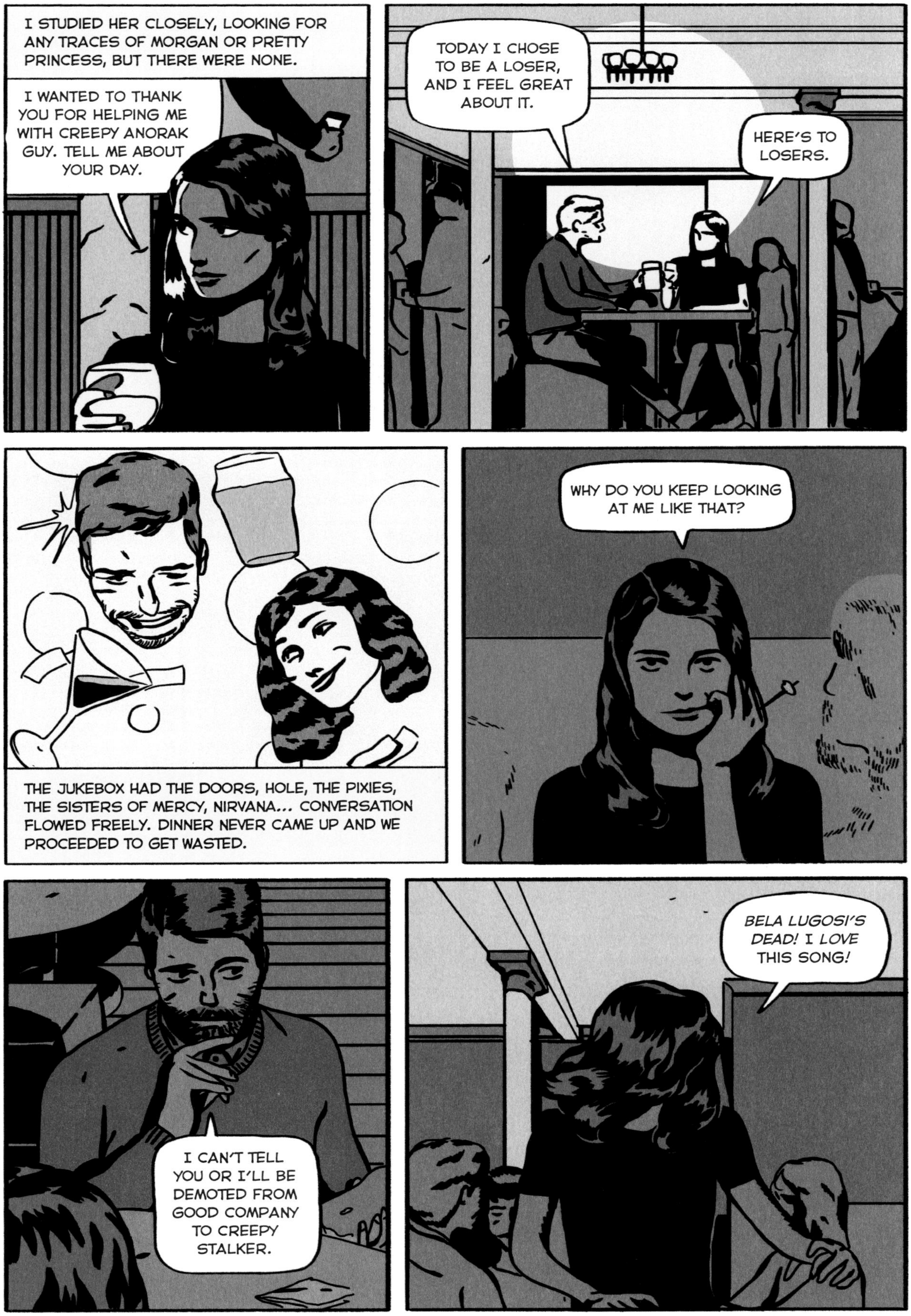
I STUDIED HER CLOSELY, LOOKING FOR ANY TRACES OF MORGAN OR PRETTY PRINCESS, BUT THERE WERE NONE.
I WANTED TO THANK YOU FOR HELPING ME WITH CREEPY ANORAK GUY. TELL ME ABOUT YOUR DAY.
TODAY I CHOSE TO BE A LOSER, AND I FEEL GREAT ABOUT IT.
HERE'S TO LOSERS.
THE JUKEBOX HAD THE DOORS, HOLE, THE PIXIES, THE SISTERS OF MERCY, NIRVANA... CONVERSATION FLOWED FREELY. DINNER NEVER CAME UP AND WE PROCEEDED TO GET WASTED.
WHY DO YOU KEEP LOOKING AT ME LIKE THAT?
I CAN'T TELL YOU OR I'LL BE DEMOTED FROM GOOD COMPANY TO CREEPY STALKER.
BELA LUGOSI'S DEAD! I *LOVE* THIS SONG!

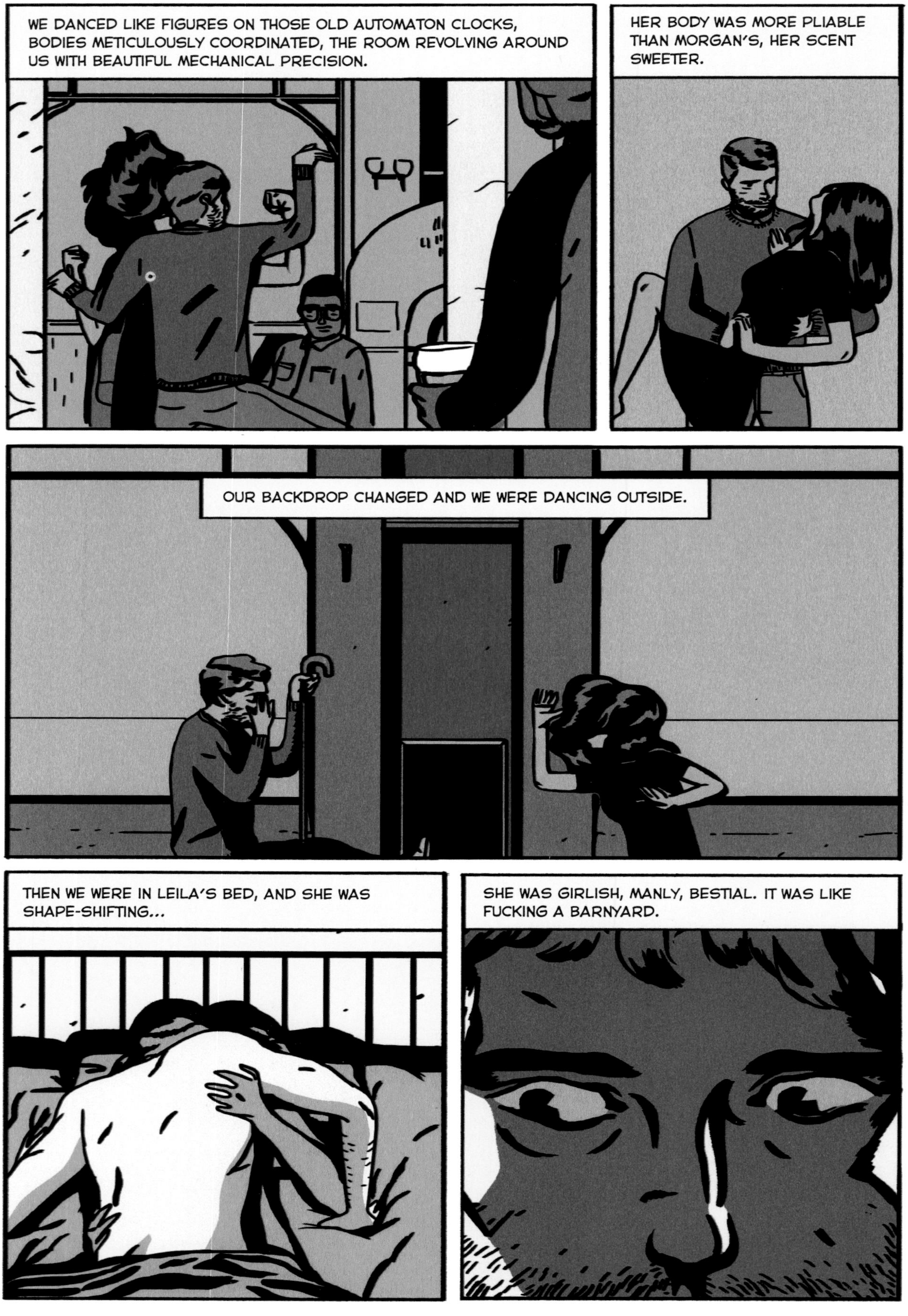
WE DANCED LIKE FIGURES ON THOSE OLD AUTOMATON CLOCKS, BODIES METICULOUSLY COORDINATED, THE ROOM REVOLVING AROUND US WITH BEAUTIFUL MECHANICAL PRECISION.
HER BODY WAS MORE PLIABLE THAN MORGAN'S, HER SCENT SWEETER.
OUR BACKDROP CHANGED AND WE WERE DANCING OUTSIDE.
THEN WE WERE IN LEILA'S BED, AND SHE WAS SHAPE-SHIFTING...
SHE WAS GIRLISH, MANLY, BESTIAL. IT WAS LIKE FUCKING A BARNYARD.

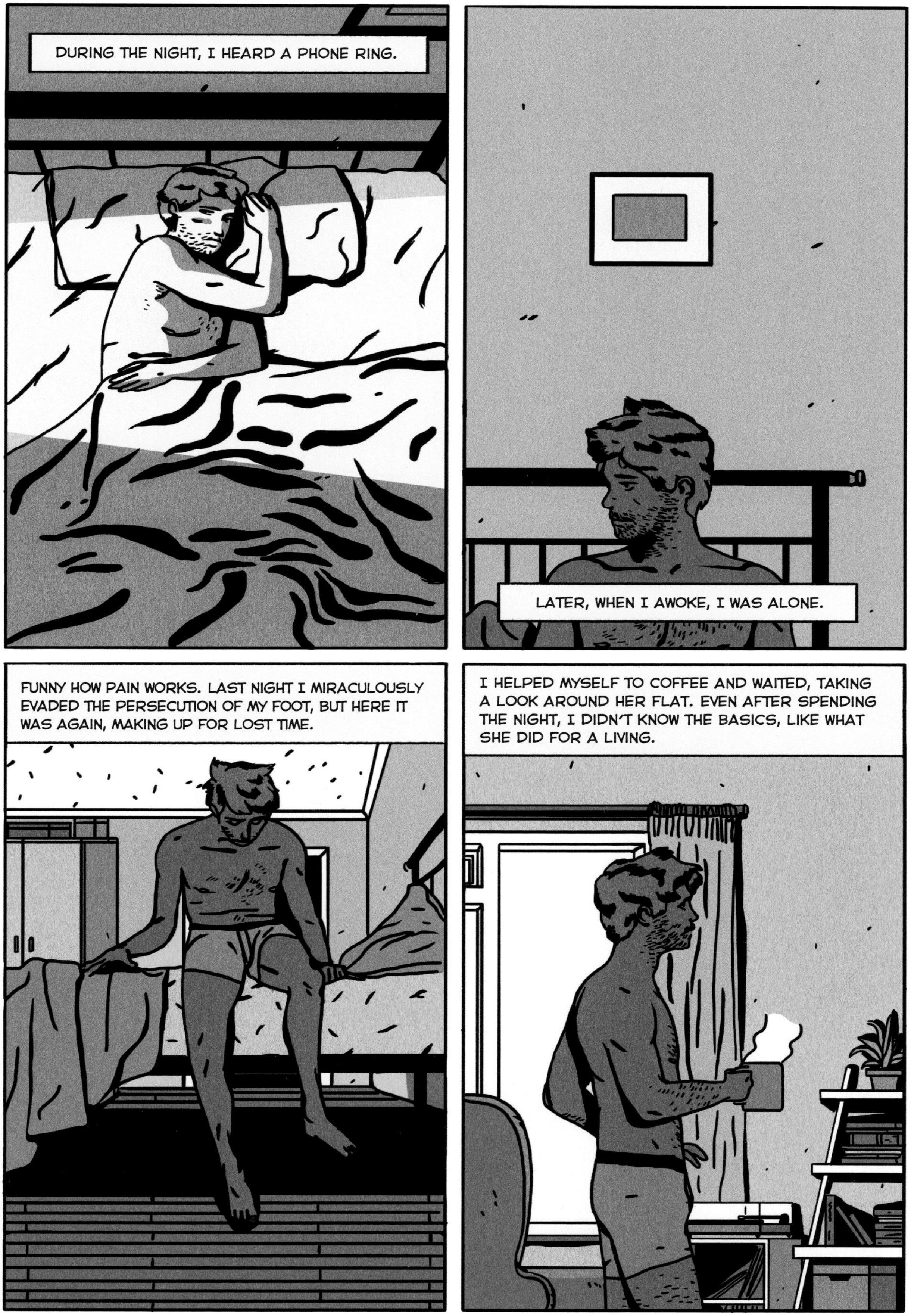
DURING THE NIGHT, I HEARD A PHONE RING.
LATER, WHEN I AWOKE, I WAS ALONE.
FUNNY HOW PAIN WORKS. LAST NIGHT I MIRACULOUSLY EVADED THE PERSECUTION OF MY FOOT, BUT HERE IT WAS AGAIN, MAKING UP FOR LOST TIME.
I HELPED MYSELF TO COFFEE AND WAITED, TAKING A LOOK AROUND HER FLAT. EVEN AFTER SPENDING THE NIGHT, I DIDN'T KNOW THE BASICS, LIKE WHAT SHE DID FOR A LIVING.

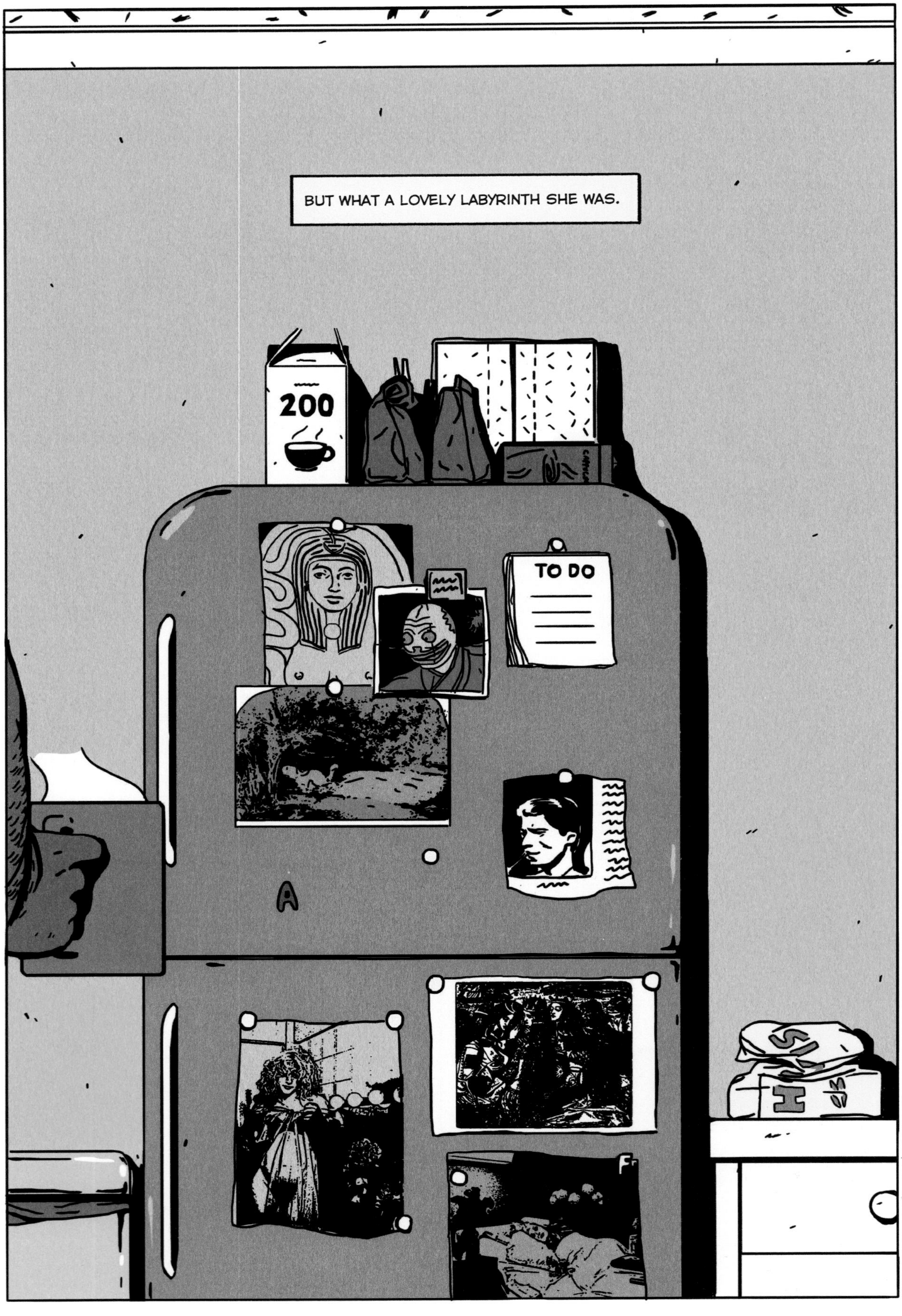
BUT WHAT A LOVELY LABYRINTH SHE WAS.
200
TO DO

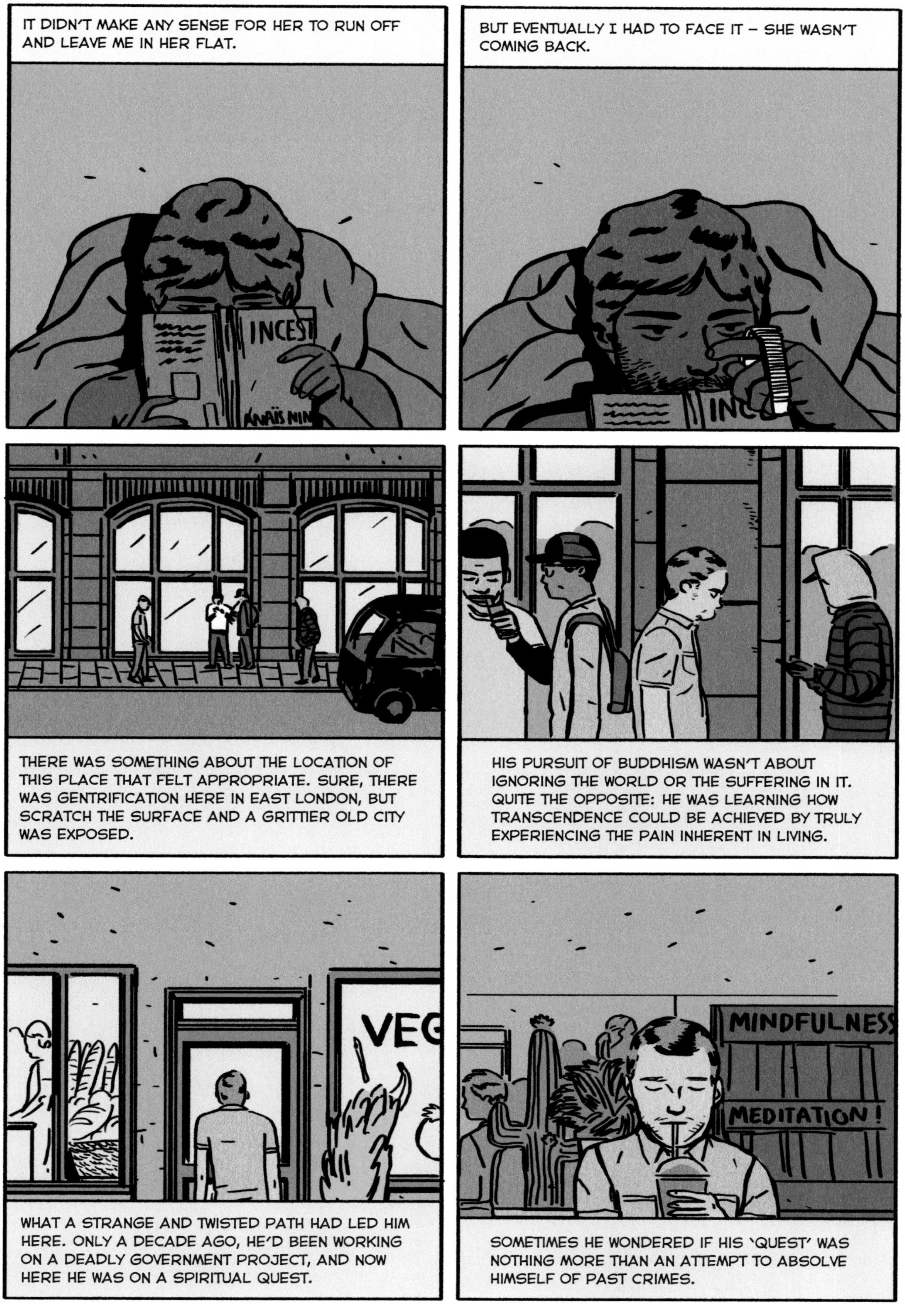
IT DIDN'T MAKE ANY SENSE FOR HER TO RUN OFF AND LEAVE ME IN HER FLAT.
INCEST
ANAÏS NIN
BUT EVENTUALLY I HAD TO FACE IT – SHE WASN'T COMING BACK.
THERE WAS SOMETHING ABOUT THE LOCATION OF THIS PLACE THAT FELT APPROPRIATE. SURE, THERE WAS GENTRIFICATION HERE IN EAST LONDON, BUT SCRATCH THE SURFACE AND A GRITTIER OLD CITY WAS EXPOSED.
HIS PURSUIT OF BUDDHISM WASN'T ABOUT IGNORING THE WORLD OR THE SUFFERING IN IT. QUITE THE OPPOSITE: HE WAS LEARNING HOW TRANSCENDENCE COULD BE ACHIEVED BY TRULY EXPERIENCING THE PAIN INHERENT IN LIVING.
VEG
WHAT A STRANGE AND TWISTED PATH HAD LED HIM HERE. ONLY A DECADE AGO, HE'D BEEN WORKING ON A DEADLY GOVERNMENT PROJECT, AND NOW HERE HE WAS ON A SPIRITUAL QUEST.
MINDFULNESS
MEDITATION!
SOMETIMES HE WONDERED IF HIS 'QUEST' WAS NOTHING MORE THAN AN ATTEMPT TO ABSOLVE HIMSELF OF PAST CRIMES.

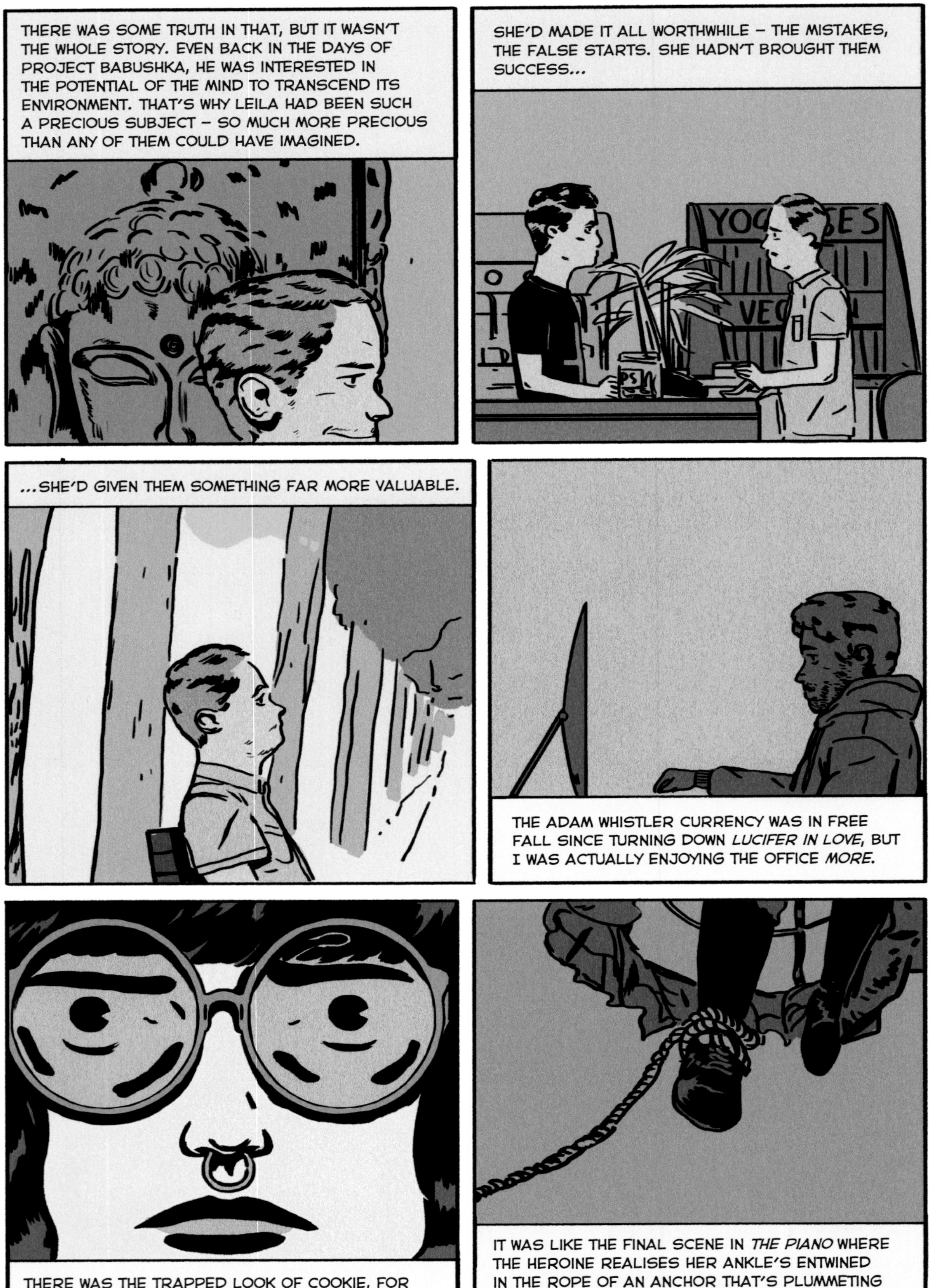
THERE WAS SOME TRUTH IN THAT, BUT IT WASN'T THE WHOLE STORY. EVEN BACK IN THE DAYS OF PROJECT BABUSHKA, HE WAS INTERESTED IN THE POTENTIAL OF THE MIND TO TRANSCEND ITS ENVIRONMENT. THAT'S WHY LEILA HAD BEEN SUCH A PRECIOUS SUBJECT – SO MUCH MORE PRECIOUS THAN ANY OF THEM COULD HAVE IMAGINED.
SHE'D MADE IT ALL WORTHWHILE – THE MISTAKES, THE FALSE STARTS. SHE HADN'T BROUGHT THEM SUCCESS...
...SHE'D GIVEN THEM SOMETHING FAR MORE VALUABLE.
THE ADAM WHISTLER CURRENCY WAS IN FREE FALL SINCE TURNING DOWN *LUCIFER IN LOVE*, BUT I WAS ACTUALLY ENJOYING THE OFFICE *MORE*.
THERE WAS THE TRAPPED LOOK OF COOKIE, FOR INSTANCE, NOW THAT SHE WAS HITCHED TO A LOSER. PRICELESS.
IT WAS LIKE THE FINAL SCENE IN *THE PIANO* WHERE THE HEROINE REALISES HER ANKLE'S ENTWINED IN THE ROPE OF AN ANCHOR THAT'S PLUMMETING TO THE SEABED, AND THAT SHE'S ABOUT TO BE DRAGGED DOWN AFTER IT...

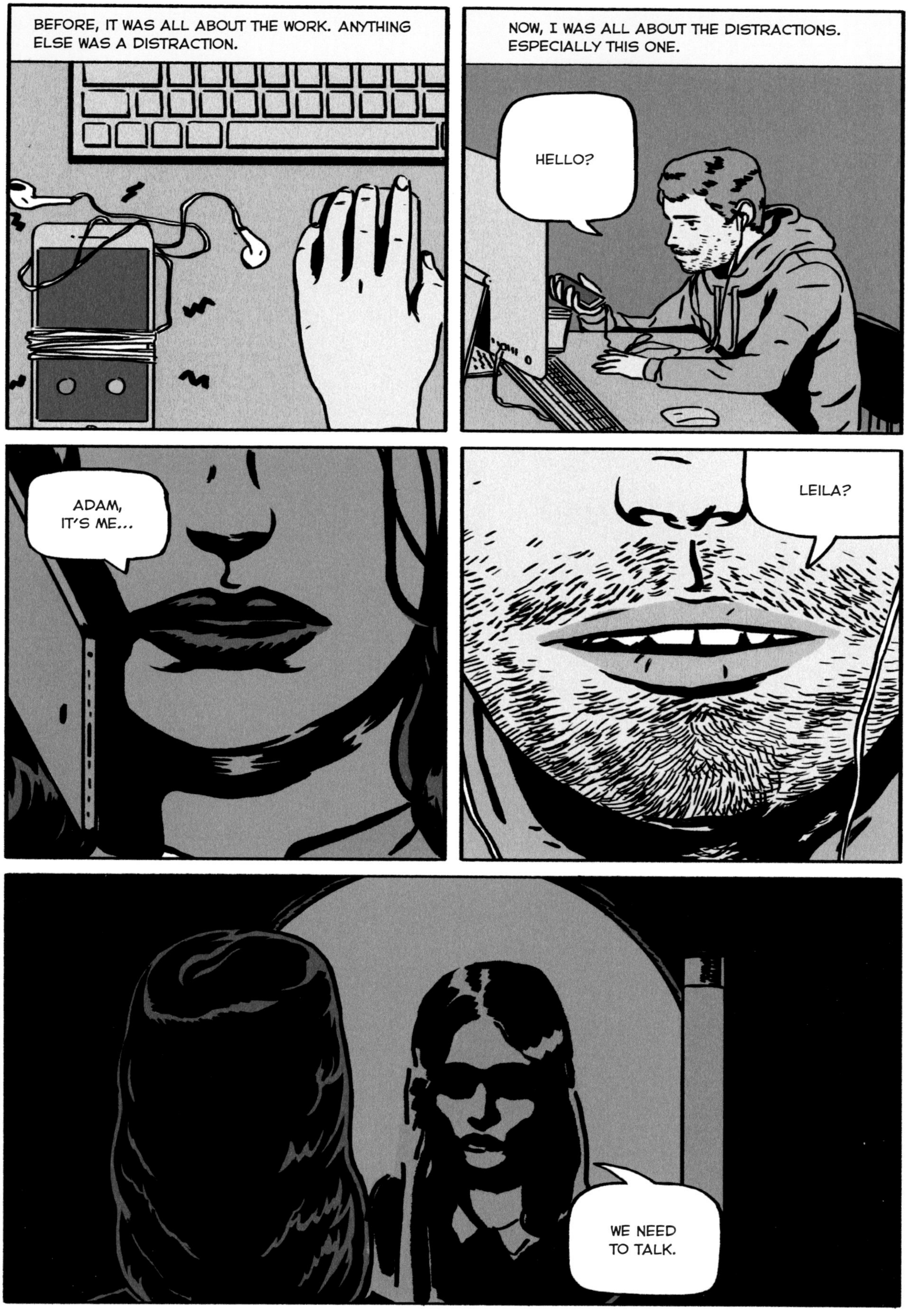
BEFORE, IT WAS ALL ABOUT THE WORK. ANYTHING ELSE WAS A DISTRACTION.
NOW, I WAS ALL ABOUT THE DISTRACTIONS. ESPECIALLY THIS ONE.
HELLO?
ADAM, IT'S ME...
LEILA?
WE NEED TO TALK.

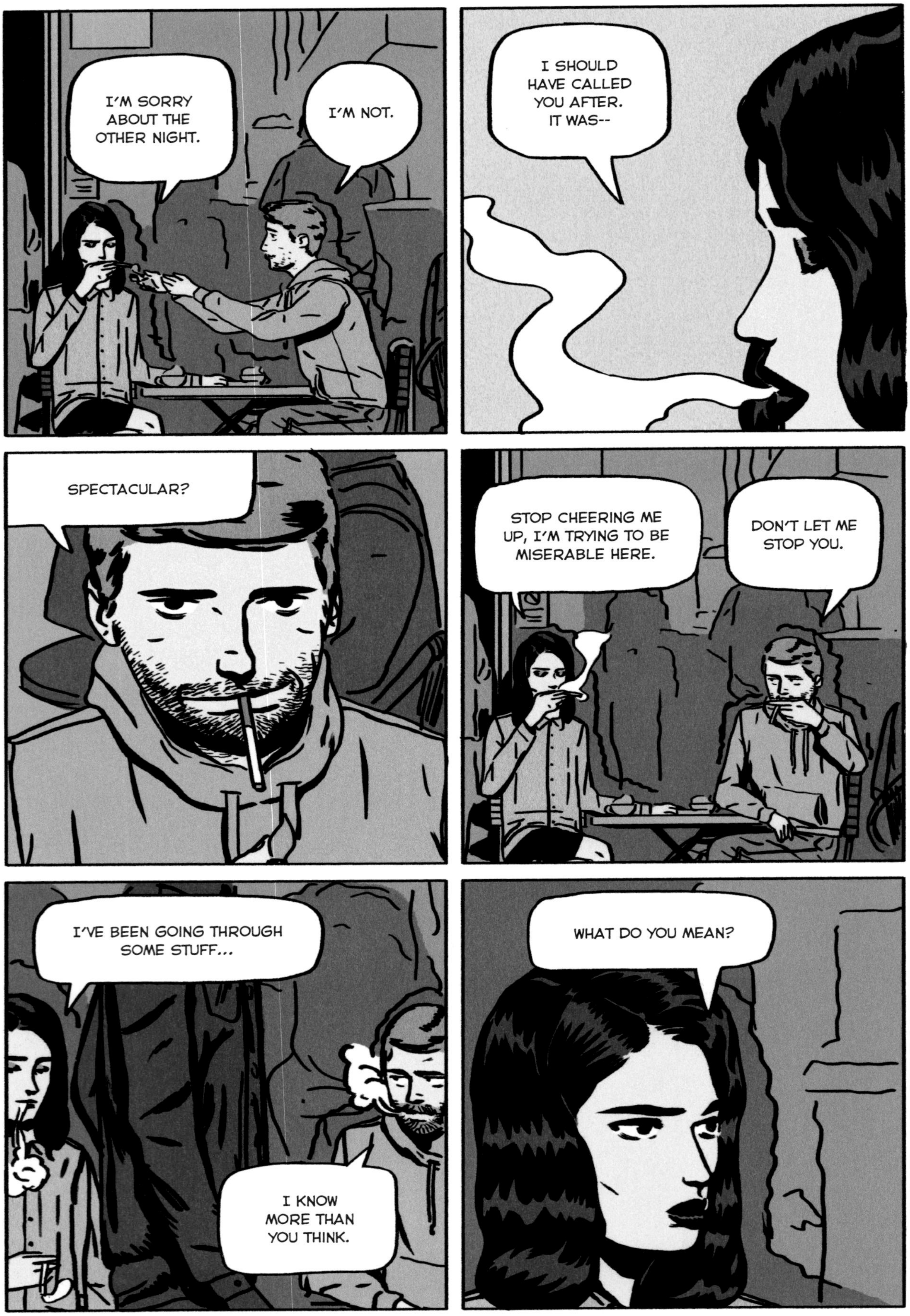
I'M SORRY ABOUT THE OTHER NIGHT.
I'M NOT.
I SHOULD HAVE CALLED YOU AFTER. IT WAS--
SPECTACULAR?
STOP CHEERING ME UP, I'M TRYING TO BE MISERABLE HERE.
DON'T LET ME STOP YOU.
I'VE BEEN GOING THROUGH SOME STUFF...
I KNOW MORE THAN YOU THINK.
WHAT DO YOU MEAN?

I'VE MET PRETTY PRINCESS.

THEN YOU KNOW...

LEILA, I DON'T HAVE THE FIRST CLUE. BUT I WANT TO UNDERSTAND.

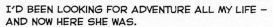

I'D BEEN LOOKING FOR ADVENTURE ALL MY LIFE — AND NOW HERE SHE WAS.

AS EVERYTHING ELSE DRAINED FROM MY LIFE, SHE FILLED THE VOID.

LEILA, I'M SO SORRY, I DIDN'T--

NO, IT'S FINE, IT'S JUST... I NEVER DISCUSS IT WITH ANYONE.

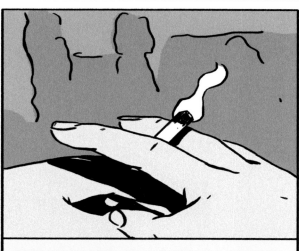

THIS WASN'T AS CALLOUS AS SIMPLY LOOKING FOR THRILLS — I WANTED TO PROTECT HER. DESPITE THE MESS MY LIFE WAS IN, SHE GAVE ME PURPOSE.

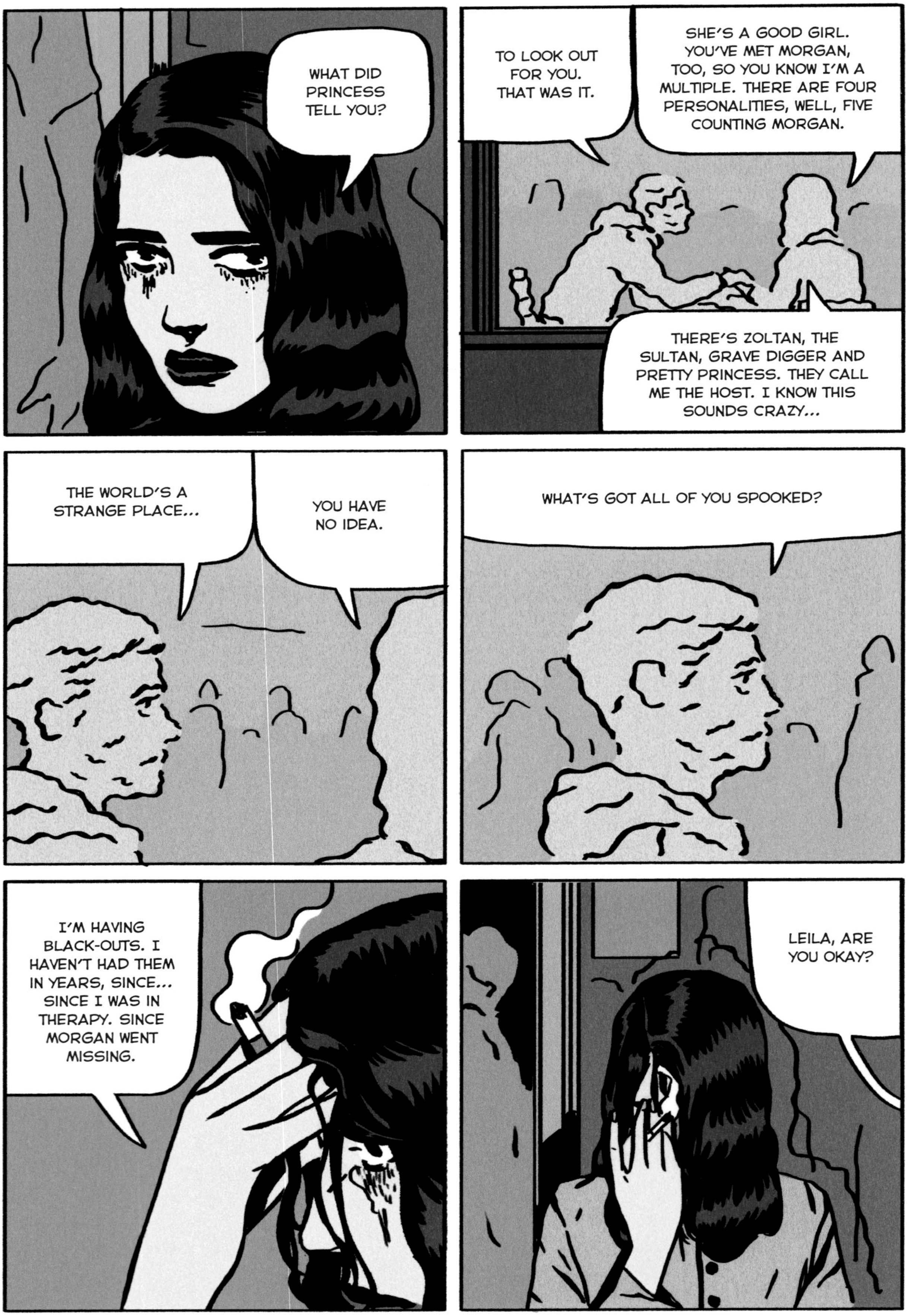
WHAT DID PRINCESS TELL YOU?
TO LOOK OUT FOR YOU. THAT WAS IT.
SHE'S A GOOD GIRL. YOU'VE MET MORGAN, TOO, SO YOU KNOW I'M A MULTIPLE. THERE ARE FOUR PERSONALITIES, WELL, FIVE COUNTING MORGAN.
THERE'S ZOLTAN, THE SULTAN, GRAVE DIGGER AND PRETTY PRINCESS. THEY CALL ME THE HOST. I KNOW THIS SOUNDS CRAZY...
THE WORLD'S A STRANGE PLACE...
YOU HAVE NO IDEA.
WHAT'S GOT ALL OF YOU SPOOKED?
I'M HAVING BLACK-OUTS. I HAVEN'T HAD THEM IN YEARS, SINCE... SINCE I WAS IN THERAPY. SINCE MORGAN WENT MISSING.
LEILA, ARE YOU OKAY?

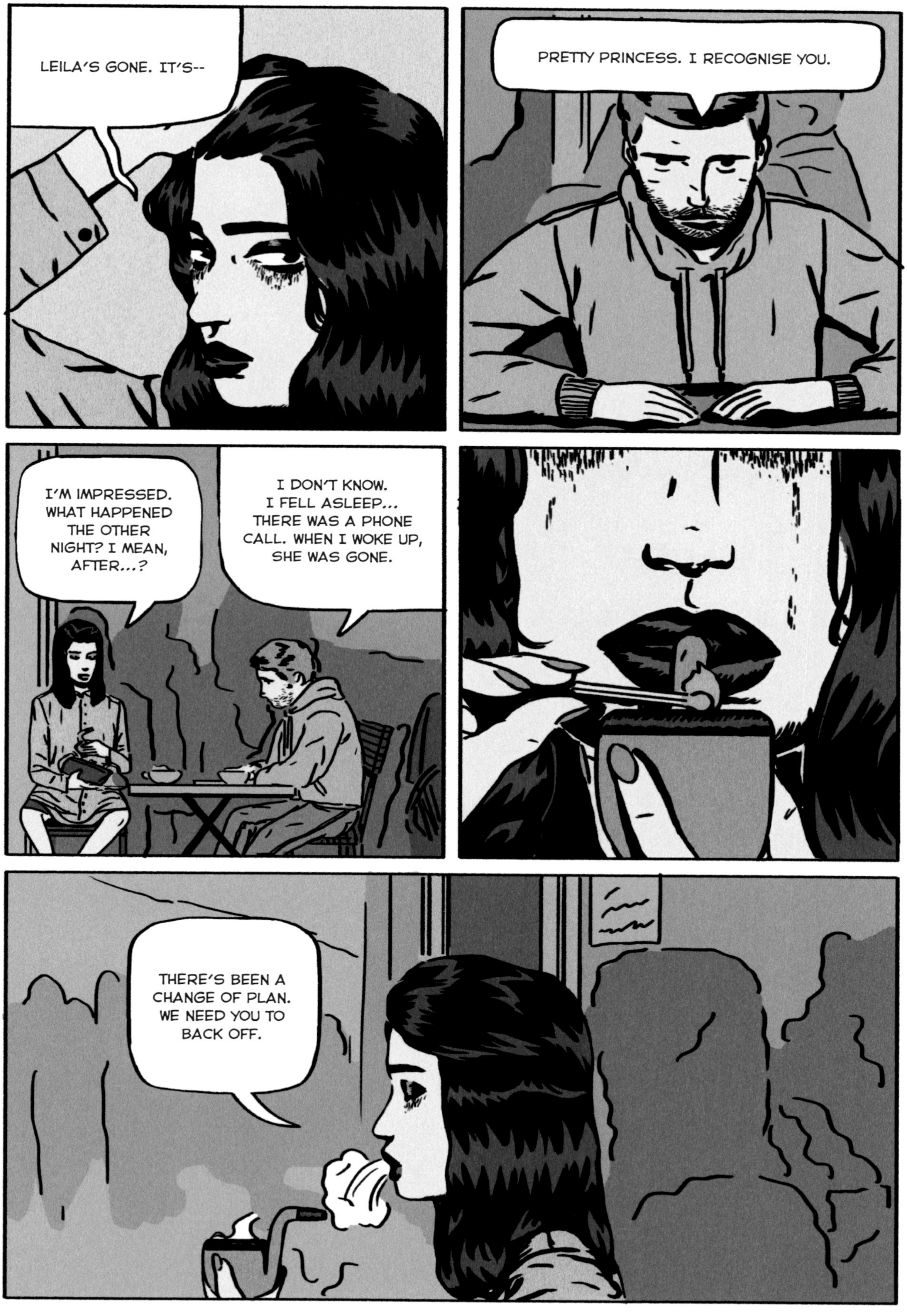
LEILA'S GONE. IT'S--
PRETTY PRINCESS. I RECOGNISE YOU.
I'M IMPRESSED. WHAT HAPPENED THE OTHER NIGHT? I MEAN, AFTER...?
I DON'T KNOW. I FELL ASLEEP... THERE WAS A PHONE CALL. WHEN I WOKE UP, SHE WAS GONE.
THERE'S BEEN A CHANGE OF PLAN. WE NEED YOU TO BACK OFF.

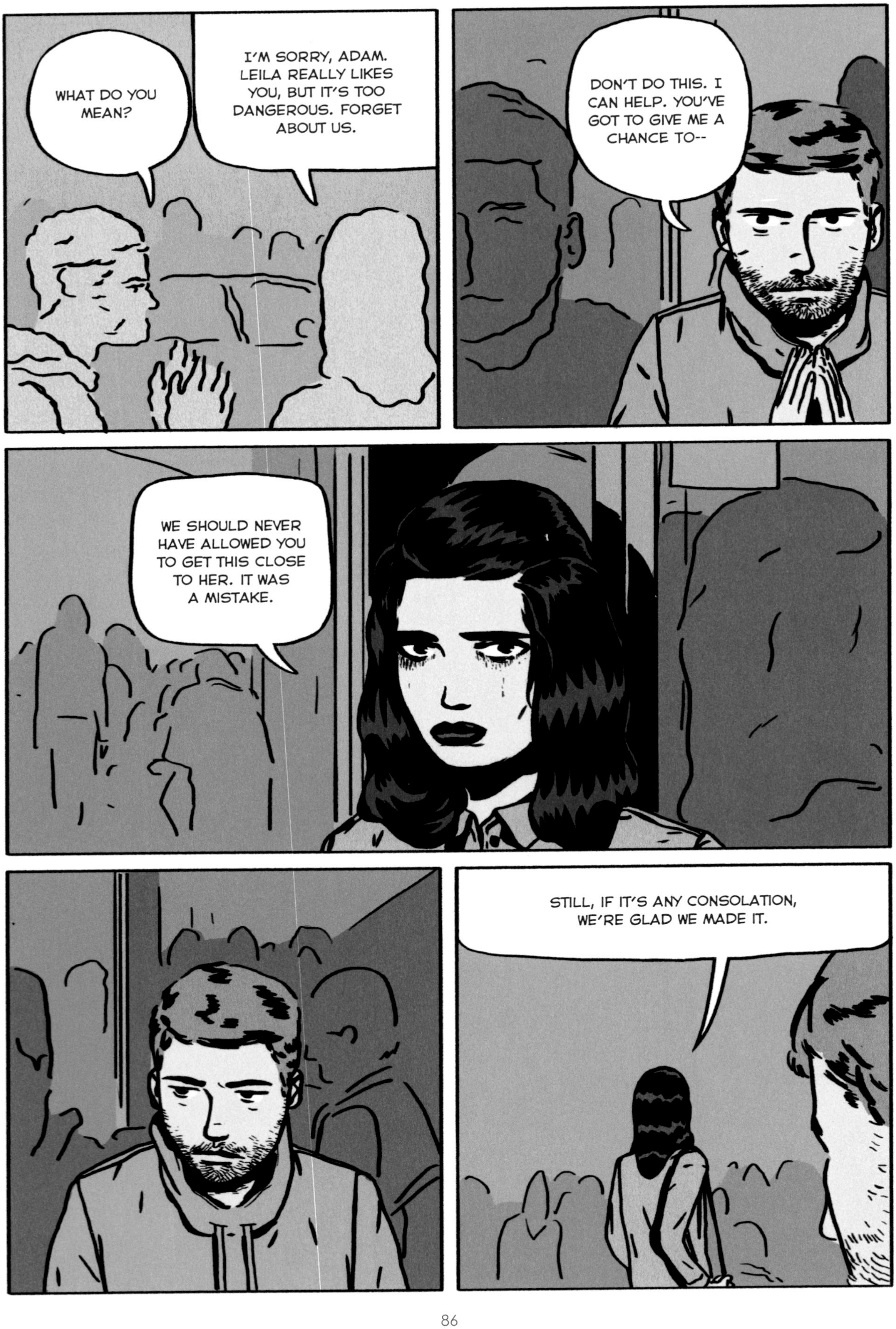
WHAT DO YOU MEAN?
I'M SORRY, ADAM. LEILA REALLY LIKES YOU, BUT IT'S TOO DANGEROUS. FORGET ABOUT US.
DON'T DO THIS. I CAN HELP. YOU'VE GOT TO GIVE ME A CHANCE TO--
WE SHOULD NEVER HAVE ALLOWED YOU TO GET THIS CLOSE TO HER. IT WAS A MISTAKE.
STILL, IF IT'S ANY CONSOLATION, WE'RE GLAD WE MADE IT.

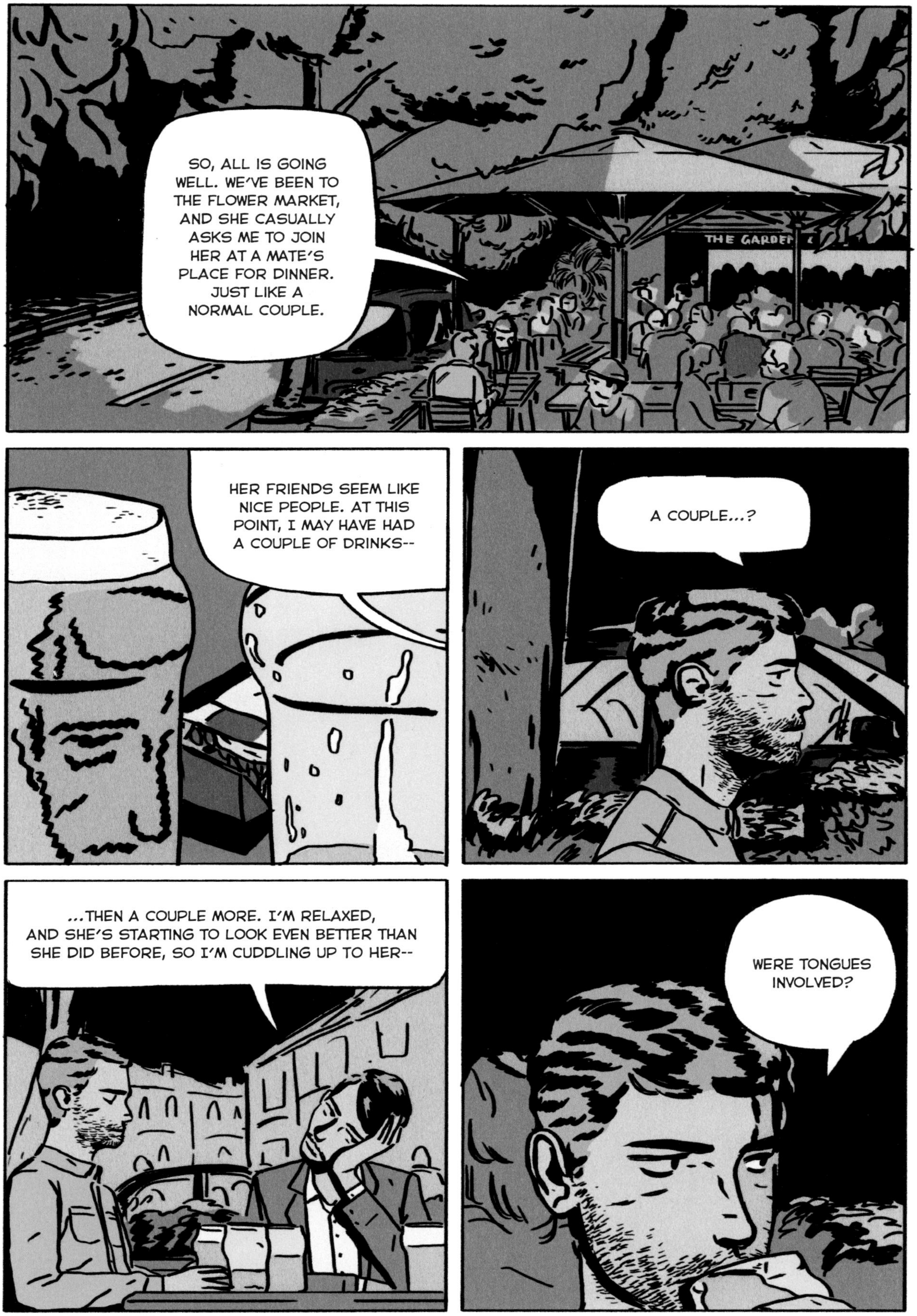
SO, ALL IS GOING WELL. WE'VE BEEN TO THE FLOWER MARKET, AND SHE CASUALLY ASKS ME TO JOIN HER AT A MATE'S PLACE FOR DINNER. JUST LIKE A NORMAL COUPLE.
HER FRIENDS SEEM LIKE NICE PEOPLE. AT THIS POINT, I MAY HAVE HAD A COUPLE OF DRINKS--
A COUPLE...?
...THEN A COUPLE MORE. I'M RELAXED, AND SHE'S STARTING TO LOOK EVEN BETTER THAN SHE DID BEFORE, SO I'M CUDDLING UP TO HER--
WERE TONGUES INVOLVED?

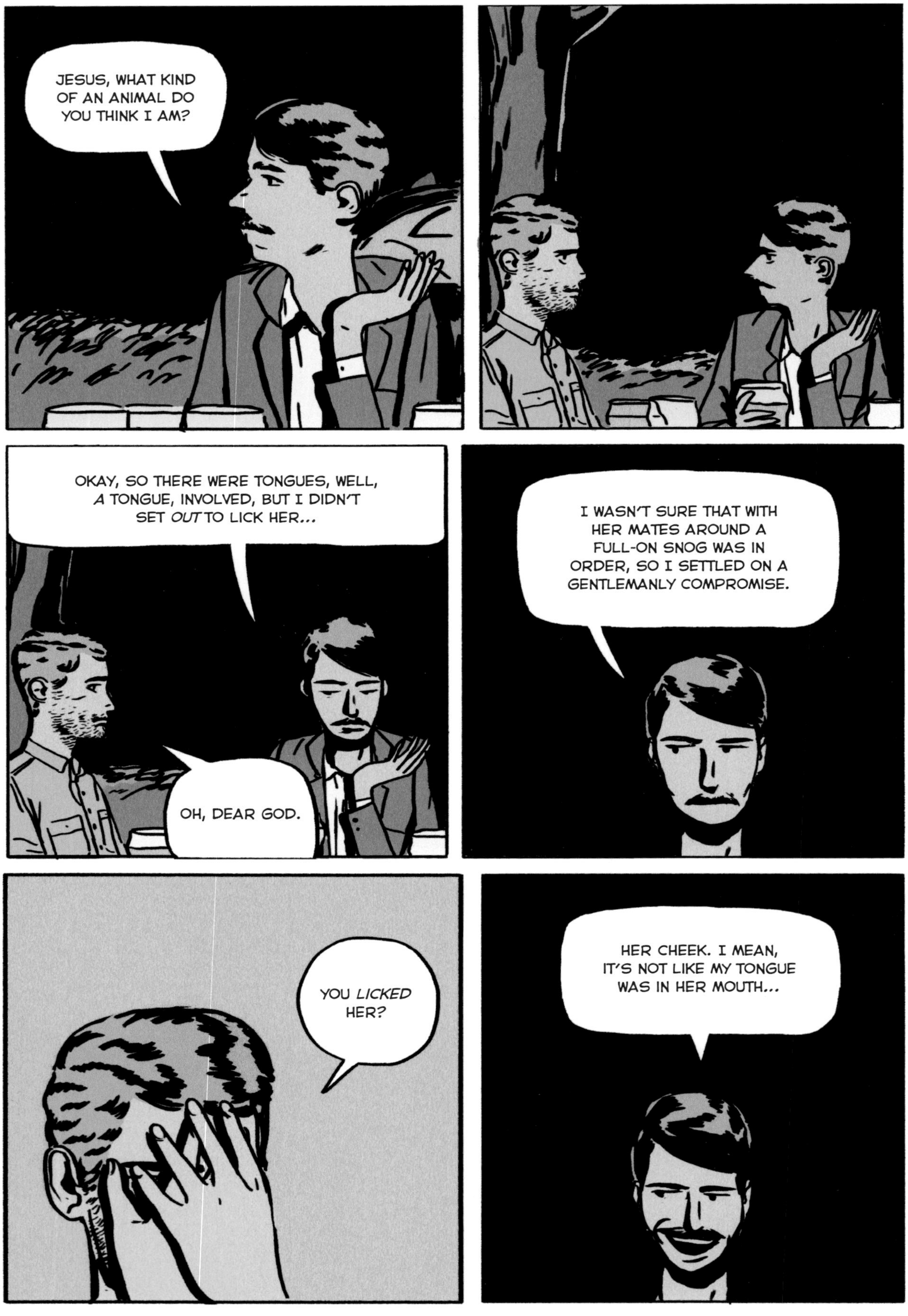
JESUS, WHAT KIND OF AN ANIMAL DO YOU THINK I AM?
OKAY, SO THERE WERE TONGUES, WELL, *A* TONGUE, INVOLVED, BUT I DIDN'T SET *OUT* TO LICK HER...
OH, DEAR GOD.
I WASN'T SURE THAT WITH HER MATES AROUND A FULL-ON SNOG WAS IN ORDER, SO I SETTLED ON A GENTLEMANLY COMPROMISE.
YOU *LICKED* HER?
HER CHEEK. I MEAN, IT'S NOT LIKE MY TONGUE WAS IN HER MOUTH...

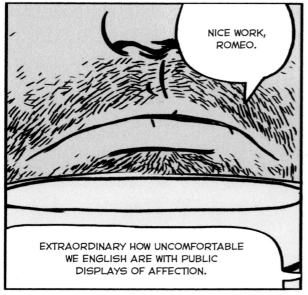

NICE WORK, ROMEO.

EXTRAORDINARY HOW UNCOMFORTABLE WE ENGLISH ARE WITH PUBLIC DISPLAYS OF AFFECTION.

HER FRIENDS SEEMED... SURPRISED, BUT I STYLED IT OUT AND STAYED PUT. I REMEMBER FALLING INTO A FLOWER BED LATER, THEN SOME HELPING HANDS ESCORTING ME OUT ONTO THE STREET...

WELL, SHE MAY AS WELL KNOW WHAT SHE'S IN FOR FROM THE GET-GO.

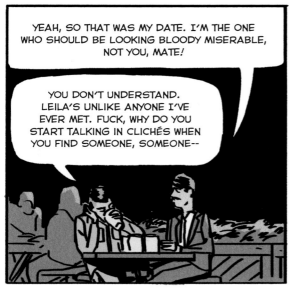

YEAH, SO THAT WAS MY DATE. I'M THE ONE WHO SHOULD BE LOOKING BLOODY MISERABLE, NOT YOU, MATE!

YOU DON'T UNDERSTAND. LEILA'S UNLIKE ANYONE I'VE EVER MET. FUCK, WHY DO YOU START TALKING IN CLICHÉS WHEN YOU FIND SOMEONE, SOMEONE--

SPECIAL? HALLMARK™.

I'M SERIOUS!

I KNOW YOU ARE, BUT COME ON, BUDDY. YOU'VE JUST BROKEN UP WITH SARAH. THE LAST THING YOU NEED IS GETTING SERIOUS WITH SOMEONE, HOWEVER SPECIAL THEY ARE.

YOU MAKE FOR AN UNLIKELY VOICE OF REASON.

GRANTED.

THERE ARE THINGS ABOUT HER I HAVEN'T TOLD YOU... I JUST CAN'T LET HER GO.

SHE'S THAT GOOD IN BED? AMAZING. WELL, IN THAT CASE, I SUPPOSE YOU'RE GOING TO HAVE TO TAKE THE *TERMINATOR* APPROACH.

I'M AFRAID TO ASK...

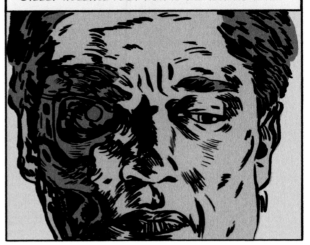

"AH, COME NOW, I NEED HARDLY REMIND YOU OF THE LOVE STORY AT THE HEART OF THE OTHERWISE STEELY VIOLENCE-FEST THAT IS *THE TERMINATOR*..."

THIS WAS THE DAWN OF A NEW AGE OF ACTION FILMS: THAT OF THE STRONG FEMALE LEAD. SURE, SARAH CONNOR WAS JUST A WAITRESS, BUT SHE HAD *BALLS*."

"AND THAT WASN'T THE ONLY INNOVATION. THERE WAS A LOVE STORY HERE."

"IT DIDN'T GO SMOOTHLY, THOUGH. AT FIRST, SARAH THOUGHT KYLE REESE WAS A STALKER. IT WAS ONLY WHEN FACED WITH A DEMENTED CYBORG FROM THE FUTURE THAT SHE FINALLY GAVE HIM THE TIME OF DAY."

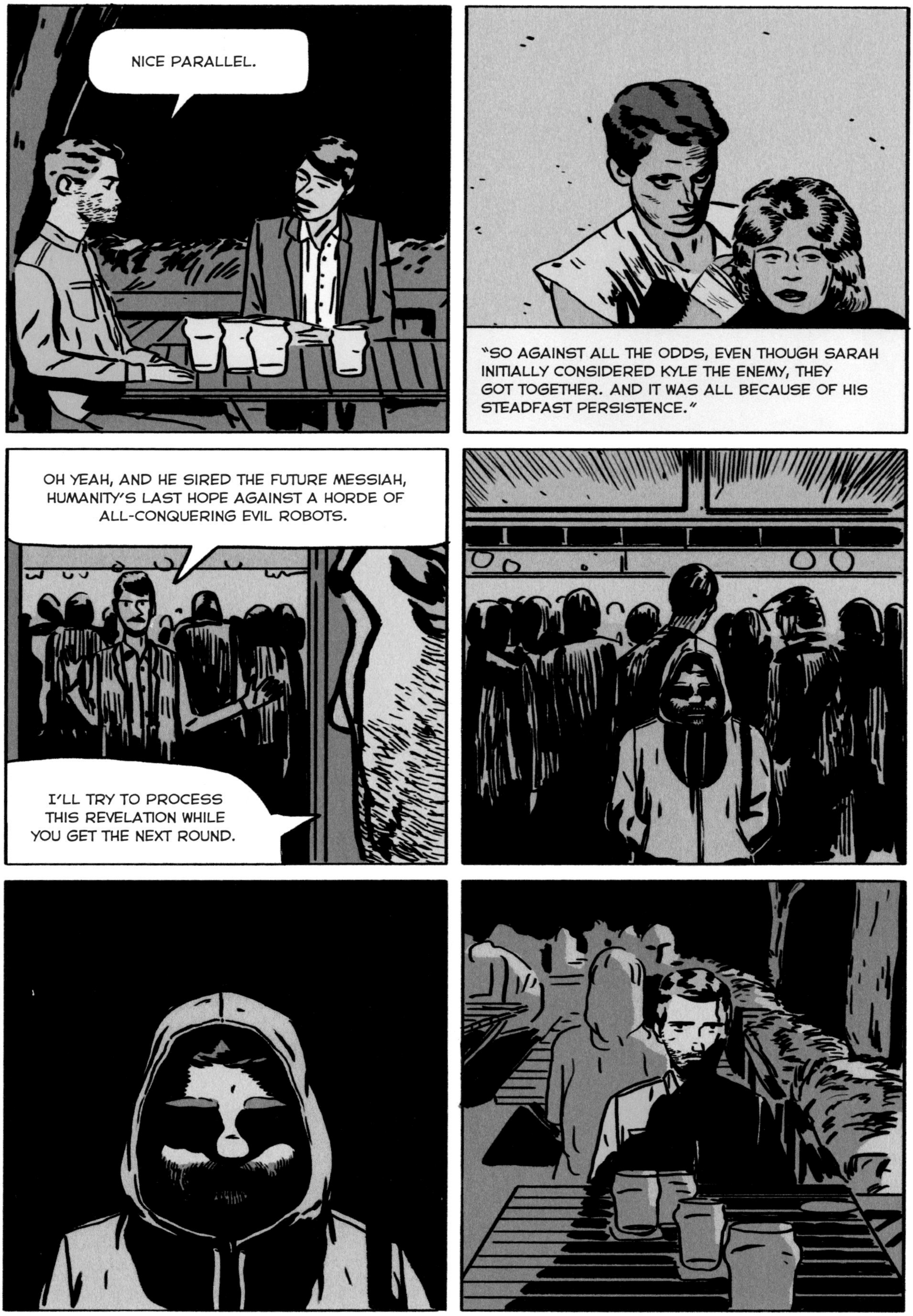
NICE PARALLEL.
"SO AGAINST ALL THE ODDS, EVEN THOUGH SARAH INITIALLY CONSIDERED KYLE THE ENEMY, THEY GOT TOGETHER. AND IT WAS ALL BECAUSE OF HIS STEADFAST PERSISTENCE."
OH YEAH, AND HE SIRED THE FUTURE MESSIAH, HUMANITY'S LAST HOPE AGAINST A HORDE OF ALL-CONQUERING EVIL ROBOTS.
I'LL TRY TO PROCESS THIS REVELATION WHILE YOU GET THE NEXT ROUND.

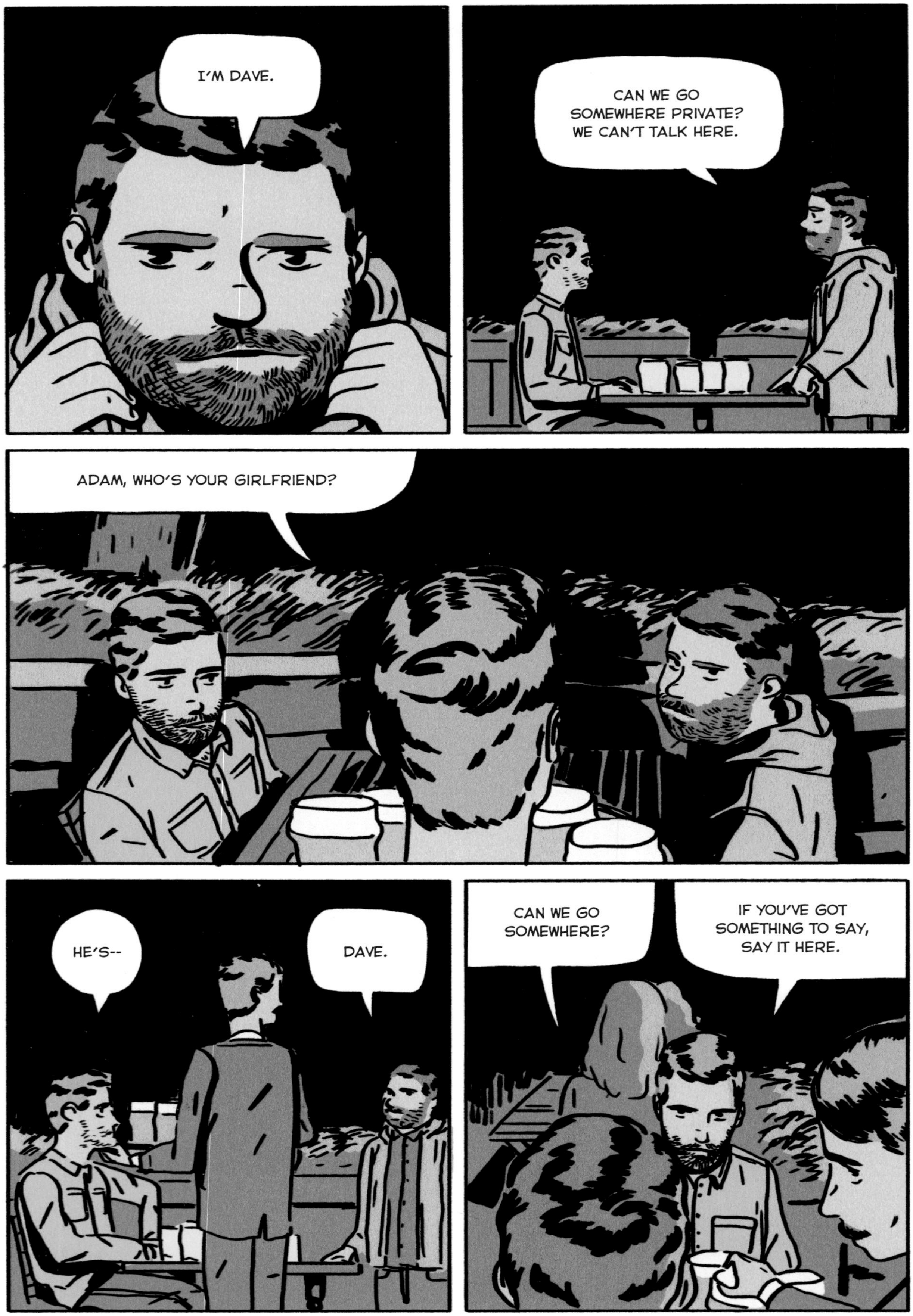
I'M DAVE.
CAN WE GO SOMEWHERE PRIVATE? WE CAN'T TALK HERE.
ADAM, WHO'S YOUR GIRLFRIEND?
HE'S--
DAVE.
CAN WE GO SOMEWHERE?
IF YOU'VE GOT SOMETHING TO SAY, SAY IT HERE.

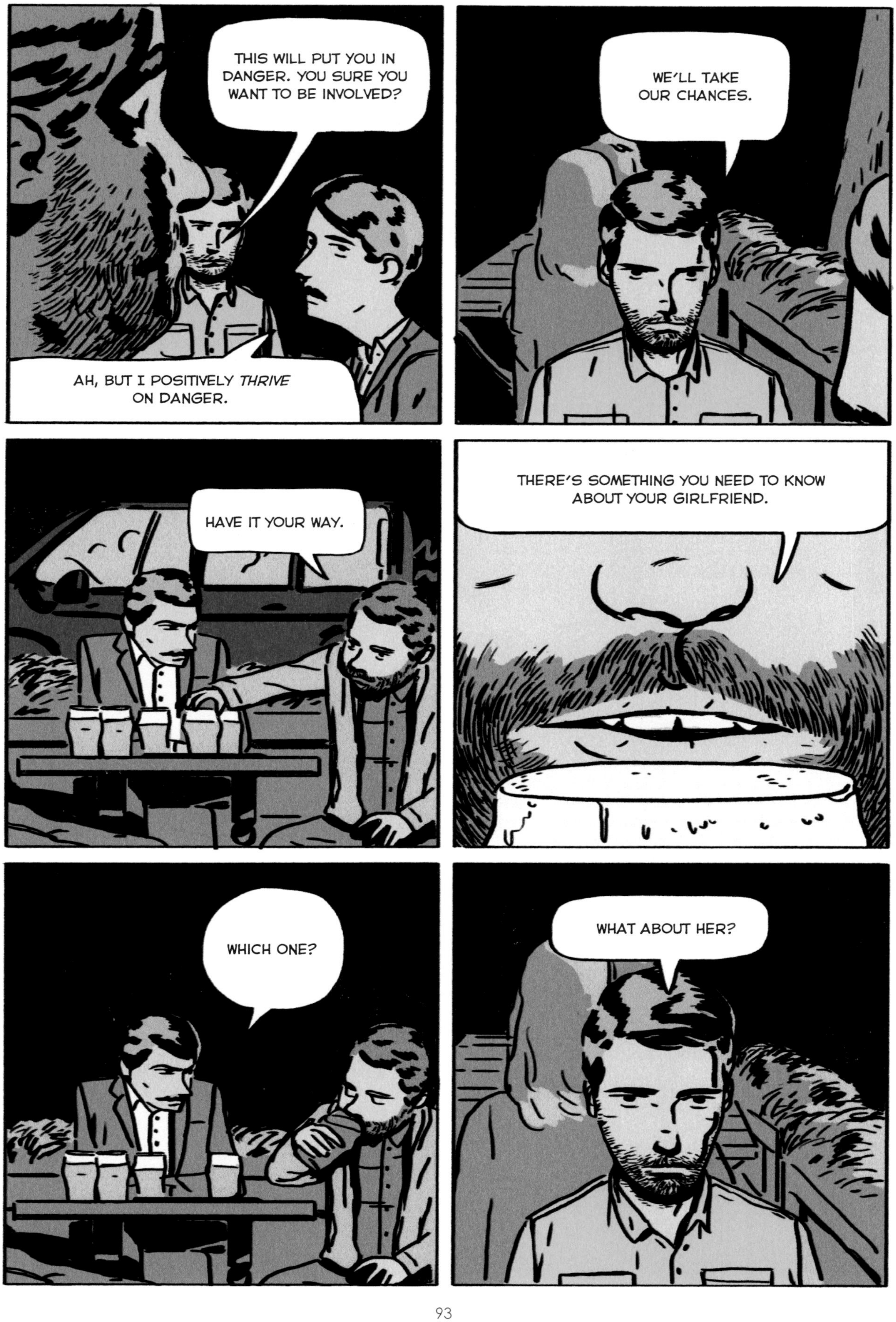
THIS WILL PUT YOU IN DANGER. YOU SURE YOU WANT TO BE INVOLVED?
AH, BUT I POSITIVELY *THRIVE* ON DANGER.
WE'LL TAKE OUR CHANCES.
HAVE IT YOUR WAY.
THERE'S SOMETHING YOU NEED TO KNOW ABOUT YOUR GIRLFRIEND.
WHICH ONE?
WHAT ABOUT HER?

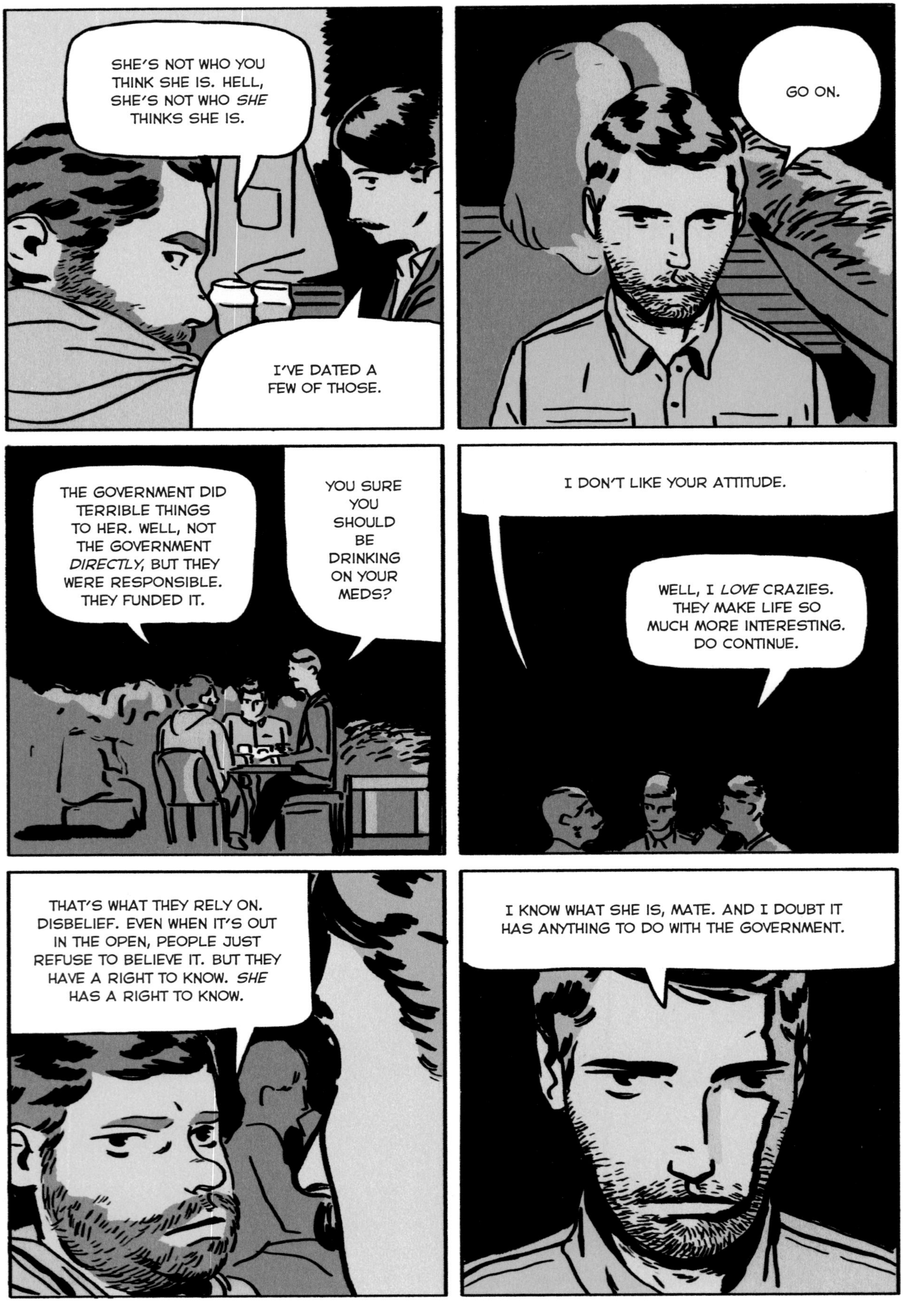
SHE'S NOT WHO YOU THINK SHE IS. HELL, SHE'S NOT WHO *SHE* THINKS SHE IS.
I'VE DATED A FEW OF THOSE.
GO ON.
THE GOVERNMENT DID TERRIBLE THINGS TO HER. WELL, NOT THE GOVERNMENT *DIRECTLY,* BUT THEY WERE RESPONSIBLE. THEY FUNDED IT.
YOU SURE YOU SHOULD BE DRINKING ON YOUR MEDS?
I DON'T LIKE YOUR ATTITUDE.
WELL, I *LOVE* CRAZIES. THEY MAKE LIFE SO MUCH MORE INTERESTING. DO CONTINUE.
THAT'S WHAT THEY RELY ON. DISBELIEF. EVEN WHEN IT'S OUT IN THE OPEN, PEOPLE JUST REFUSE TO BELIEVE IT. BUT THEY HAVE A RIGHT TO KNOW. *SHE* HAS A RIGHT TO KNOW.
I KNOW WHAT SHE IS, MATE. AND I DOUBT IT HAS ANYTHING TO DO WITH THE GOVERNMENT.

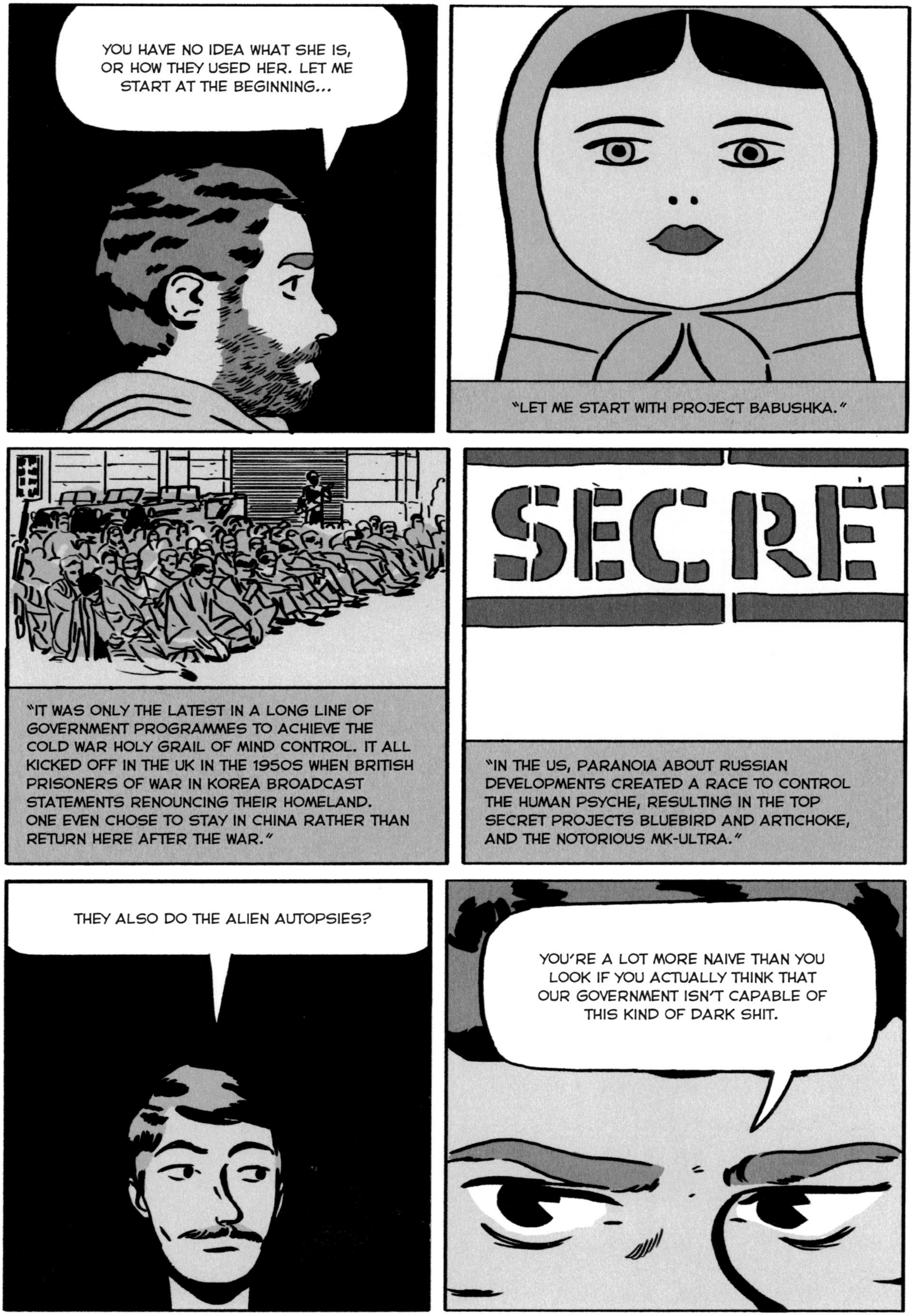

YOU HAVE NO IDEA WHAT SHE IS, OR HOW THEY USED HER. LET ME START AT THE BEGINNING...
"LET ME START WITH PROJECT BABUSHKA."
"IT WAS ONLY THE LATEST IN A LONG LINE OF GOVERNMENT PROGRAMMES TO ACHIEVE THE COLD WAR HOLY GRAIL OF MIND CONTROL. IT ALL KICKED OFF IN THE UK IN THE 1950S WHEN BRITISH PRISONERS OF WAR IN KOREA BROADCAST STATEMENTS RENOUNCING THEIR HOMELAND. ONE EVEN CHOSE TO STAY IN CHINA RATHER THAN RETURN HERE AFTER THE WAR."
SECRET
"IN THE US, PARANOIA ABOUT RUSSIAN DEVELOPMENTS CREATED A RACE TO CONTROL THE HUMAN PSYCHE, RESULTING IN THE TOP SECRET PROJECTS BLUEBIRD AND ARTICHOKE, AND THE NOTORIOUS MK-ULTRA."
THEY ALSO DO THE ALIEN AUTOPSIES?
YOU'RE A LOT MORE NAIVE THAN YOU LOOK IF YOU ACTUALLY THINK THAT OUR GOVERNMENT ISN'T CAPABLE OF THIS KIND OF DARK SHIT.

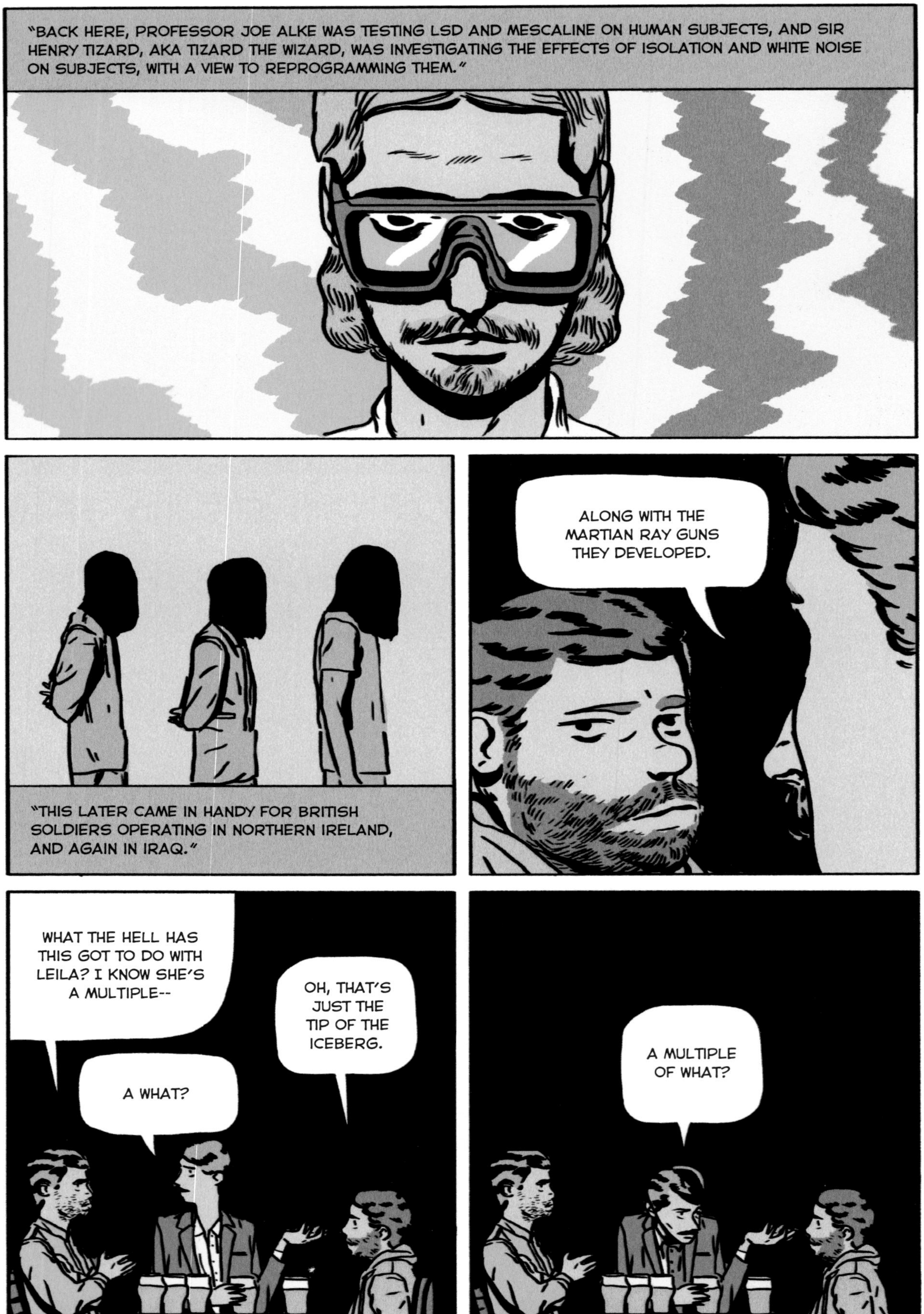
"BACK HERE, PROFESSOR JOE ALKE WAS TESTING LSD AND MESCALINE ON HUMAN SUBJECTS, AND SIR HENRY TIZARD, AKA TIZARD THE WIZARD, WAS INVESTIGATING THE EFFECTS OF ISOLATION AND WHITE NOISE ON SUBJECTS, WITH A VIEW TO REPROGRAMMING THEM."
"THIS LATER CAME IN HANDY FOR BRITISH SOLDIERS OPERATING IN NORTHERN IRELAND, AND AGAIN IN IRAQ."
ALONG WITH THE MARTIAN RAY GUNS THEY DEVELOPED.
WHAT THE HELL HAS THIS GOT TO DO WITH LEILA? I KNOW SHE'S A MULTIPLE--
A WHAT?
OH, THAT'S JUST THE TIP OF THE ICEBERG.
A MULTIPLE OF WHAT?

"THE WAR ON TERROR IS WHAT KICK-STARTED PROJECT BABUSHKA. THE AIM WAS SIMPLE: CREATE THE PERFECT ASSASSIN. AND WHAT BETTER WAY OF GUARANTEEING COMPLETE DISCRETION THAN BY KEEPING THE ASSASSIN IGNORANT OF THEIR OWN ACTIONS?"

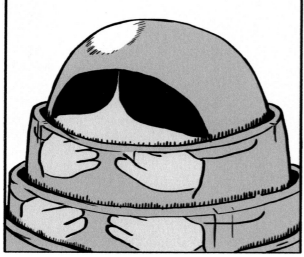

I DON'T FOLLOW YOU.

THEY WERE EXPERIMENTING ON SUBJECTS WITH MULTIPLE PERSONALITIES, TRYING TO ISOLATE ONE TO DO THE GOVERNMENT'S DIRTY WORK.

THIS IS RIDICULOUS. COME ON, YOU CAN'T POSSIBLY BELIEVE...?

I'M NOT STUPID. OF COURSE I DON'T BELIEVE IT'S POSSIBLE, BUT I *DO* BELIEVE SOME AGENCY THOUGHT IT WAS. AND THAT THEY USED SOME VERY VULNERABLE PEOPLE, INCLUDING LEILA HARRISON, WITHOUT ANY THOUGHT FOR THE CONSEQUENCES.

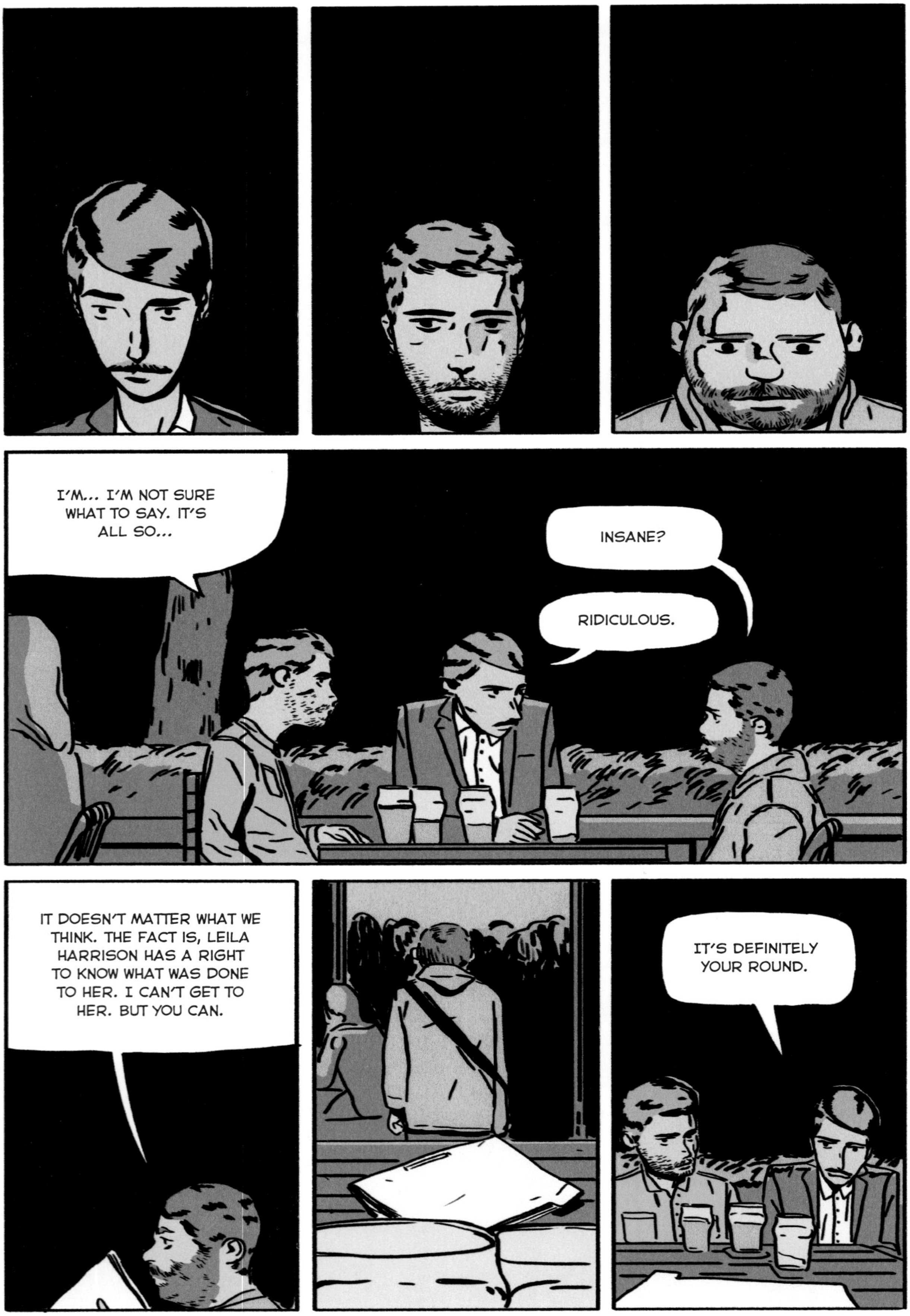
I'M... I'M NOT SURE WHAT TO SAY. IT'S ALL SO...
INSANE?
RIDICULOUS.
IT DOESN'T MATTER WHAT WE THINK. THE FACT IS, LEILA HARRISON HAS A RIGHT TO KNOW WHAT WAS DONE TO HER. I CAN'T GET TO HER. BUT YOU CAN.
IT'S DEFINITELY YOUR ROUND.

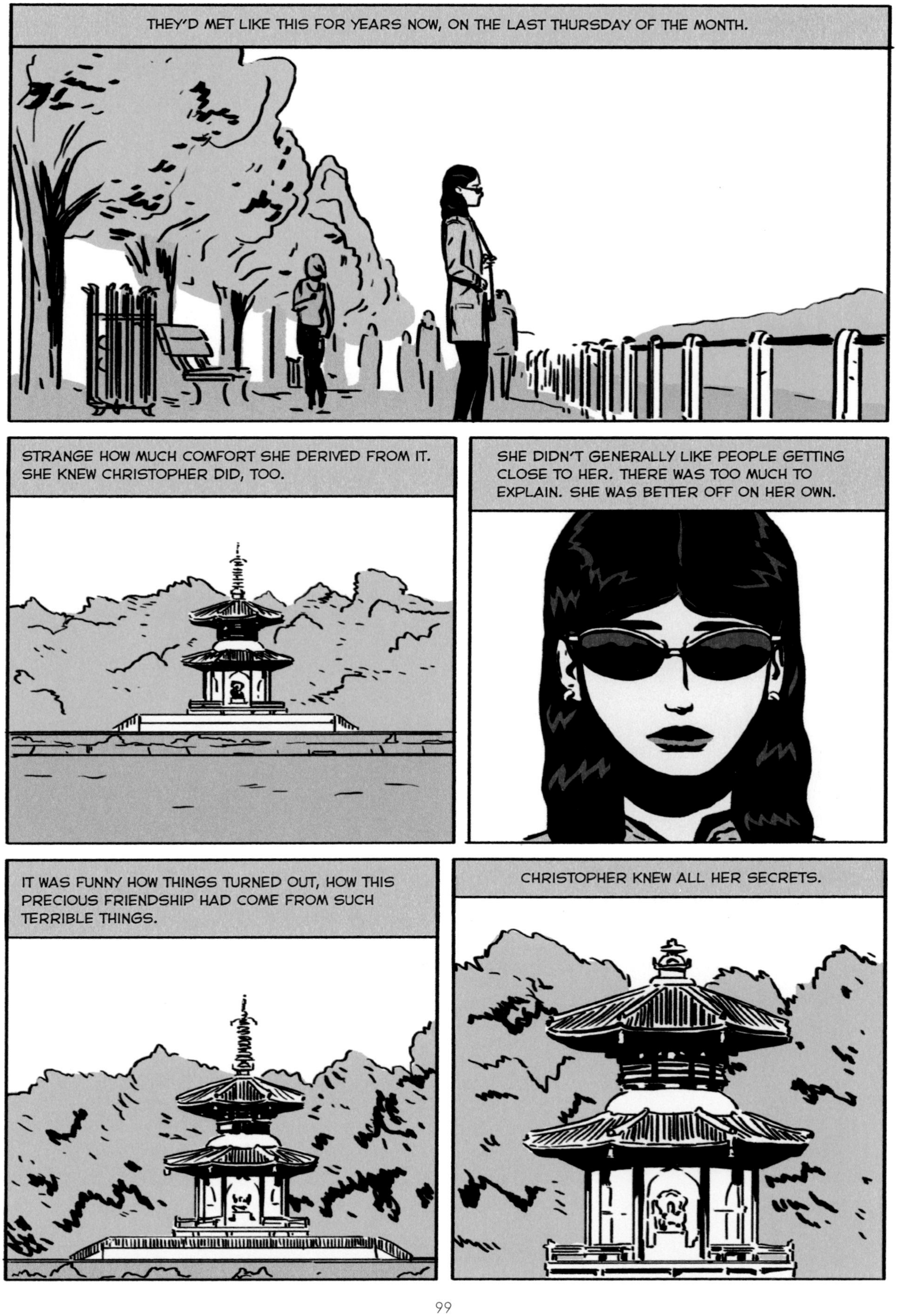
THEY'D MET LIKE THIS FOR YEARS NOW, ON THE LAST THURSDAY OF THE MONTH.
STRANGE HOW MUCH COMFORT SHE DERIVED FROM IT. SHE KNEW CHRISTOPHER DID, TOO.
SHE DIDN'T GENERALLY LIKE PEOPLE GETTING CLOSE TO HER. THERE WAS TOO MUCH TO EXPLAIN. SHE WAS BETTER OFF ON HER OWN.
IT WAS FUNNY HOW THINGS TURNED OUT, HOW THIS PRECIOUS FRIENDSHIP HAD COME FROM SUCH TERRIBLE THINGS.
CHRISTOPHER KNEW ALL HER SECRETS.

EVEN THEN SHE'D SEEN IT IN HIM: KINDNESS.

IT'S VERY BRAVE OF YOU TO SEEK HELP.

LOOKING BACK, SHE HAD TO AGREE: IT *HAD* BEEN BRAVE. SHE'D BEEN DETERMINED NOT TO LET HER MOTHER WIN.

WHAT YOU HAVE TO UNDERSTAND IS THAT YOUR REACTION WAS PERFECTLY NORMAL. THE THINGS YOU WERE SUBJECTED TO... SENSORY DEPRIVATION HAS A HUGE IMPACT ON US. ALL OF US. HALLUCINATIONS, AUDITORY AND VISUAL, PANIC...

PANIC.

PANIC.

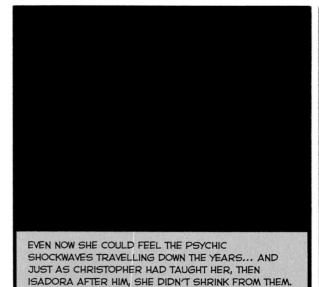

EVEN NOW SHE COULD FEEL THE PSYCHIC SHOCKWAVES TRAVELLING DOWN THE YEARS... AND JUST AS CHRISTOPHER HAD TAUGHT HER, THEN ISADORA AFTER HIM, SHE DIDN'T SHRINK FROM THEM.

THERE SHE WAS, BACK IN THAT CUPBOARD, DRIFTING LIKE A FOETUS IN DARKNESS. TIME WAS MEANINGLESS. EVEN HUNGER WAS A WELCOME COMPANION IN THIS ENDLESS OBLIVION...

THEN IT WAS OVER, AND IN THAT TERRIFYING FIRST MOMENT, SHE CLUNG TO THE DARK, TO ITS CERTAINTY, NEVER KNOWING WHAT WOULD GREET HER.

ANGEL...

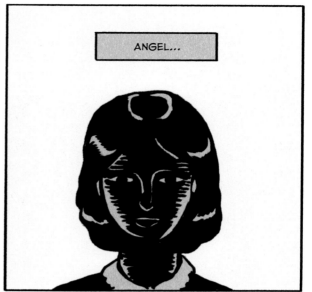

...OR DEMON?

BUT SHE'D SURVIVED. AND IF CHRISTOPHER WAS TO BE BELIEVED...

I'M NOT TRYING TO BELITTLE WHAT YOU'VE BEEN THROUGH, BUT ALL LIFE IS SUFFERING. TIBETAN BUDDHISTS HAVE SOMETHING THEY CALL THE PRACTICE IN THE DARK. THEY SHUT THEMSELVES AWAY IN THE DARK FOR MONTHS, EVEN *YEARS*, TO ACHIEVE NIRVANA.

...PERHAPS SHE'D EVEN BEEN ENRICHED BY THE EXPERIENCE.

PAIN IS THE ULTIMATE TEACHER.

THE VERY IDEA WAS A GIFT.

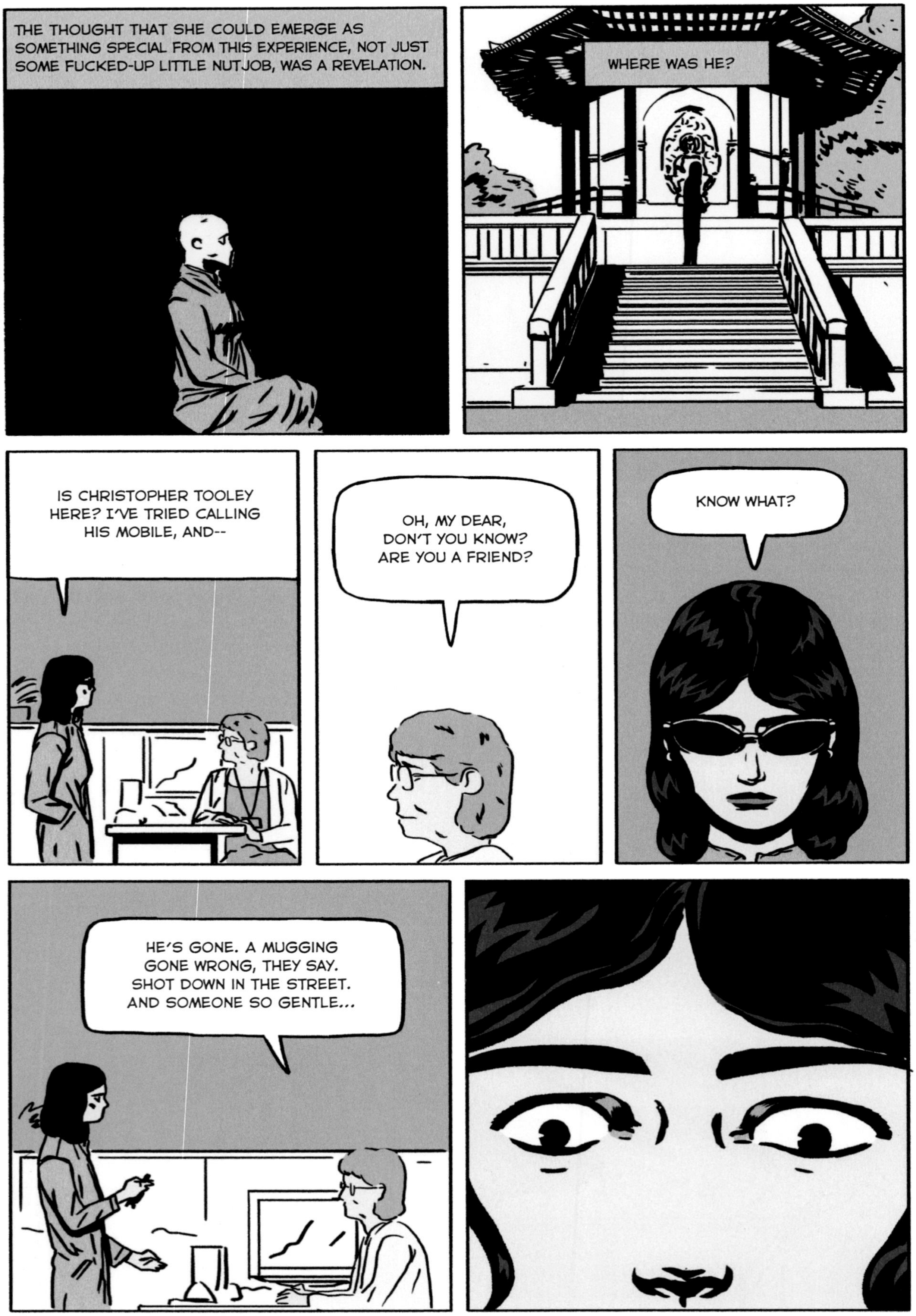
THE THOUGHT THAT SHE COULD EMERGE AS SOMETHING SPECIAL FROM THIS EXPERIENCE, NOT JUST SOME FUCKED-UP LITTLE NUTJOB, WAS A REVELATION.
WHERE WAS HE?
IS CHRISTOPHER TOOLEY HERE? I'VE TRIED CALLING HIS MOBILE, AND--
OH, MY DEAR, DON'T YOU KNOW? ARE YOU A FRIEND?
KNOW WHAT?
HE'S GONE. A MUGGING GONE WRONG, THEY SAY. SHOT DOWN IN THE STREET. AND SOMEONE SO GENTLE...

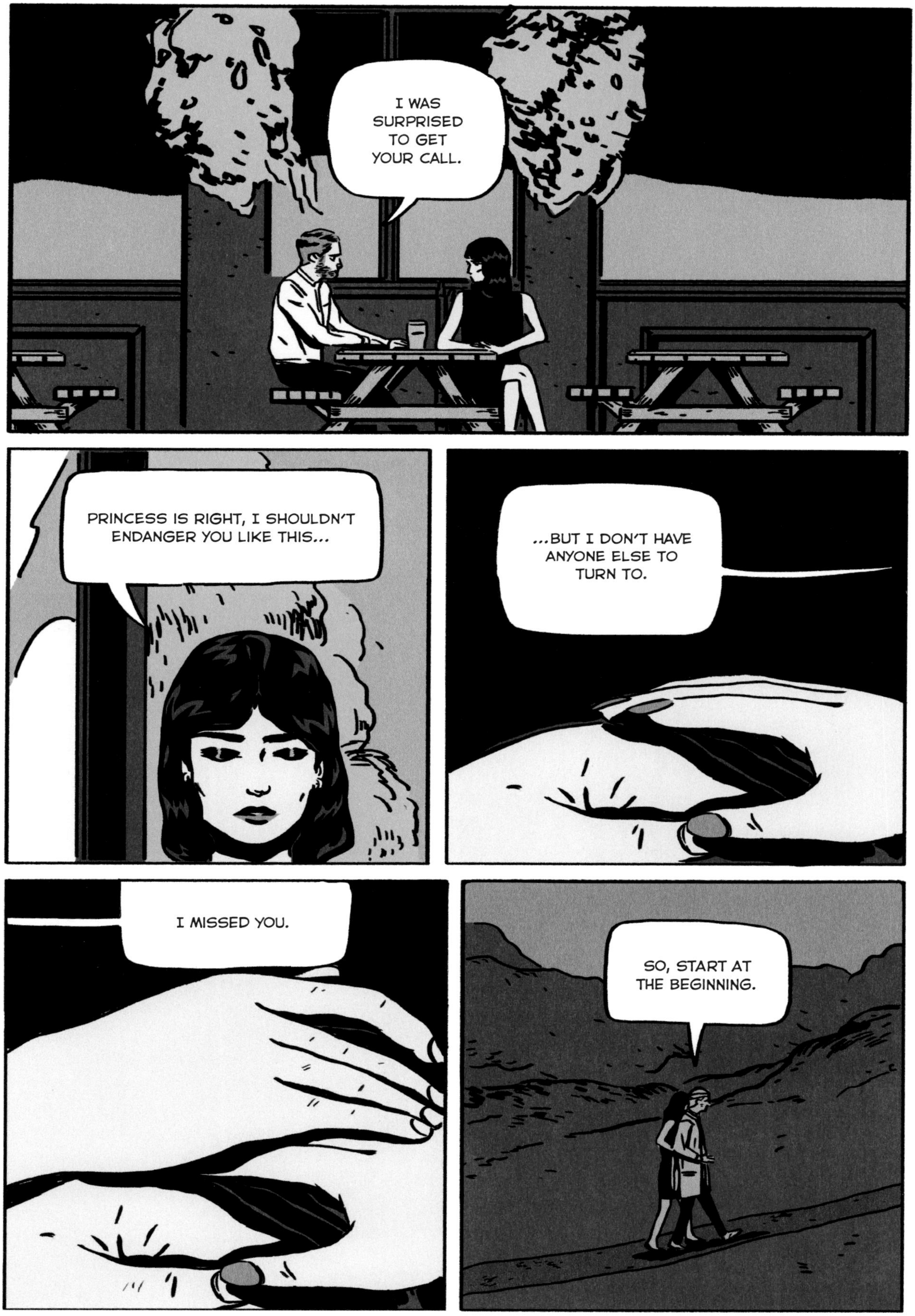
I WAS SURPRISED TO GET YOUR CALL.
PRINCESS IS RIGHT, I SHOULDN'T ENDANGER YOU LIKE THIS...
...BUT I DON'T HAVE ANYONE ELSE TO TURN TO.
I MISSED YOU.
SO, START AT THE BEGINNING.

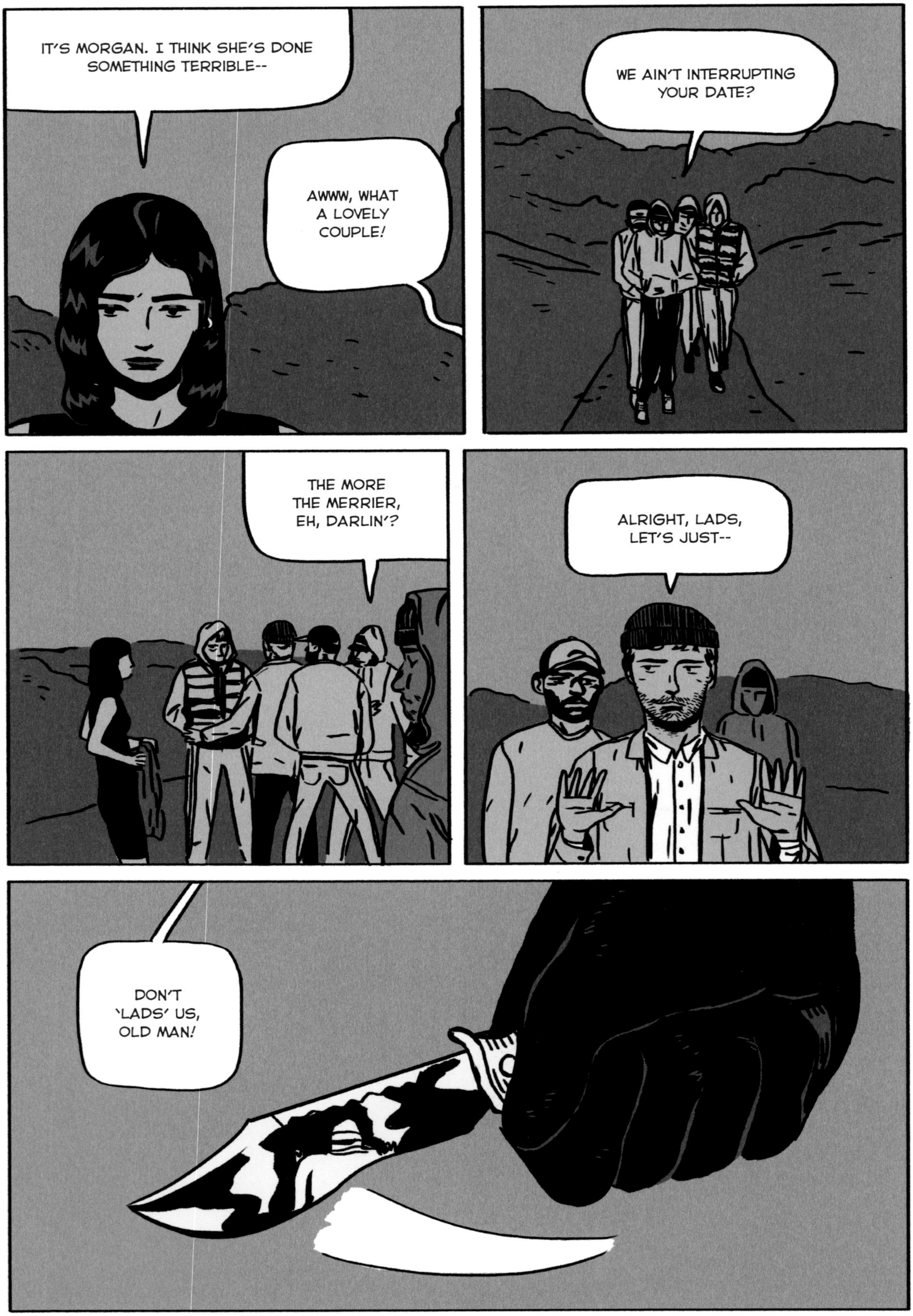
IT'S MORGAN. I THINK SHE'S DONE SOMETHING TERRIBLE--
AWWW, WHAT A LOVELY COUPLE!
WE AIN'T INTERRUPTING YOUR DATE?
THE MORE THE MERRIER, EH, DARLIN'?
ALRIGHT, LADS, LET'S JUST--
DON'T 'LADS' US, OLD MAN!

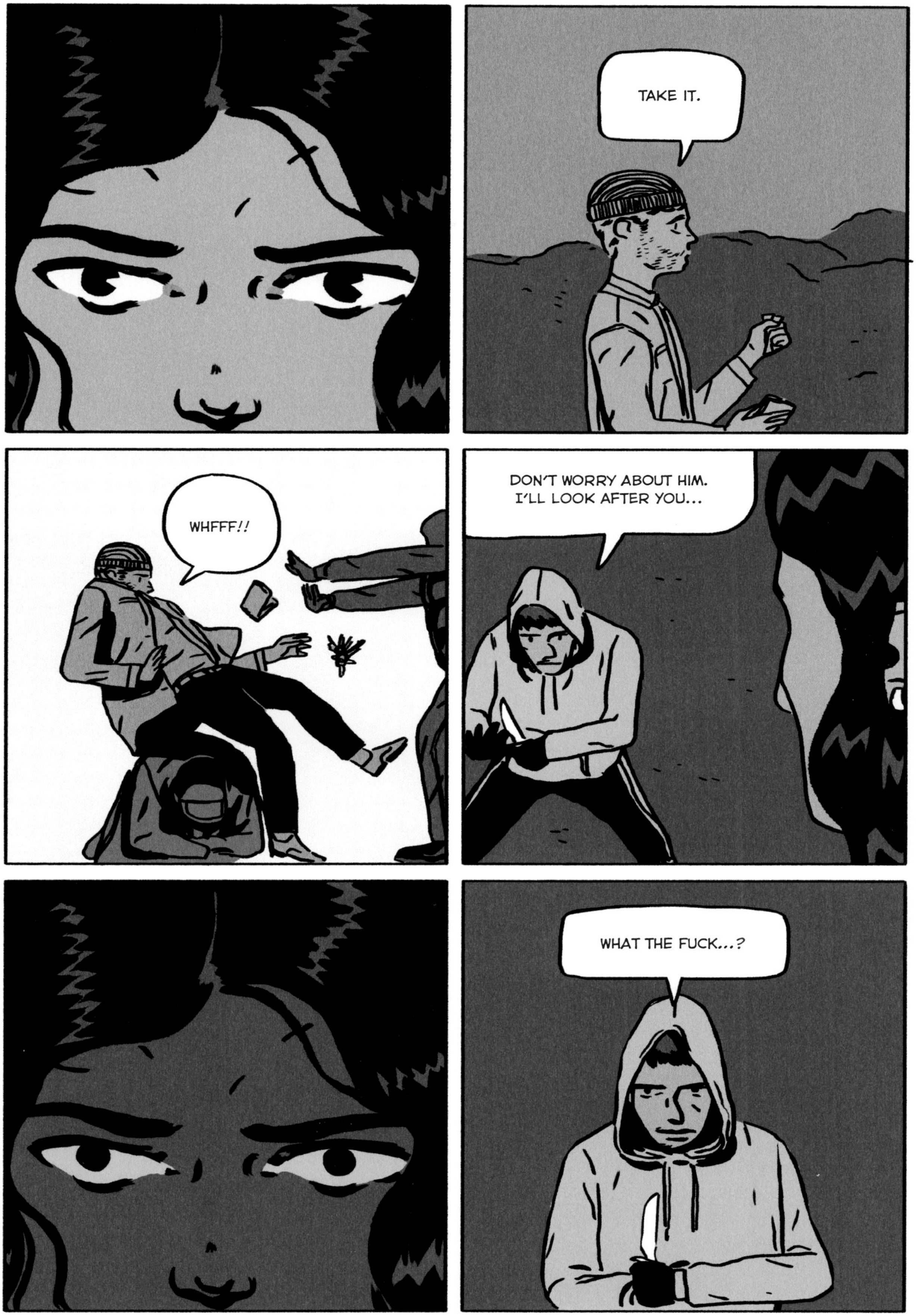
TAKE IT.
WHFFF!!
DON'T WORRY ABOUT HIM.
I'LL LOOK AFTER YOU...
WHAT THE FUCK...?

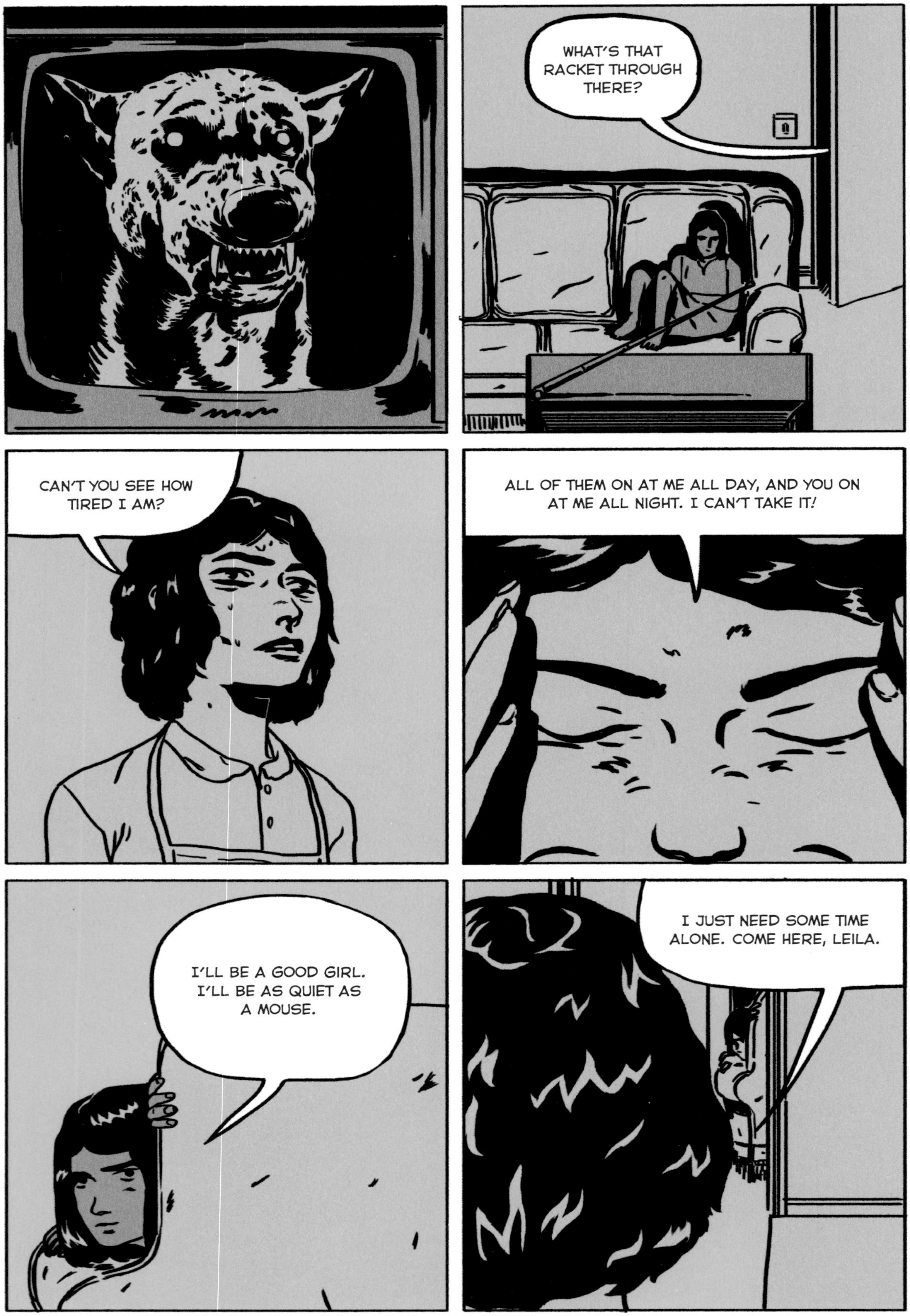
WHAT'S THAT RACKET THROUGH THERE?
CAN'T YOU SEE HOW TIRED I AM?
ALL OF THEM ON AT ME ALL DAY, AND YOU ON AT ME ALL NIGHT. I CAN'T TAKE IT!
I'LL BE A GOOD GIRL. I'LL BE AS QUIET AS A MOUSE.
I JUST NEED SOME TIME ALONE. COME HERE, LEILA.

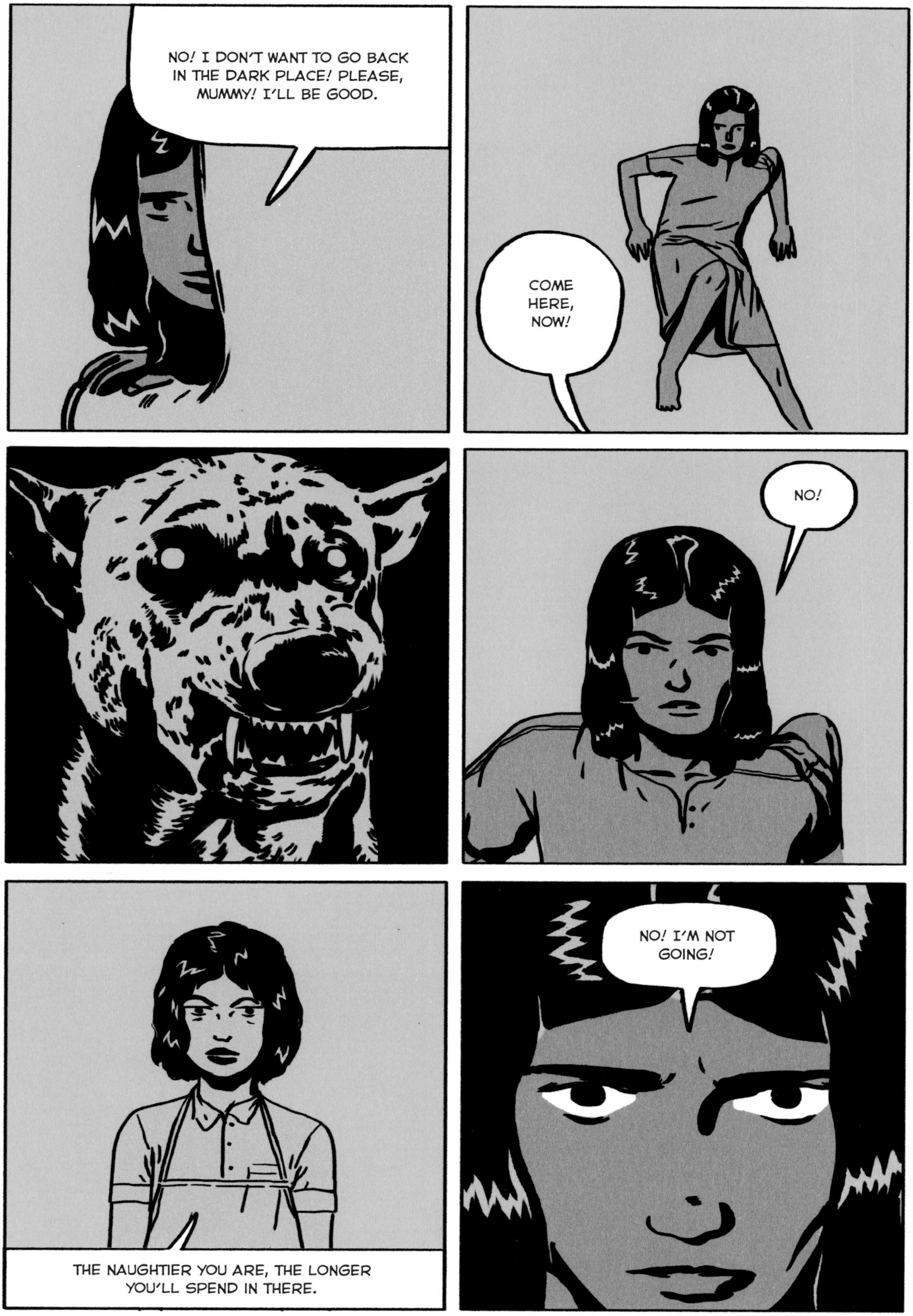
NO! I DON'T WANT TO GO BACK IN THE DARK PLACE! PLEASE, MUMMY! I'LL BE GOOD.
COME HERE, NOW!
NO!
THE NAUGHTIER YOU ARE, THE LONGER YOU'LL SPEND IN THERE.
NO! I'M NOT GOING!

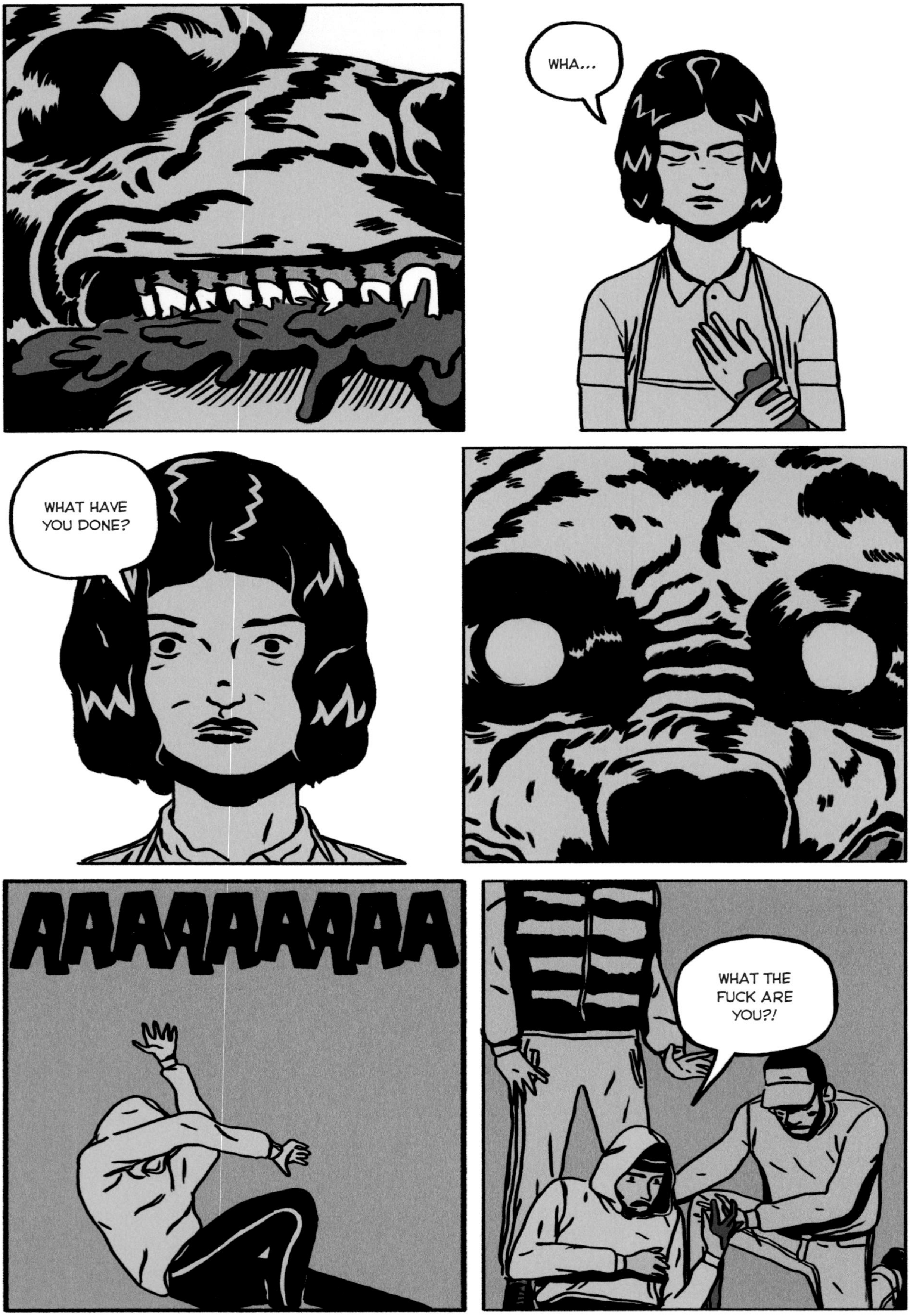
WHA...
WHAT HAVE YOU DONE?
AAAAAAAAA
WHAT THE FUCK ARE YOU?!

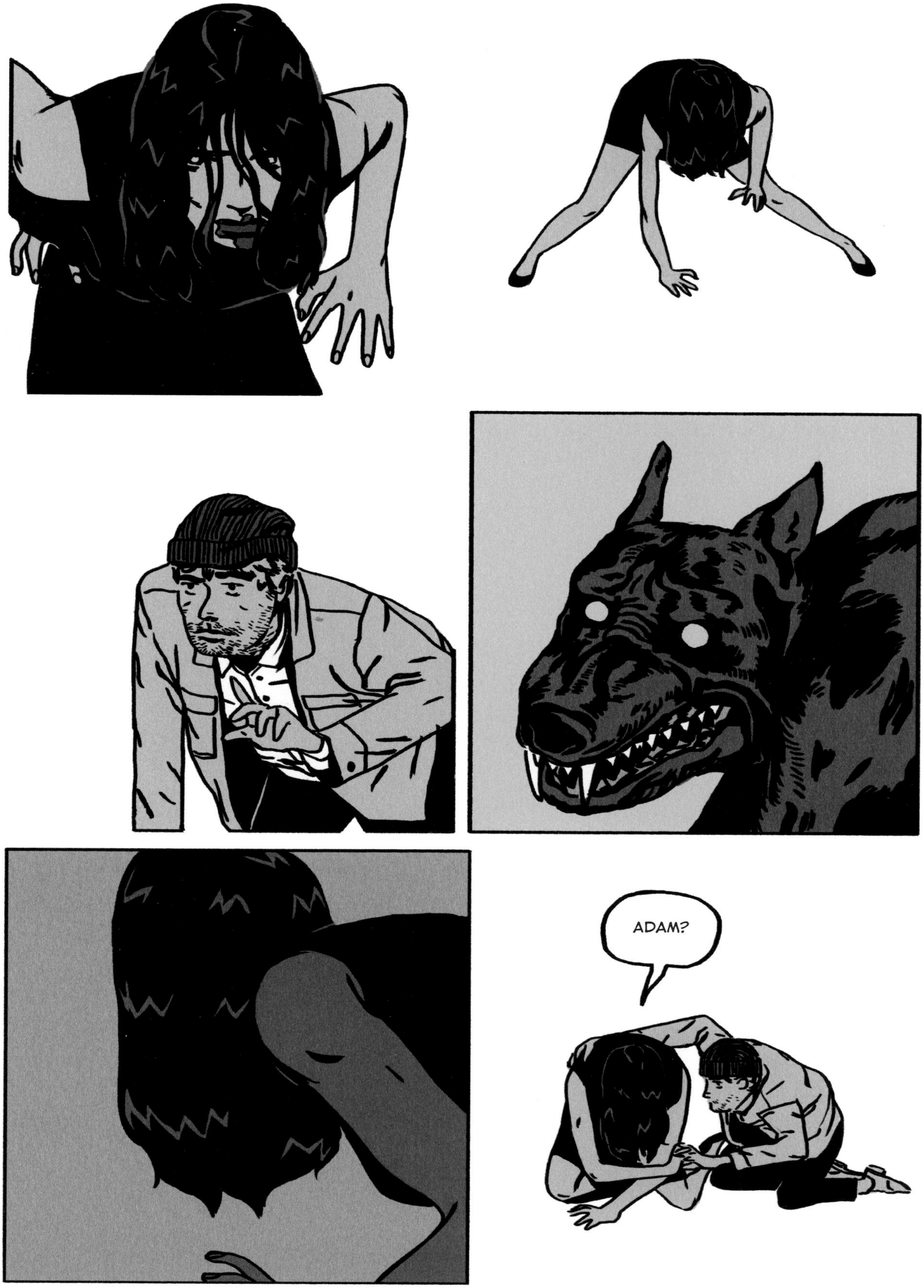
ADAM?

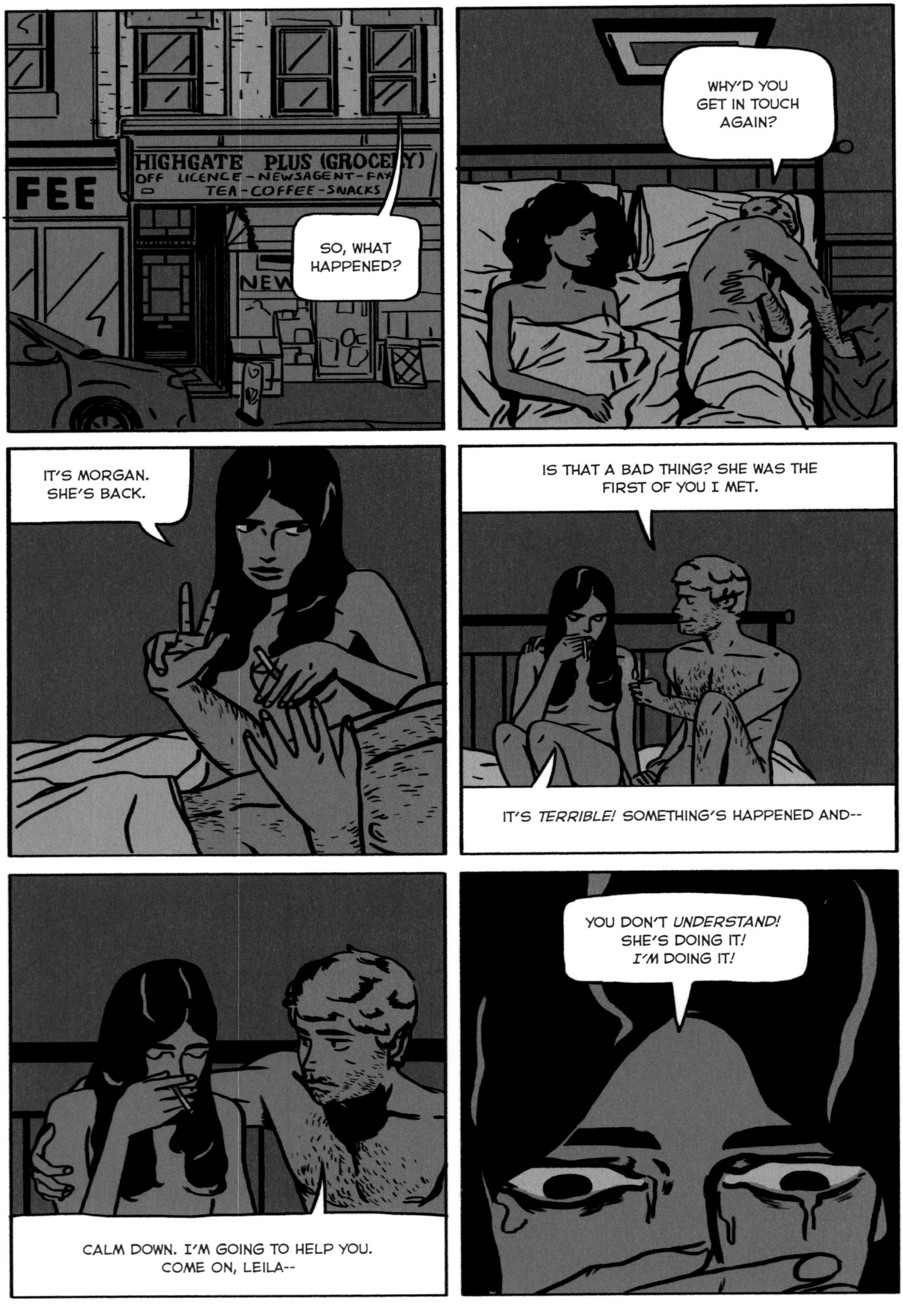
HIGHGATE PLUS (GROCERY)
OFF LICENCE - NEWSAGENT - FAX
TEA - COFFEE - SNACKS
FEE
SO, WHAT HAPPENED?
WHY'D YOU GET IN TOUCH AGAIN?
IT'S MORGAN. SHE'S BACK.
IS THAT A BAD THING? SHE WAS THE FIRST OF YOU I MET.
IT'S *TERRIBLE!* SOMETHING'S HAPPENED AND--
CALM DOWN. I'M GOING TO HELP YOU. COME ON, LEILA--
YOU DON'T *UNDERSTAND!* SHE'S DOING IT! *I'M* DOING IT!

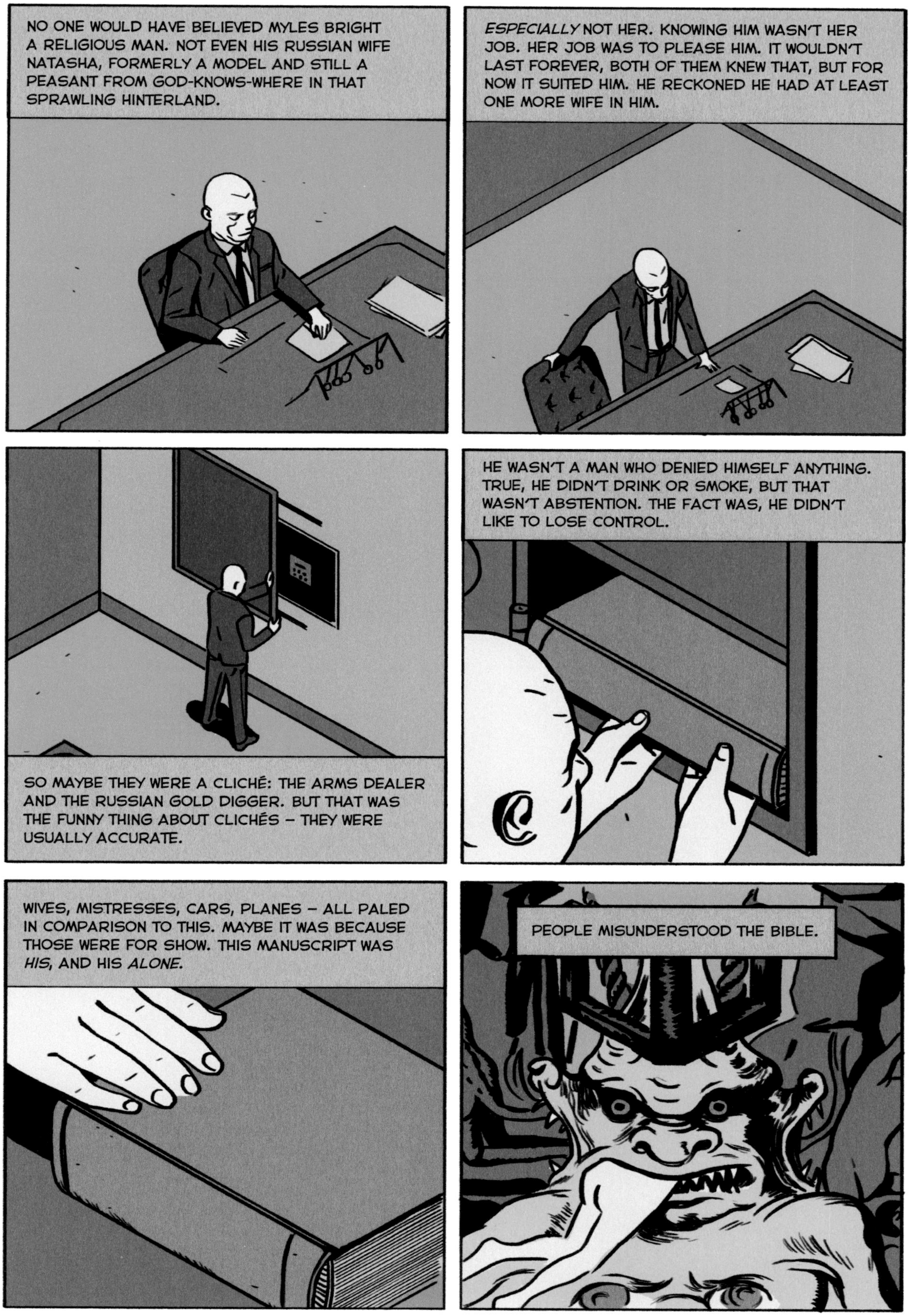
NO ONE WOULD HAVE BELIEVED MYLES BRIGHT A RELIGIOUS MAN. NOT EVEN HIS RUSSIAN WIFE NATASHA, FORMERLY A MODEL AND STILL A PEASANT FROM GOD-KNOWS-WHERE IN THAT SPRAWLING HINTERLAND.
ESPECIALLY NOT HER. KNOWING HIM WASN'T HER JOB. HER JOB WAS TO PLEASE HIM. IT WOULDN'T LAST FOREVER, BOTH OF THEM KNEW THAT, BUT FOR NOW IT SUITED HIM. HE RECKONED HE HAD AT LEAST ONE MORE WIFE IN HIM.
SO MAYBE THEY WERE A CLICHÉ: THE ARMS DEALER AND THE RUSSIAN GOLD DIGGER. BUT THAT WAS THE FUNNY THING ABOUT CLICHÉS – THEY WERE USUALLY ACCURATE.
HE WASN'T A MAN WHO DENIED HIMSELF ANYTHING. TRUE, HE DIDN'T DRINK OR SMOKE, BUT THAT WASN'T ABSTENTION. THE FACT WAS, HE DIDN'T LIKE TO LOSE CONTROL.
WIVES, MISTRESSES, CARS, PLANES – ALL PALED IN COMPARISON TO THIS. MAYBE IT WAS BECAUSE THOSE WERE FOR SHOW. THIS MANUSCRIPT WAS *HIS*, AND HIS *ALONE*.
PEOPLE MISUNDERSTOOD THE BIBLE.

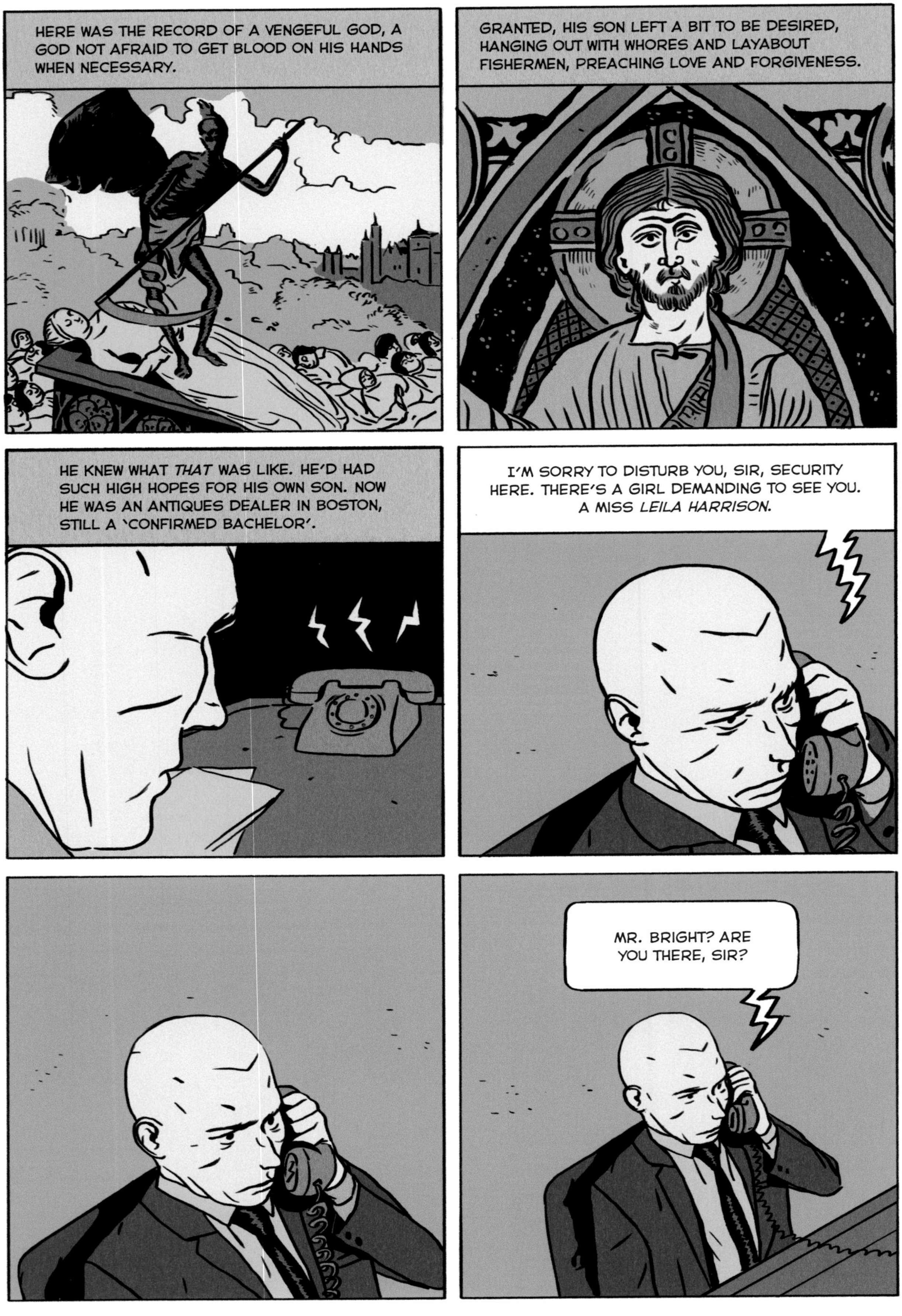
HERE WAS THE RECORD OF A VENGEFUL GOD, A GOD NOT AFRAID TO GET BLOOD ON HIS HANDS WHEN NECESSARY.
GRANTED, HIS SON LEFT A BIT TO BE DESIRED, HANGING OUT WITH WHORES AND LAYABOUT FISHERMEN, PREACHING LOVE AND FORGIVENESS.
HE KNEW WHAT *THAT* WAS LIKE. HE'D HAD SUCH HIGH HOPES FOR HIS OWN SON. NOW HE WAS AN ANTIQUES DEALER IN BOSTON, STILL A 'CONFIRMED BACHELOR'.
I'M SORRY TO DISTURB YOU, SIR, SECURITY HERE. THERE'S A GIRL DEMANDING TO SEE YOU. A MISS *LEILA HARRISON*.
MR. BRIGHT? ARE YOU THERE, SIR?

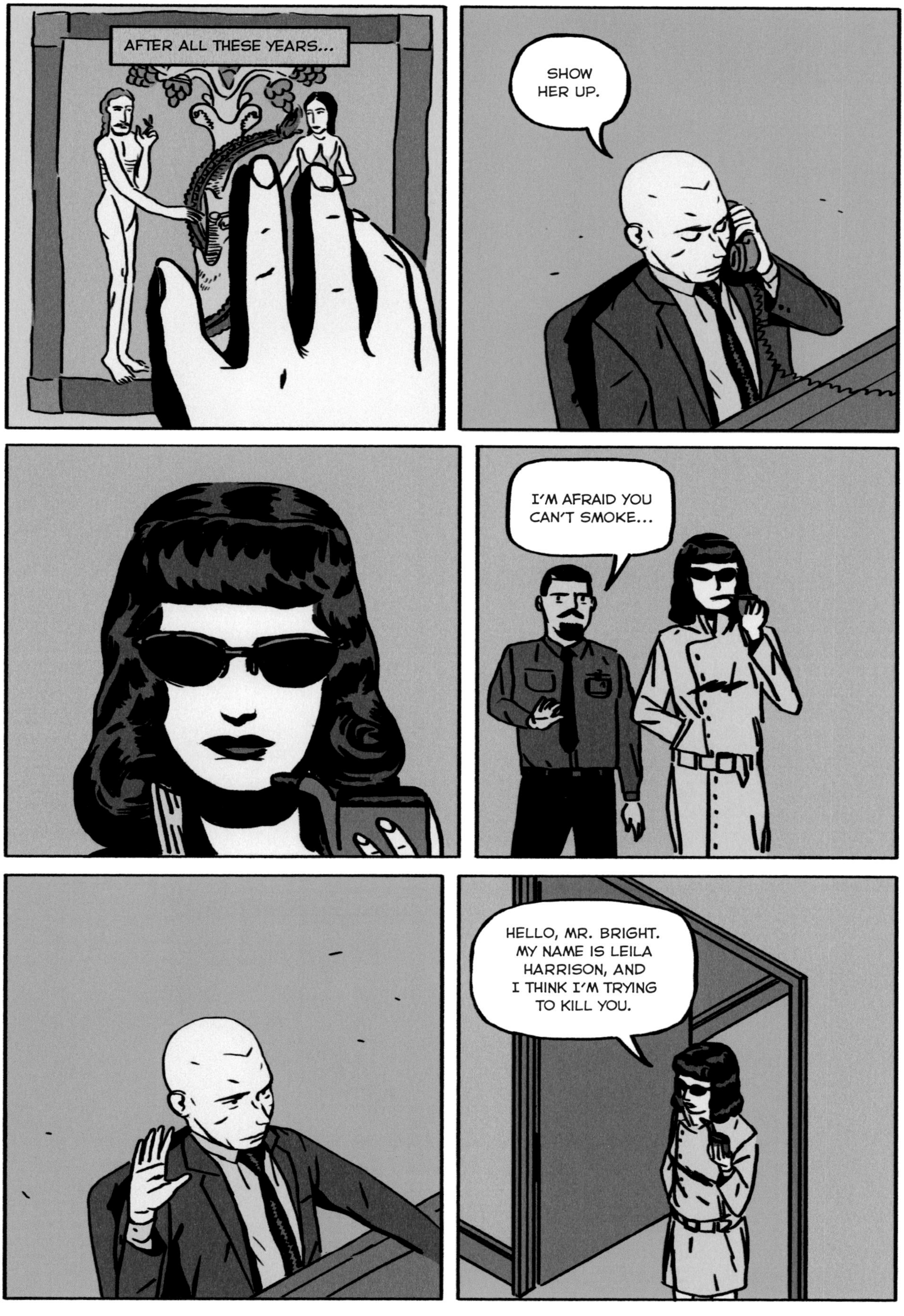
AFTER ALL THESE YEARS...
SHOW HER UP.
I'M AFRAID YOU CAN'T SMOKE...
HELLO, MR. BRIGHT. MY NAME IS LEILA HARRISON, AND I THINK I'M TRYING TO KILL YOU.

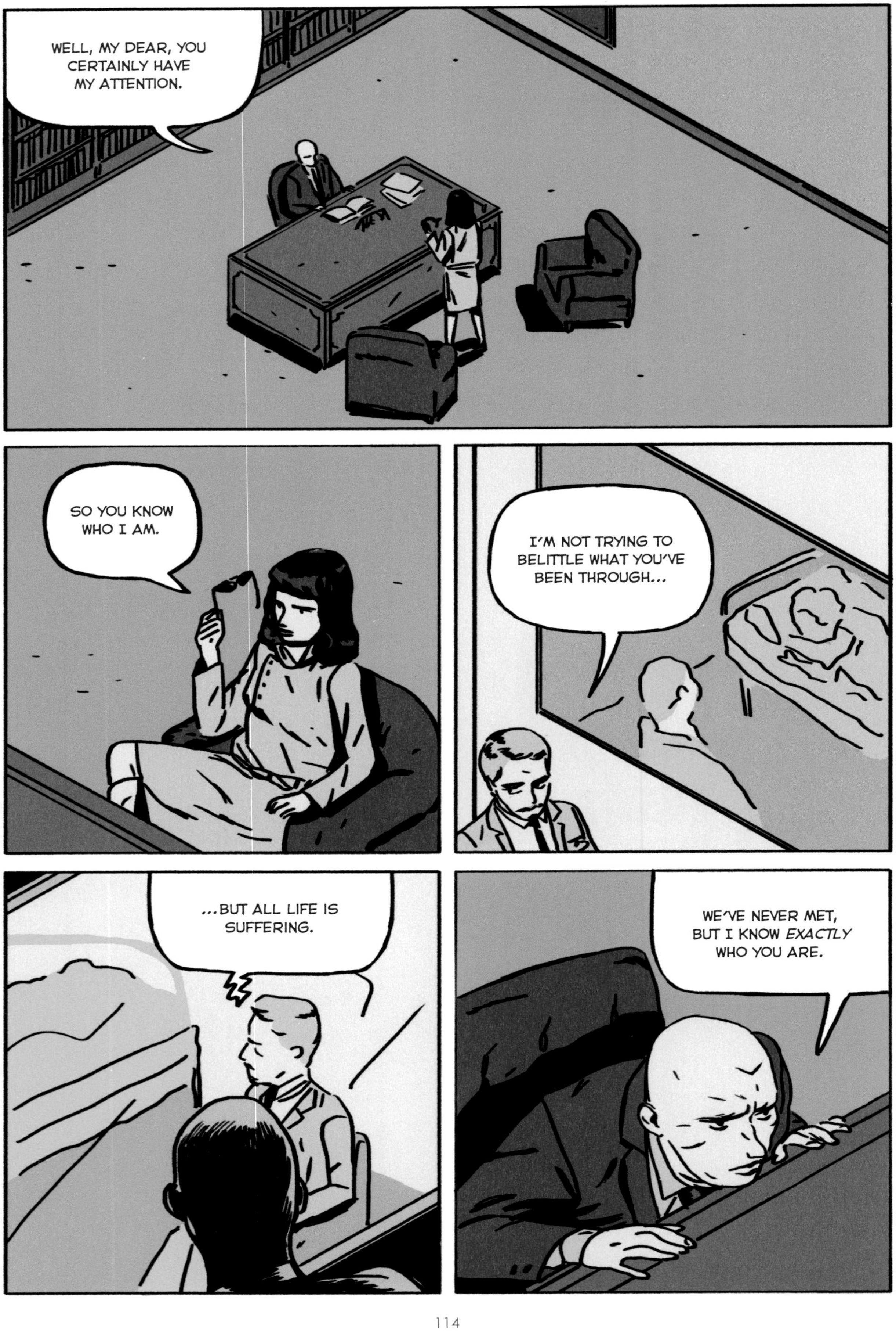
WELL, MY DEAR, YOU CERTAINLY HAVE MY ATTENTION.
SO YOU KNOW WHO I AM.
I'M NOT TRYING TO BELITTLE WHAT YOU'VE BEEN THROUGH...
...BUT ALL LIFE IS SUFFERING.
WE'VE NEVER MET, BUT I KNOW *EXACTLY* WHO YOU ARE.

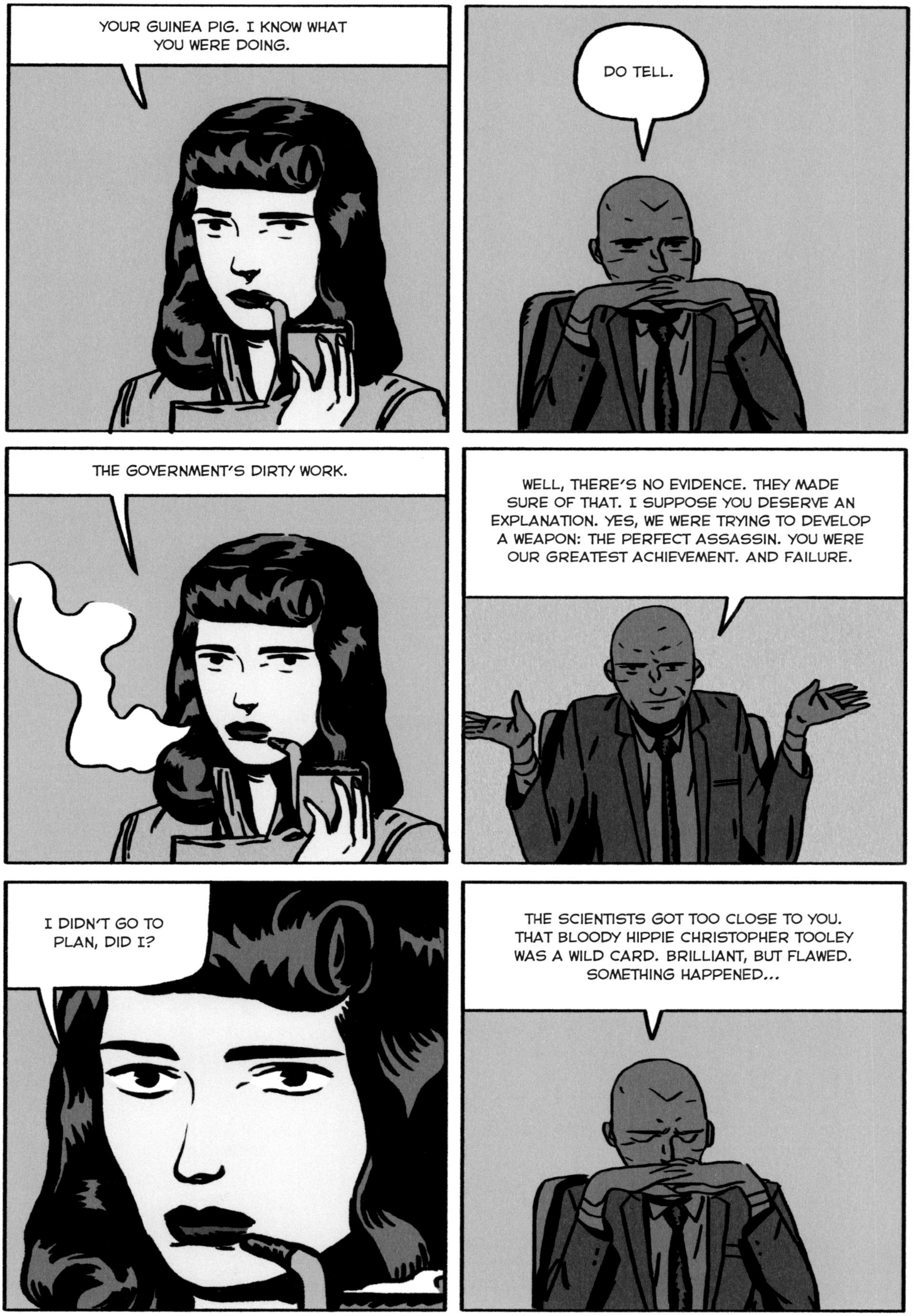
YOUR GUINEA PIG. I KNOW WHAT YOU WERE DOING.
DO TELL.
THE GOVERNMENT'S DIRTY WORK.
WELL, THERE'S NO EVIDENCE. THEY MADE SURE OF THAT. I SUPPOSE YOU DESERVE AN EXPLANATION. YES, WE WERE TRYING TO DEVELOP A WEAPON: THE PERFECT ASSASSIN. YOU WERE OUR GREATEST ACHIEVEMENT. AND FAILURE.
I DIDN'T GO TO PLAN, DID I?
THE SCIENTISTS GOT TOO CLOSE TO YOU. THAT BLOODY HIPPIE CHRISTOPHER TOOLEY WAS A WILD CARD. BRILLIANT, BUT FLAWED. SOMETHING HAPPENED...

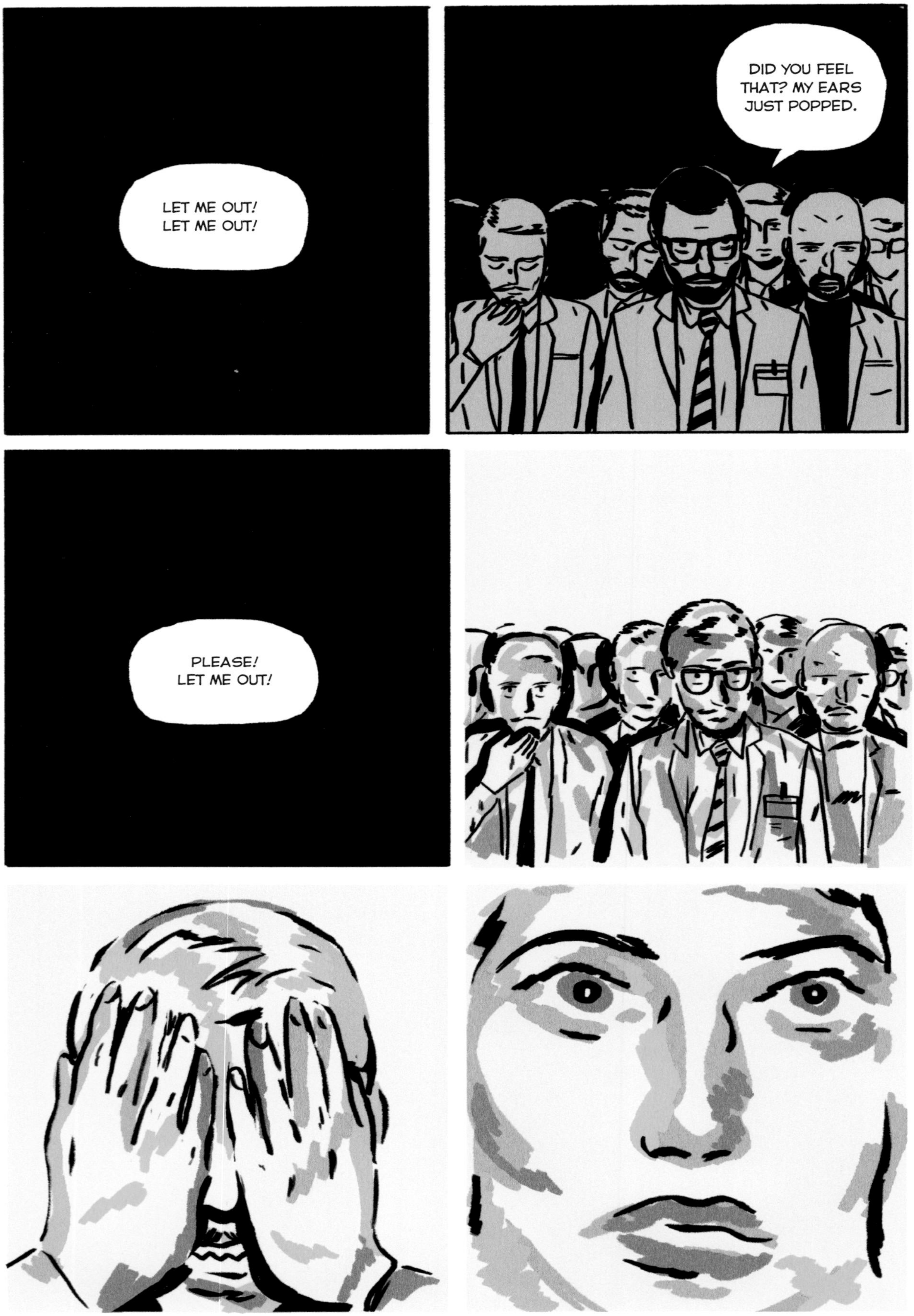
LET ME OUT!
LET ME OUT!
DID YOU FEEL THAT? MY EARS JUST POPPED.
PLEASE!
LET ME OUT!

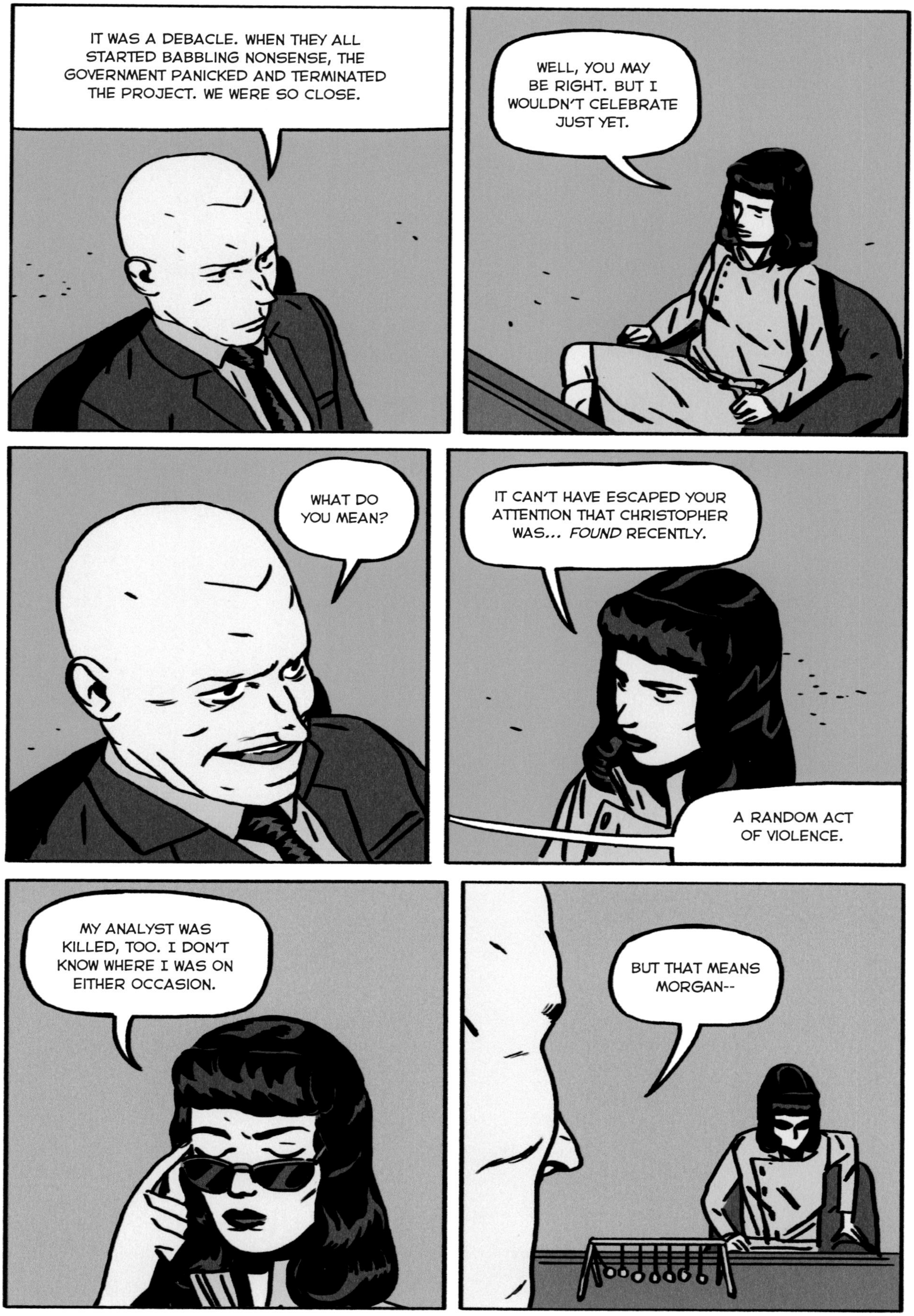
IT WAS A DEBACLE. WHEN THEY ALL STARTED BABBLING NONSENSE, THE GOVERNMENT PANICKED AND TERMINATED THE PROJECT. WE WERE SO CLOSE.
WELL, YOU MAY BE RIGHT. BUT I WOULDN'T CELEBRATE JUST YET.
WHAT DO YOU MEAN?
IT CAN'T HAVE ESCAPED YOUR ATTENTION THAT CHRISTOPHER WAS... *FOUND* RECENTLY.
A RANDOM ACT OF VIOLENCE.
MY ANALYST WAS KILLED, TOO. I DON'T KNOW WHERE I WAS ON EITHER OCCASION.
BUT THAT MEANS MORGAN--

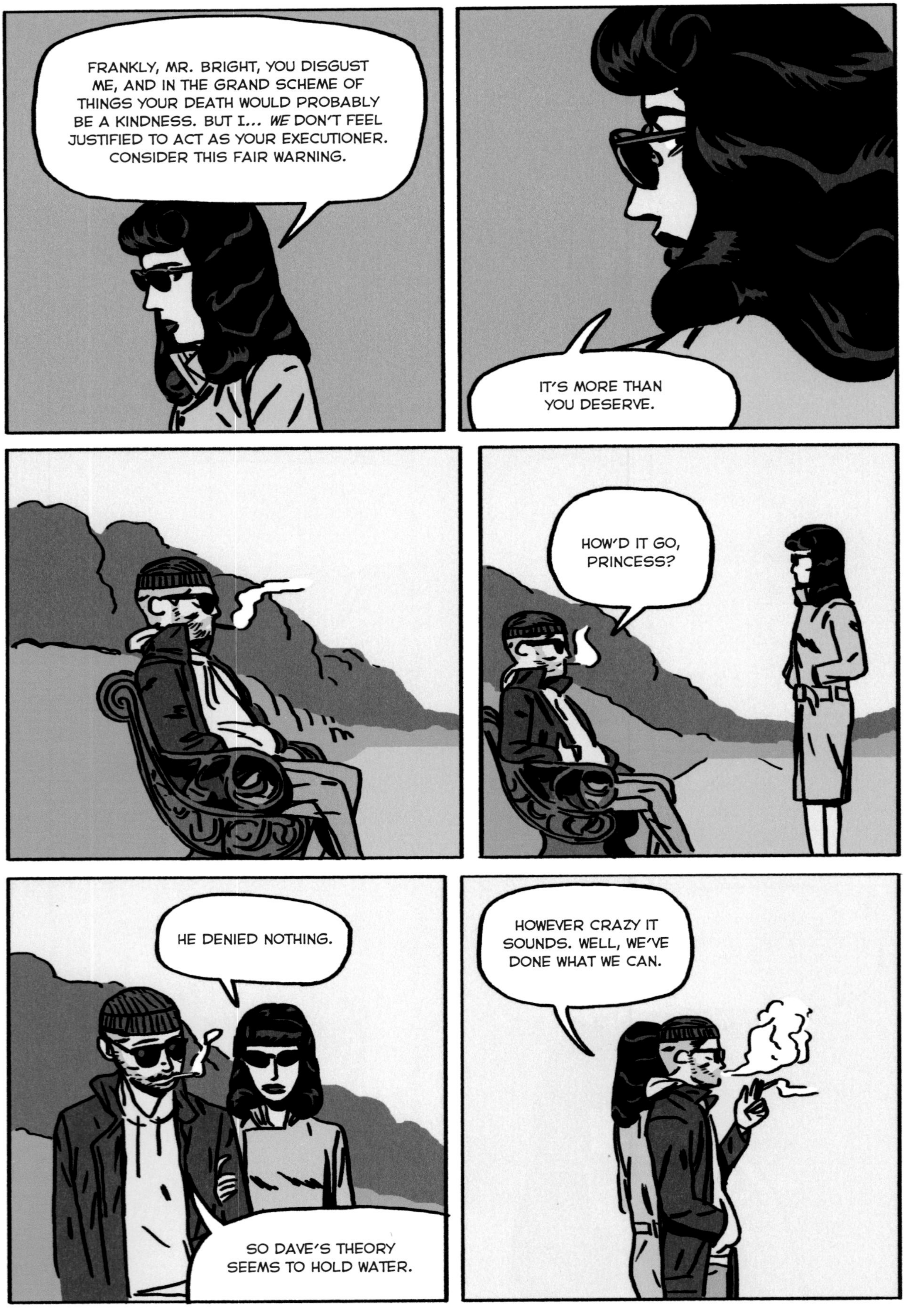
FRANKLY, MR. BRIGHT, YOU DISGUST ME, AND IN THE GRAND SCHEME OF THINGS YOUR DEATH WOULD PROBABLY BE A KINDNESS. BUT I... *WE* DON'T FEEL JUSTIFIED TO ACT AS YOUR EXECUTIONER. CONSIDER THIS FAIR WARNING.
IT'S MORE THAN YOU DESERVE.
HOW'D IT GO, PRINCESS?
HE DENIED NOTHING.
SO DAVE'S THEORY SEEMS TO HOLD WATER.
HOWEVER CRAZY IT SOUNDS. WELL, WE'VE DONE WHAT WE CAN.

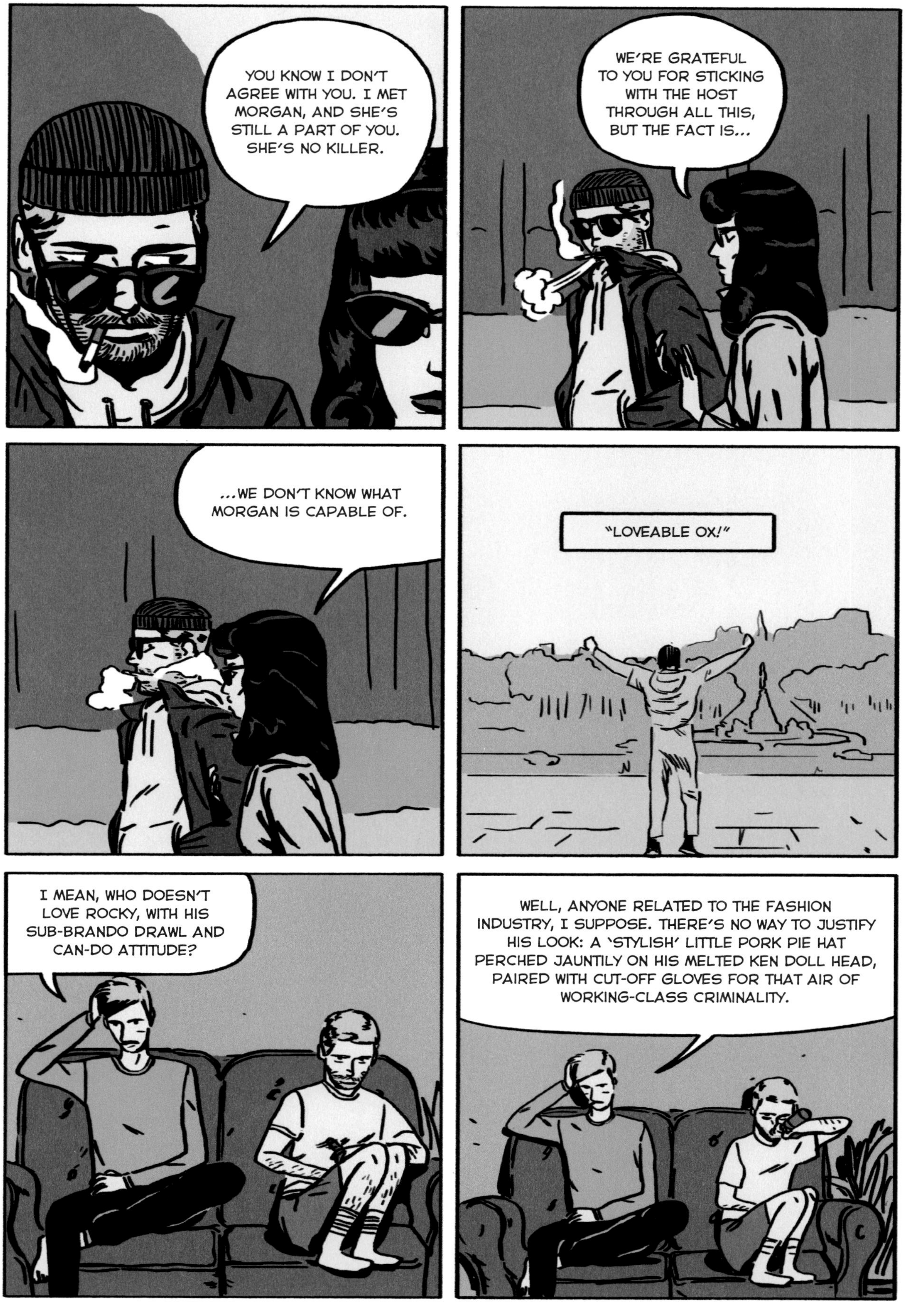
YOU KNOW I DON'T AGREE WITH YOU. I MET MORGAN, AND SHE'S STILL A PART OF YOU. SHE'S NO KILLER.
WE'RE GRATEFUL TO YOU FOR STICKING WITH THE HOST THROUGH ALL THIS, BUT THE FACT IS...
...WE DON'T KNOW WHAT MORGAN IS CAPABLE OF.
"LOVEABLE OX!"
I MEAN, WHO DOESN'T LOVE ROCKY, WITH HIS SUB-BRANDO DRAWL AND CAN-DO ATTITUDE?
WELL, ANYONE RELATED TO THE FASHION INDUSTRY, I SUPPOSE. THERE'S NO WAY TO JUSTIFY HIS LOOK: A 'STYLISH' LITTLE PORK PIE HAT PERCHED JAUNTILY ON HIS MELTED KEN DOLL HEAD, PAIRED WITH CUT-OFF GLOVES FOR THAT AIR OF WORKING-CLASS CRIMINALITY.

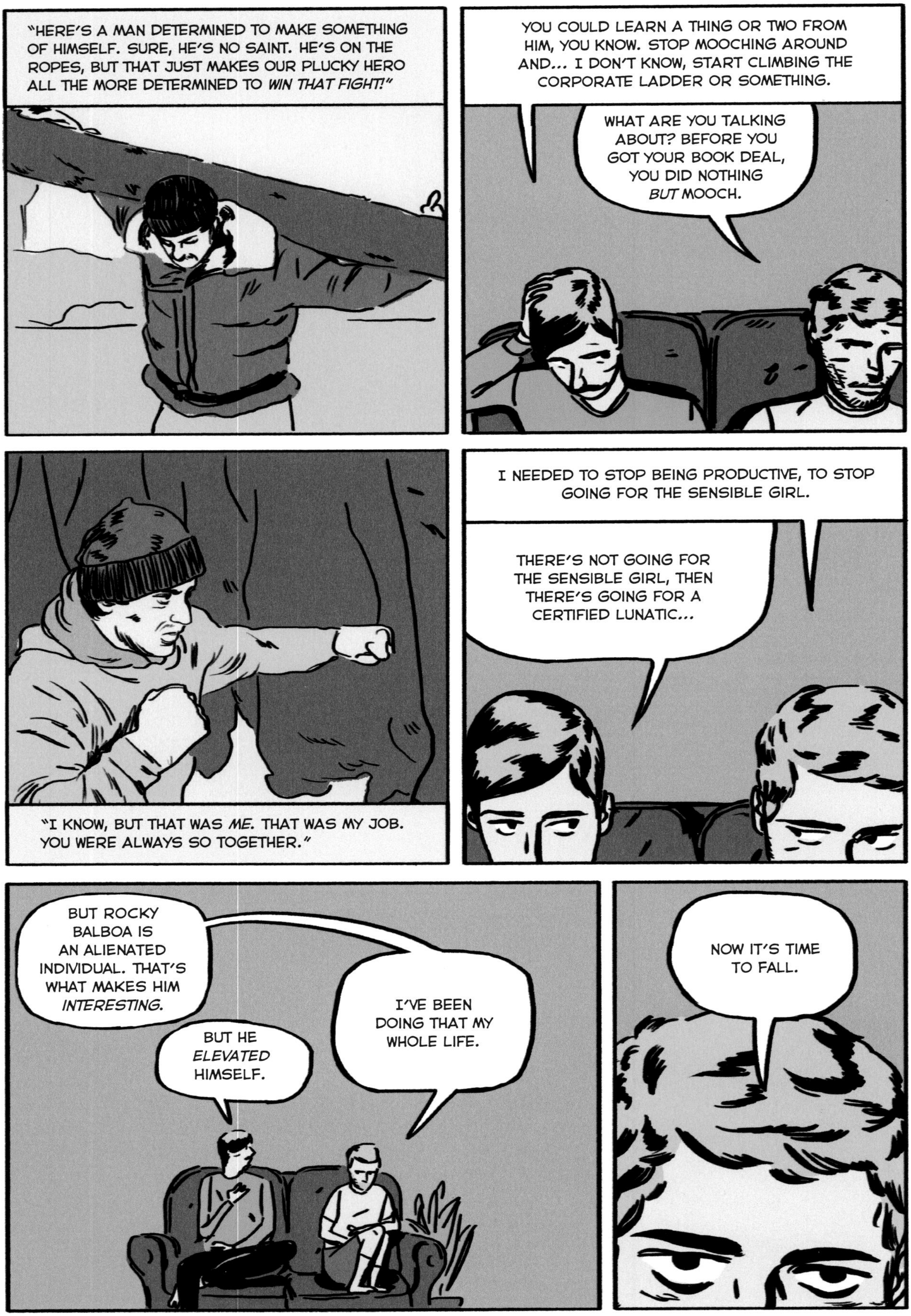
"HERE'S A MAN DETERMINED TO MAKE SOMETHING OF HIMSELF. SURE, HE'S NO SAINT. HE'S ON THE ROPES, BUT THAT JUST MAKES OUR PLUCKY HERO ALL THE MORE DETERMINED TO *WIN THAT FIGHT!*"
YOU COULD LEARN A THING OR TWO FROM HIM, YOU KNOW. STOP MOOCHING AROUND AND... I DON'T KNOW, START CLIMBING THE CORPORATE LADDER OR SOMETHING.
WHAT ARE YOU TALKING ABOUT? BEFORE YOU GOT YOUR BOOK DEAL, YOU DID NOTHING *BUT* MOOCH.
"I KNOW, BUT THAT WAS *ME*. THAT WAS MY JOB. YOU WERE ALWAYS SO TOGETHER."
I NEEDED TO STOP BEING PRODUCTIVE, TO STOP GOING FOR THE SENSIBLE GIRL.
THERE'S NOT GOING FOR THE SENSIBLE GIRL, THEN THERE'S GOING FOR A CERTIFIED LUNATIC...
BUT ROCKY BALBOA IS AN ALIENATED INDIVIDUAL. THAT'S WHAT MAKES HIM *INTERESTING*.
BUT HE *ELEVATED* HIMSELF.
I'VE BEEN DOING THAT MY WHOLE LIFE.
NOW IT'S TIME TO FALL.

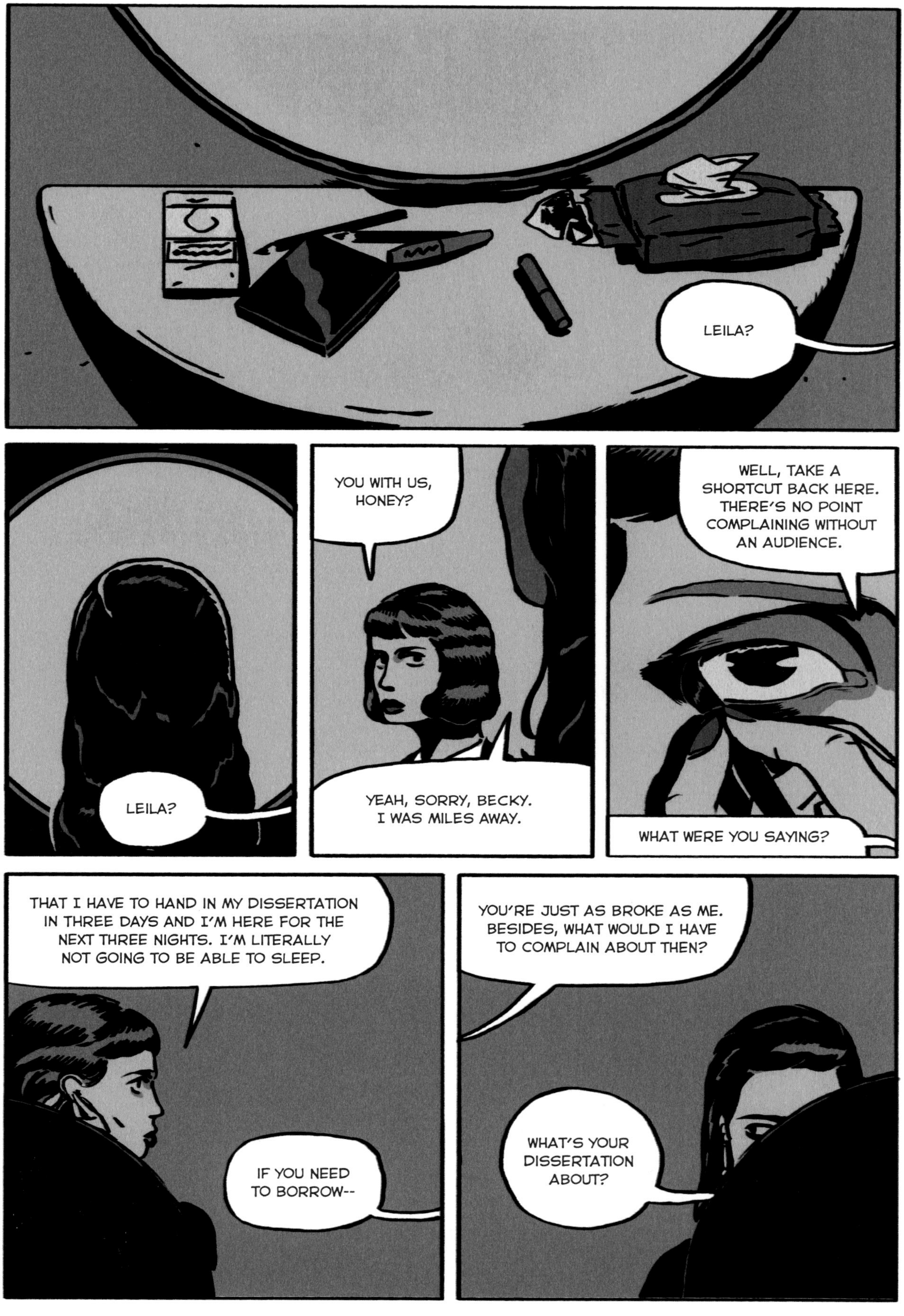
LEILA?
LEILA?
YOU WITH US, HONEY?
YEAH, SORRY, BECKY. I WAS MILES AWAY.
WELL, TAKE A SHORTCUT BACK HERE. THERE'S NO POINT COMPLAINING WITHOUT AN AUDIENCE.
WHAT WERE YOU SAYING?
THAT I HAVE TO HAND IN MY DISSERTATION IN THREE DAYS AND I'M HERE FOR THE NEXT THREE NIGHTS. I'M LITERALLY NOT GOING TO BE ABLE TO SLEEP.
IF YOU NEED TO BORROW--
YOU'RE JUST AS BROKE AS ME. BESIDES, WHAT WOULD I HAVE TO COMPLAIN ABOUT THEN?
WHAT'S YOUR DISSERTATION ABOUT?

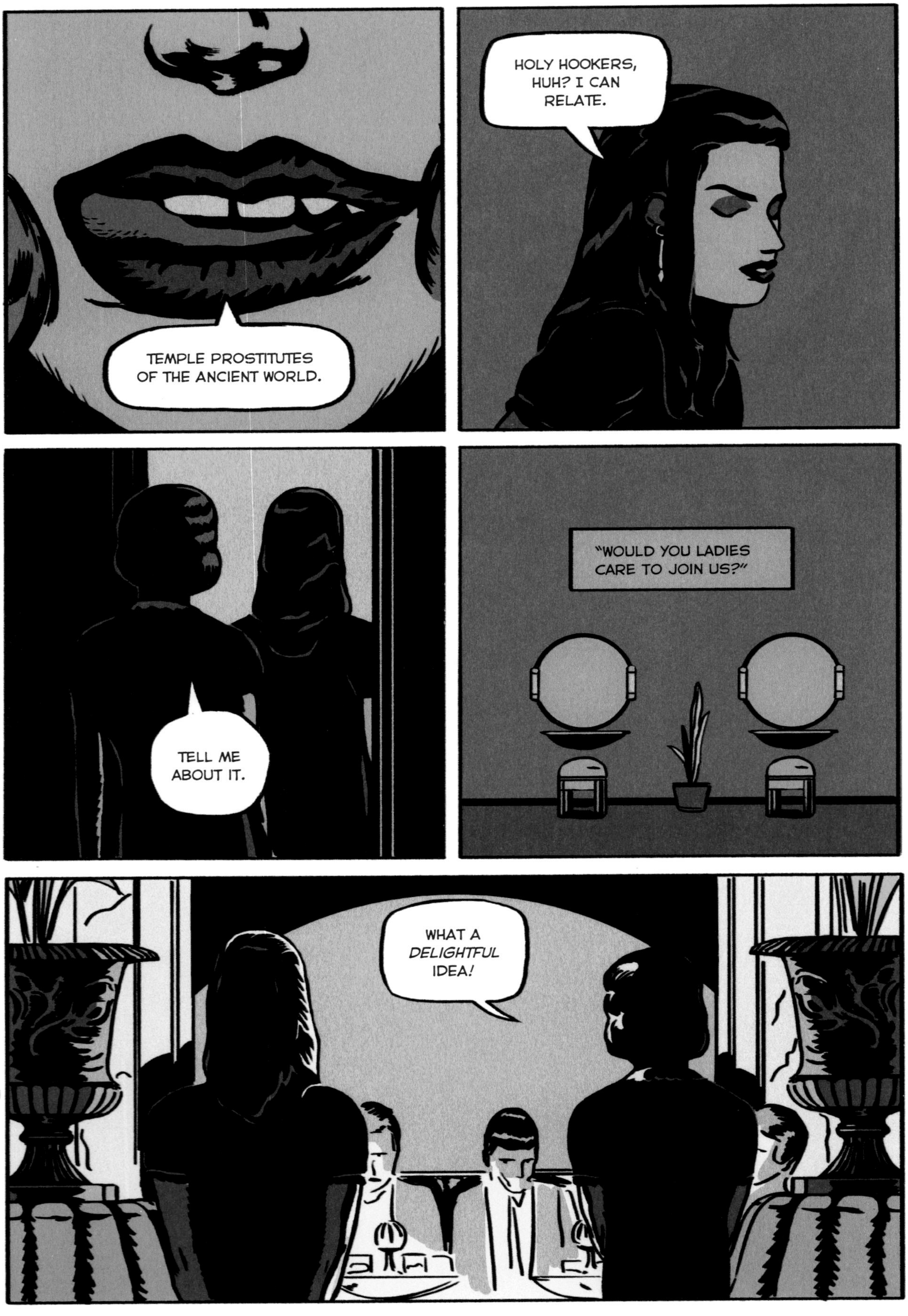
TEMPLE PROSTITUTES OF THE ANCIENT WORLD.
HOLY HOOKERS, HUH? I CAN RELATE.
TELL ME ABOUT IT.
"WOULD YOU LADIES CARE TO JOIN US?"
WHAT A *DELIGHTFUL* IDEA!

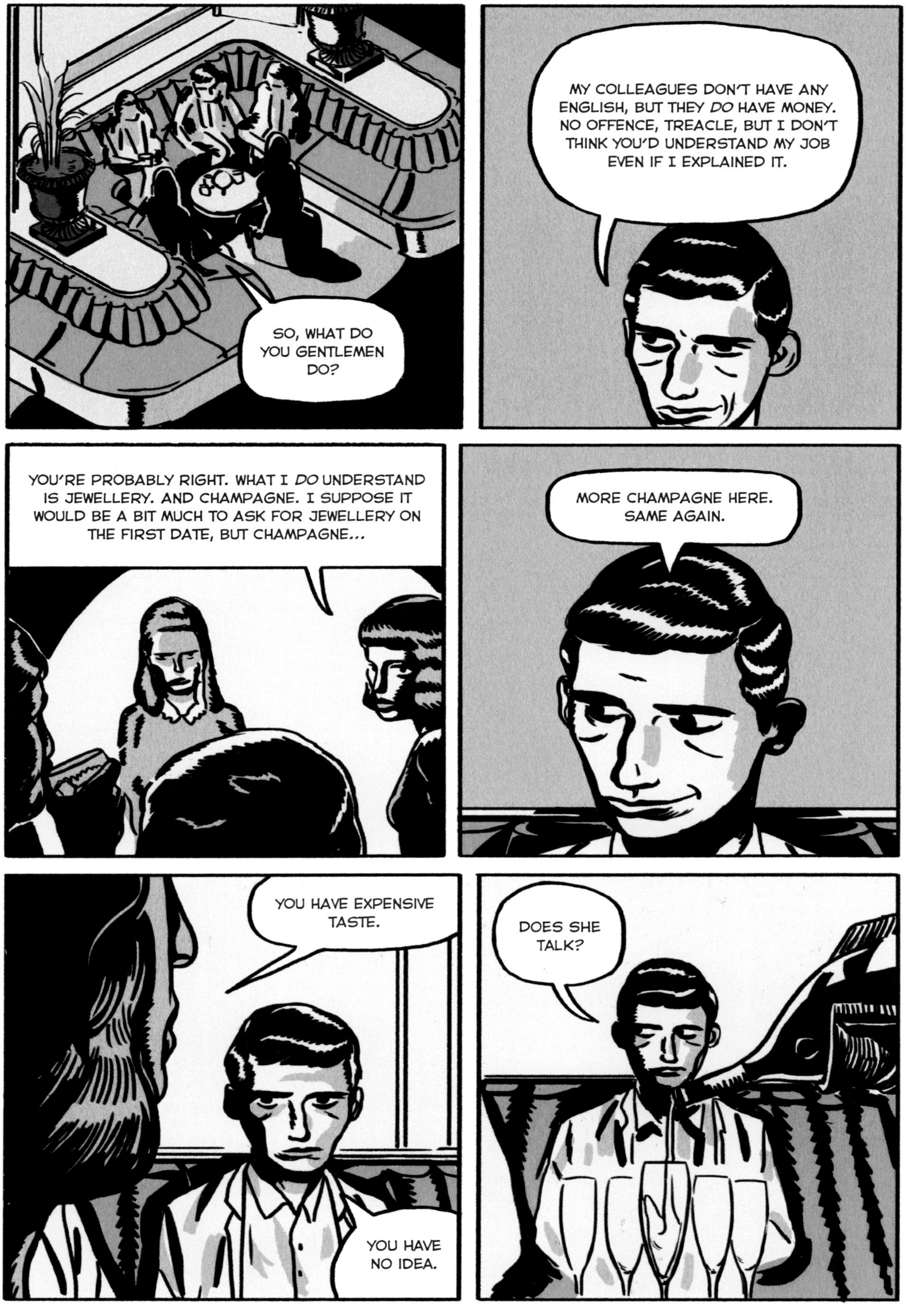
SO, WHAT DO YOU GENTLEMEN DO?
MY COLLEAGUES DON'T HAVE ANY ENGLISH, BUT THEY *DO* HAVE MONEY. NO OFFENCE, TREACLE, BUT I DON'T THINK YOU'D UNDERSTAND MY JOB EVEN IF I EXPLAINED IT.
YOU'RE PROBABLY RIGHT. WHAT I *DO* UNDERSTAND IS JEWELLERY. AND CHAMPAGNE. I SUPPOSE IT WOULD BE A BIT MUCH TO ASK FOR JEWELLERY ON THE FIRST DATE, BUT CHAMPAGNE...
MORE CHAMPAGNE HERE. SAME AGAIN.
YOU HAVE EXPENSIVE TASTE.
YOU HAVE NO IDEA.
DOES SHE TALK?

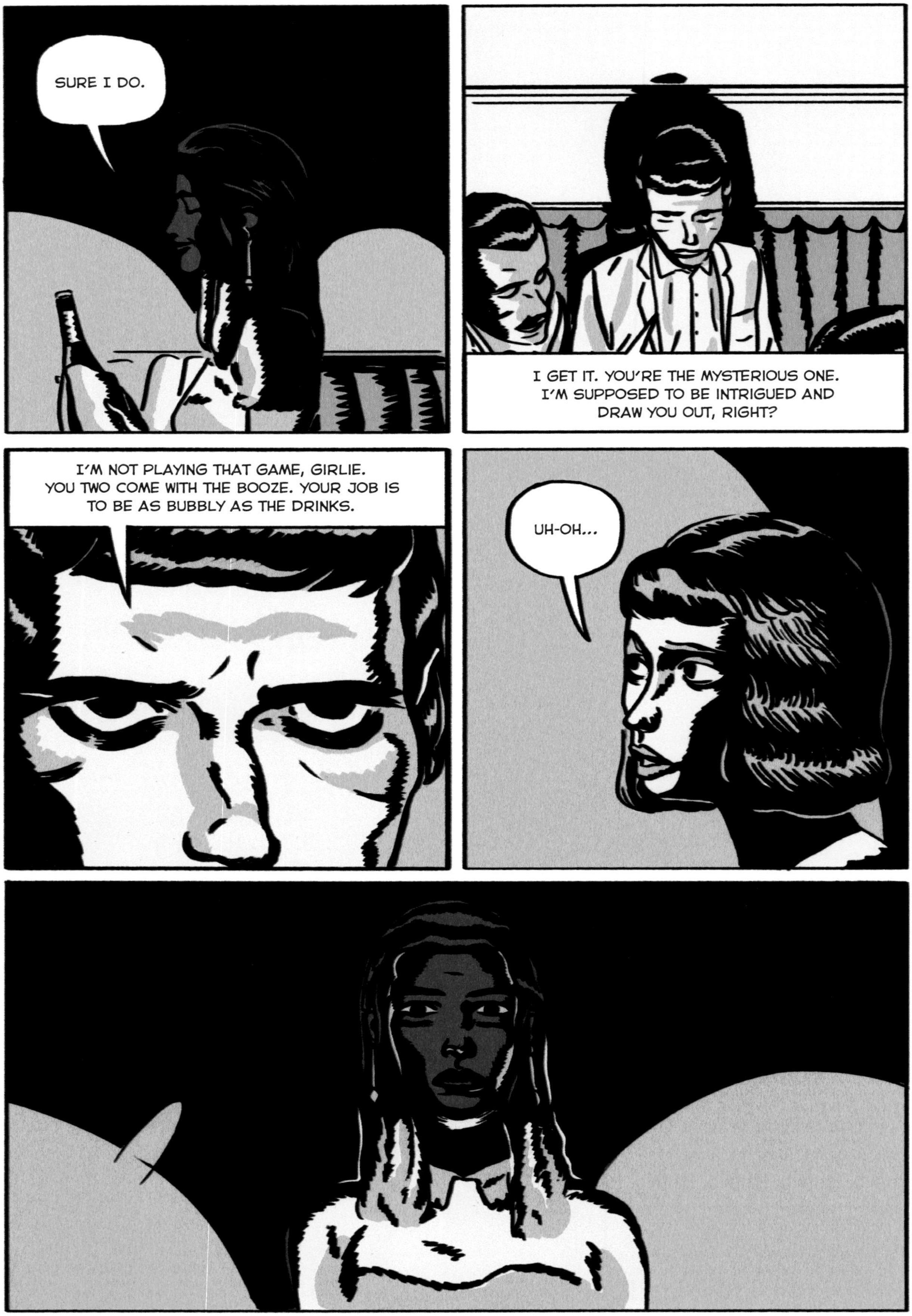
SURE I DO.
I GET IT. YOU'RE THE MYSTERIOUS ONE. I'M SUPPOSED TO BE INTRIGUED AND DRAW YOU OUT, RIGHT?
I'M NOT PLAYING THAT GAME, GIRLIE. YOU TWO COME WITH THE BOOZE. YOUR JOB IS TO BE AS BUBBLY AS THE DRINKS.
UH-OH...

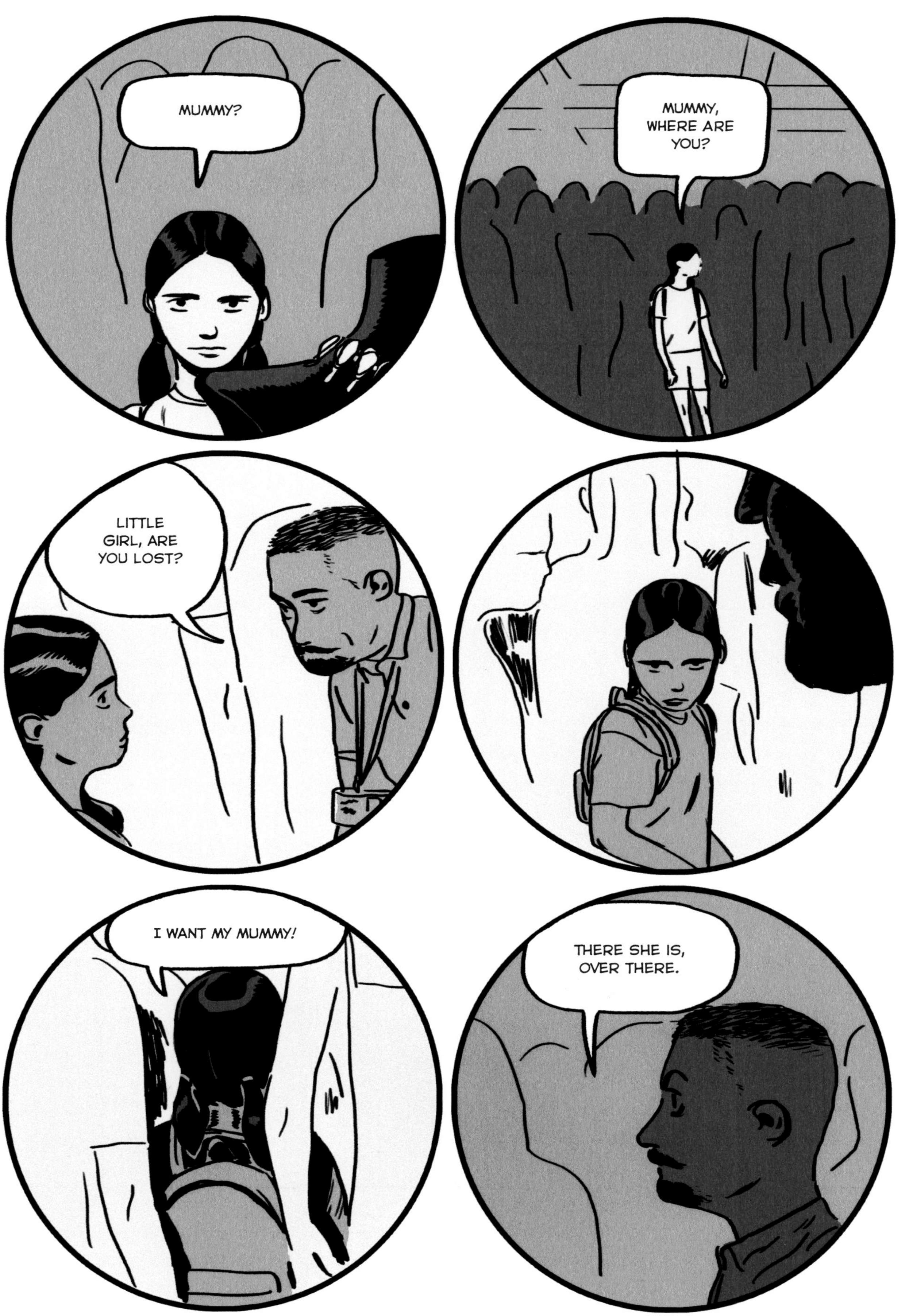
MUMMY?
MUMMY, WHERE ARE YOU?
LITTLE GIRL, ARE YOU LOST?
I WANT MY MUMMY!
THERE SHE IS, OVER THERE.

YOU FOOLISH LITTLE MAN, I WILL HAVE YOUR ENTRAILS FED TO YOU AS YOU BEG FOR MERCY.

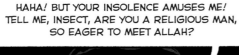

HAHA! BUT YOUR INSOLENCE AMUSES ME! TELL ME, INSECT, ARE YOU A RELIGIOUS MAN, SO EAGER TO MEET ALLAH?

I'M NOT SURE I...

PERHAPS I CAN FIND A USE FOR YOU, AFTER ALL. I'LL HAVE YOU CASTRATED. YOU CAN JOIN THE ESTEEMED RANKS OF MY EUNUCHS.

CASTRATED...?

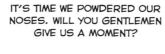

IT'S TIME WE POWDERED OUR NOSES. WILL YOU GENTLEMEN GIVE US A MOMENT?

BRING THE INSECT WITH US. MY SURGEONS WILL HAVE HIM SMOOTH BETWEEN THE LEGS IN NO TIME.

ARE YOU OKAY, HONEY?

I... I'LL BE FINE.

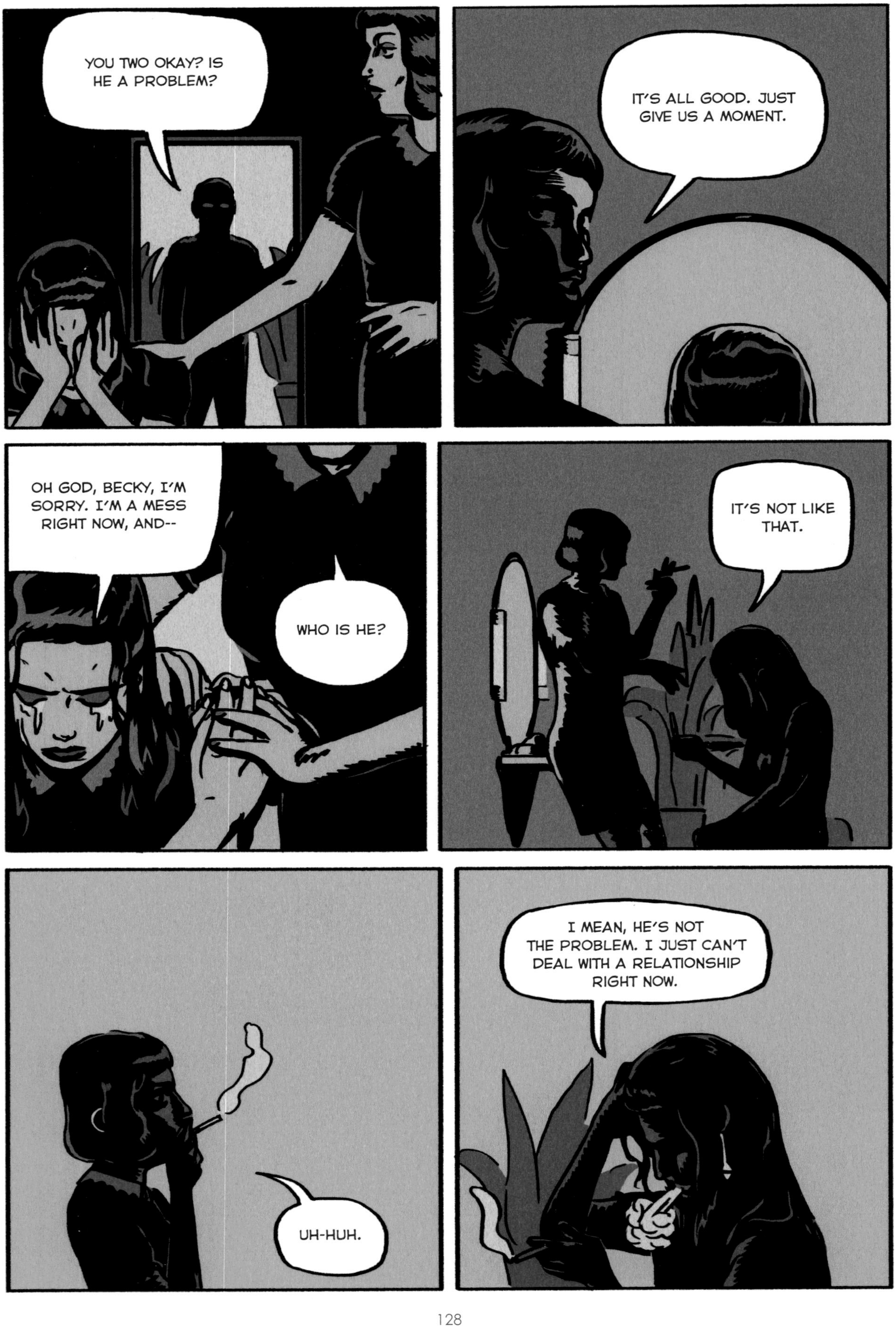
YOU TWO OKAY? IS HE A PROBLEM?
IT'S ALL GOOD. JUST GIVE US A MOMENT.
OH GOD, BECKY, I'M SORRY. I'M A MESS RIGHT NOW, AND--
WHO IS HE?
IT'S NOT LIKE THAT.
UH-HUH.
I MEAN, HE'S NOT THE PROBLEM. I JUST CAN'T DEAL WITH A RELATIONSHIP RIGHT NOW.

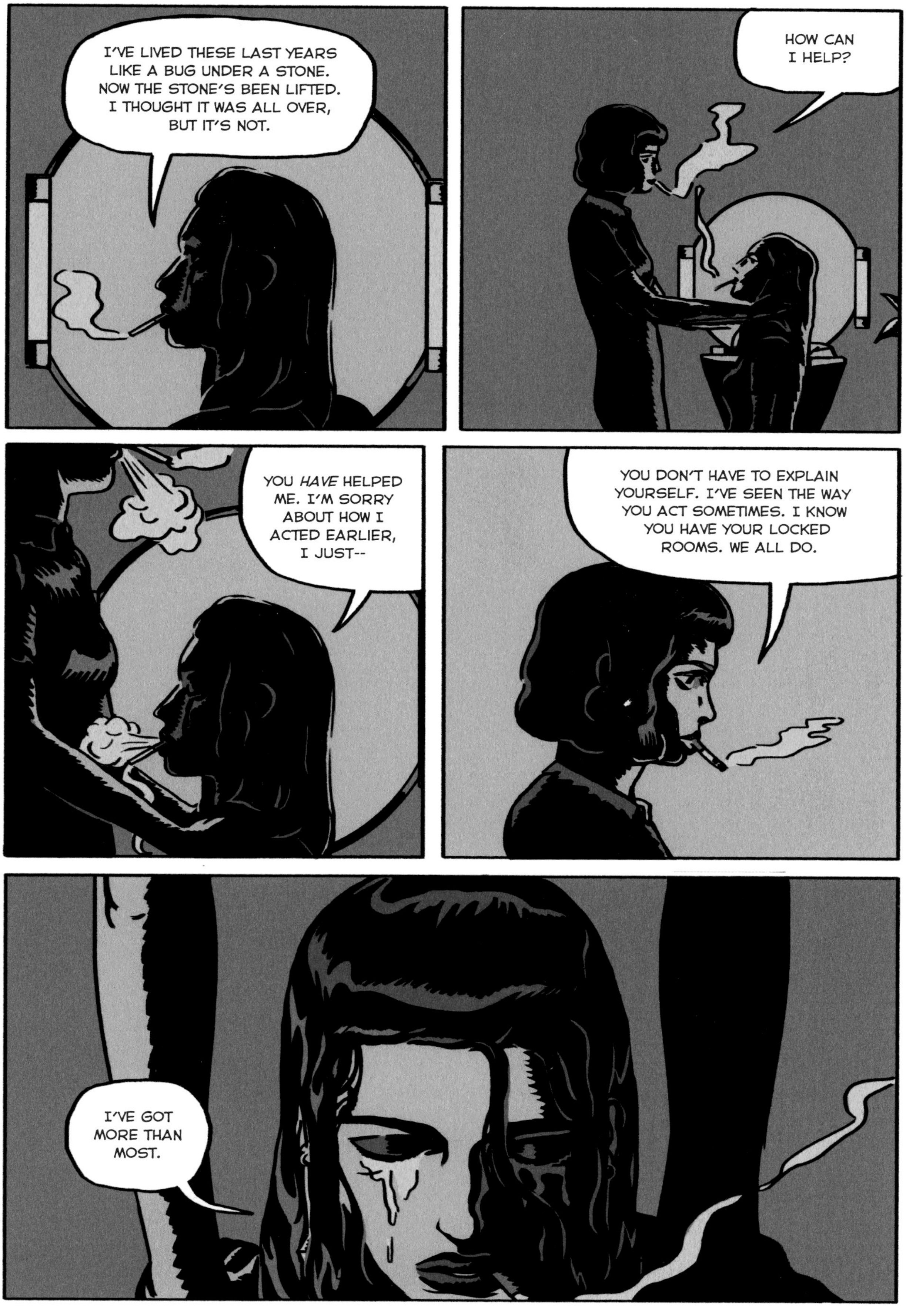
I'VE LIVED THESE LAST YEARS LIKE A BUG UNDER A STONE. NOW THE STONE'S BEEN LIFTED. I THOUGHT IT WAS ALL OVER, BUT IT'S NOT.
HOW CAN I HELP?
YOU *HAVE* HELPED ME. I'M SORRY ABOUT HOW I ACTED EARLIER, I JUST--
YOU DON'T HAVE TO EXPLAIN YOURSELF. I'VE SEEN THE WAY YOU ACT SOMETIMES. I KNOW YOU HAVE YOUR LOCKED ROOMS. WE ALL DO.
I'VE GOT MORE THAN MOST.

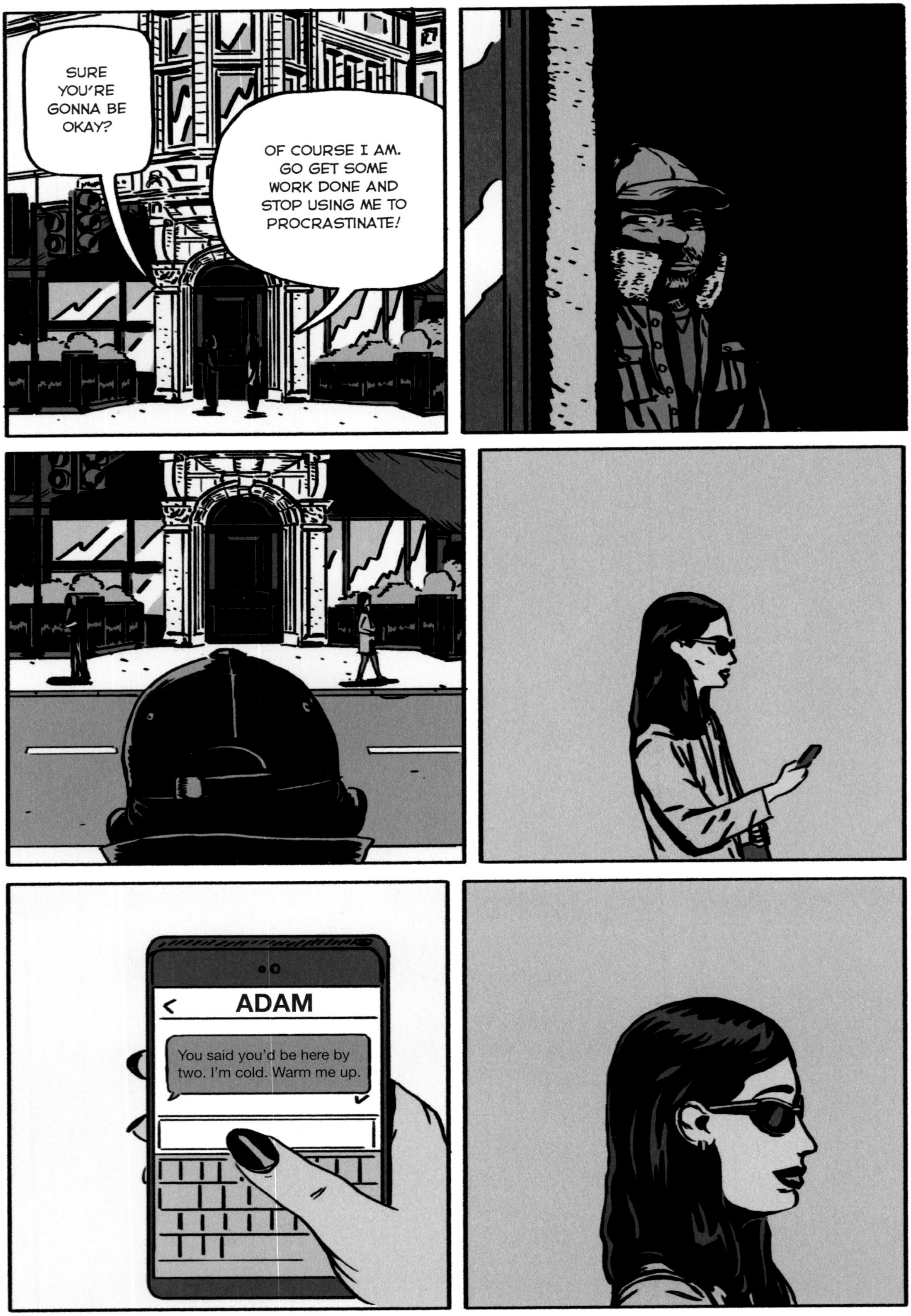
SURE YOU'RE GONNA BE OKAY?
OF COURSE I AM. GO GET SOME WORK DONE AND STOP USING ME TO PROCRASTINATE!
ADAM
You said you'd be here by two. I'm cold. Warm me up.

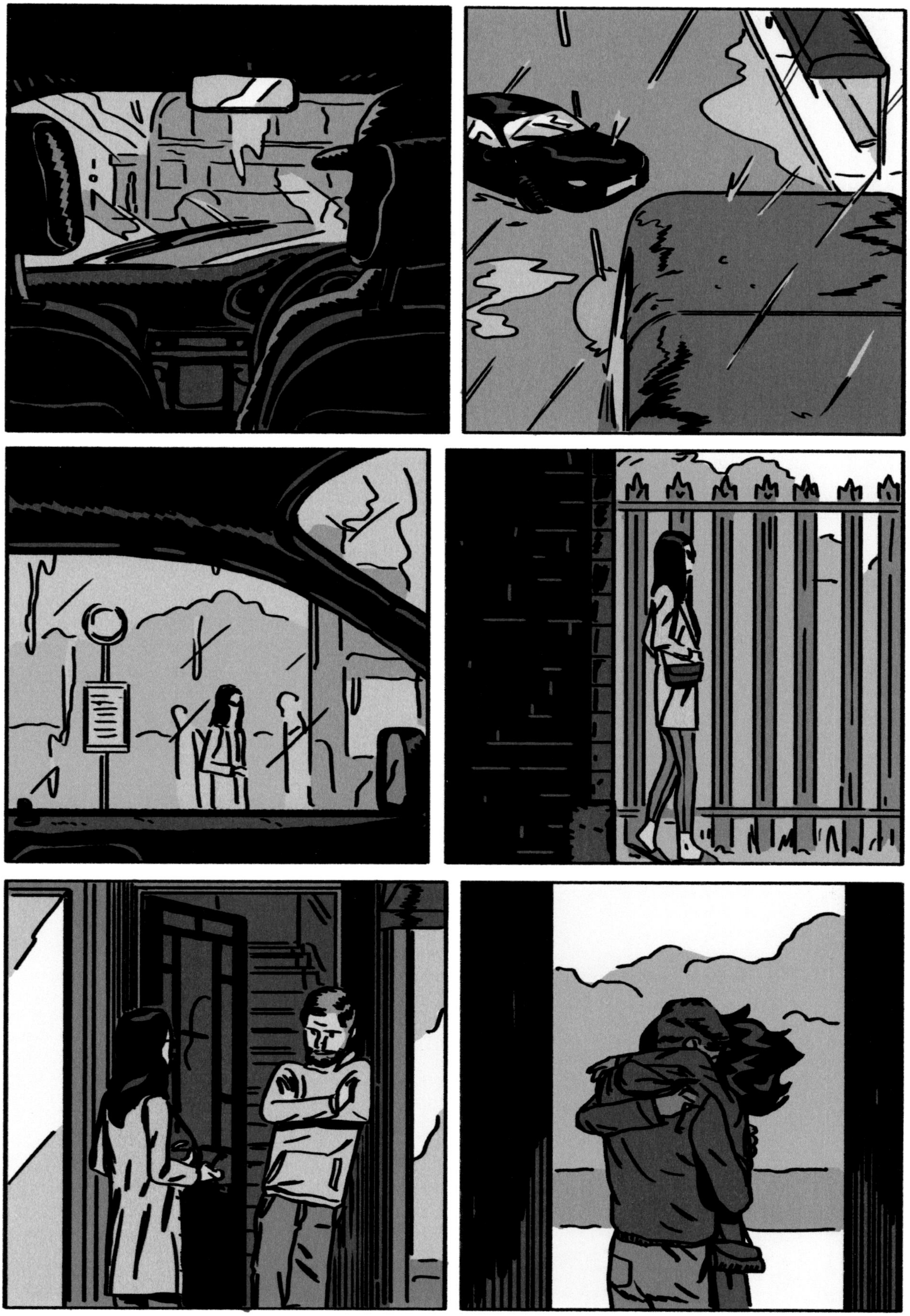

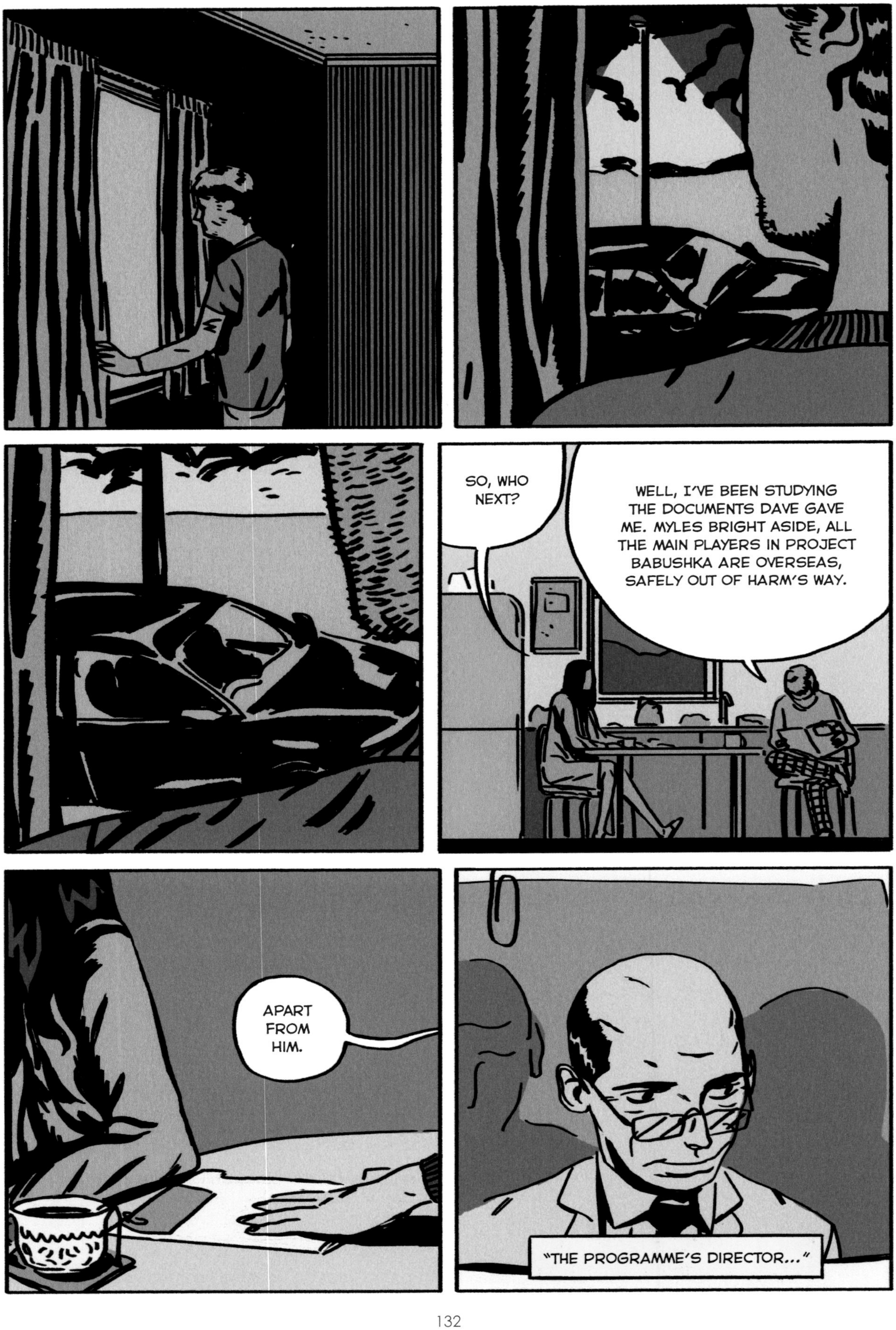
SO, WHO NEXT?
WELL, I'VE BEEN STUDYING THE DOCUMENTS DAVE GAVE ME. MYLES BRIGHT ASIDE, ALL THE MAIN PLAYERS IN PROJECT BABUSHKA ARE OVERSEAS, SAFELY OUT OF HARM'S WAY.
APART FROM HIM.
"THE PROGRAMME'S DIRECTOR..."

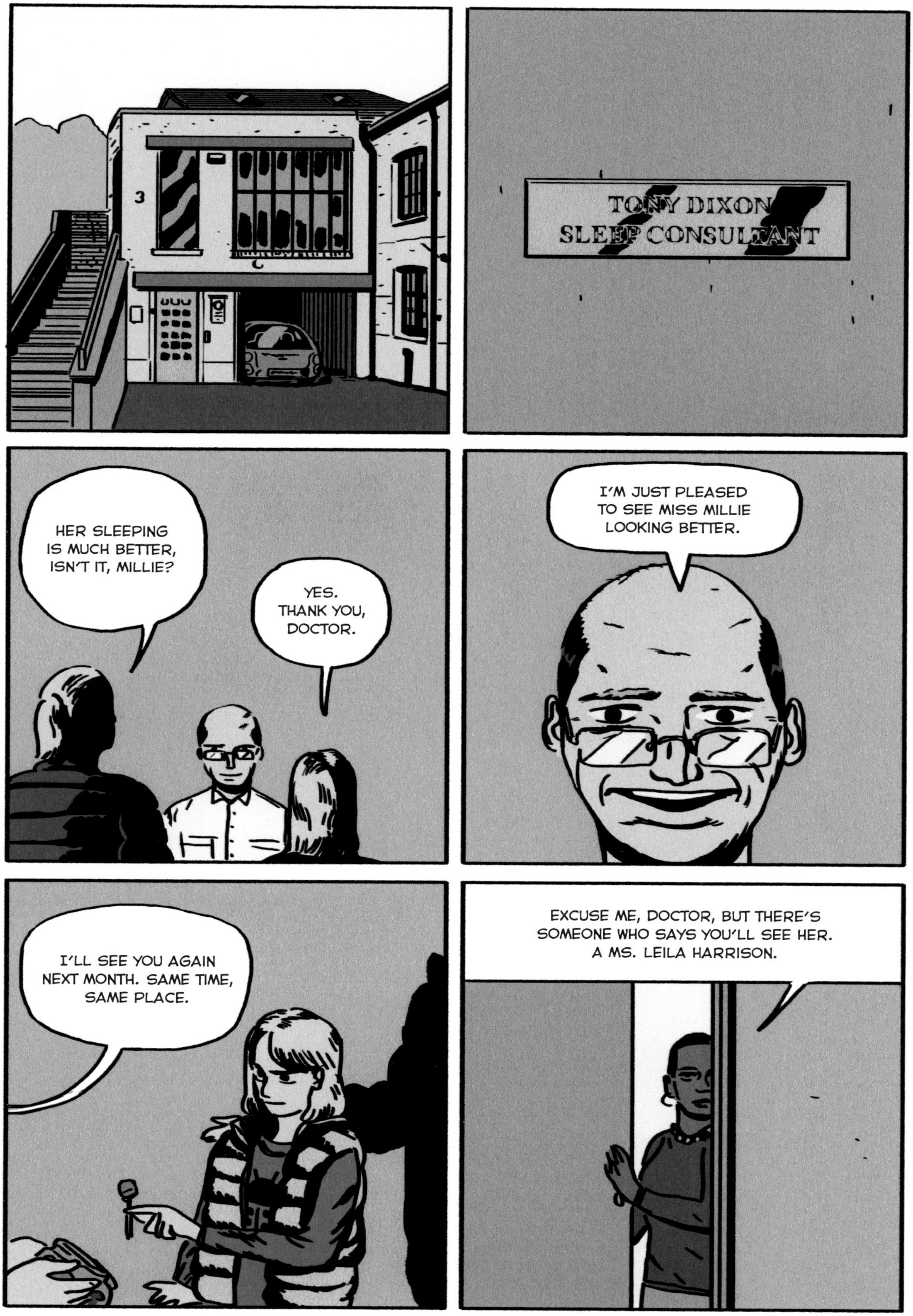
3
TONY DIXON
SLEEP CONSULTANT
HER SLEEPING IS MUCH BETTER, ISN'T IT, MILLIE?
YES. THANK YOU, DOCTOR.
I'M JUST PLEASED TO SEE MISS MILLIE LOOKING BETTER.
I'LL SEE YOU AGAIN NEXT MONTH. SAME TIME, SAME PLACE.
EXCUSE ME, DOCTOR, BUT THERE'S SOMEONE WHO SAYS YOU'LL SEE HER. A MS. LEILA HARRISON.

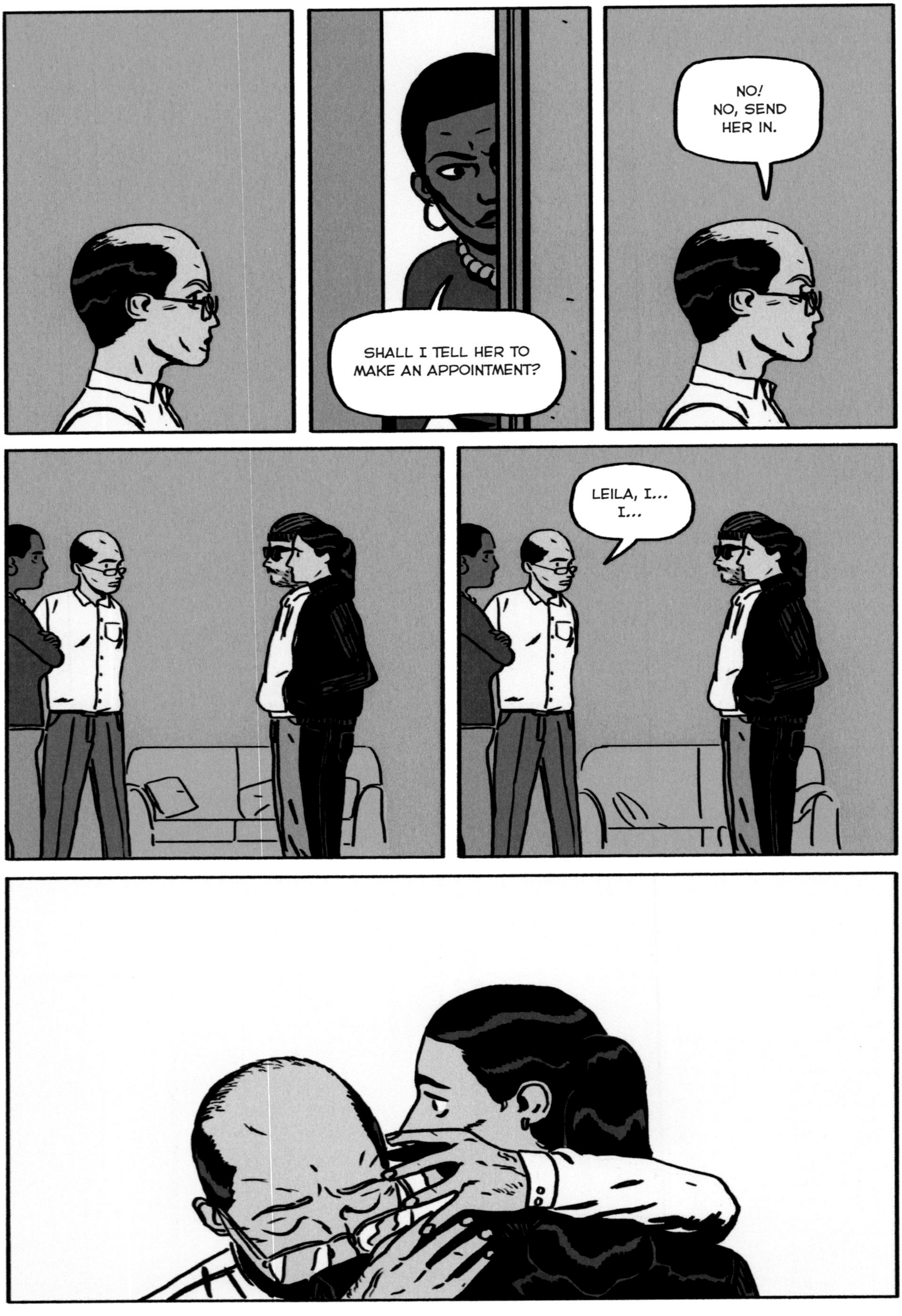
SHALL I TELL HER TO MAKE AN APPOINTMENT?
NO! NO, SEND HER IN.
LEILA, I... I...

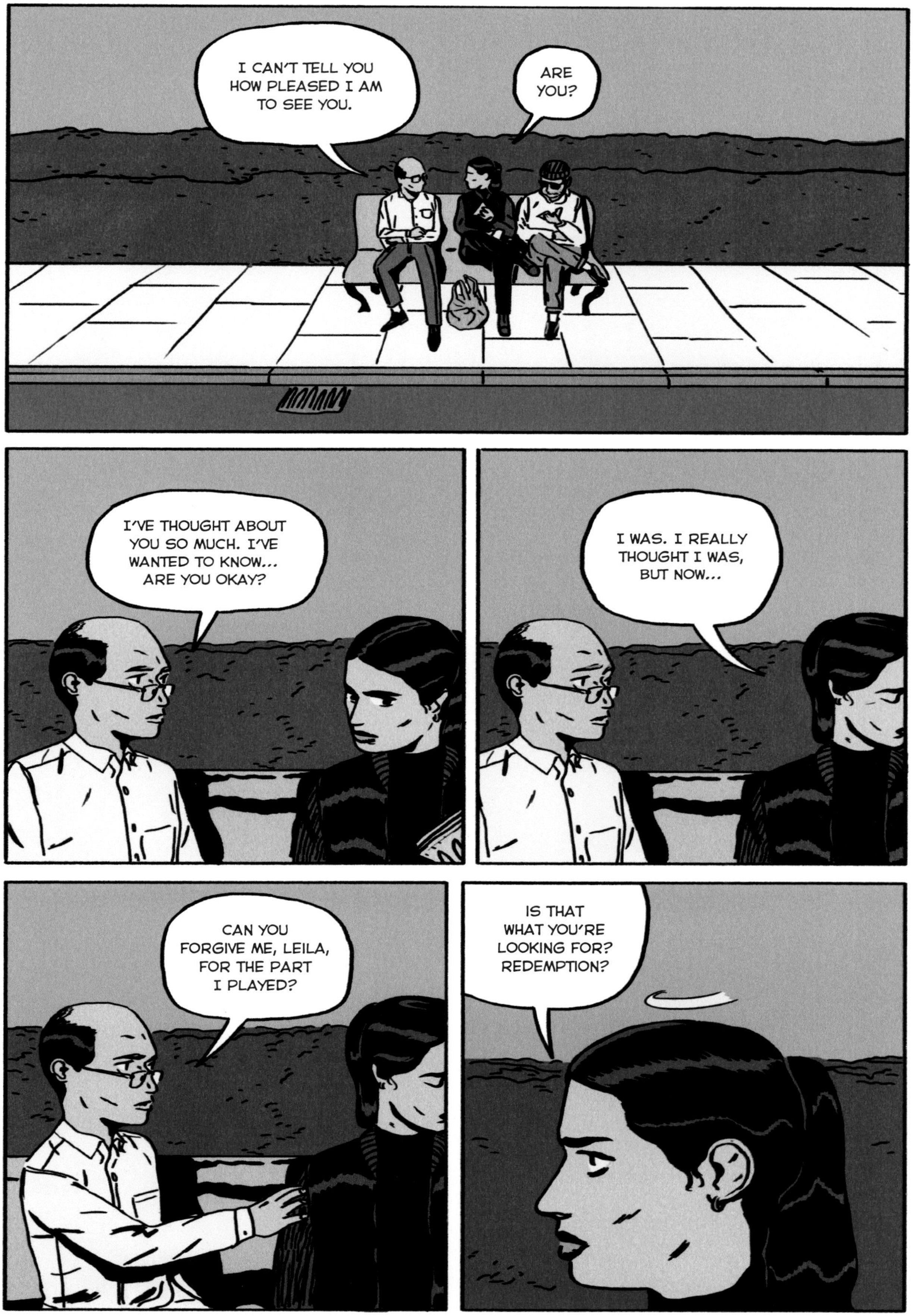
I CAN'T TELL YOU HOW PLEASED I AM TO SEE YOU.
ARE YOU?
I'VE THOUGHT ABOUT YOU SO MUCH. I'VE WANTED TO KNOW... ARE YOU OKAY?
I WAS. I REALLY THOUGHT I WAS, BUT NOW...
CAN YOU FORGIVE ME, LEILA, FOR THE PART I PLAYED?
IS THAT WHAT YOU'RE LOOKING FOR? REDEMPTION?

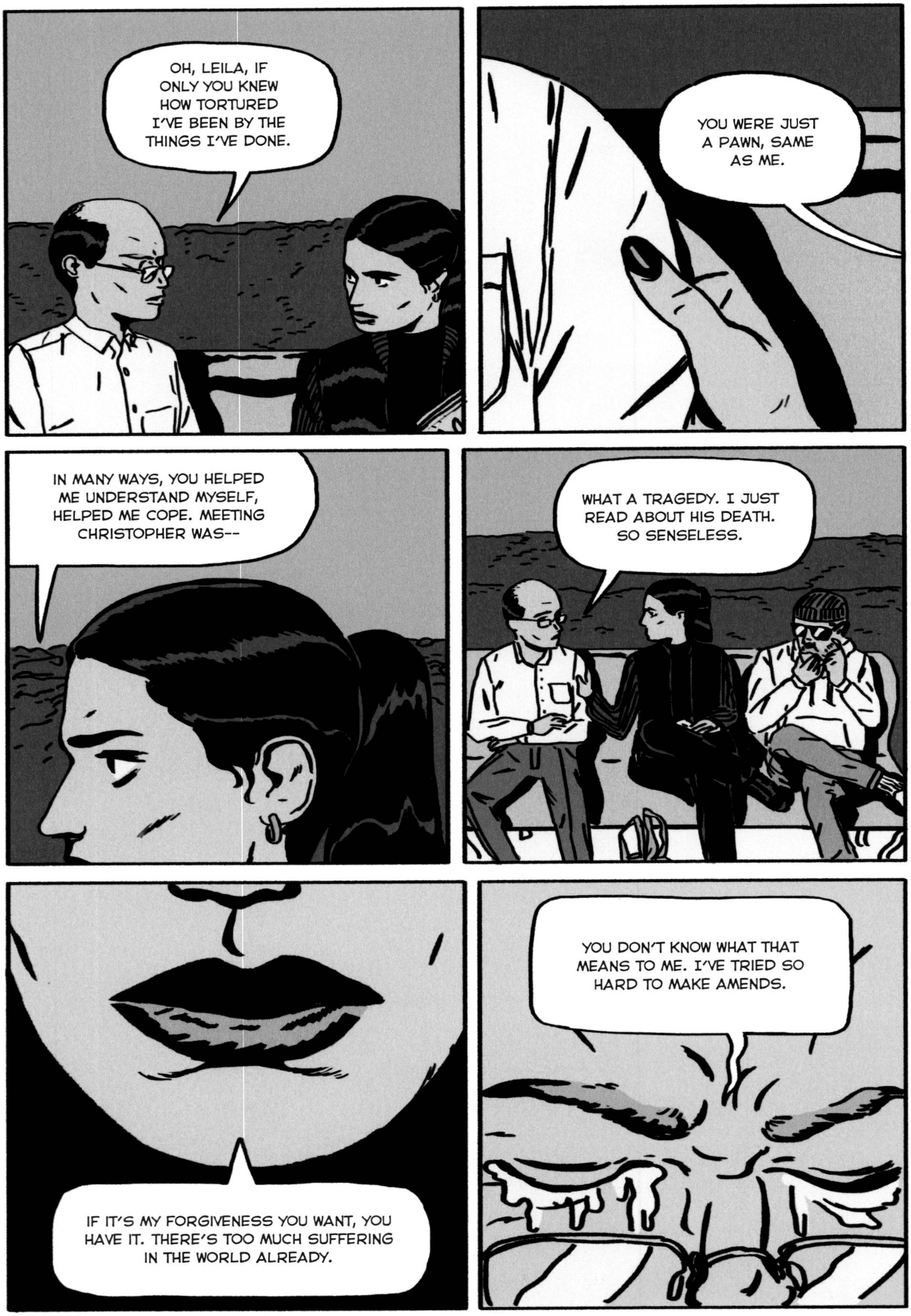
OH, LEILA, IF ONLY YOU KNEW HOW TORTURED I'VE BEEN BY THE THINGS I'VE DONE.
YOU WERE JUST A PAWN, SAME AS ME.
IN MANY WAYS, YOU HELPED ME UNDERSTAND MYSELF, HELPED ME COPE. MEETING CHRISTOPHER WAS--
WHAT A TRAGEDY. I JUST READ ABOUT HIS DEATH. SO SENSELESS.
IF IT'S MY FORGIVENESS YOU WANT, YOU HAVE IT. THERE'S TOO MUCH SUFFERING IN THE WORLD ALREADY.
YOU DON'T KNOW WHAT THAT MEANS TO ME. I'VE TRIED SO HARD TO MAKE AMENDS.

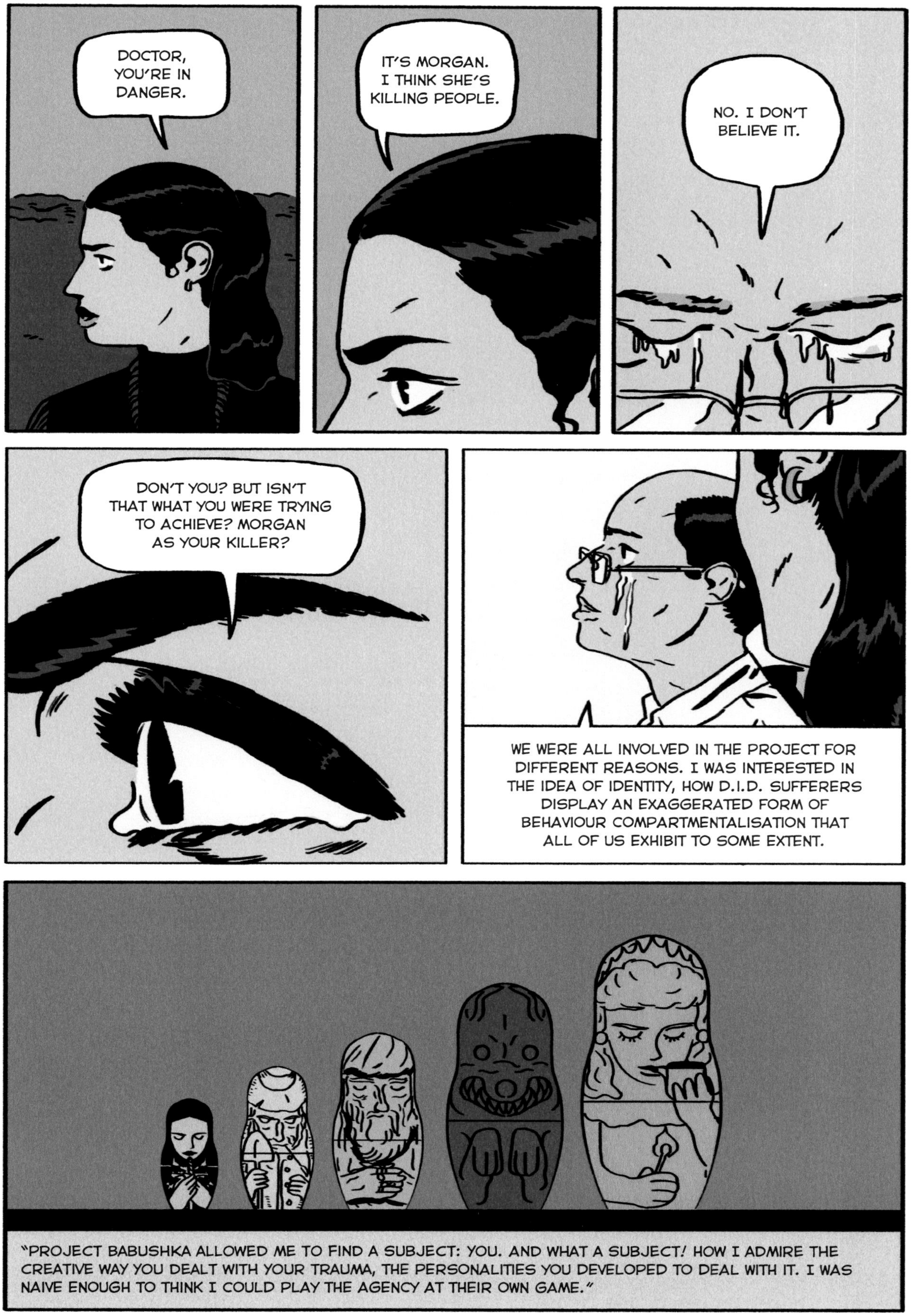

DOCTOR, YOU'RE IN DANGER.
IT'S MORGAN. I THINK SHE'S KILLING PEOPLE.
NO. I DON'T BELIEVE IT.
DON'T YOU? BUT ISN'T THAT WHAT YOU WERE TRYING TO ACHIEVE? MORGAN AS YOUR KILLER?
WE WERE ALL INVOLVED IN THE PROJECT FOR DIFFERENT REASONS. I WAS INTERESTED IN THE IDEA OF IDENTITY, HOW D.I.D. SUFFERERS DISPLAY AN EXAGGERATED FORM OF BEHAVIOUR COMPARTMENTALISATION THAT ALL OF US EXHIBIT TO SOME EXTENT.
"PROJECT BABUSHKA ALLOWED ME TO FIND A SUBJECT: YOU. AND WHAT A SUBJECT! HOW I ADMIRE THE CREATIVE WAY YOU DEALT WITH YOUR TRAUMA, THE PERSONALITIES YOU DEVELOPED TO DEAL WITH IT. I WAS NAIVE ENOUGH TO THINK I COULD PLAY THE AGENCY AT THEIR OWN GAME."

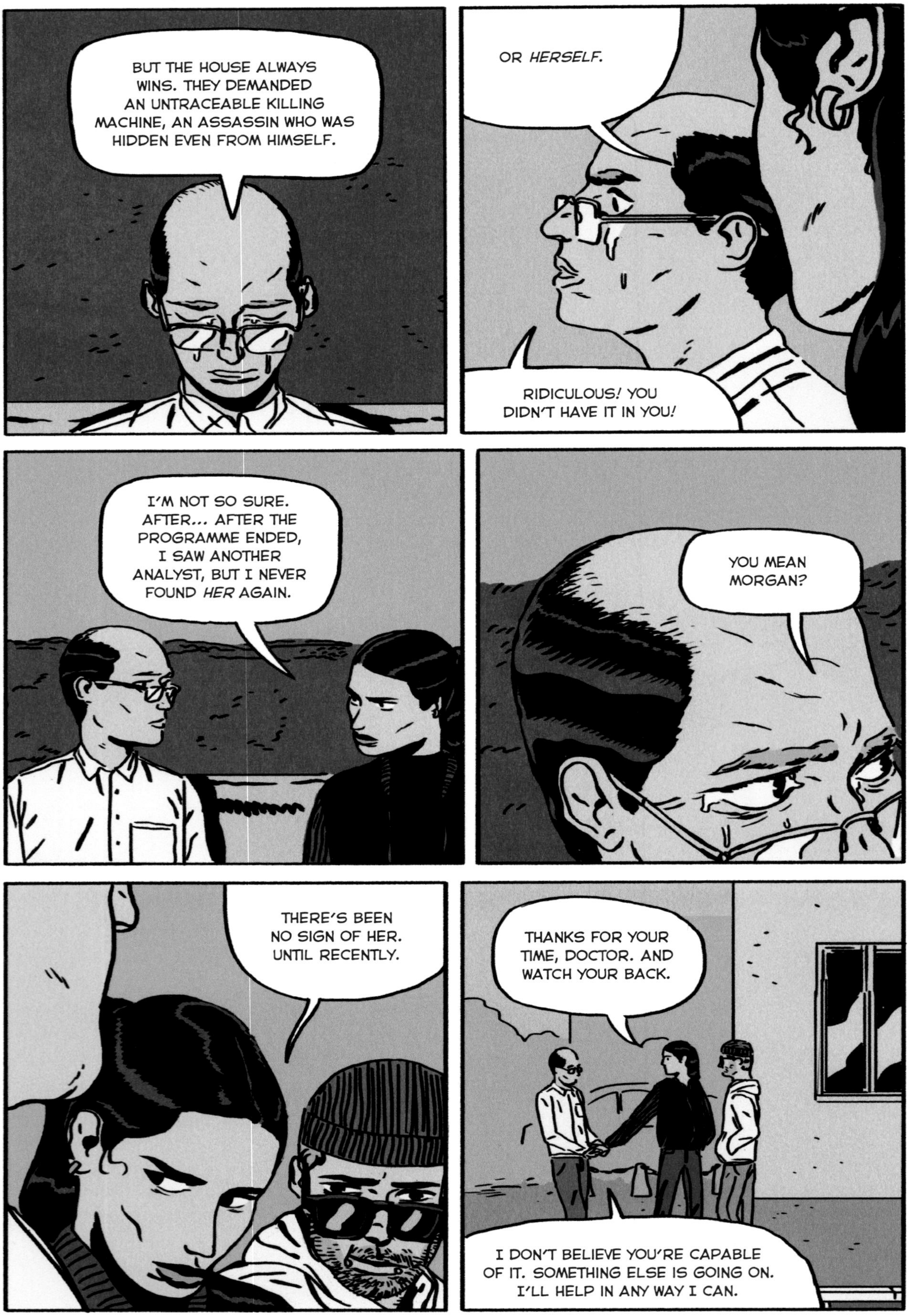
BUT THE HOUSE ALWAYS WINS. THEY DEMANDED AN UNTRACEABLE KILLING MACHINE, AN ASSASSIN WHO WAS HIDDEN EVEN FROM HIMSELF.
OR *HERSELF*.
RIDICULOUS! YOU DIDN'T HAVE IT IN YOU!
I'M NOT SO SURE. AFTER... AFTER THE PROGRAMME ENDED, I SAW ANOTHER ANALYST, BUT I NEVER FOUND *HER* AGAIN.
YOU MEAN MORGAN?
THERE'S BEEN NO SIGN OF HER. UNTIL RECENTLY.
THANKS FOR YOUR TIME, DOCTOR. AND WATCH YOUR BACK.
I DON'T BELIEVE YOU'RE CAPABLE OF IT. SOMETHING ELSE IS GOING ON. I'LL HELP IN ANY WAY I CAN.

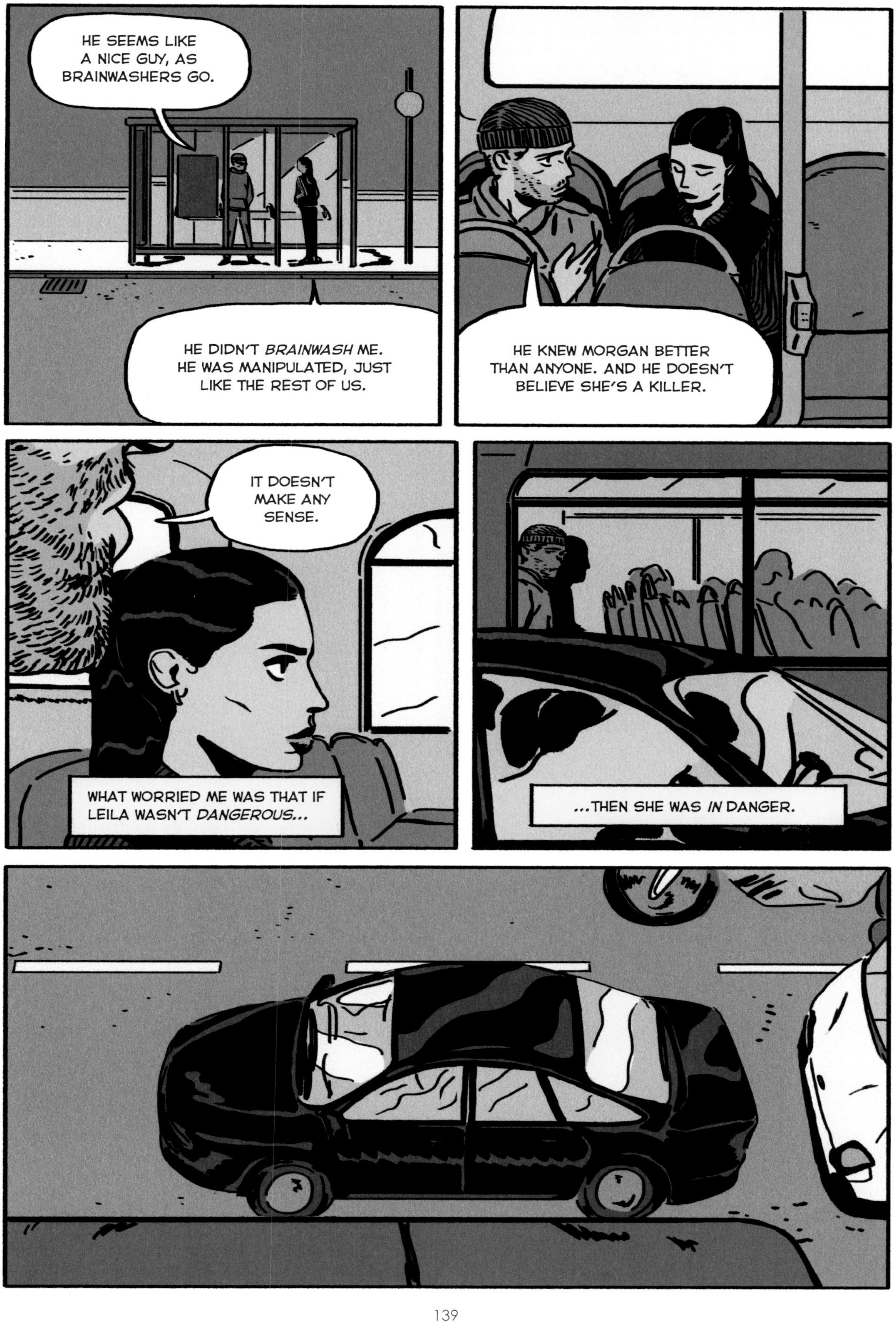
HE SEEMS LIKE A NICE GUY, AS BRAINWASHERS GO.
HE DIDN'T *BRAINWASH* ME. HE WAS MANIPULATED, JUST LIKE THE REST OF US.
HE KNEW MORGAN BETTER THAN ANYONE. AND HE DOESN'T BELIEVE SHE'S A KILLER.
IT DOESN'T MAKE ANY SENSE.
WHAT WORRIED ME WAS THAT IF LEILA WASN'T *DANGEROUS*...
...THEN SHE WAS *IN* DANGER.

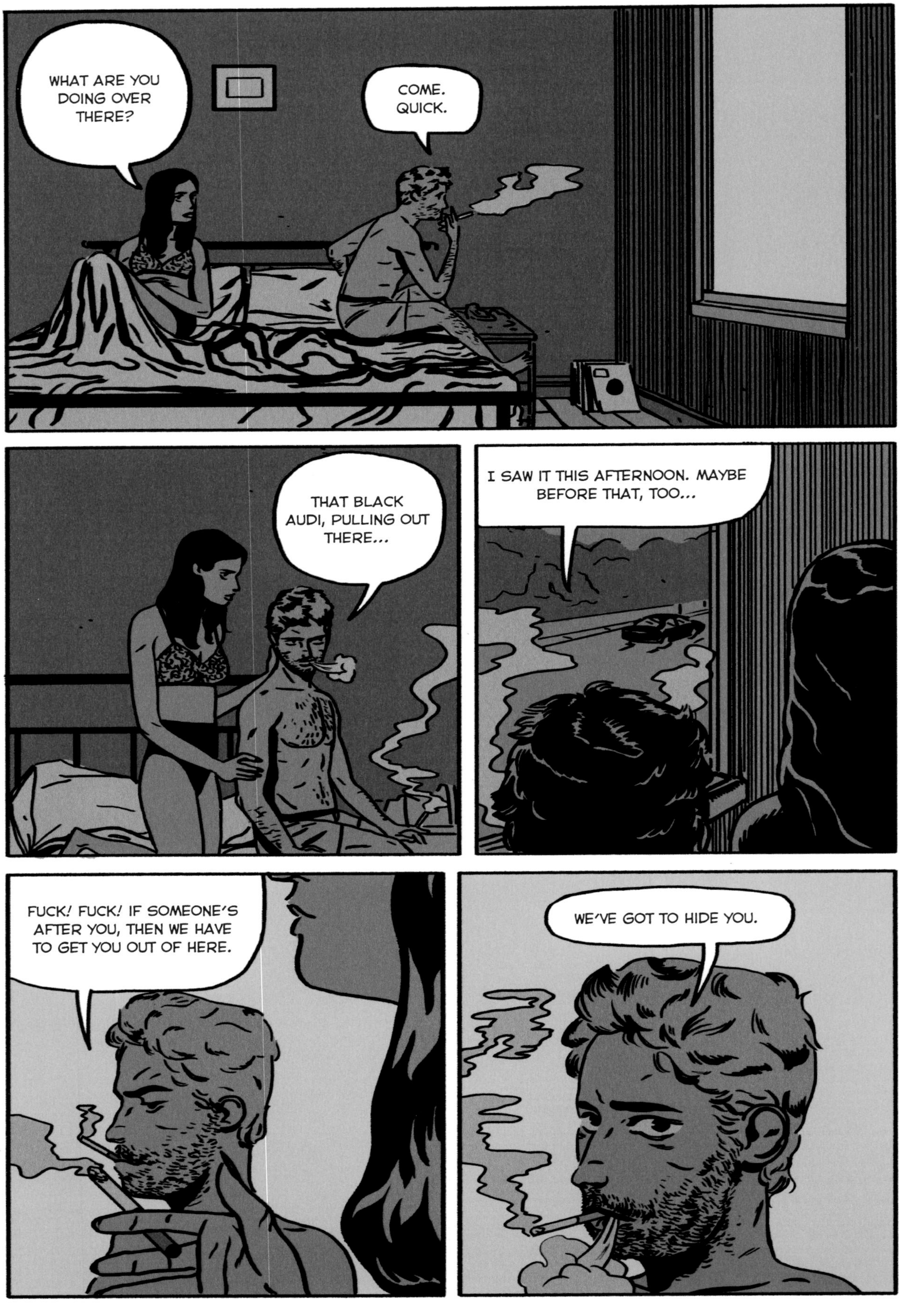

WHAT ARE YOU DOING OVER THERE?
COME. QUICK.
THAT BLACK AUDI, PULLING OUT THERE...
I SAW IT THIS AFTERNOON. MAYBE BEFORE THAT, TOO...
FUCK! FUCK! IF SOMEONE'S AFTER YOU, THEN WE HAVE TO GET YOU OUT OF HERE.
WE'VE GOT TO HIDE YOU.

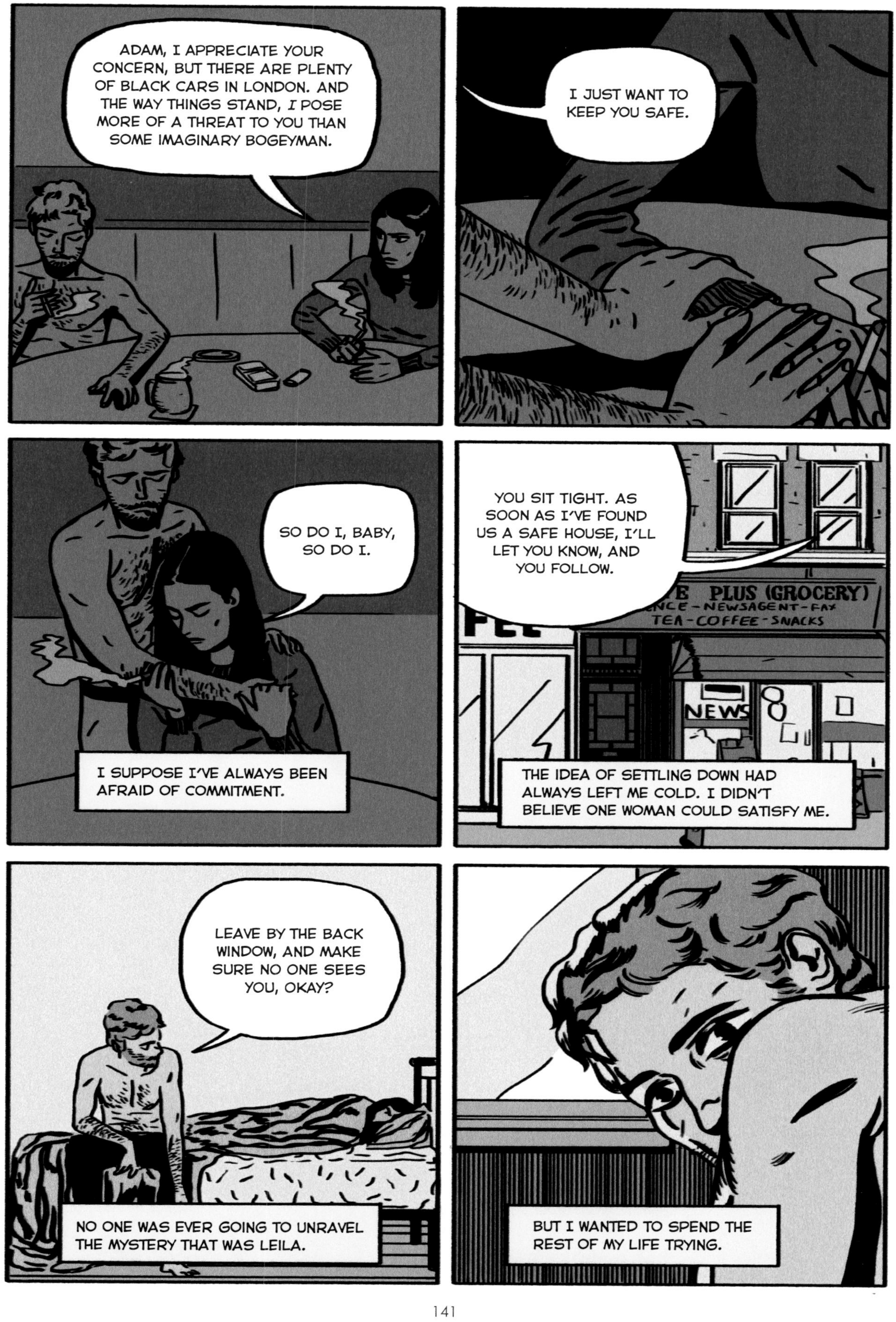
ADAM, I APPRECIATE YOUR CONCERN, BUT THERE ARE PLENTY OF BLACK CARS IN LONDON. AND THE WAY THINGS STAND, *I* POSE MORE OF A THREAT TO YOU THAN SOME IMAGINARY BOGEYMAN.
I JUST WANT TO KEEP YOU SAFE.
SO DO I, BABY, SO DO I.
I SUPPOSE I'VE ALWAYS BEEN AFRAID OF COMMITMENT.
YOU SIT TIGHT. AS SOON AS I'VE FOUND US A SAFE HOUSE, I'LL LET YOU KNOW, AND YOU FOLLOW.
PLUS (GROCERY)
NEWSAGENT-FAX
TEA-COFFEE-SNACKS
NEWS
THE IDEA OF SETTLING DOWN HAD ALWAYS LEFT ME COLD. I DIDN'T BELIEVE ONE WOMAN COULD SATISFY ME.
LEAVE BY THE BACK WINDOW, AND MAKE SURE NO ONE SEES YOU, OKAY?
NO ONE WAS EVER GOING TO UNRAVEL THE MYSTERY THAT WAS LEILA.
BUT I WANTED TO SPEND THE REST OF MY LIFE TRYING.

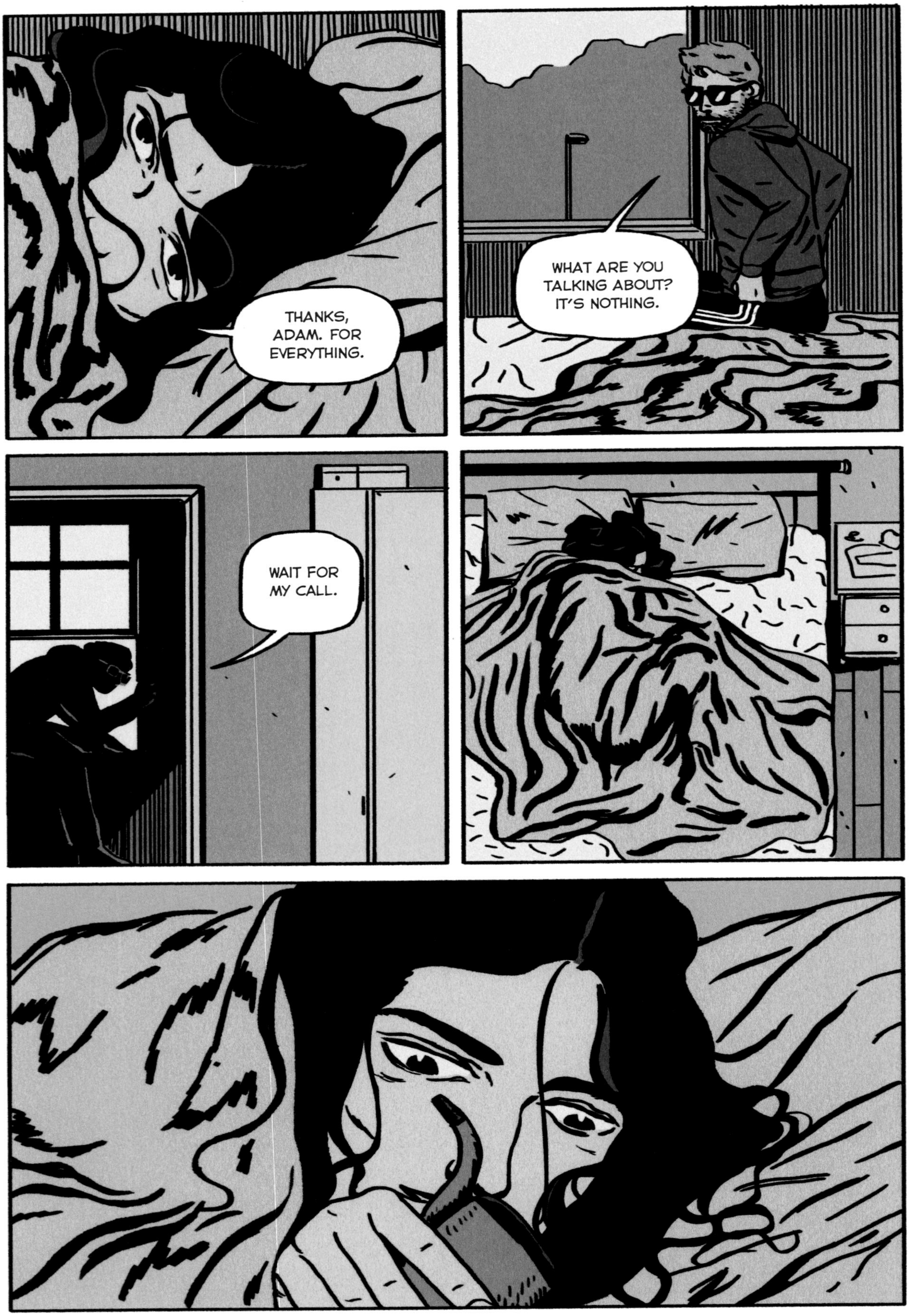
THANKS, ADAM. FOR EVERYTHING.
WHAT ARE YOU TALKING ABOUT? IT'S NOTHING.
WAIT FOR MY CALL.

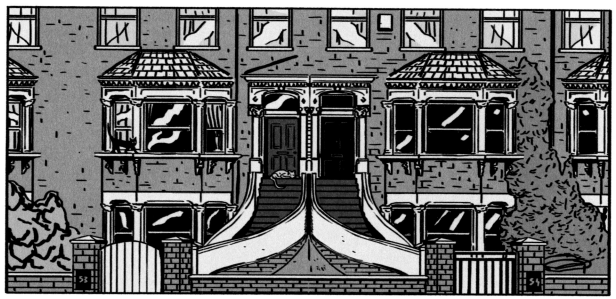

...'SMALL TOWN', OKAY, I'VE GOT THAT.

HUH?

LISTEN, MATE, ARE YOU SURE YOU'RE OKAY TO HELP WITH THIS?

YOU'RE ALREADY LATE HANDING IN YOUR MANUSCRIPT. LET'S DO THIS THING.

SURE, BUT I KNOW HOW WORRIED YOU'VE BEEN SINCE SHE TOOK OFF.

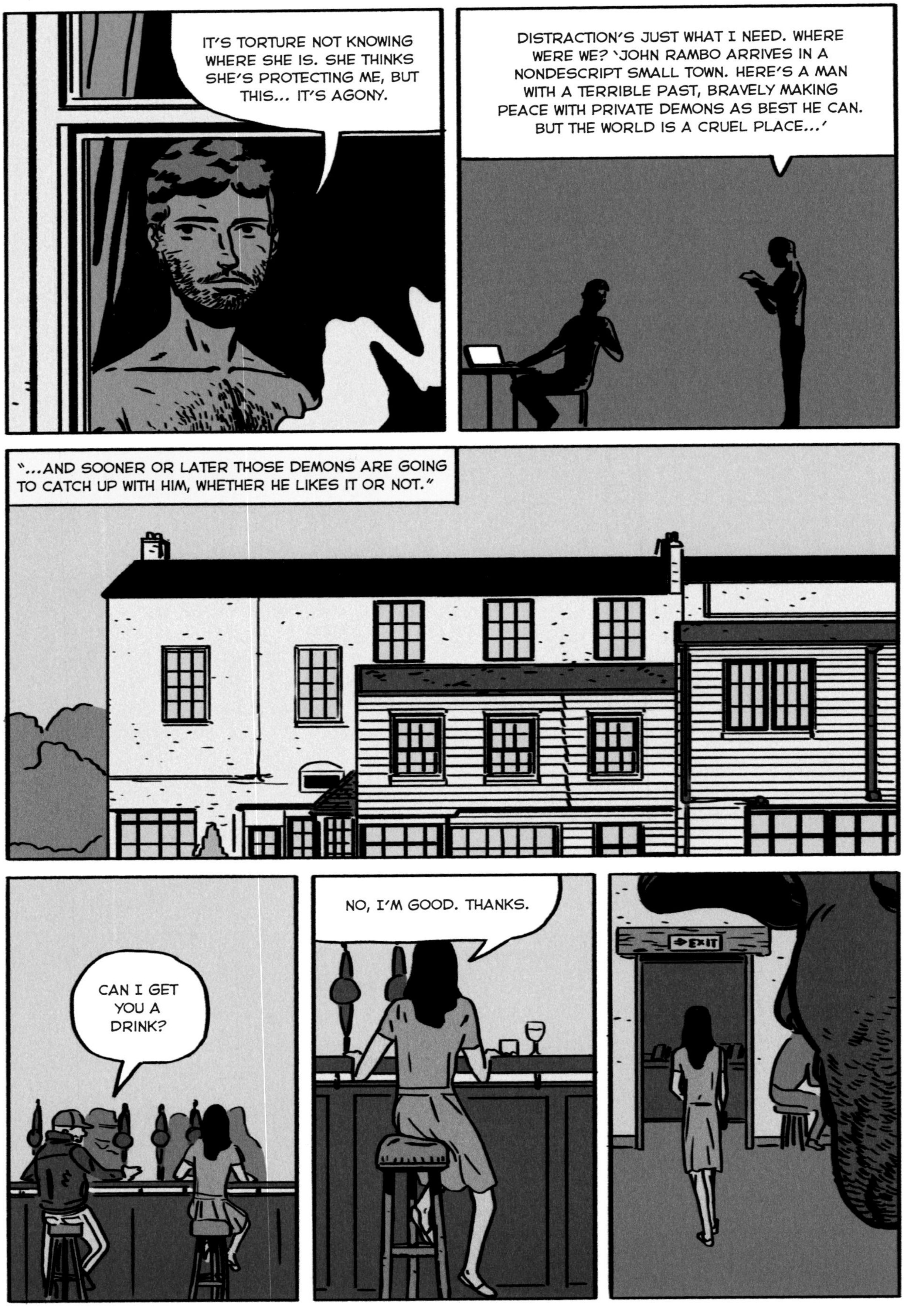
IT'S TORTURE NOT KNOWING WHERE SHE IS. SHE THINKS SHE'S PROTECTING ME, BUT THIS... IT'S AGONY.
DISTRACTION'S JUST WHAT I NEED. WHERE WERE WE? 'JOHN RAMBO ARRIVES IN A NONDESCRIPT SMALL TOWN. HERE'S A MAN WITH A TERRIBLE PAST, BRAVELY MAKING PEACE WITH PRIVATE DEMONS AS BEST HE CAN. BUT THE WORLD IS A CRUEL PLACE...'
"...AND SOONER OR LATER THOSE DEMONS ARE GOING TO CATCH UP WITH HIM, WHETHER HE LIKES IT OR NOT."
CAN I GET YOU A DRINK?
NO, I'M GOOD. THANKS.
EXIT

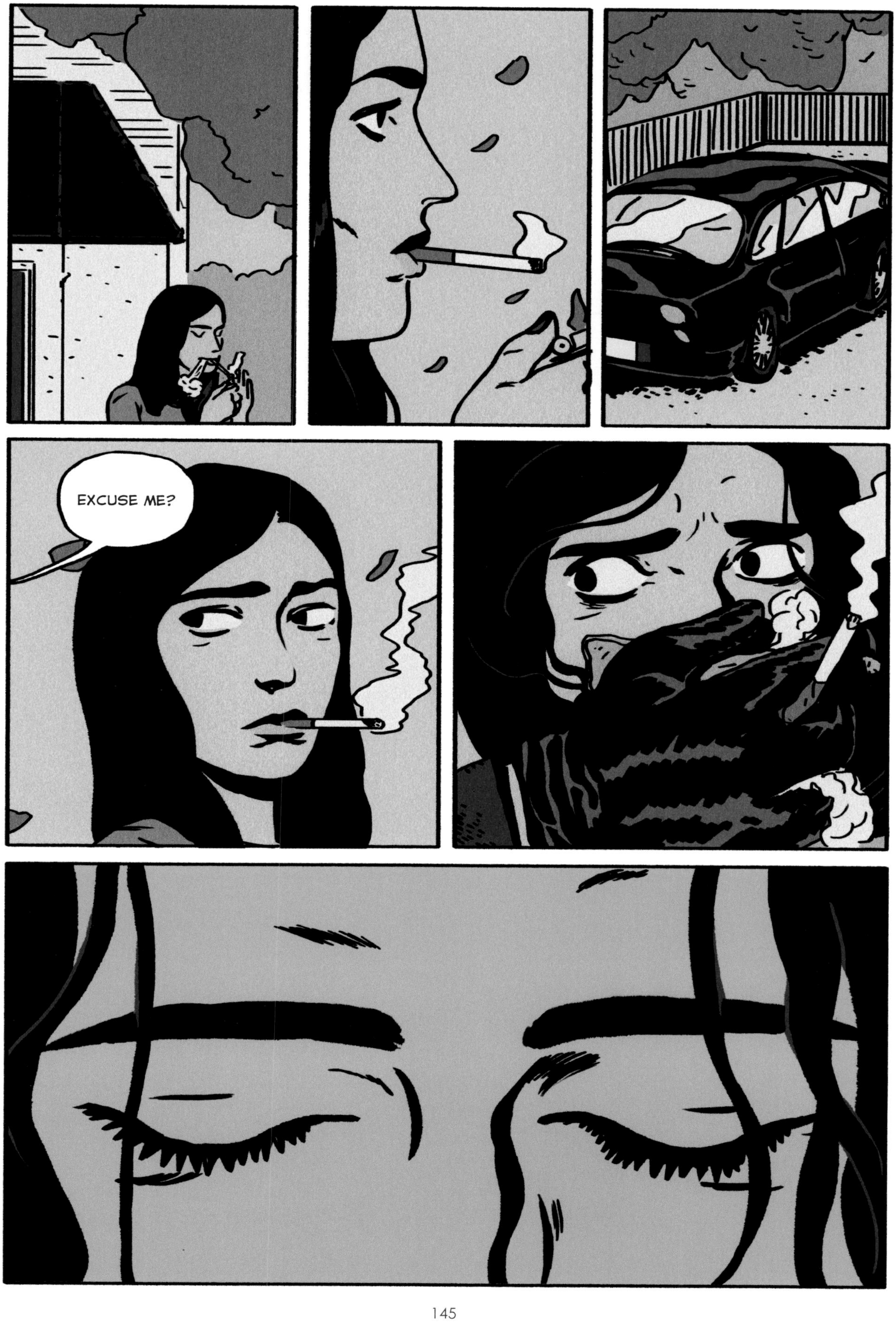
EXCUSE ME?

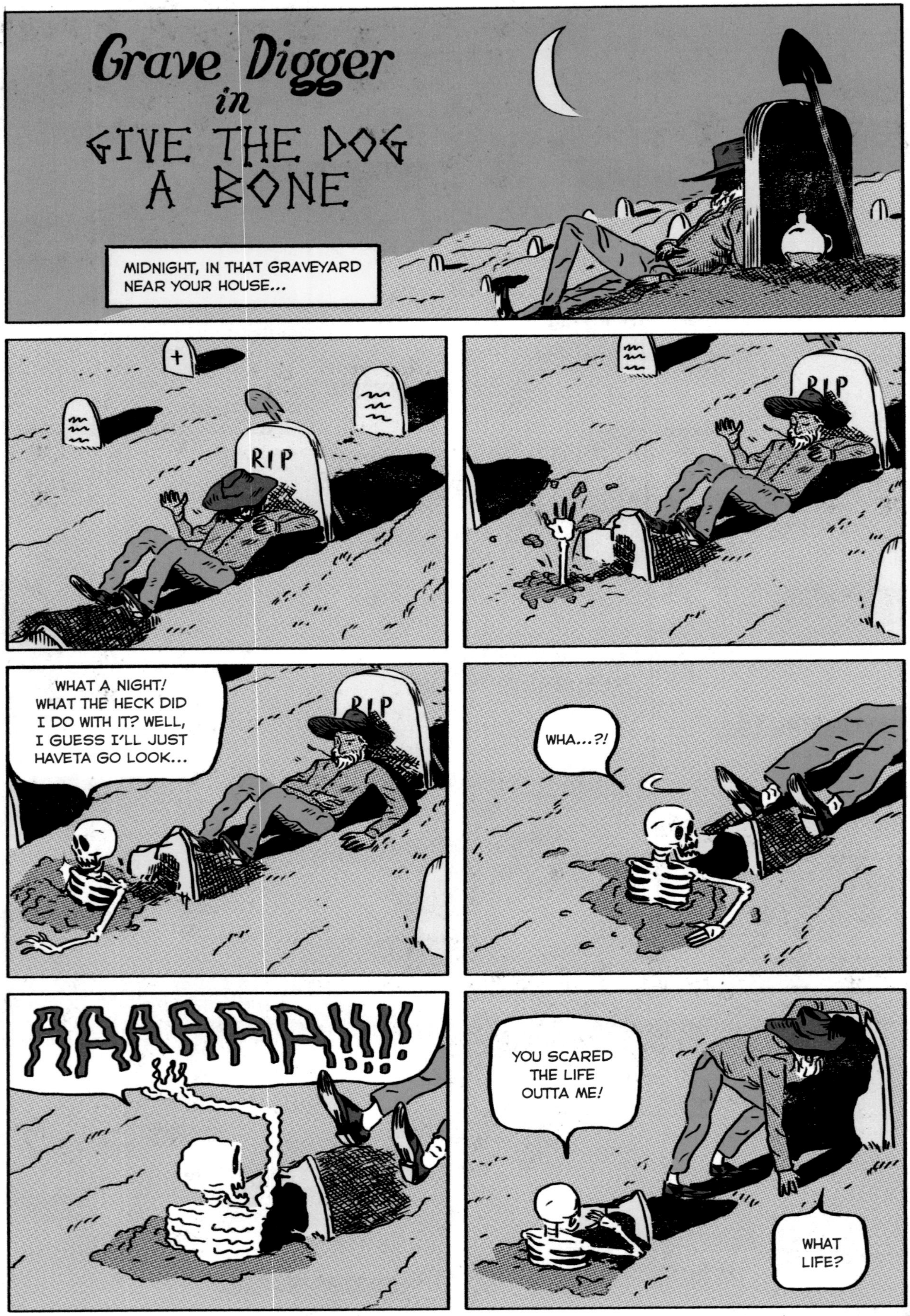
Grave Digger in
GIVE THE DOG A BONE
MIDNIGHT, IN THAT GRAVEYARD NEAR YOUR HOUSE...
RIP
RIP
WHAT A NIGHT! WHAT THE HECK DID I DO WITH IT? WELL, I GUESS I'LL JUST HAVETA GO LOOK...
WHA...?!
AAAAAA!!!!
YOU SCARED THE LIFE OUTTA ME!
WHAT LIFE?

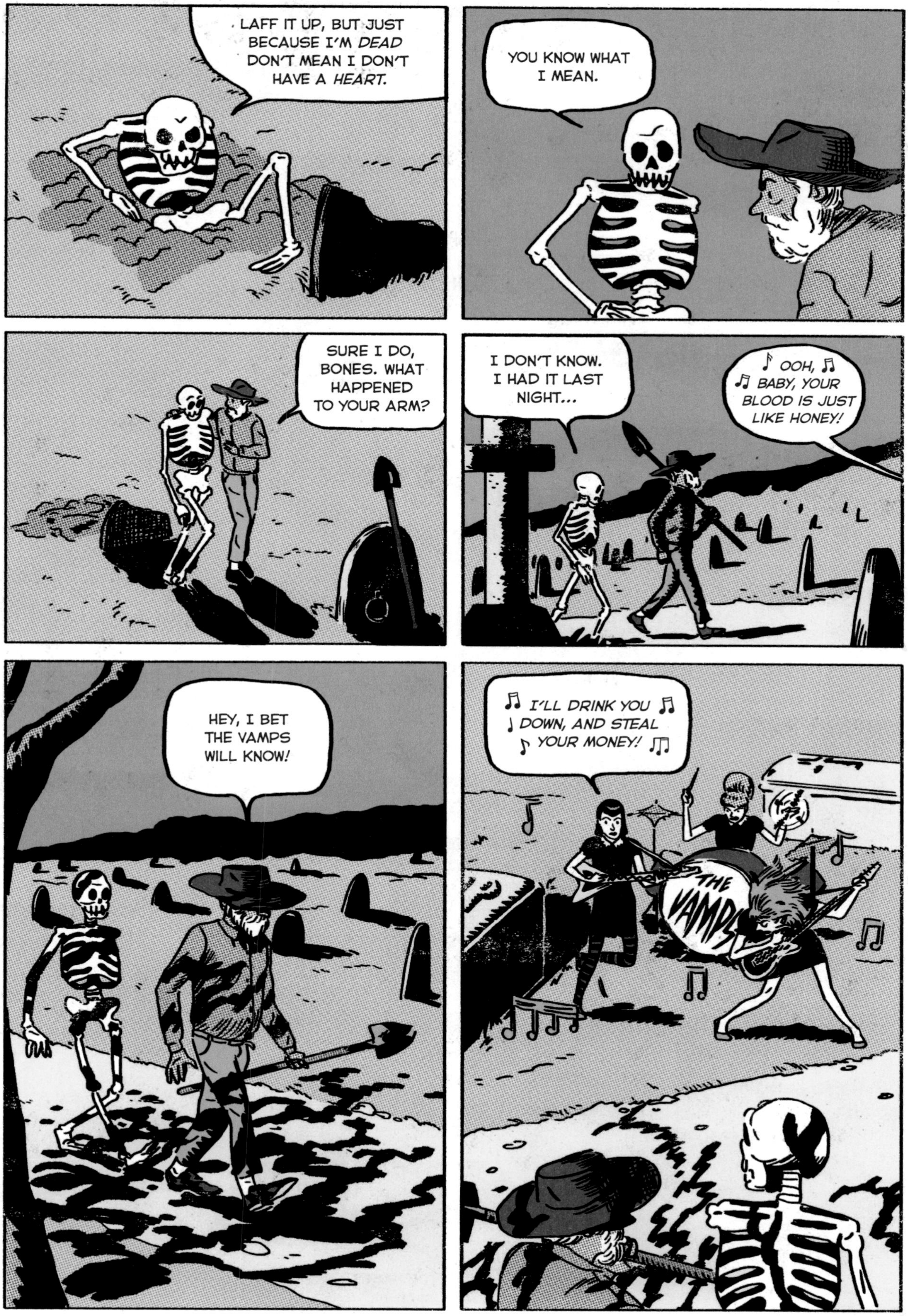
LAFF IT UP, BUT JUST BECAUSE I'M *DEAD* DON'T MEAN I DON'T HAVE A *HEART.*
YOU KNOW WHAT I MEAN.
SURE I DO, BONES. WHAT HAPPENED TO YOUR ARM?
I DON'T KNOW. I HAD IT LAST NIGHT...
♪ OOH, ♫ ♫ BABY, YOUR BLOOD IS JUST LIKE HONEY!
HEY, I BET THE VAMPS WILL KNOW!
♫ I'LL DRINK YOU ♫ ♩ DOWN, AND STEAL ♪ YOUR MONEY! ♫
THE VAMPS

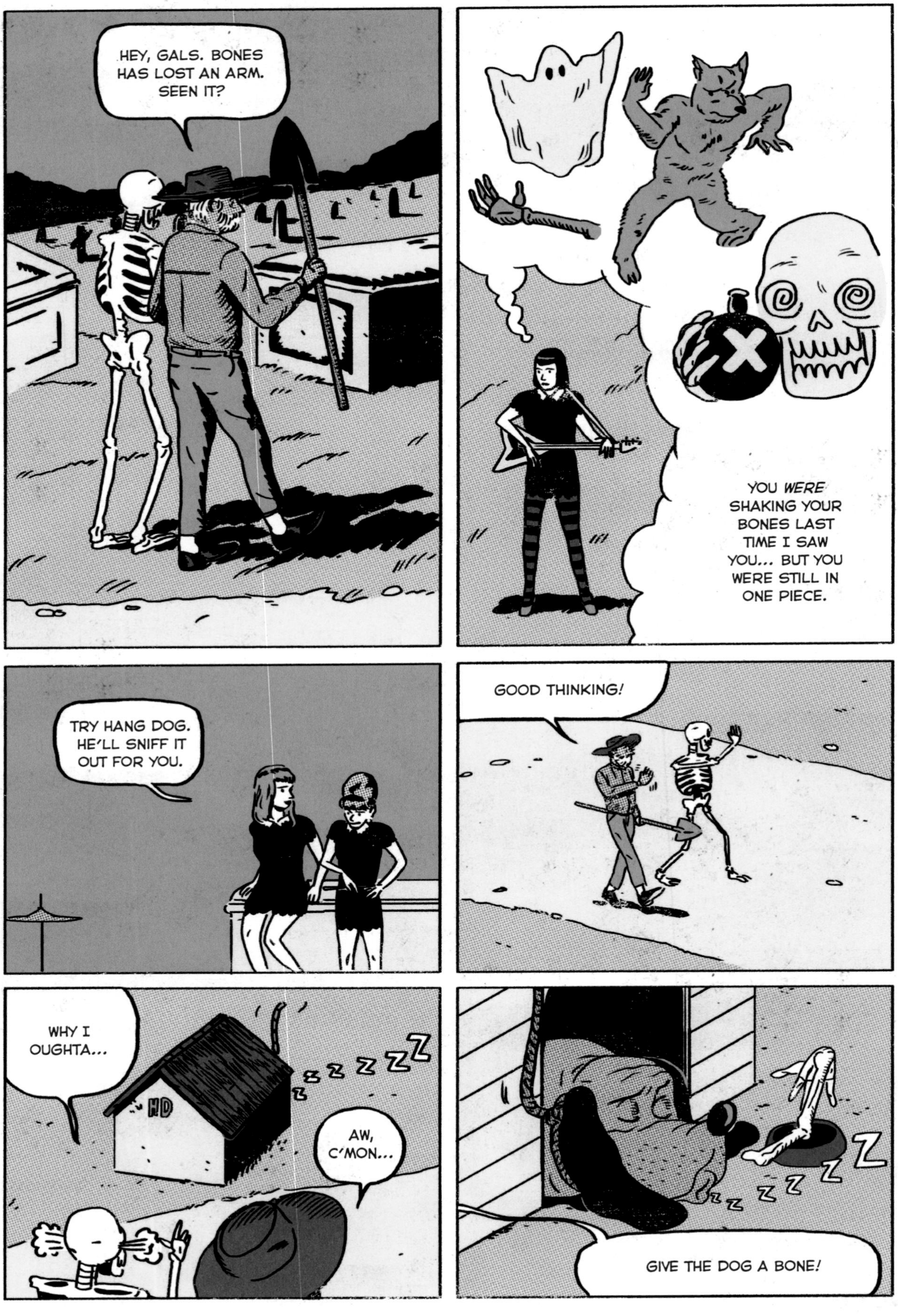
HEY, GALS. BONES HAS LOST AN ARM. SEEN IT?
YOU *WERE* SHAKING YOUR BONES LAST TIME I SAW YOU... BUT YOU WERE STILL IN ONE PIECE.
TRY HANG DOG. HE'LL SNIFF IT OUT FOR YOU.
GOOD THINKING!
WHY I OUGHTA...
HD
Z Z Z Z Z Z
AW, C'MON...
Z Z Z Z Z Z
GIVE THE DOG A BONE!

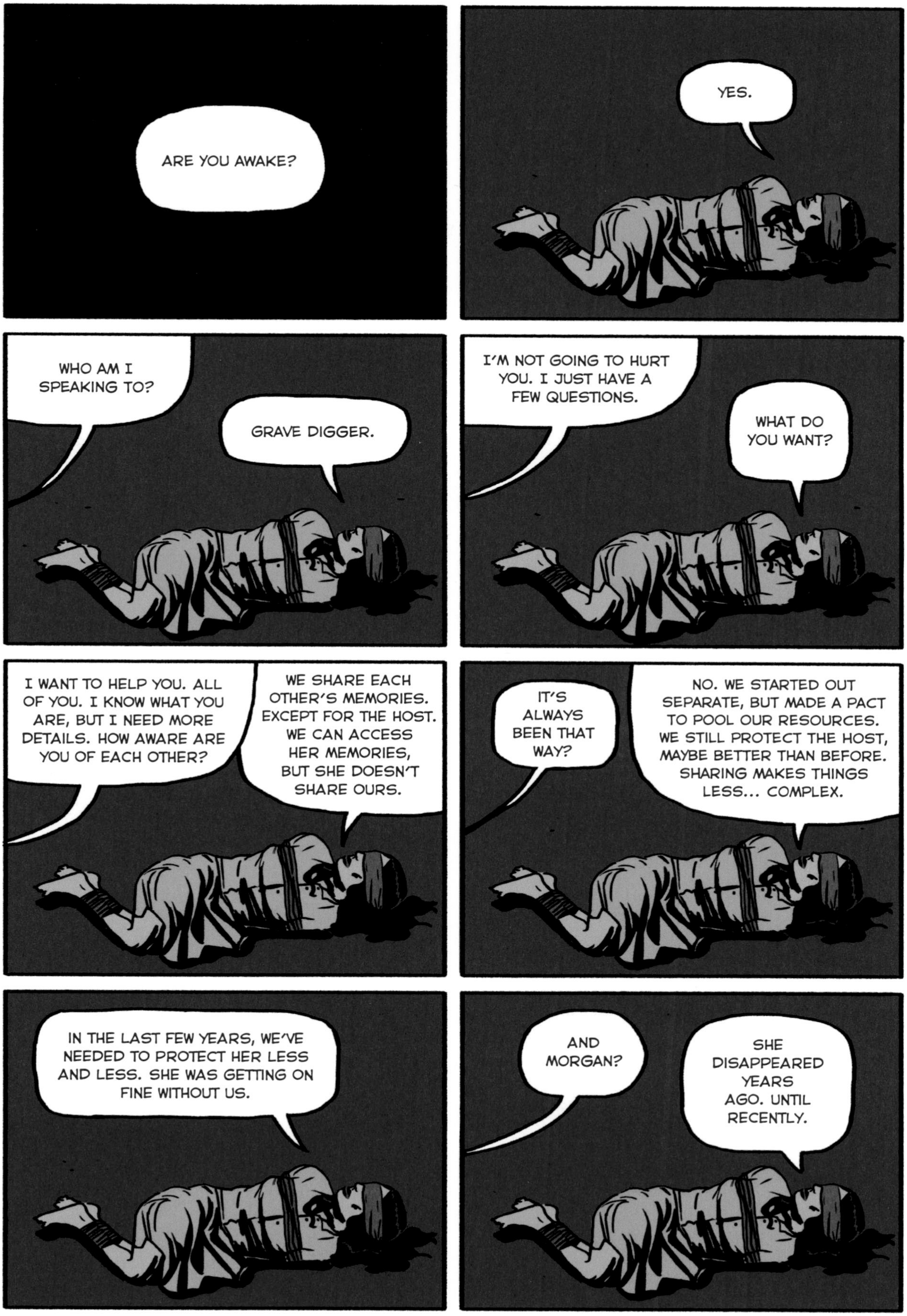
ARE YOU AWAKE?
YES.
WHO AM I SPEAKING TO?
GRAVE DIGGER.
I'M NOT GOING TO HURT YOU. I JUST HAVE A FEW QUESTIONS.
WHAT DO YOU WANT?
I WANT TO HELP YOU. ALL OF YOU. I KNOW WHAT YOU ARE, BUT I NEED MORE DETAILS. HOW AWARE ARE YOU OF EACH OTHER?
WE SHARE EACH OTHER'S MEMORIES. EXCEPT FOR THE HOST. WE CAN ACCESS HER MEMORIES, BUT SHE DOESN'T SHARE OURS.
IT'S ALWAYS BEEN THAT WAY?
NO. WE STARTED OUT SEPARATE, BUT MADE A PACT TO POOL OUR RESOURCES. WE STILL PROTECT THE HOST, MAYBE BETTER THAN BEFORE. SHARING MAKES THINGS LESS... COMPLEX.
IN THE LAST FEW YEARS, WE'VE NEEDED TO PROTECT HER LESS AND LESS. SHE WAS GETTING ON FINE WITHOUT US.
AND MORGAN?
SHE DISAPPEARED YEARS AGO. UNTIL RECENTLY.

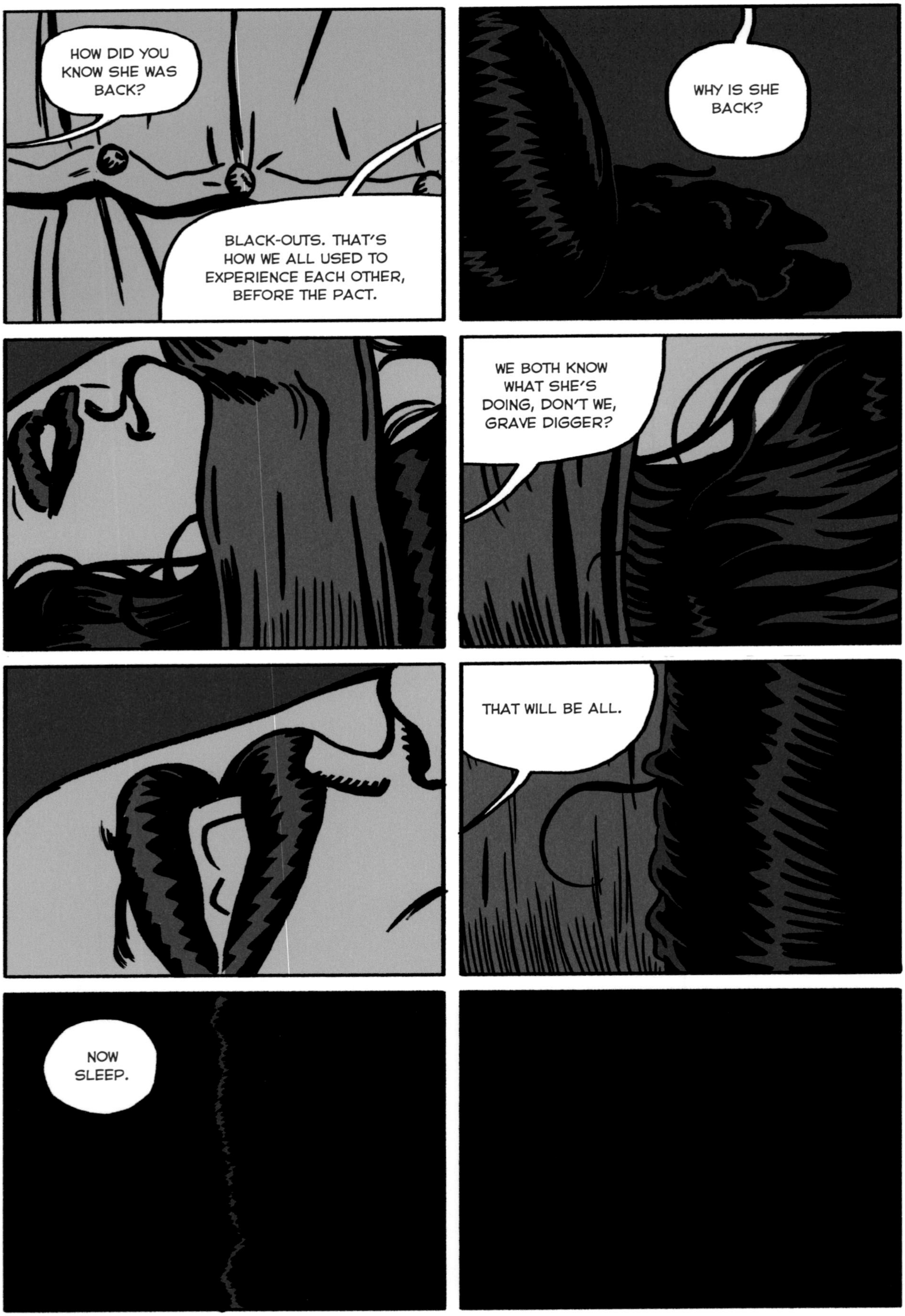
HOW DID YOU KNOW SHE WAS BACK?
BLACK-OUTS. THAT'S HOW WE ALL USED TO EXPERIENCE EACH OTHER, BEFORE THE PACT.
WHY IS SHE BACK?
WE BOTH KNOW WHAT SHE'S DOING, DON'T WE, GRAVE DIGGER?
THAT WILL BE ALL.
NOW SLEEP.

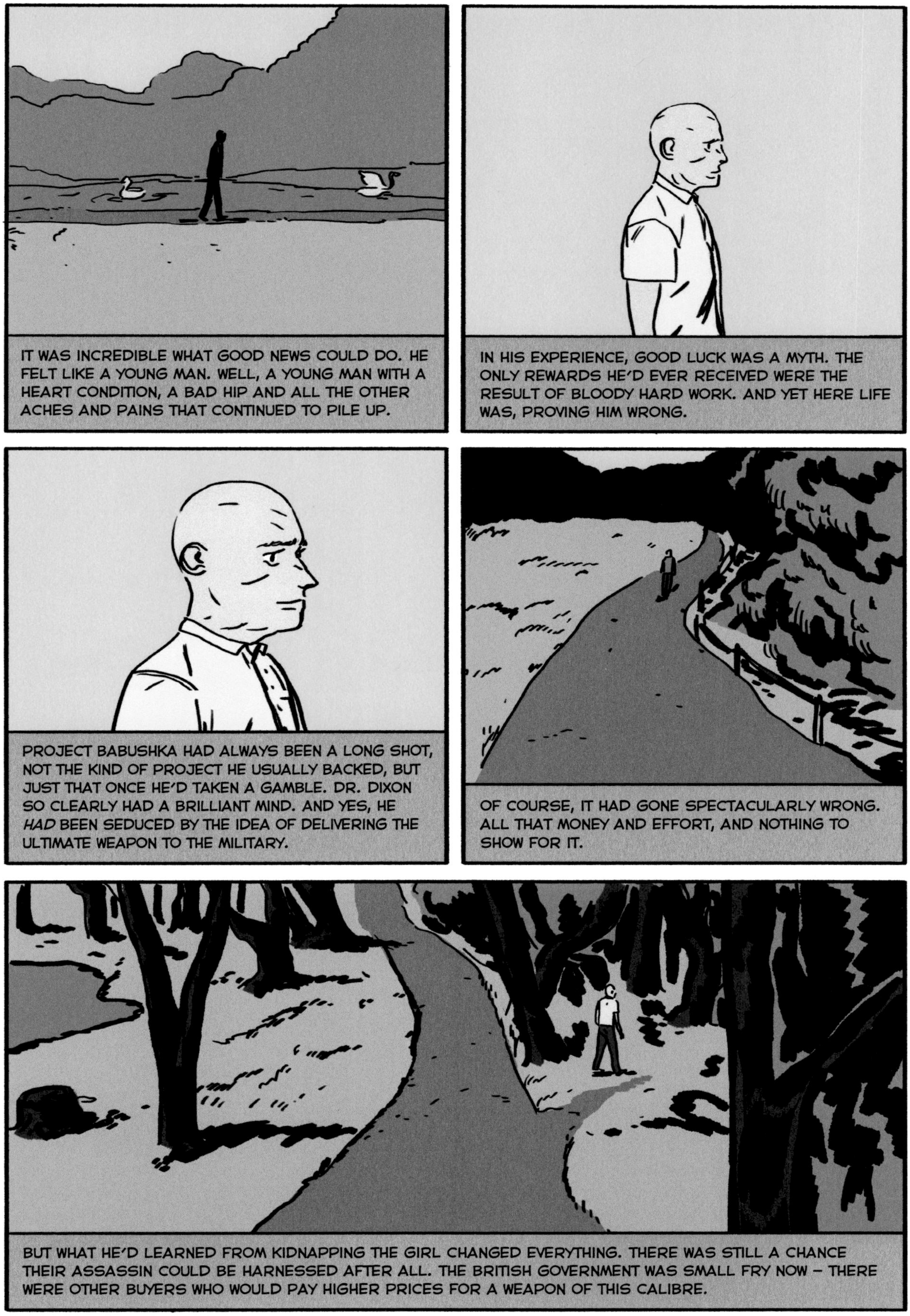
IT WAS INCREDIBLE WHAT GOOD NEWS COULD DO. HE FELT LIKE A YOUNG MAN. WELL, A YOUNG MAN WITH A HEART CONDITION, A BAD HIP AND ALL THE OTHER ACHES AND PAINS THAT CONTINUED TO PILE UP.
IN HIS EXPERIENCE, GOOD LUCK WAS A MYTH. THE ONLY REWARDS HE'D EVER RECEIVED WERE THE RESULT OF BLOODY HARD WORK. AND YET HERE LIFE WAS, PROVING HIM WRONG.
PROJECT BABUSHKA HAD ALWAYS BEEN A LONG SHOT, NOT THE KIND OF PROJECT HE USUALLY BACKED, BUT JUST THAT ONCE HE'D TAKEN A GAMBLE. DR. DIXON SO CLEARLY HAD A BRILLIANT MIND. AND YES, HE *HAD* BEEN SEDUCED BY THE IDEA OF DELIVERING THE ULTIMATE WEAPON TO THE MILITARY.
OF COURSE, IT HAD GONE SPECTACULARLY WRONG. ALL THAT MONEY AND EFFORT, AND NOTHING TO SHOW FOR IT.
BUT WHAT HE'D LEARNED FROM KIDNAPPING THE GIRL CHANGED EVERYTHING. THERE WAS STILL A CHANCE THEIR ASSASSIN COULD BE HARNESSED AFTER ALL. THE BRITISH GOVERNMENT WAS SMALL FRY NOW – THERE WERE OTHER BUYERS WHO WOULD PAY HIGHER PRICES FOR A WEAPON OF THIS CALIBRE.

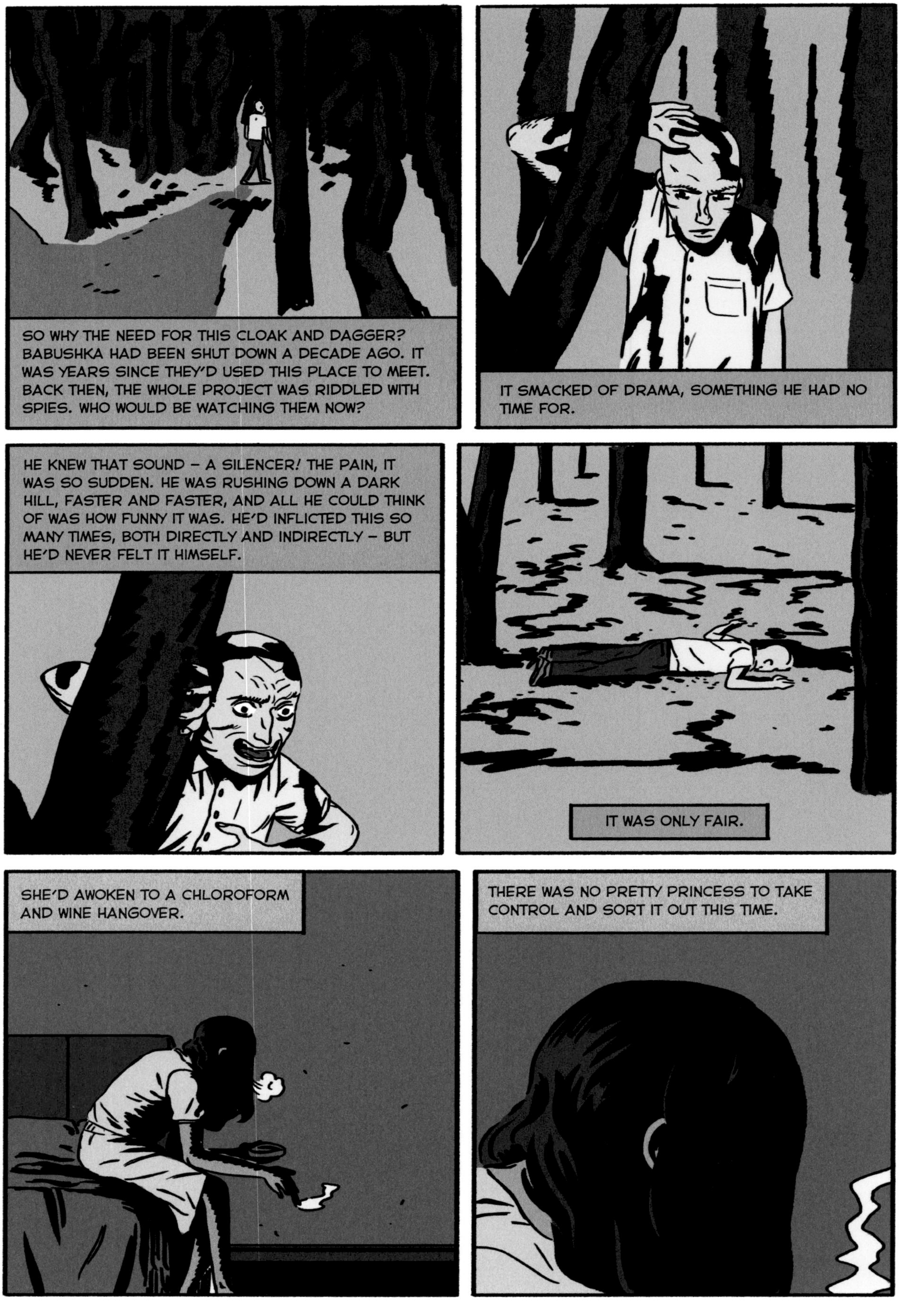
SO WHY THE NEED FOR THIS CLOAK AND DAGGER? BABUSHKA HAD BEEN SHUT DOWN A DECADE AGO. IT WAS YEARS SINCE THEY'D USED THIS PLACE TO MEET. BACK THEN, THE WHOLE PROJECT WAS RIDDLED WITH SPIES. WHO WOULD BE WATCHING THEM NOW?
IT SMACKED OF DRAMA, SOMETHING HE HAD NO TIME FOR.
HE KNEW THAT SOUND – A SILENCER! THE PAIN, IT WAS SO SUDDEN. HE WAS RUSHING DOWN A DARK HILL, FASTER AND FASTER, AND ALL HE COULD THINK OF WAS HOW FUNNY IT WAS. HE'D INFLICTED THIS SO MANY TIMES, BOTH DIRECTLY AND INDIRECTLY – BUT HE'D NEVER FELT IT HIMSELF.
IT WAS ONLY FAIR.
SHE'D AWOKEN TO A CHLOROFORM AND WINE HANGOVER.
THERE WAS NO PRETTY PRINCESS TO TAKE CONTROL AND SORT IT OUT THIS TIME.

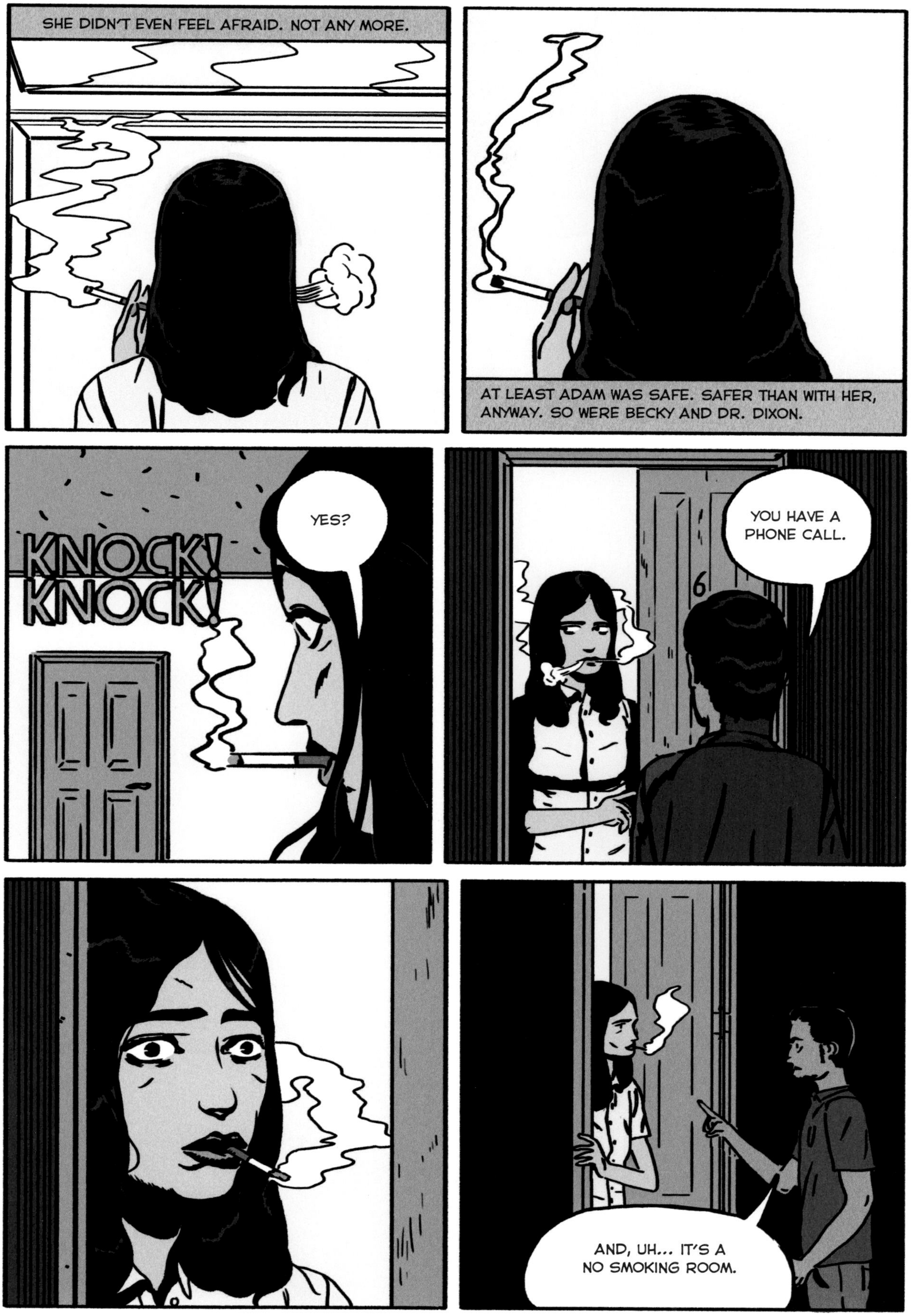
SHE DIDN'T EVEN FEEL AFRAID. NOT ANY MORE.
AT LEAST ADAM WAS SAFE. SAFER THAN WITH HER, ANYWAY. SO WERE BECKY AND DR. DIXON.
KNOCK! KNOCK!
YES?
6
YOU HAVE A PHONE CALL.
AND, UH... IT'S A NO SMOKING ROOM.

HELLO...?

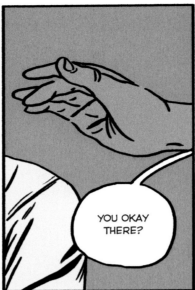

YOU OKAY THERE?

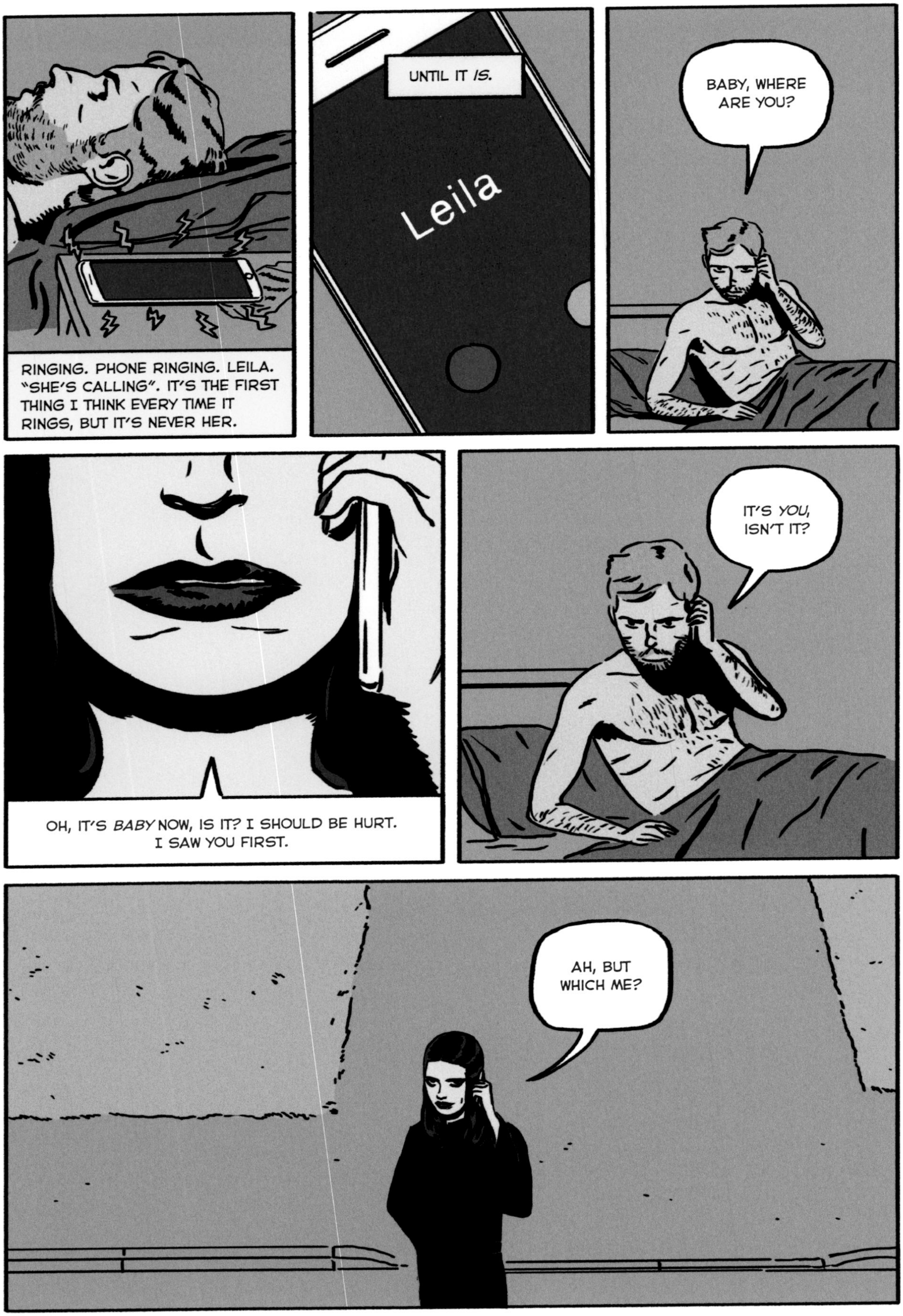
RINGING. PHONE RINGING. LEILA. "SHE'S CALLING". IT'S THE FIRST THING I THINK EVERY TIME IT RINGS, BUT IT'S NEVER HER.
UNTIL IT *IS*.
Leila
BABY, WHERE ARE YOU?
OH, IT'S *BABY* NOW, IS IT? I SHOULD BE HURT. I SAW YOU FIRST.
IT'S *YOU*, ISN'T IT?
AH, BUT WHICH ME?

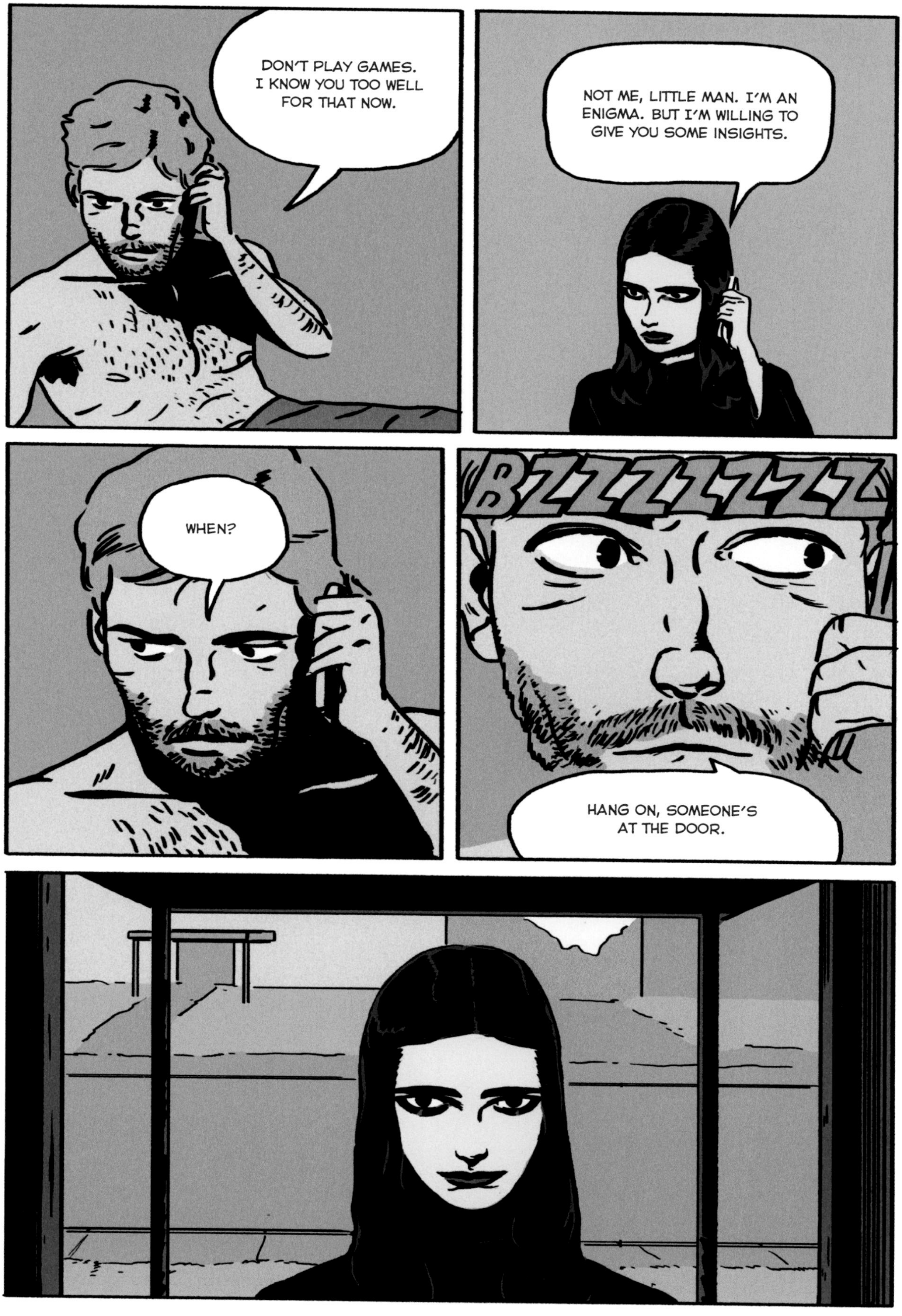
DON'T PLAY GAMES. I KNOW YOU TOO WELL FOR THAT NOW.
NOT ME, LITTLE MAN. I'M AN ENIGMA. BUT I'M WILLING TO GIVE YOU SOME INSIGHTS.
WHEN?
BZZZZZZZZ
HANG ON, SOMEONE'S AT THE DOOR.

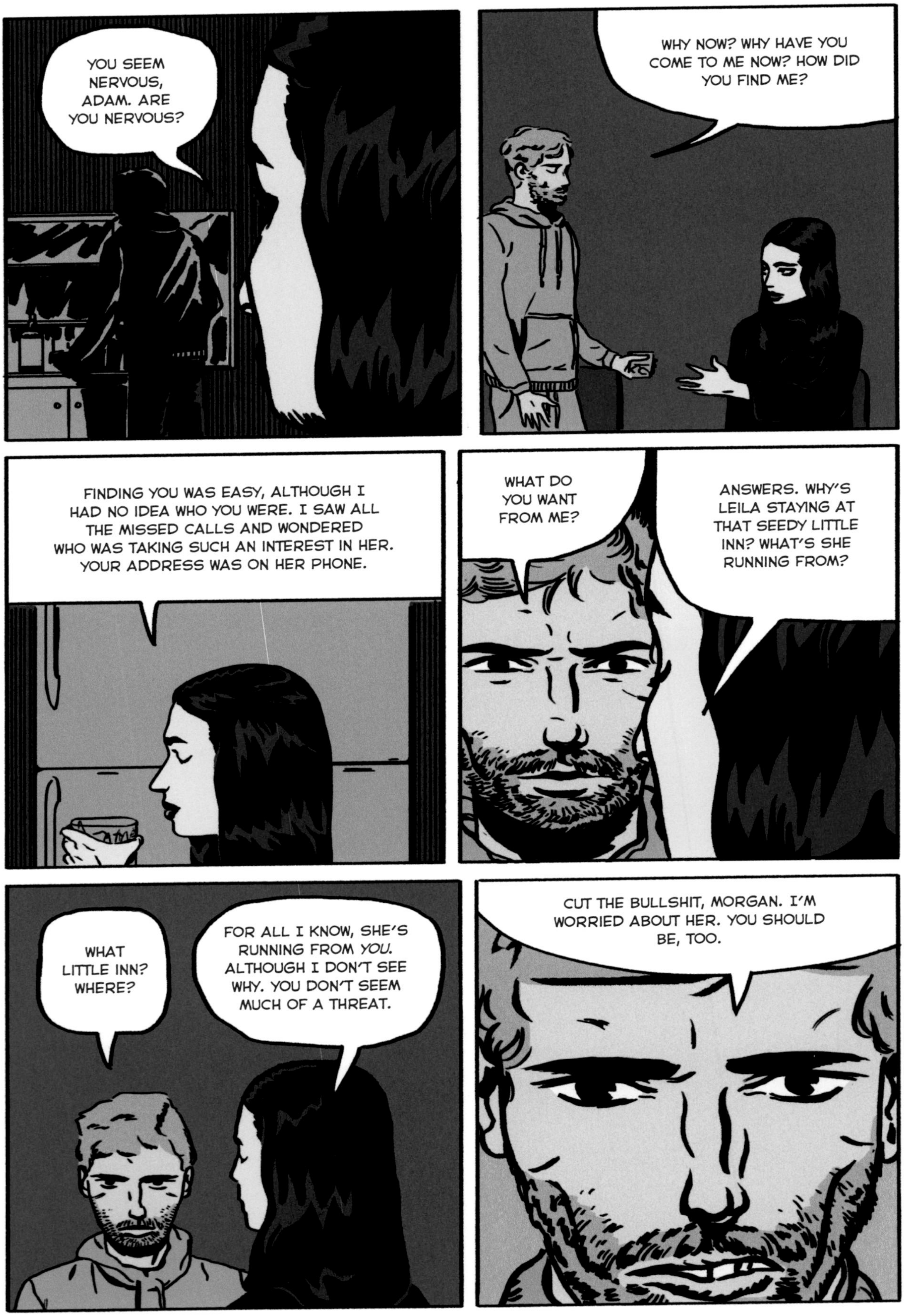
YOU SEEM NERVOUS, ADAM. ARE YOU NERVOUS?
WHY NOW? WHY HAVE YOU COME TO ME NOW? HOW DID YOU FIND ME?
FINDING YOU WAS EASY, ALTHOUGH I HAD NO IDEA WHO YOU WERE. I SAW ALL THE MISSED CALLS AND WONDERED WHO WAS TAKING SUCH AN INTEREST IN HER. YOUR ADDRESS WAS ON HER PHONE.
WHAT DO YOU WANT FROM ME?
ANSWERS. WHY'S LEILA STAYING AT THAT SEEDY LITTLE INN? WHAT'S SHE RUNNING FROM?
WHAT LITTLE INN? WHERE?
FOR ALL I KNOW, SHE'S RUNNING FROM *YOU*. ALTHOUGH I DON'T SEE WHY. YOU DON'T SEEM MUCH OF A THREAT.
CUT THE BULLSHIT, MORGAN. I'M WORRIED ABOUT HER. YOU SHOULD BE, TOO.

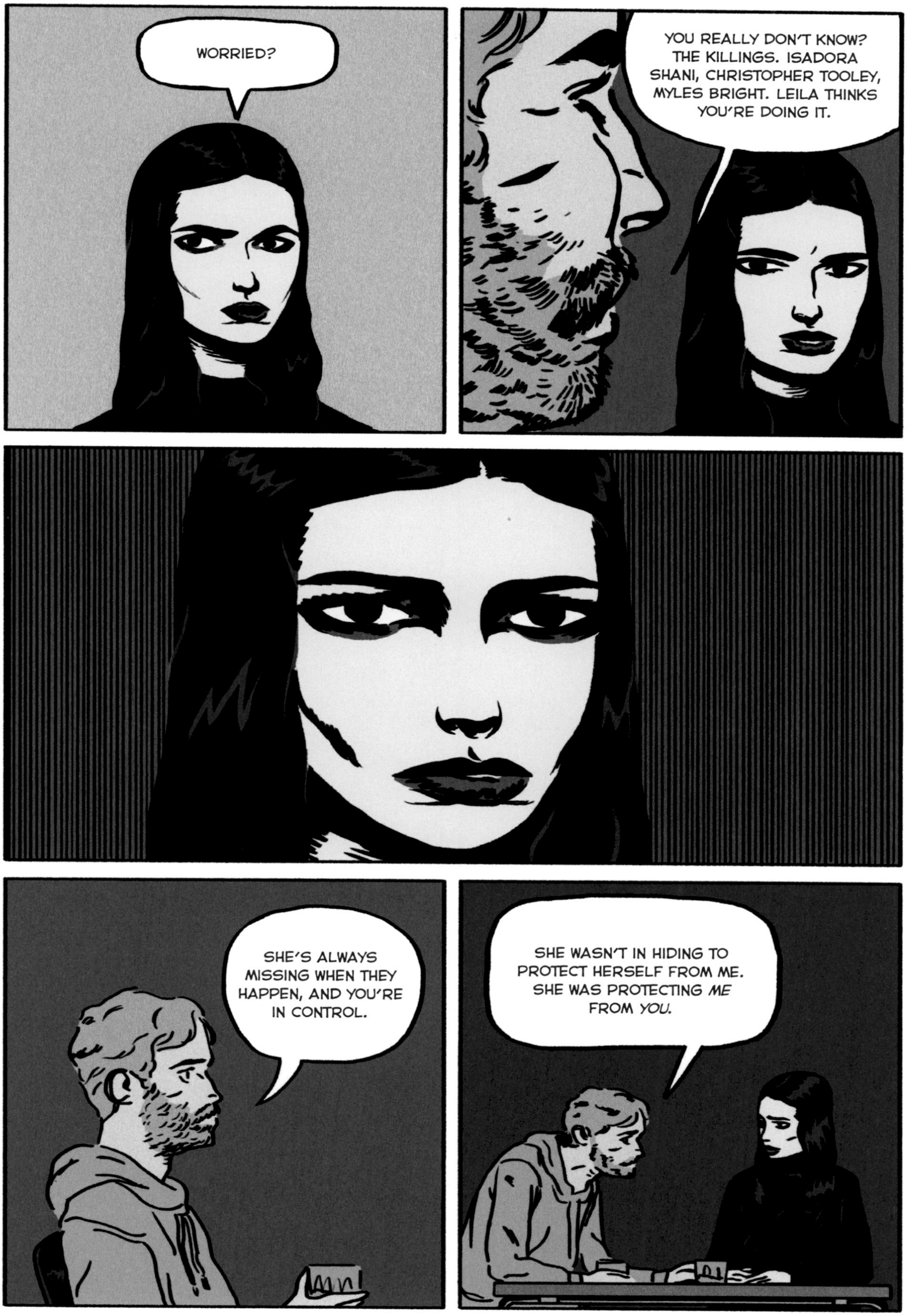
WORRIED?
YOU REALLY DON'T KNOW? THE KILLINGS. ISADORA SHANI, CHRISTOPHER TOOLEY, MYLES BRIGHT. LEILA THINKS YOU'RE DOING IT.
SHE'S ALWAYS MISSING WHEN THEY HAPPEN, AND YOU'RE IN CONTROL.
SHE WASN'T IN HIDING TO PROTECT HERSELF FROM ME. SHE WAS PROTECTING *ME* FROM *YOU*.

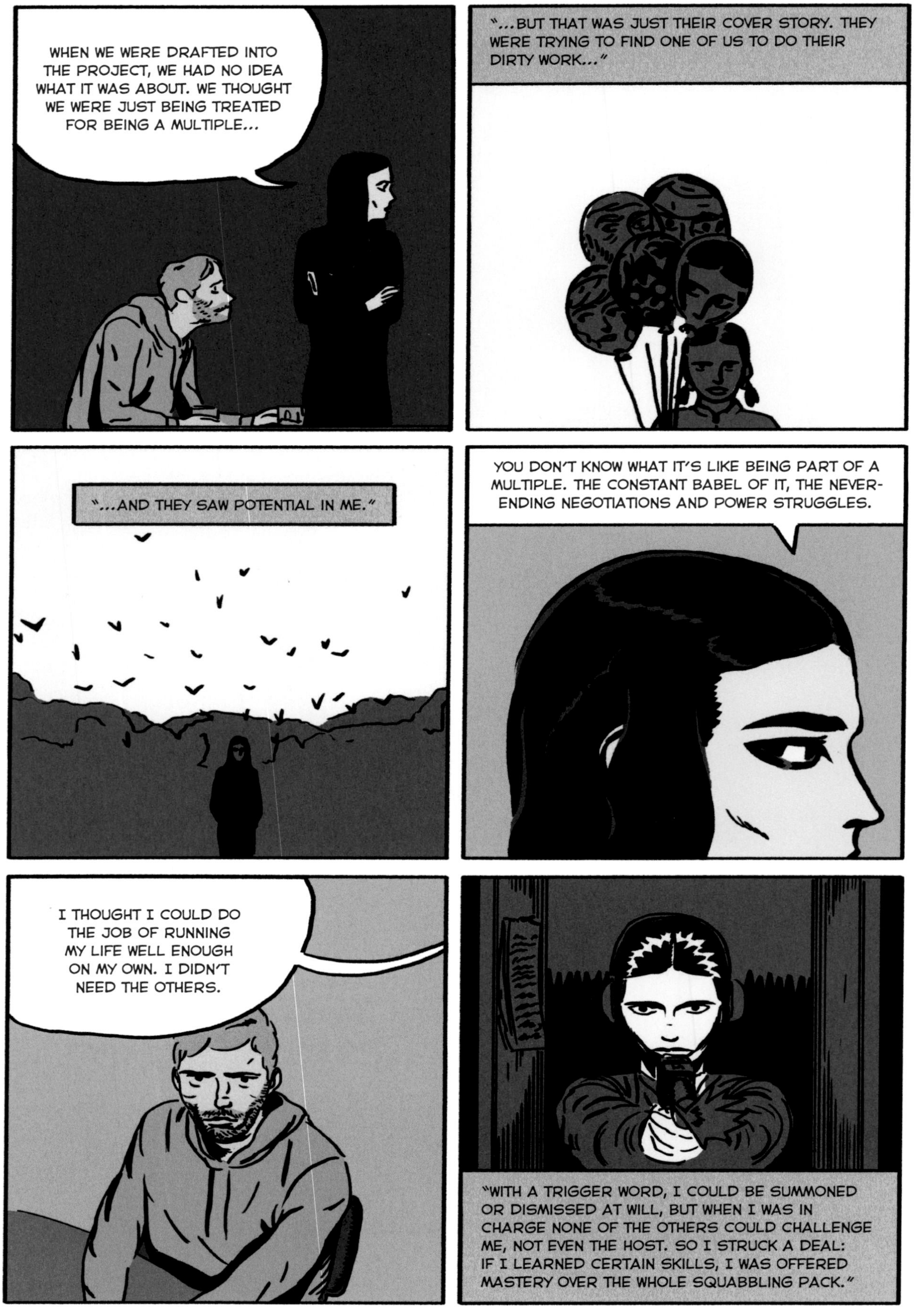

WHEN WE WERE DRAFTED INTO THE PROJECT, WE HAD NO IDEA WHAT IT WAS ABOUT. WE THOUGHT WE WERE JUST BEING TREATED FOR BEING A MULTIPLE...
"...BUT THAT WAS JUST THEIR COVER STORY. THEY WERE TRYING TO FIND ONE OF US TO DO THEIR DIRTY WORK..."
"...AND THEY SAW POTENTIAL IN ME."
YOU DON'T KNOW WHAT IT'S LIKE BEING PART OF A MULTIPLE. THE CONSTANT BABEL OF IT, THE NEVER-ENDING NEGOTIATIONS AND POWER STRUGGLES.
I THOUGHT I COULD DO THE JOB OF RUNNING MY LIFE WELL ENOUGH ON MY OWN. I DIDN'T NEED THE OTHERS.
"WITH A TRIGGER WORD, I COULD BE SUMMONED OR DISMISSED AT WILL, BUT WHEN I WAS IN CHARGE NONE OF THE OTHERS COULD CHALLENGE ME, NOT EVEN THE HOST. SO I STRUCK A DEAL: IF I LEARNED CERTAIN SKILLS, I WAS OFFERED MASTERY OVER THE WHOLE SQUABBLING PACK."

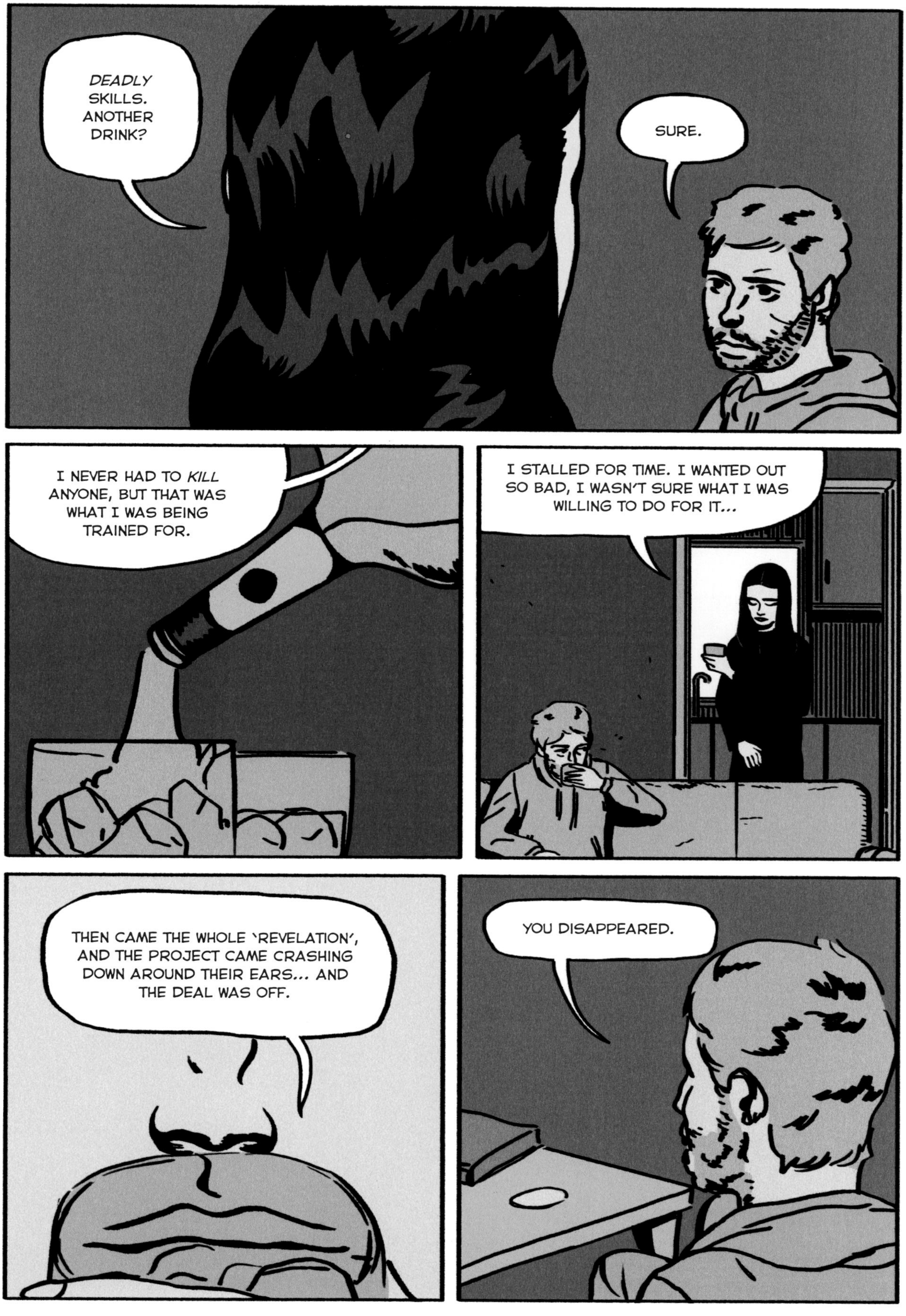
DEADLY SKILLS. ANOTHER DRINK?
SURE.
I NEVER HAD TO *KILL* ANYONE, BUT THAT WAS WHAT I WAS BEING TRAINED FOR.
I STALLED FOR TIME. I WANTED OUT SO BAD, I WASN'T SURE WHAT I WAS WILLING TO DO FOR IT...
THEN CAME THE WHOLE 'REVELATION', AND THE PROJECT CAME CRASHING DOWN AROUND THEIR EARS... AND THE DEAL WAS OFF.
YOU DISAPPEARED.

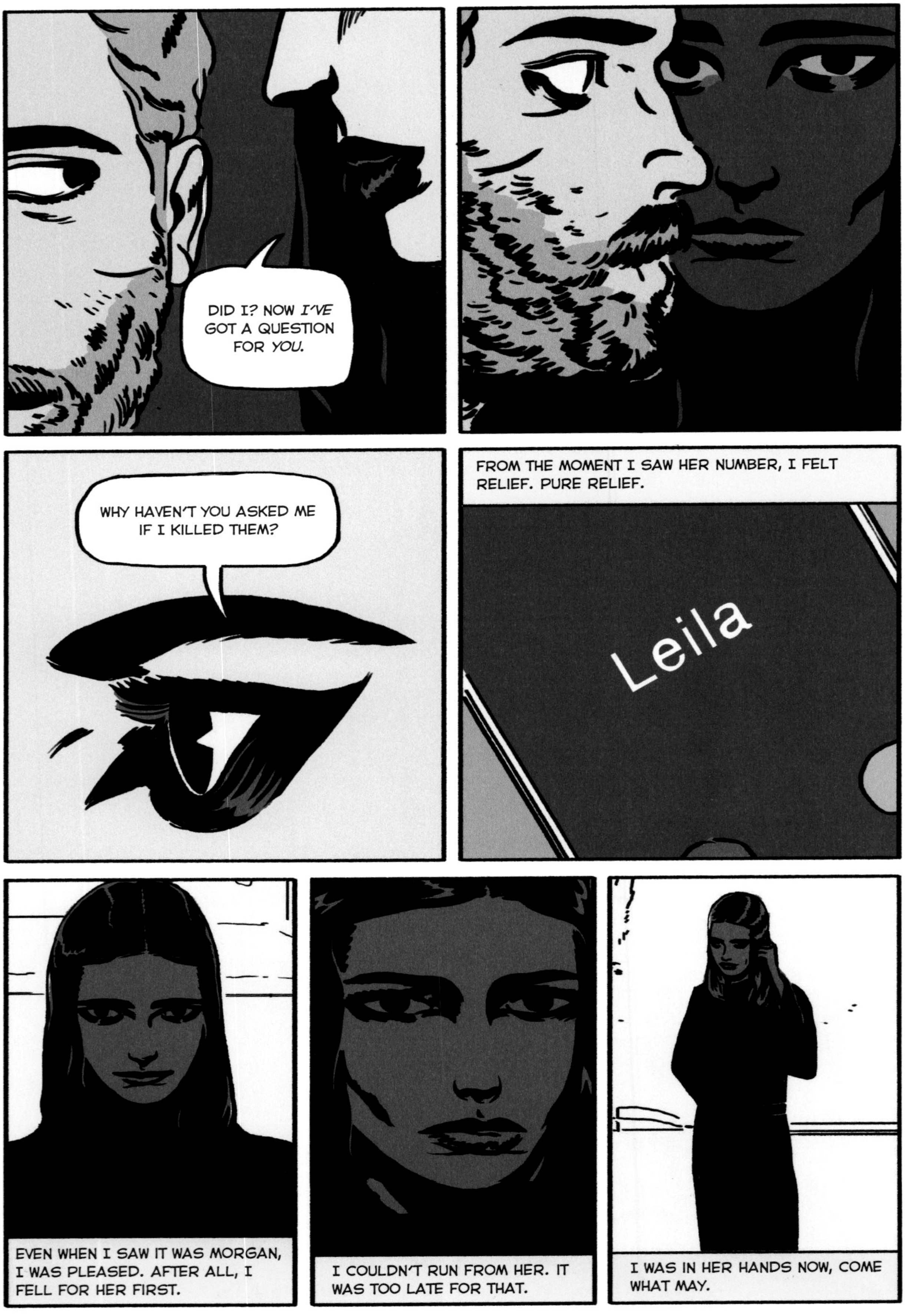
DID I? NOW I'VE GOT A QUESTION FOR YOU.
WHY HAVEN'T YOU ASKED ME IF I KILLED THEM?
FROM THE MOMENT I SAW HER NUMBER, I FELT RELIEF. PURE RELIEF.
Leila
EVEN WHEN I SAW IT WAS MORGAN, I WAS PLEASED. AFTER ALL, I FELL FOR HER FIRST.
I COULDN'T RUN FROM HER. IT WAS TOO LATE FOR THAT.
I WAS IN HER HANDS NOW, COME WHAT MAY.

I TRUST YOU.

SHE WAS SO DIFFERENT FROM LEILA, THE SMELL OF HER, THE AGGRESSIVE HUNGER...

I MET HER WITH ANOTHER ME...

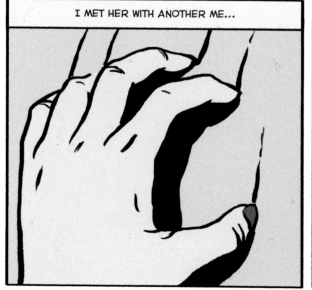

...ONE THAT COULD MATCH HER FEROCITY.

AFTERWARDS, SLEEP DRAGGED ME DOWN LIKE A POWERFUL UNDERTOW.

YOU'VE DRUGGED ME.

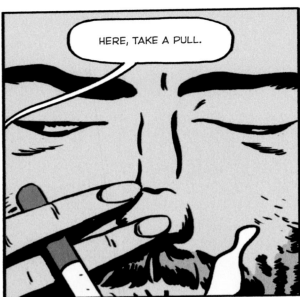

HERE, TAKE A PULL.

WHAT ARE YOU GOING TO DO?

WHAT I HAVE TO. GOODBYE, ADAM.

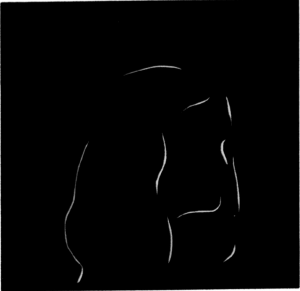

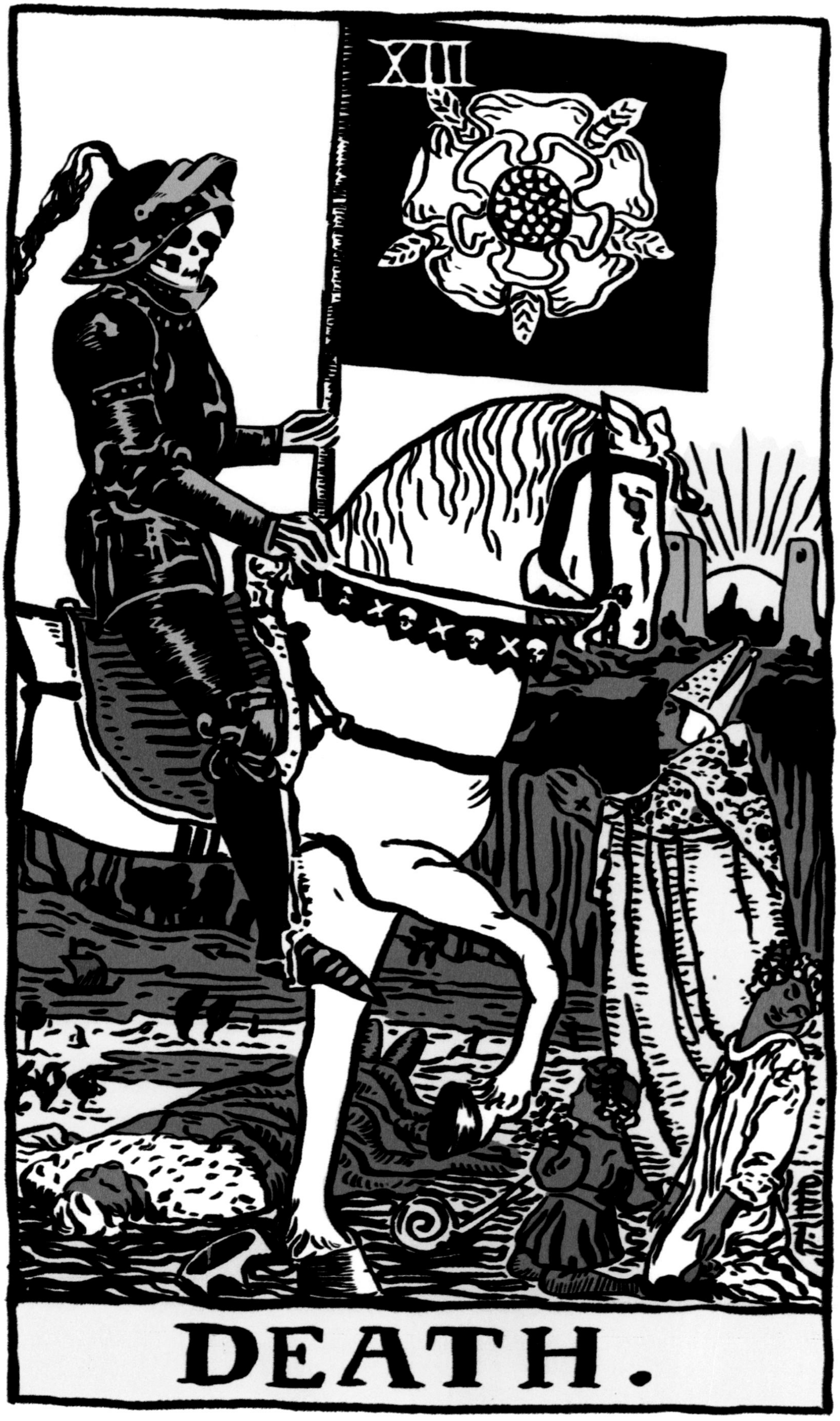
XIII

DEATH.

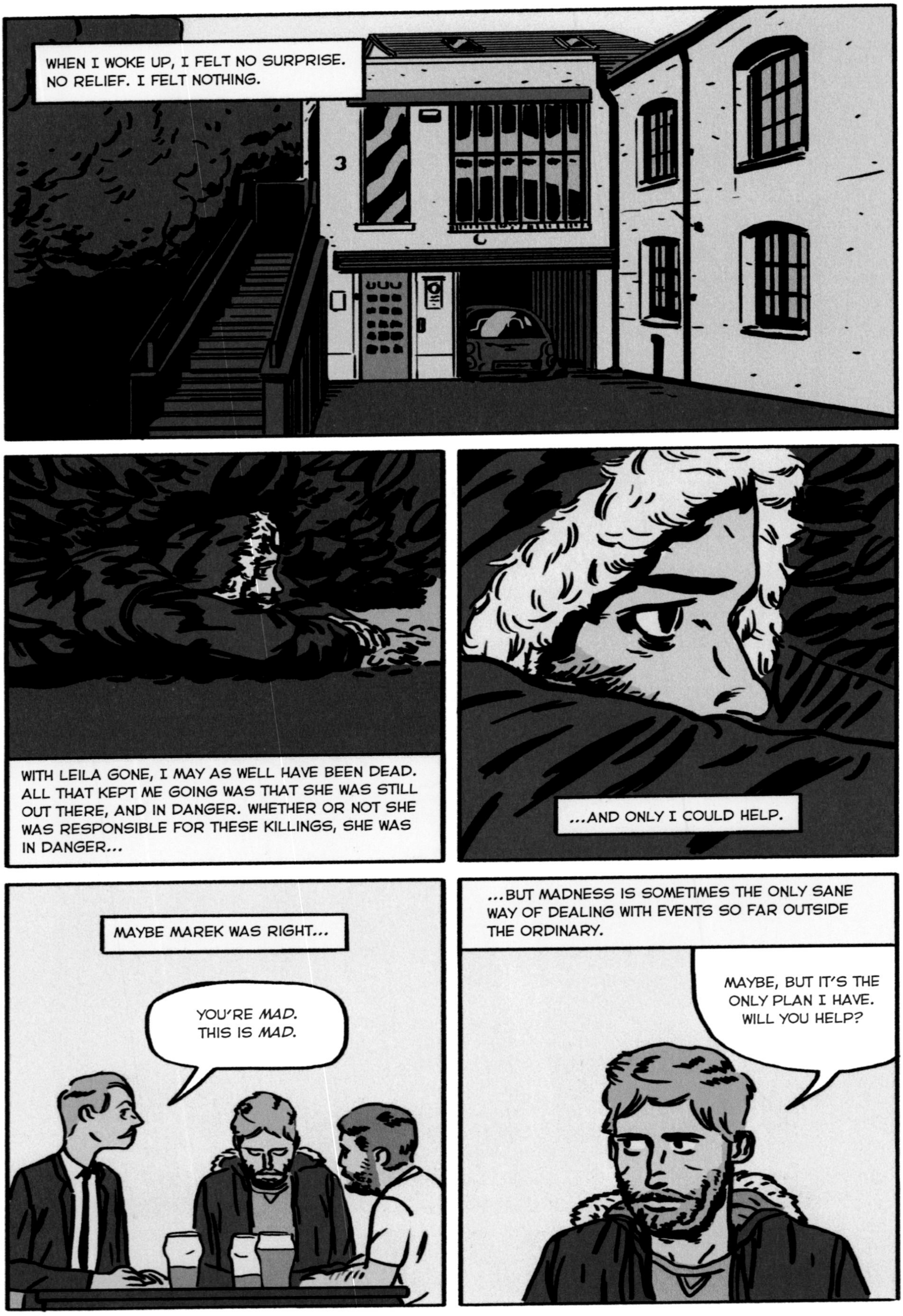
WHEN I WOKE UP, I FELT NO SURPRISE. NO RELIEF. I FELT NOTHING.
WITH LEILA GONE, I MAY AS WELL HAVE BEEN DEAD. ALL THAT KEPT ME GOING WAS THAT SHE WAS STILL OUT THERE, AND IN DANGER. WHETHER OR NOT SHE WAS RESPONSIBLE FOR THESE KILLINGS, SHE WAS IN DANGER...
...AND ONLY I COULD HELP.
MAYBE MAREK WAS RIGHT...
YOU'RE MAD. THIS IS MAD.
...BUT MADNESS IS SOMETIMES THE ONLY SANE WAY OF DEALING WITH EVENTS SO FAR OUTSIDE THE ORDINARY.
MAYBE, BUT IT'S THE ONLY PLAN I HAVE. WILL YOU HELP?

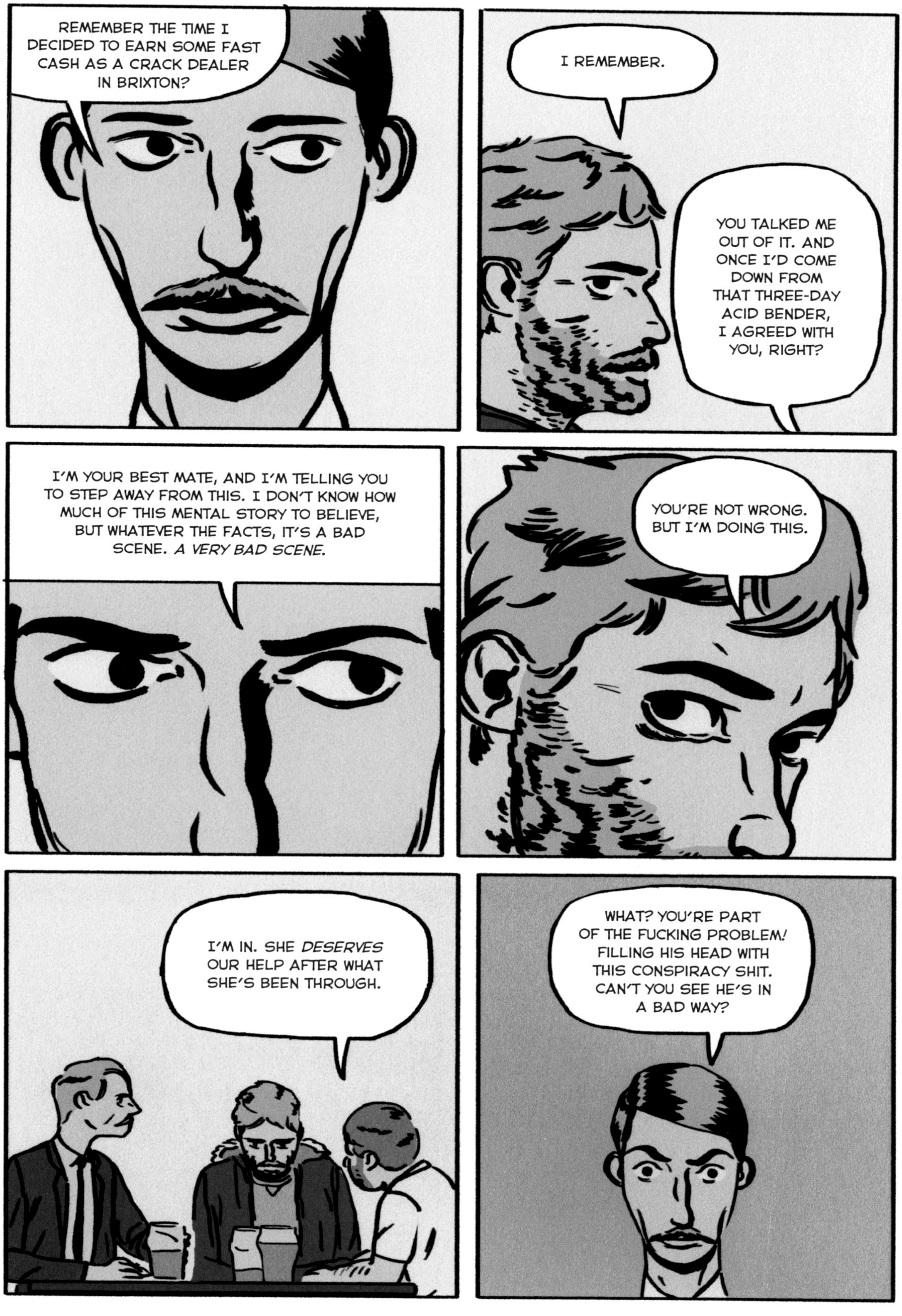
REMEMBER THE TIME I DECIDED TO EARN SOME FAST CASH AS A CRACK DEALER IN BRIXTON?
I REMEMBER.
YOU TALKED ME OUT OF IT. AND ONCE I'D COME DOWN FROM THAT THREE-DAY ACID BENDER, I AGREED WITH YOU, RIGHT?
I'M YOUR BEST MATE, AND I'M TELLING YOU TO STEP AWAY FROM THIS. I DON'T KNOW HOW MUCH OF THIS MENTAL STORY TO BELIEVE, BUT WHATEVER THE FACTS, IT'S A BAD SCENE. *A VERY BAD SCENE.*
YOU'RE NOT WRONG. BUT I'M DOING THIS.
I'M IN. SHE *DESERVES* OUR HELP AFTER WHAT SHE'S BEEN THROUGH.
WHAT? YOU'RE PART OF THE FUCKING PROBLEM! FILLING HIS HEAD WITH THIS CONSPIRACY SHIT. CAN'T YOU SEE HE'S IN A BAD WAY?

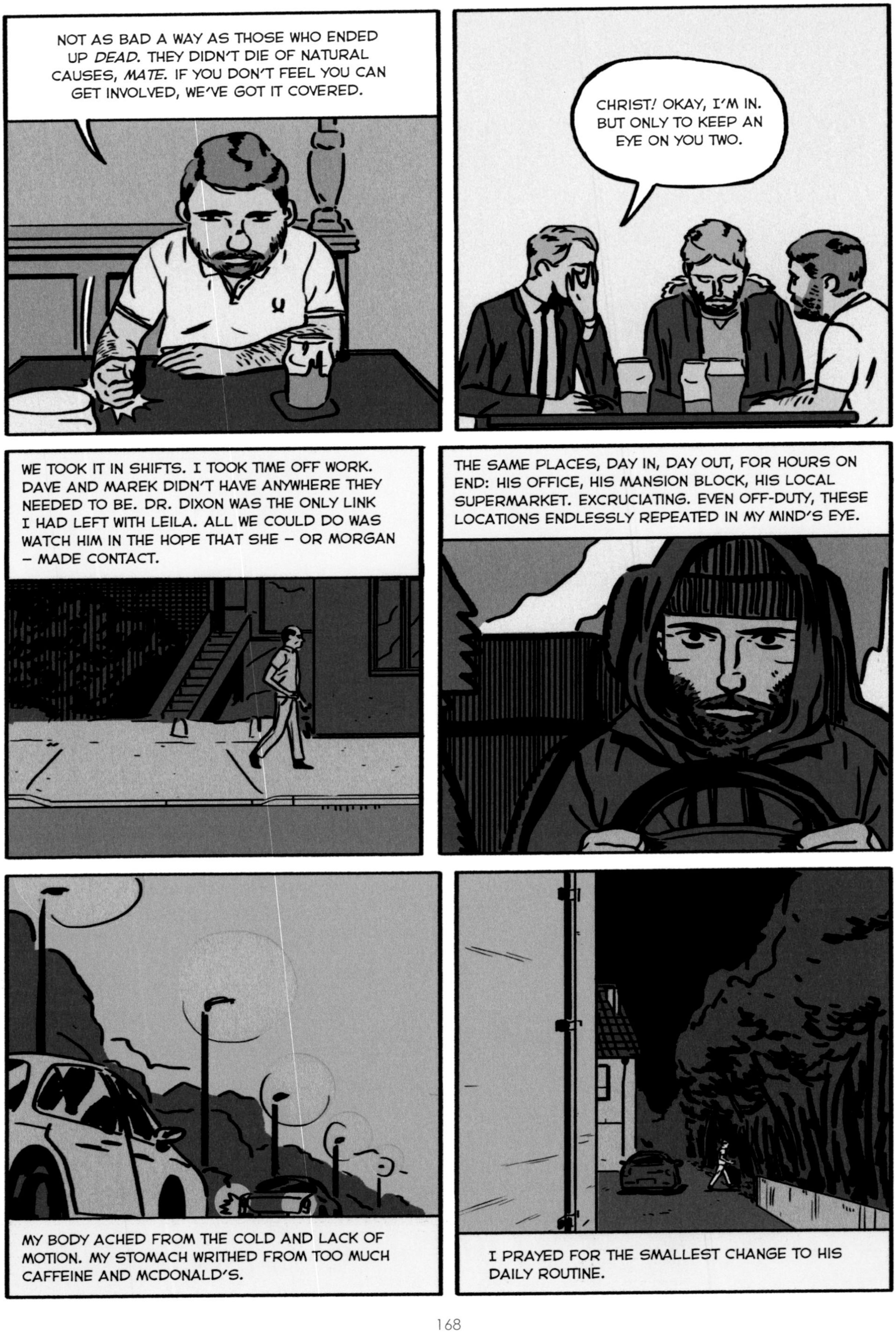
NOT AS BAD A WAY AS THOSE WHO ENDED UP *DEAD*. THEY DIDN'T DIE OF NATURAL CAUSES, *MATE*. IF YOU DON'T FEEL YOU CAN GET INVOLVED, WE'VE GOT IT COVERED.
CHRIST! OKAY, I'M IN. BUT ONLY TO KEEP AN EYE ON YOU TWO.
WE TOOK IT IN SHIFTS. I TOOK TIME OFF WORK. DAVE AND MAREK DIDN'T HAVE ANYWHERE THEY NEEDED TO BE. DR. DIXON WAS THE ONLY LINK I HAD LEFT WITH LEILA. ALL WE COULD DO WAS WATCH HIM IN THE HOPE THAT SHE – OR MORGAN – MADE CONTACT.
THE SAME PLACES, DAY IN, DAY OUT, FOR HOURS ON END: HIS OFFICE, HIS MANSION BLOCK, HIS LOCAL SUPERMARKET. EXCRUCIATING. EVEN OFF-DUTY, THESE LOCATIONS ENDLESSLY REPEATED IN MY MIND'S EYE.
MY BODY ACHED FROM THE COLD AND LACK OF MOTION. MY STOMACH WRITHED FROM TOO MUCH CAFFEINE AND MCDONALD'S.
I PRAYED FOR THE SMALLEST CHANGE TO HIS DAILY ROUTINE.

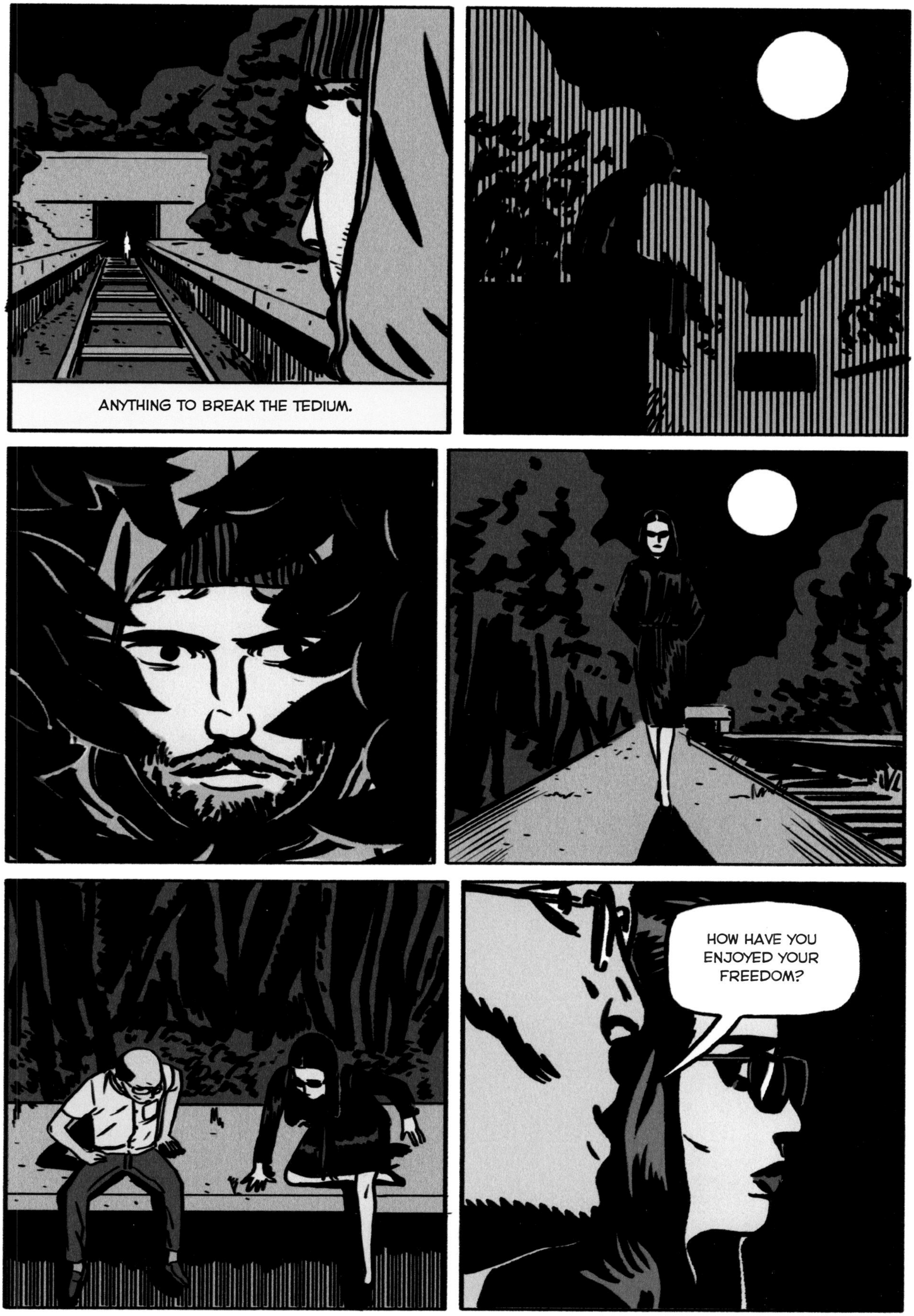
ANYTHING TO BREAK THE TEDIUM.
HOW HAVE YOU ENJOYED YOUR FREEDOM?

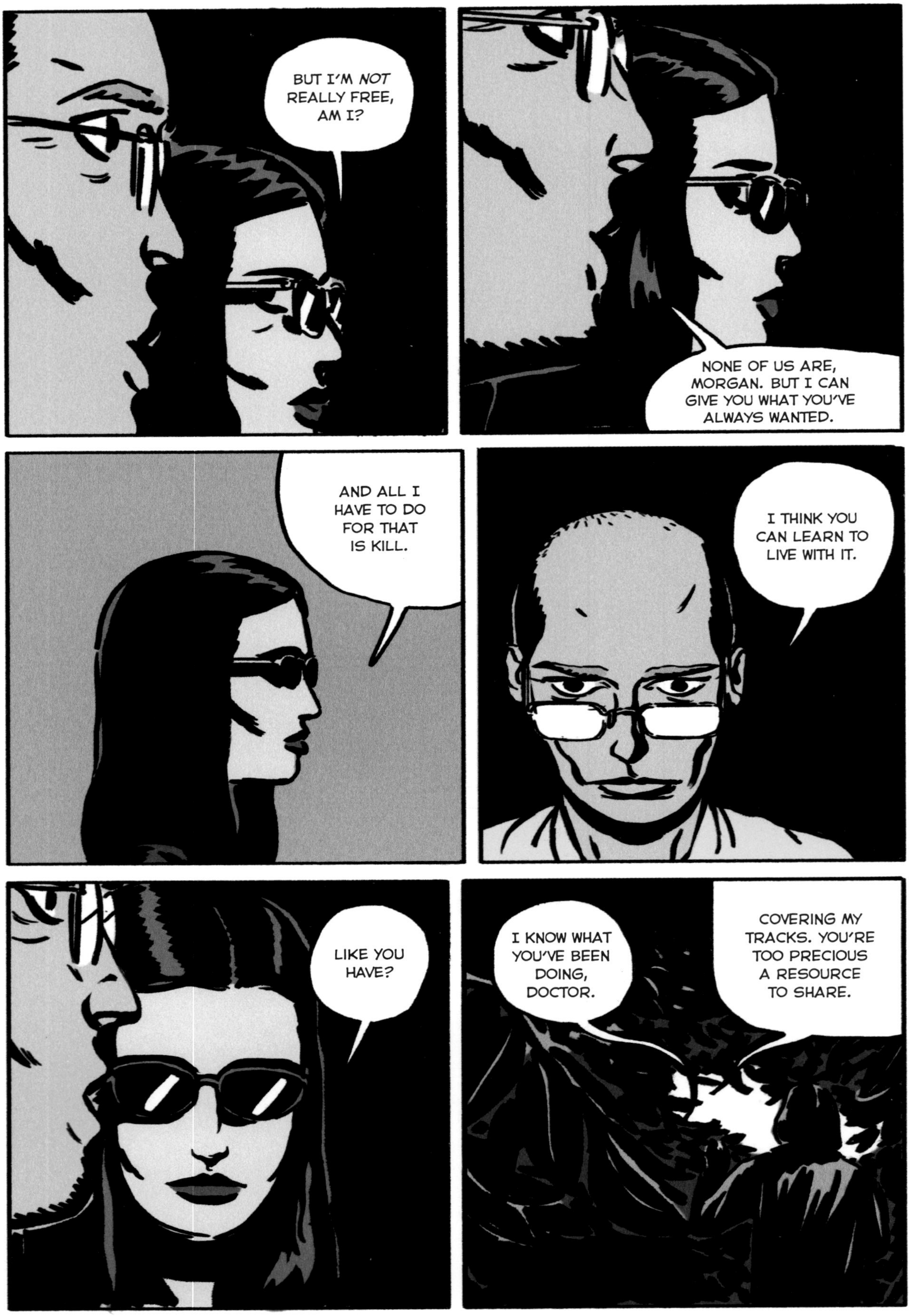
BUT I'M *NOT* REALLY FREE, AM I?
NONE OF US ARE, MORGAN. BUT I CAN GIVE YOU WHAT YOU'VE ALWAYS WANTED.
AND ALL I HAVE TO DO FOR THAT IS KILL.
I THINK YOU CAN LEARN TO LIVE WITH IT.
LIKE YOU HAVE?
I KNOW WHAT YOU'VE BEEN DOING, DOCTOR.
COVERING MY TRACKS. YOU'RE TOO PRECIOUS A RESOURCE TO SHARE.

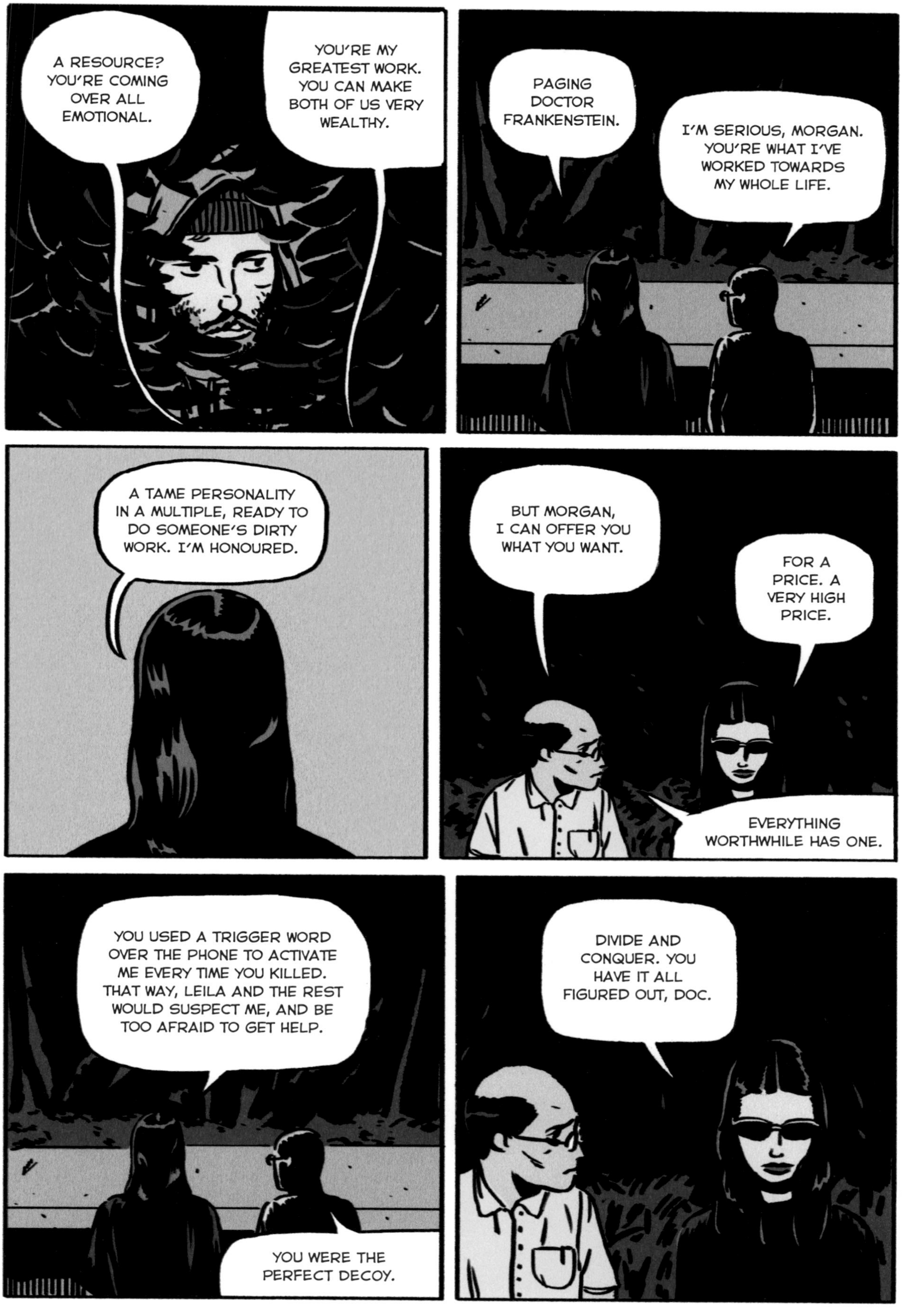
A RESOURCE? YOU'RE COMING OVER ALL EMOTIONAL.
YOU'RE MY GREATEST WORK. YOU CAN MAKE BOTH OF US VERY WEALTHY.
PAGING DOCTOR FRANKENSTEIN.
I'M SERIOUS, MORGAN. YOU'RE WHAT I'VE WORKED TOWARDS MY WHOLE LIFE.
A TAME PERSONALITY IN A MULTIPLE, READY TO DO SOMEONE'S DIRTY WORK. I'M HONOURED.
BUT MORGAN, I CAN OFFER YOU WHAT YOU WANT.
FOR A PRICE. A VERY HIGH PRICE.
EVERYTHING WORTHWHILE HAS ONE.
YOU USED A TRIGGER WORD OVER THE PHONE TO ACTIVATE ME EVERY TIME YOU KILLED. THAT WAY, LEILA AND THE REST WOULD SUSPECT ME, AND BE TOO AFRAID TO GET HELP.
YOU WERE THE PERFECT DECOY.
DIVIDE AND CONQUER. YOU HAVE IT ALL FIGURED OUT, DOC.

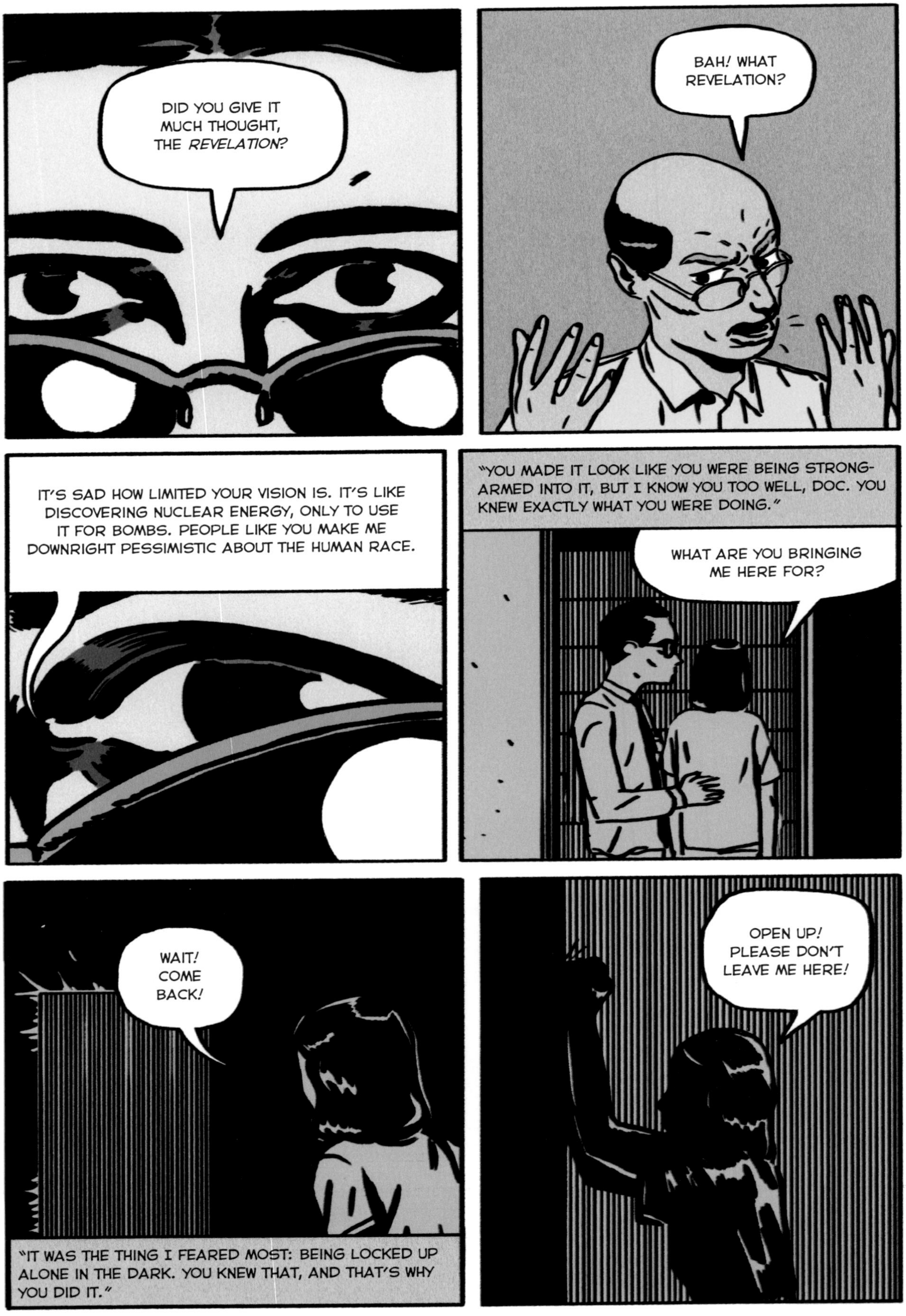
DID YOU GIVE IT MUCH THOUGHT, THE *REVELATION*?
BAH! WHAT REVELATION?
IT'S SAD HOW LIMITED YOUR VISION IS. IT'S LIKE DISCOVERING NUCLEAR ENERGY, ONLY TO USE IT FOR BOMBS. PEOPLE LIKE YOU MAKE ME DOWNRIGHT PESSIMISTIC ABOUT THE HUMAN RACE.
"YOU MADE IT LOOK LIKE YOU WERE BEING STRONG-ARMED INTO IT, BUT I KNOW YOU TOO WELL, DOC. YOU KNEW EXACTLY WHAT YOU WERE DOING."
WHAT ARE YOU BRINGING ME HERE FOR?
WAIT! COME BACK!
"IT WAS THE THING I FEARED MOST: BEING LOCKED UP ALONE IN THE DARK. YOU KNEW THAT, AND THAT'S WHY YOU DID IT."
OPEN UP! PLEASE DON'T LEAVE ME HERE!

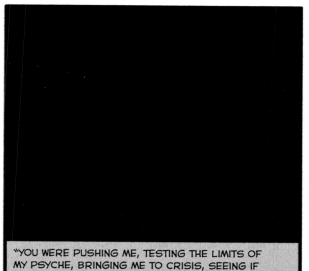

"YOU WERE PUSHING ME, TESTING THE LIMITS OF MY PSYCHE, BRINGING ME TO CRISIS, SEEING IF WHAT YOU'D PUT IN PLACE COULD BE SHAKEN APART."

PLEASE! LET ME *OUT!*

"THE FEAR OVERWHELMED ME, EXPANDING UNTIL I DIDN'T FEEL I COULD CONTAIN SOMETHING SO HUGE."

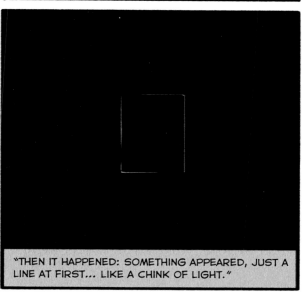

"THEN IT HAPPENED: SOMETHING APPEARED, JUST A LINE AT FIRST... LIKE A CHINK OF LIGHT."

"IT GOT CLEARER AND CLEARER, LIKE A DOOR..."

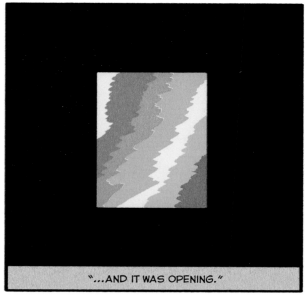

"...AND IT WAS OPENING."

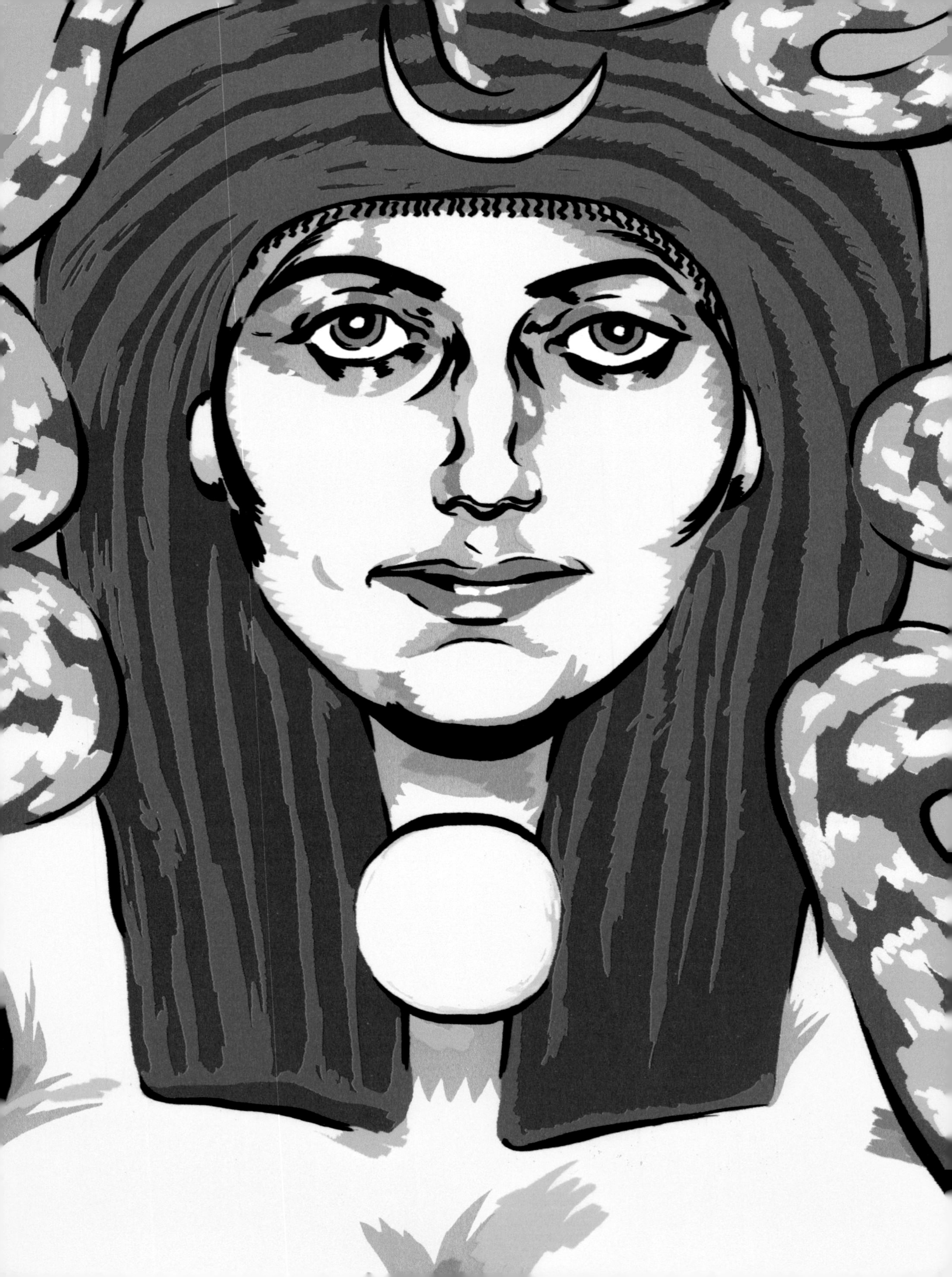

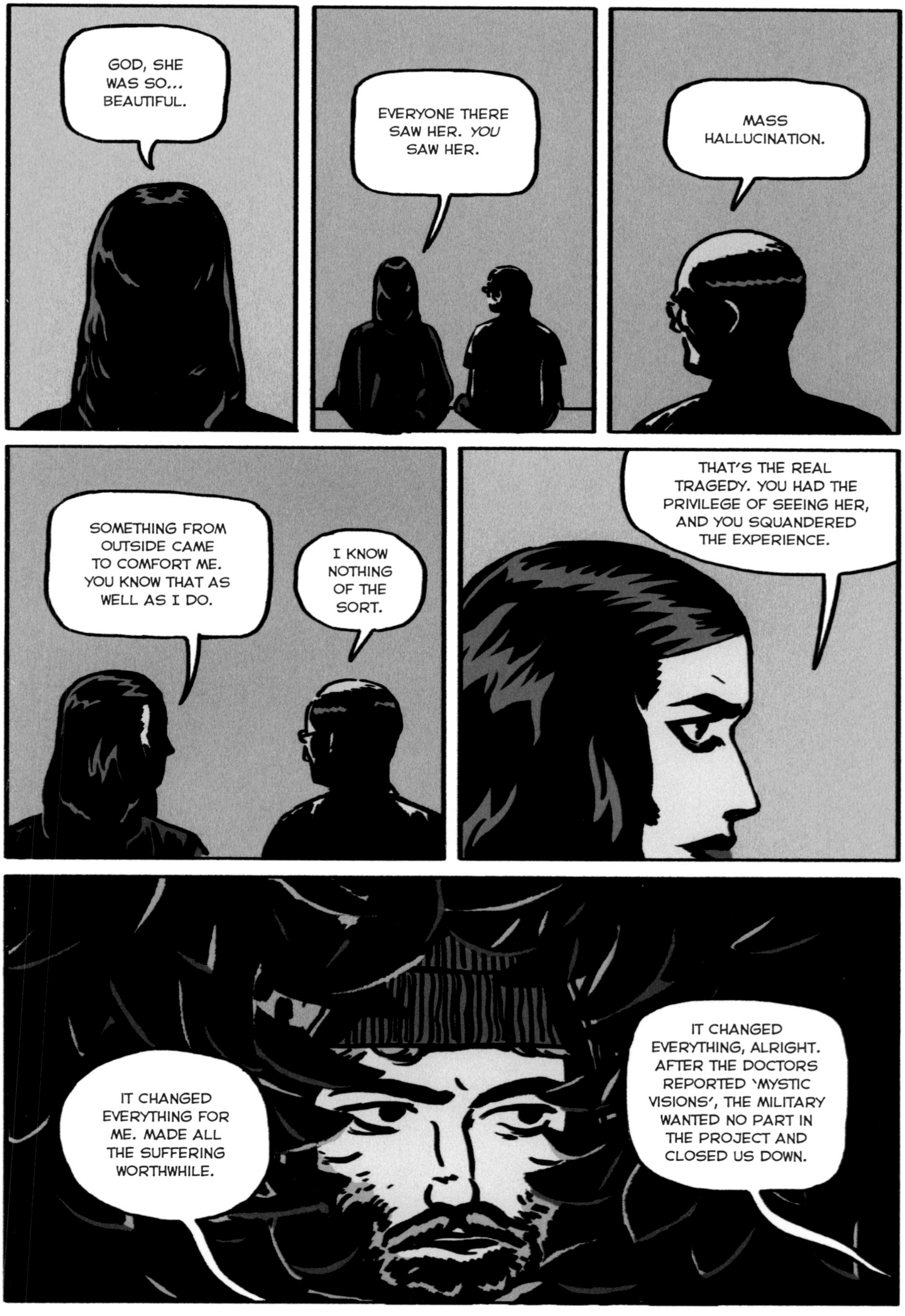
GOD, SHE WAS SO... BEAUTIFUL.
EVERYONE THERE SAW HER. *YOU* SAW HER.
MASS HALLUCINATION.
SOMETHING FROM OUTSIDE CAME TO COMFORT ME. YOU KNOW THAT AS WELL AS I DO.
I KNOW NOTHING OF THE SORT.
THAT'S THE REAL TRAGEDY. YOU HAD THE PRIVILEGE OF SEEING HER, AND YOU SQUANDERED THE EXPERIENCE.
IT CHANGED EVERYTHING FOR ME. MADE ALL THE SUFFERING WORTHWHILE.
IT CHANGED EVERYTHING, ALRIGHT. AFTER THE DOCTORS REPORTED 'MYSTIC VISIONS', THE MILITARY WANTED NO PART IN THE PROJECT AND CLOSED US DOWN.

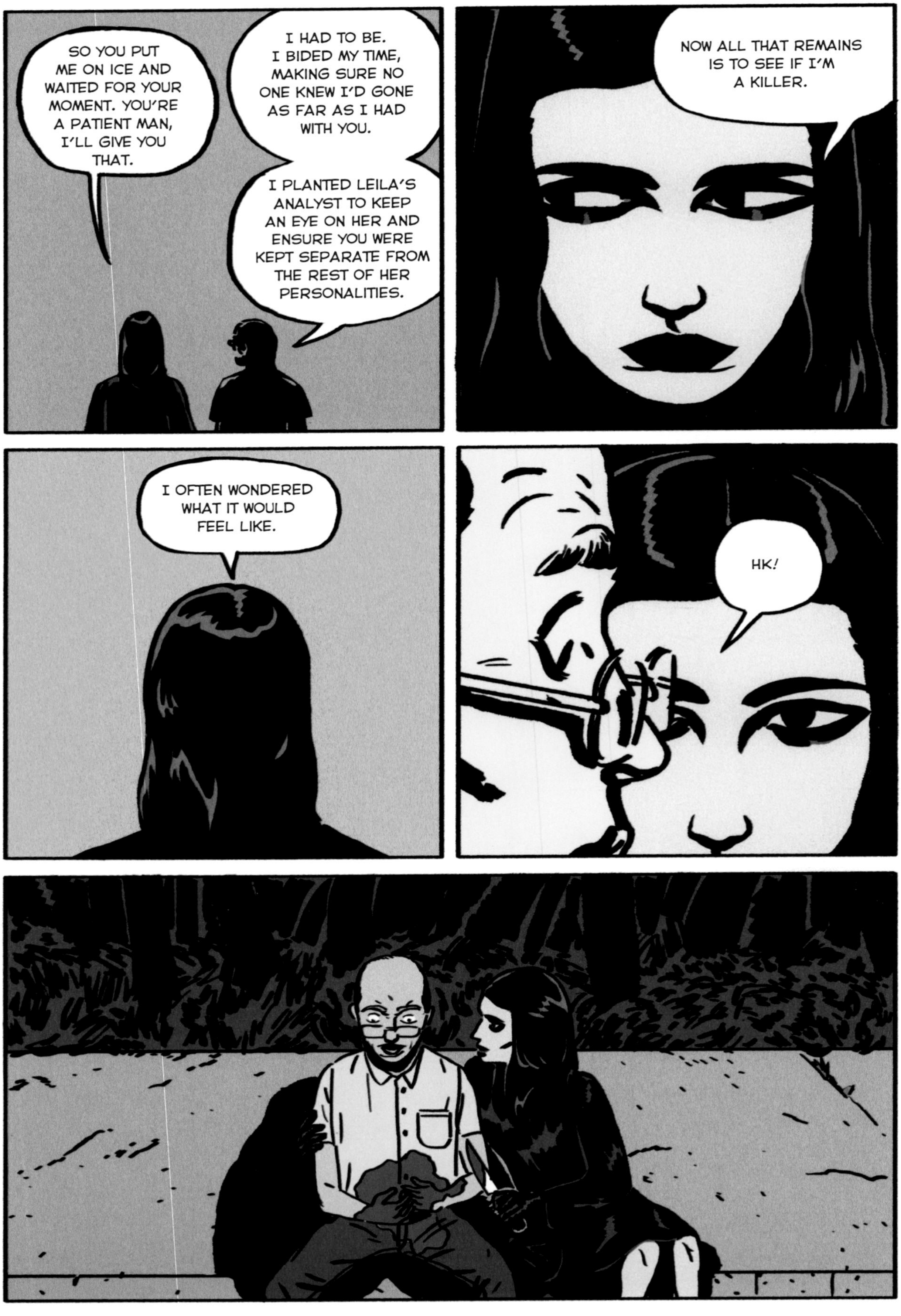
SO YOU PUT ME ON ICE AND WAITED FOR YOUR MOMENT. YOU'RE A PATIENT MAN, I'LL GIVE YOU THAT.
I HAD TO BE. I BIDED MY TIME, MAKING SURE NO ONE KNEW I'D GONE AS FAR AS I HAD WITH YOU.
I PLANTED LEILA'S ANALYST TO KEEP AN EYE ON HER AND ENSURE YOU WERE KEPT SEPARATE FROM THE REST OF HER PERSONALITIES.
NOW ALL THAT REMAINS IS TO SEE IF I'M A KILLER.
I OFTEN WONDERED WHAT IT WOULD FEEL LIKE.
HK!

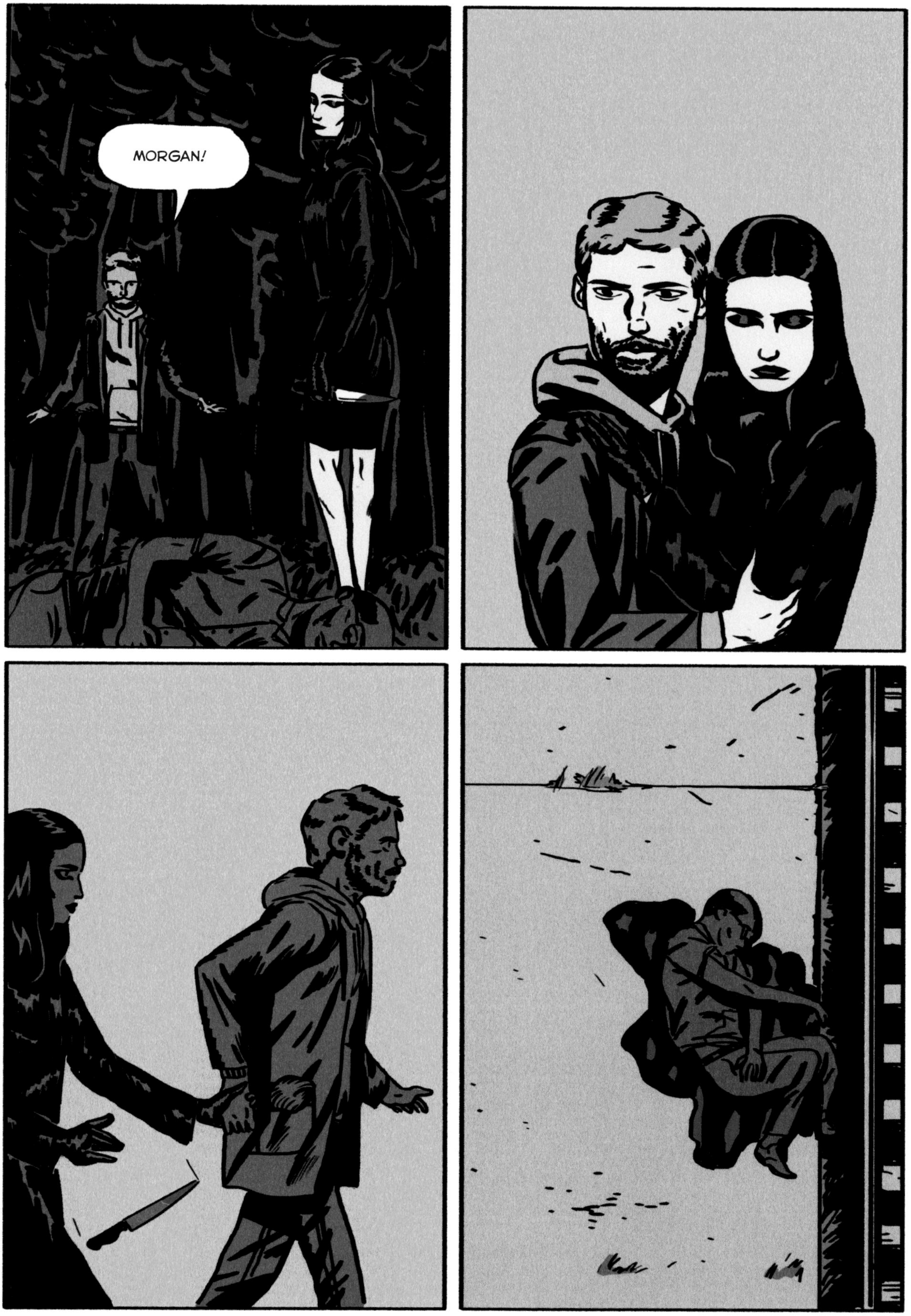
MORGAN!

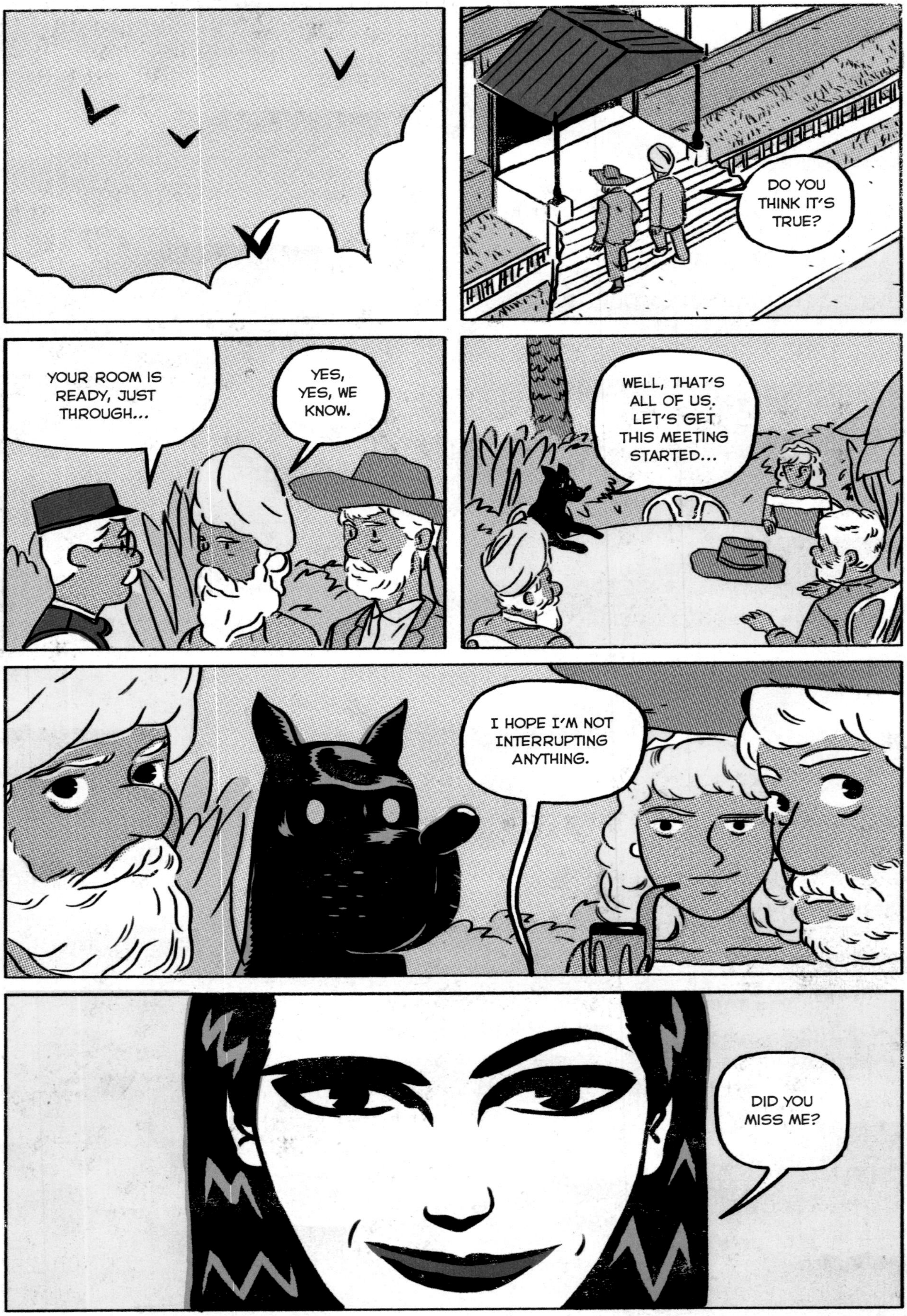
DO YOU THINK IT'S TRUE?
YOUR ROOM IS READY, JUST THROUGH...
YES, YES, WE KNOW.
WELL, THAT'S ALL OF US. LET'S GET THIS MEETING STARTED...
I HOPE I'M NOT INTERRUPTING ANYTHING.
DID YOU MISS ME?

ACKNOWLEDGEMENTS

John Harris Dunning wishes to thank the Arts Council, Adrian & Amber Baillie, Talitha Bell, Will Clarke, Carol Dunning, Maggie Dunning, Simon Dunning, Roland Erasmus, Sylvia Farago, Paul Gravett, Emma Hayley, Rohne Hill, Alyn Horton, Sam Humphrey, Simon Jablonski, Richard James, Txabi Jones, the brilliant Michael Kennedy, Dan Lockwood, Sacha Mardou, Fiona McMorrough, Mike Medaglia, Abigail, Dylan, Georgia & Imogen Morris, Emma Pettit, Sophie Pittaway, Mark Pool, Guillaume Rater, Annushka Shani, Paul Smith, Rory Stead, Sarah Such, Jeremy Thomas, Robert Van Zyl, Peter Watson and Adam Woodward.

Michael Kennedy wishes to thank Mom, Dad, Nan, Reece, Elyse, Ben, Callum, Greg, Emily, Ian, John, Sarah, the SelfMadeHero team and the Arts Council. This is in addition to anyone else who has wondered what I've been up to this past year.

ABOUT THE AUTHORS

 **John Harris Dunning** is the writer of graphic novel *Salem Brownstone*. He instigated and curated the *Comics Unmasked: Art and Anarchy in the UK* exhibition at the British Library, the most prestigious exhibition of comics to be held in Britain. He's written for *GQ*, *Esquire*, *Dazed*, *iD*, the *Guardian* and *Metro*.

 **Michael Kennedy** is a cartoonist from Tamworth, Staffordshire. He is the artist on *Spiritus* from Vault Comics and has produced comics in the small press and independent scene. This is his first graphic novel.

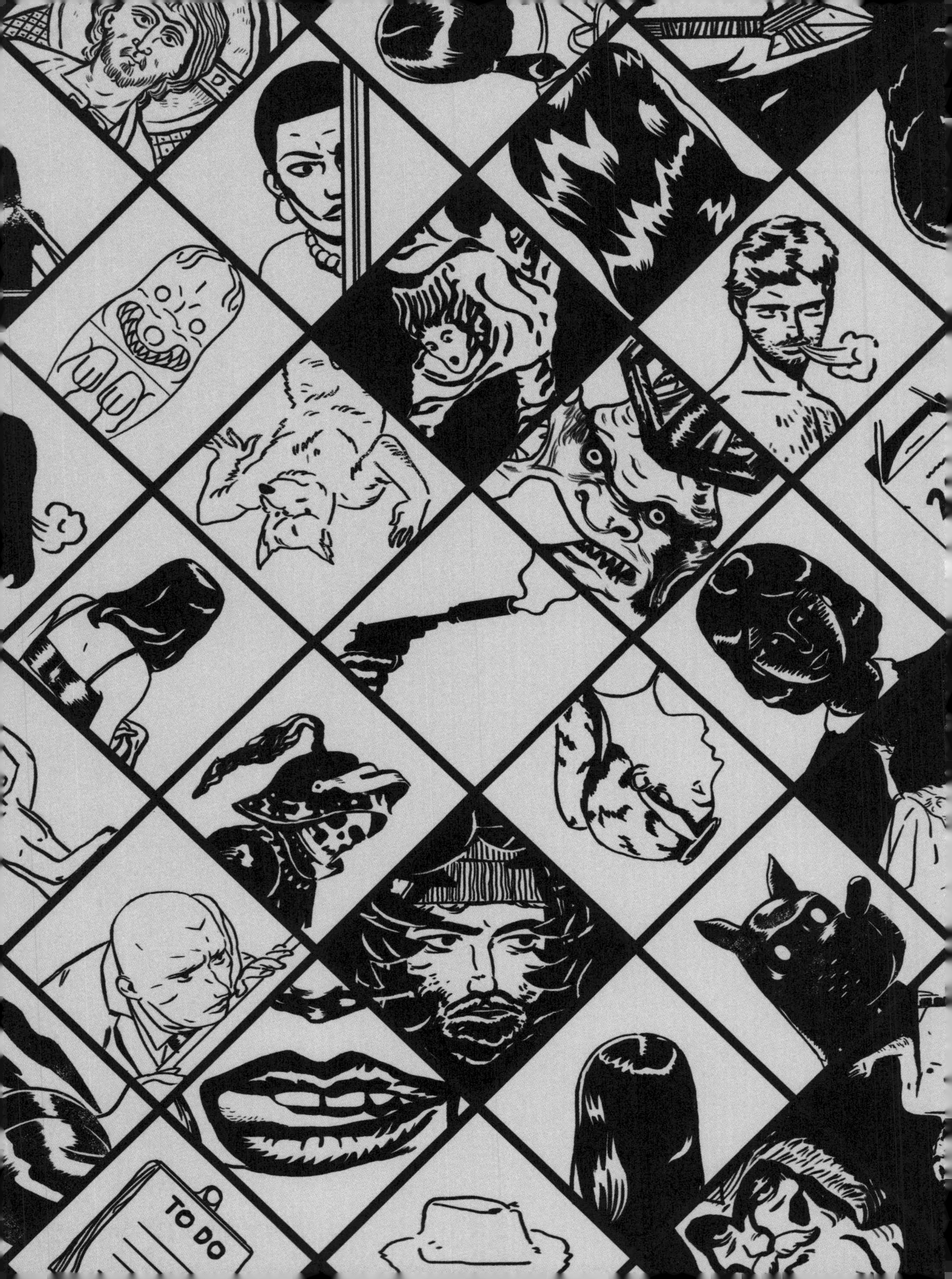
TO DO